WINGS
of the
WIND

Books by Connilyn Cossette

OUT FROM EGYPT

Counted With the Stars
Shadow of the Storm
Wings of the Wind

CITIES OF REFUGE

A Light on the Hill
Shelter of the Most High
Until the Mountains Fall

WINGS *of the* WIND

CONNILYN COSSETTE

BETHANYHOUSE

a division of Baker Publishing Group
Minneapolis, Minnesota

Published by Bethany House Publishers
Minneapolis, Minnesota
www.bethanyhouse.com

Bethany House Publishers is a division of
Baker Publishing Group, Grand Rapids, Michigan

Printed in the United States of America

Library of Congress Cataloging-in-Publication Data
Names: Cossette, Connilyn, author.
Title: Wings of the wind / Connilyn Cossette.
Description: Minneapolis, Minnesota : Bethany House, a division of Baker
    Publishing Group, [2017] | Series: Out from Egypt ; 3
Identifiers: LCCN 2016048832 | ISBN 9780764218224 (trade paper) | ISBN
    9780764230370 (hardcover)
Subjects: | GSAFD: Christian fiction.
Classification: LCC PS3603.O8655 W54 2017 | DDC 813/.6—dc23
LC record available at https://lccn.loc.gov/2016048832

Cover design by Jennifer Parker
Cover photography by Mike Habermann Photography, LLC

Author is represented by The Steve Laube Agency.

Baker Publishing Group publications use paper produced from sustainable forestry practices and post-consumer waste whenever possible.

For Juli

A true sister-of-the-heart
with a gift for asking the right questions
and a passion for setting captives free.
Your encouragement, support,
and vision are invaluable to me.

I, the Lord, have called you in righteousness;
I will take hold of your hand.
I will keep you and will make you
to be a covenant for the people
and a light for the Gentiles, to open eyes that are blind,
to free captives from prison and to release from the dungeon
those who sit in darkness.

—Isaiah 42:6–7

When the Canaanite king of Arad, who lived in the Negev, heard that Israel was coming along the road to Atharim, he attacked the Israelites and captured some of them. Then Israel made this vow to the Lord: "If you will deliver these people into our hands, we will totally destroy their cities."

Numbers 21:1–2

ALANAH

14 NISSAN
1407 BC
NEGEV DESERT

Forging through the teeming mass of Canaanite soldiers in this vast army camp, I'd never felt more alone. A tendril of hair tickled the side of my neck and I jammed the errant strand under my bronze helmet, hoping no one had glimpsed the flash of red against my shoulder. The scaled armor I wore, heavy as it was, disguised my form to good effect. If I was vigilant to keep my guard raised, no one would ever know a woman walked among them until they found my body on the battlefield tomorrow.

Careful to widen my stance and tread with a heavier step, I ran my brother's name through my mind again and again, then repeated it under my breath for good measure. If I was questioned, the name *Davash* must spring easily to my lips, instead of my own. Any hesitation and there would be suspicion. I could not afford suspicion.

My build, my hands, or the pitch of my voice could reveal my gender in the span of a breath. When it happened—for surely it would happen at some point—it must be after my bow took its revenge. My makeshift beard, a thin layer of dirt smudged across my cheeks and chin, had begun to peel and itch, but evening shadows would aid my deception.

Drunken laughter swirled around the sea of black tents, mixing with the bray of horses and clanging of weapons meeting in practice, a wild cacophony that only grew louder as twilight advanced. Perhaps hiding in plain sight would be easier than I'd expected.

Beneath my brother's gray wool tunic, a copper amulet hung from a leather strip around my neck. The gift from my father depicted a raised-relief image of the warrior goddess Anat, battle axe and spear in hand, and had inspired the courage I needed to leave my village when the king of Arad again called for defenders of his lands. Although I had little respect for any deity, the weight of the cool metal against my skin and the reminder of my family bolstered my resolve. The quiver slung over my shoulder was full, each arrow tipped with vengeance. I had no delusions that I would live through the battle tomorrow, but when the arrows I had made with my own hands found Hebrew flesh, I would finally have satisfaction for the deaths of my father and my three brothers.

Amorites and Jebusites, and even some Moabites and Edomites, numbered among this fierce but fragile coalition. Tribal grudges had been set aside to come together against the swarm of Hebrews invading our lands.

Crude language tossed across campfires had little effect on me, for I had grown up with three older brothers. But the lisp of female voices floating through flimsy tent walls soured my stomach. Lonely soldiers with extra war rations made for good business, so women who traded in their own flesh were never far from the battlefront. The seductive laughter and brazen display of their wares made my skin crawl. I would rather die than number among them—in fact, I planned on it.

A group of men huddled around a fire at the edge of camp, slapping backs and comparing weapons. I slipped behind them and settled near a boulder, breathing easier as shadows deepened and night advanced.

Days of trudging through the desert to meet the army in this valley had wreaked havoc on my body. Wounded skin flamed and throbbed where my sandals had stripped my heels and ankles raw during the long walk across blazing sand and stone. I closed my eyes and breathed steady, imagining the pain lessened with every slow exhale.

Rich smoke emanated from the cookfires and the meat of prebattle offerings to the gods. To distance myself from my empty stomach's violent reaction to the smell, I focused on the conversations around me and attempted to lift useful details from the overlapping chatter. Perhaps if I feigned sleep well enough, no one would take notice and I would be rewarded with information on tomorrow's strategy—and our enemy.

A slurred voice rose above the rest. "How many of those Hebrews did we take last month?"

"Five hundred, at least. Frightened little hares, all of them," a gruff voice responded.

Someone else snorted. "The rest of them will scatter tomorrow. And any that don't will be made into girls by my dagger."

Raucous laughter erupted, startling my eyes open. I squeezed them shut before anyone noticed or questioned me. Drunk as they were, if I answered with my own voice, I would be on my back in one of those tents within moments. Would I have the courage to grab the dagger at my hip and plunge it into my heart?

The slurred voice rose to the top again. "You seen their women? They worth keeping?"

Lewd comments followed, assaulting my ears and curling my insides. My brothers, much as I admired them, had been no different than these soldiers—coarse and savage with their enemies. No wonder they had found such pleasure in war. It was a surprise they'd survived long enough to be murdered by the Hebrews.

The name of the hated invaders tasted bitter, even in my mind. I swallowed hard and imagined loading my first arrow and letting it fly toward the faceless intruders who had stolen everything from me. I'd heard the stories of the slaves who'd thwarted Pharaoh nearly forty years ago, as well as the rumors that their sights were set on Canaan. Fools. They would be crushed. Decimated. And I would ensure that I killed my fair share of them before my blood soaked the sands tomorrow.

Sour, wine-laden breath suddenly filled my senses, and a voice was in my ear. "How 'bout you, little man? You going to keep a couple Hebrew fillies for yourself? Even a young one's got needs? Eh?"

There was no time to hesitate. Grabbing for his throat, I dug my fingers deep into his windpipe and emptied the depth of my hate and fear into my voice. "I. Am. Trying. To. Sleep."

He was twice my size, built like a bull, and thankfully almost gone with drink. His black eyes went wide. Even through his haze, he must have seen something in my expression that gave him pause. He stood, mumbled a curse, and staggered out of the circle of firelight.

I tensed my body. *Do not tremble. Confidence. Swagger. Be Davash.*

Rising, I ignored the myriad eyes on me and stomped away.

But in the blackness between campfires, my breath came fast and my body vibrated like a discharged bowstring. I should have stayed away until morning. Why had I risked discovery? Skirting clusters of tents and the glow of fires, I kept my head down and my hand on my dagger hilt.

The sharp-ridged hills around this valley were shod with lime shale, too noisy to climb even with my well-practiced light step. A river of stones would clatter down if I attempted it in the dark.

A tent, butted up against the hill, stood deep in shadow. I slid behind it, silently pressing my body into the gap between the tent and the limestone behind. There was only enough room to lay with my leather satchel beneath my helmeted head and my bow and quiver against my back. Sleeping in armor would be uncomfortable, but necessary.

My mind touched on the faces of each of my brothers as they'd left our village to head off the invaders. Zealous to protect our farm after reports that the Hebrews were moving north, my father and brothers had heeded the call from the king of Arad to band together and go on the offensive. They'd left, more than confident they would return and sure that a horde of slaves wandering aimlessly in the wilderness would have no chance against the united warrior tribes of Canaan.

And yet, here I lay, a woman alone in the middle of this immense army, preparing to finish what the men of my family had started. Or, at the least, to meet them in death. Curling in on myself, I rubbed my thumb over the four jagged wounds on my wrist as I braced against the numbing cold and the howling emptiness, and forced sleep.

Morning could not come fast enough—even if it was to be the last dawn I would see with earthly eyes.

2

"Wake up!"

Someone booted my backside, hard. A jolt of realization cleared sleep from my brain in an instant. My pulse went wild. Had my hair come loose? Was I discovered? How foolish to sleep so close to a tent! I peered through my eyelashes, and my stomach hollowed. I was inside the tent. I must have rolled over in my sleep and slipped beneath the wall. What would I say to the man who had awoken me? Claim I had been drunk and wandered in?

Shrugging a shoulder, I released a low groan, hoping to stall the inevitable. How long would it take him to realize I was a woman and take advantage? My dagger was still tucked under my hip. Slowly, as if I was stretching to shake off sleep, I slid my hand toward the hilt. One breath. Two.

"Get up, soldier. Sun'll be up soon, time to move." The man prodded my leg again with his boot and left the tent, obviously not the least bit surprised to find a stranger here. I released a measured breath and turned over. A lone oil lamp in the corner flicked shadows around the empty tent. Relief spilled itself into my veins in a rush.

My satchel lay nearby. Thankfully, no one had pilfered the few items I carried. I snaked my hand under the black goat-hair wall and hunted for my quiver and bow, breathing easier when my fingertips met the treasures.

After devouring the last stale piece of flatbread from my satchel and slaking my thirst with tepid water from a scavenged water-skin, I adjusted the leather shoulder straps of Davash's leather-scaled armor and pulled it tighter against my chest, wincing as it smashed my breasts and dug the edge of my amulet into my skin.

Good. I yanked the side clasp again. The less like a woman I looked, the better. Besides, I needed the copper amulet as close to my heart as possible, a reminder of why I was here today.

After ensuring my braid was still secure under my helmet, and my wrist guard tied tightly, I lifted the tent flap. The sun had not quite breached the hills. Anat, the bright star, clung to the last of the night. The warrior goddess had freed her brother-god from the Underworld and in her name I would avenge my own brothers today.

Lines were forming to the south. I followed a group with quivers slung across their shoulders, head down, determination in my every step.

The Hebrews knew we were coming. Why would they provoke another battle with those who had beaten them so handily the first time they tried to invade this land? Why weren't they running back to wherever they'd come from?

Only a few weeks ago, they had swarmed up from the south like a plague, and the army of Arad had routed them. But not before my brothers and father were slain. And yet here the Hebrews were again, meeting us in the very same valley, as if we had not ground them to dust and taken many captives.

How many prisoners had that drunk last night bragged about? Five hundred? Today it would be five thousand, or fifty thousand.

My eyes would not see the sunset this day. My father may have trained me to shoot an arrow true, but I would not survive. Better to be slain on the battlefield than succumb to the only other choice I had left. Death was far preferable to following the path of my mother—a priestess who reveled in her wanton duties and abandoned her three-year-old daughter to flee north and return to the temple.

A ram's horn ripped a shrill cry before our lines had fully formed, and I jerked my neck toward the unexpected call. Panic rippled through the ranks, along with the hiss of a thousand surprised curses, as stones flew through the air from the west, clanking and pinging against helmets and armor. More stones whizzed in from the east before the archers around me could even arm themselves. One slammed against my helmet from behind, knocking my head forward with a jarring crash. Had I been hit by a stone, or a boulder? Disoriented, I turned in a circle, peering into the shadowy edges of the valley. The enemy was upon us, seeming to appear from everywhere, advancing like a horde of locusts. Had they been hiding in the rocks around the valley? Were we surrounded?

The clanging of thousands of swords reverberated, and arrows silhouetted high against the dawn. Urgency rushed through my limbs. What was I waiting for? Another knock on the head? I whipped a few arrows from my full quiver, gathering them in my right hand, ready to shoot one after another without hesitation.

Fitting one nock against the string, I raised the bow to my shoulder. Lifting the copper tip high, I pulled back with every bit of strength in my arm and, not bothering to aim, released.

The instant my arrow flew, the man to my right fell, screaming, a Hebrew arrow protruding from his cheek. An irrational urge to stop and aid him tugged at me, but I could not hesitate.

I slipped another arrow into position. Only a wisp of sun peeked above the eastern horizon, so my vision was limited, but there was no mistake: We were surrounded. Hebrews flooded into the valley on all sides, hemming us in.

I picked one black-bearded enemy not too far off, sighed a breath, and let loose. The arrow hit him square on the head but glanced off his helmet. A curse flew past my lips. *No time. Do it again.*

A sea of men riddled with Hebrew arrows writhed around me. My whole body trembled and I fell to my knees as my stomach threatened to empty itself on the ground. Why had I come here? *Foolish. Foolish!*

Distorted figures rushed at me. I blinked away the blur in my vision. Thousands of Hebrew soldiers, swords waving, fury on their faces, charged across the battlefield. How could they already have broken through and reached the archers? A gleaming golden chariot thundered by, destroying what was left of our lines, throwing us into confusion. A Hebrew with an Egyptian-style chariot?

Horns screamed all around the wide basin. The violent sound reverberated off the ridge-backed hills and crashed around inside my skull. Although I was tempted to cover my ears against the painful screech, at least it obscured the shrieks of the dying for a few seconds. All too soon the fanfare ended and the horrific tumult overwhelmed me again.

Where to aim? There were so many. I could not find a fixed point. With one knee still on the ground, I shot arrow after arrow into the crush of flailing bodies. Perhaps one of my enemies might be at the end of their random arc.

A snarling, bloody-faced Hebrew charged toward me, sword high. But when he tripped over a fallen man, I fled before he could regain his footing. A battered shield had fallen at my feet, so I snatched it up. Grasping the handle in white-knuckled panic, I cowered beneath it and fled.

Dodging clumps and pairs of men working to hack one another to pieces, I wound through the melee. I tripped over a body, scrambled back to my feet without looking behind me, and pressed on. The screams of the fallen and the full-throated roars of the soldiers made my teeth vibrate. The false image I'd conjured of gaunt, weak-willed Hebrew slaves had been replaced by the reality of fierce, full-bearded warriors clad in well-crafted armor and with expressions devoid of fear.

Somehow I reached the edge of the valley with my head attached to my body. Panting, bruised, and bloodied, I ducked beside a large boulder, making myself small and scanning the unimaginable scene with horror. Death surrounded me on every side, and the Hebrews continued to advance like an endless river. How many were there?

There was only one more arrow in my quiver. Should I shoot? Or save it? I was going to die regardless. What did it matter?

I reached behind me and pulled out the arrow, one made by my own hand. In one swift move, I ran my thumb across the feathers of the fletching—the offering of a turquoise-winged kingfisher I had snared near my village cistern—and fit the nock against the bowstring. Aiming for the nearest Hebrew, I held my breath, focusing on the pulse where my fingers met sinew, waiting for the silence between thundering heartbeats before I released.

Victory! He fell to the ground, clutching his side.

However, instead of feeling the pride I expected, my stomach threatened to rebel again, and my eyes burned. *What have I done?*

Pain slammed into my left shoulder, twisting me around

and buckling my knees. My temple collided with the boulder. Whooshing swirled through my head, crashed against the wall of consciousness, and pulled me into a black abyss of silence.

Fire burned against my shoulder. I tried to shift away, but it followed. Flames licked at my skin, the flash of pain spreading like lightning. I forced my eyes open. My vision blurred and the flames glowed red, like blood.

It *was* blood. An arrow had pierced my shoulder. I attempted to roll to my back and then cursed myself for doing so; the arrowhead shifted against bone, cutting new teeth of agony into my body. I should not have tried; my legs were pinned under a dead man and another corpse lay across my abdomen.

Clear, deep blue and a searing sun, now high in the sky, hung over me. My mouth ached for water. Someone blocked my view, silhouetted against the light. I blinked, but even such a small action was torture.

"This one's alive." The declaration seemed to come from far away, as if floating high above me, the familiar language weighted with a foreign accent.

"Finish it," yelled another disembodied voice. "We are to leave no man breathing."

My eyes closed and I drew a deep breath, a shuddering inhale that would be my last. The enemy sword would cleave the last of the life from my body, and I could sleep, fly to the gods, if they deigned to receive one who had shunned them.

Nothing came. No sword. No end. I opened my eyes and a blood-spattered, bearded face hovered over me with a confused expression. Soundless words formed on his lips. *A woman?*

My helmet was gone and my braid free. There was no escaping the fate that would now meet me on this battlefield. My brothers, unrestrained even around their sister, had drunkenly regaled me with stories of women in battle camps. Victors plundered women along with weapons and supplies. Perhaps I would again lose consciousness from the pain of my wound and he would kill me quickly after he sated his—

"Can you move?" His surprising question scattered my disturbing thoughts. The man thrust his sword into his scabbard, pushed the dead men off my legs and body, and knelt beside me. Cinnamon-brown eyes, full of conflict, met mine. A thick, ragged beard covered his face and met long, brown hair streaked with gold from the sun.

In my confusion and haze, I could not answer. Why was he waiting? Was he drawing out the terror? Even if I could reach the dagger at my belt with my useless arm, there was no strength left in me to fight.

He looked around, as if searching out someone to aid him. But instead of calling out for another enemy to help slaughter me, he checked me for weapons and, finding my dagger, relieved me of my last defense. "Rather not have that jammed between my ribs," he muttered.

Then, in a baffling move, he slipped a small skin-bag from his shoulder and held it to my parched lips. An explosion of cool, clean water poured into my mouth. I choked and coughed. He placed a hand behind my good shoulder and lifted me, guiding me into a sitting position. "Here. Drink."

With only a brief pause to consider his intentions, I lifted my mouth to the spout and guzzled. The sweetest mountain-fresh water I had ever tasted doused the burn in my throat, stirring a spark of life, of unwelcome hope, into my desiccated body.

"That arrow is in deep." He examined my back but did not touch the wound. "I'll find a healer."

Why would this enemy, one whose face was streaked and speckled with the blood of my countrymen, take me to a healer?

He checked my other limbs and, satisfied that I was able, helped me stand. A spasm of searing pain spiked down my arm and across my chest. The world swayed and tilted. My knees collapsed. I was locked in his arms for a moment before blackness engulfed me again.

3

TOBIAH

Why would a woman be here? Did these cursed Canaanites force girls to fight their battles? No wonder Yahweh had directed us to drive out these people—they were nothing but savages. I would no more send my sister into battle than surrender my sword.

Corpses littered the valley floor, thousands upon thousands, as lifeless as the shifting sands in which I had buried so many loved ones. Yahweh had delivered this enemy into our hands as he had promised, retribution for the unprovoked attack by Arad's forces only a few weeks ago.

Taking advantage of the woman's faint, I laid her on the ground again and broke off the hollow arrow shaft with my hands. She winced and moaned, but her eyes did not open.

Her hair, braided around her head and red like a flame, was the only clue she was female. Her helmet lay in the sand, but she wore the leather-scaled armor and tunic of a man, a quiver

20

strapped across her back. Four red slashes stood out on her forearm, jagged wounds I suspected had been self-inflicted.

I had been so close to shoving my sword through her still-rising chest. In the heartbeat it took to comprehend she was not a man, she had looked up at me. No anger. No fear in her peculiar blue-green eyes. Just pure acquiescence. As if she welcomed death.

Something shifted inside me in that moment. Although driven by fury at the Canaanites, bloodied and bruised by their hands and anxious to find my friend Shimon, I could not do the deed.

Shofarim sounded close by—the horns' call a declaration of victory. The tactic planned by Yehoshua, the commander of our army and second in command only to Mosheh, had been flawless. We had crept through the dark, surrounding the arrogant Canaanites and sweeping them into a writhing circle of confusion and panic before their charioteers had even mounted to ride. This woman must have been hit early on, and the two bodies sprawled across her had protected her from further damage by sword or arrow.

Hebrew wounded and dying were being removed from the field, but no one must notice that I carried a woman, especially a Canaanite one. With a quick glance around to ensure no one was watching, I unwound a turban from a nearby corpse and wrapped it around her head, hoping my hasty knot would hold.

Then, with careful movements so as not to jostle her wounded shoulder, I pulled her up and over my own. She groaned but did not struggle, yet somehow she retained a death grip on her bow until I pried it from her fingers. I nearly tossed it aside, but something about the way she'd clung to the weapon compelled me to bring it along.

As I walked back to our camp, I continued scanning the milling Hebrew soldiers for Shimon's black hair and the Egyptian features he'd inherited from his father. Although we'd been separated early in the conflict, he'd surely be at the tent when I returned, for there was no more skilled swordsman than Shimon. What would he say when I appeared with a bleeding woman slung over my shoulder? No doubt some mocking quip about my inability to resist taking battle spoils.

To avoid prying eyes, I skirted the perimeter of the battle encampment and ducked into the small, black tent Shimon and I had pitched at the far edge. The defensive jest I'd prepared withered on my lips, the silence inside the tent mocking me instead. *Where is he?*

Forced to push aside the uneasiness that surfaced with the question, I carefully laid the Canaanite woman on my pallet, but she jerked and cried out when her shoulder hit the ground. A jolt of phantom pain shot through me at her outburst, but she stayed beyond the realm of awareness, her face pale even through the dirt that disguised her features. What would she look like when the filth was washed away?

With a start, I stumbled backward a step. What was I doing bringing this unknown woman into my tent? I needed to find Shimon, not waste my time trying to save an enemy, even a female one.

Indecision yanked at both sides of me as blood seeped around the arrow shaft in her shoulder, dripping onto my blanket. If I didn't go now, she would die. Biting back a snarl of frustration, I slipped out of the tent, throwing a prayer skyward that she might stay unconscious until I brought back a healer—and another, more fervent one that Shimon would be here when I returned.

Men lay on the ground all around the healers' tents, their blood soaking the sand. Groans and cries filled the air. Two healers knelt in the dirt, washing wounds and applying strong-smelling poultices. I asked for help from both, but their vacant-eyed stares told me every hand was occupied.

The Canaanite woman would die on my pallet. I would never know her name, or why she chose to fight today. I turned to go and prayed those beautiful eyes would not open again, that she might drift into the next world in peace. Perhaps my sword should have delivered swift mercy on the battlefield.

A hand on my arm stopped me. "Can I help you?" A tiny woman stood beside me, silver brows furrowed in concern.

"I need a healer. There is a wom—a wounded soldier in my tent."

She lifted a reassuring smile. "I am not a physician, but I am a midwife. I came to help attend to the wounded." She gestured for me to lead the way.

Another prayer flew from my lips to Yahweh. Perhaps the woman might yet live. I pushed aside all the questions that came with that possibility and concentrated on weaving my way through the multitude of tents back to my own.

Before entering, I turned back to the midwife, my hand on the door flap. "Can you be discreet?"

Her eyes widened, but she agreed, her sober expression assuring me of her sincerity. She gasped at the sight of the red-haired woman on my bed, but before I could open my mouth to explain, the midwife was on her knees, examining the wound.

"Almost all the way through. Can you help me to prop her on her side so we can remove the shaft?" She asked for my knife, cut the leather bindings off the woman's armor, removed the breast-plate, and then cut the bloodied tunic away from the wound.

As I held the woman's shoulders, the midwife pushed on the end of the arrow shaft with a rock until the head broke free of the gash and she was able to pull the shaft clean through.

Blood gushed from the wound, front and back, but the mid-wife did not pale. Calmly, as if she were instructing me how to prepare a meal, she ordered me to press fresh linen against both sides of the woman's shoulder until the flow subsided.

She washed the shoulder with water from my goat-skin bag and packed the wound with a thick salve of honey, salts, and strong-smelling herbs from the satchel around her waist. She bound the woman's shoulder in strips of clean linen.

"She is fortunate. Her collarbone may be broken and she may not regain full use of that arm, but unless infection sets in, she should live." The midwife stood and turned to leave. "We must watch for sign of fever." She spun her tiny body back around with a fierce gleam in her eyes. "You know the law."

It was not a question. Every Hebrew knew the laws of war. Yehoshua had repeated them again last night as we prepared for battle. Women in enemy camps were not to be violated. If one was taken captive, provisions were allotted to protect her. I nodded my head. I had no intention of forcing myself on a wounded woman. Canaanite or not.

Her narrowed eyes pinned me. "Then you will marry her?"

The demand slammed me in the gut. "Marry her? Of course not!" The law provided for a Hebrew to claim a captive woman as a wife if he so desired, but the thought had not crossed my mind.

"If you don't, she could be violated, or killed, or both." The midwife's tiny fists were on her hips.

I stuttered, my tongue tangling. "But . . . she's a Canaanite . . . and out there on the field with a bow in her hands. Fighting against us. She's not my responsibility."

She came close to me, lifted her chin, and searched my face with intense scrutiny. She was strong, this midwife, and obviously one of the few left who had come out of Egypt and through the sea almost forty years ago. Her iron will was evident in the intensity of her gray eyes. "Of course she is. She became such the moment you brought her into your tent." She gestured to the bleeding woman with a frown. "Look at her. Poor thing. I cannot imagine the desperation that would drive her to plunge into such horror."

"No." I shook my head to clear the haze that had clouded over my arguments. "I cannot. My family—"

She interrupted with a smile and a gentle pat to my arm. "You are an honorable young man, I can see it in your face. You saved this woman for a reason. Don't let it be for naught. Yahweh guided you. As part of this nation, you have been given mercy. And mercy is a gift best passed along."

"I can't decide . . . not now . . . I need to go find my friend." Stumbling over my cluttered thoughts, I nodded toward the empty, rumpled pallet on the far side of the tent, and her eyes followed the gesture.

Compassion weighted her brow. "Go. I will stay with her until you return."

The last rock was heavier than all the rest. I clenched it in my fist. Unwilling to release its weight. Unwilling to place it atop the pile of stones that covered Shimon's still body. A body devoid of the friend who had sustained me through some of my darkest days. A friend who would not be here to walk beside me as I mourned his death.

This wilderness consumed everything. Sand whipped around my legs, stirred by a hot breeze, scraping my skin before lifting into the air with a gritty rush. I dropped the stone into its greedy clutches and turned away.

All around me, grim-faced men dug graves in which to lay bodies of friends and brothers. The thought that this was only the beginning, only the first of many battles that would be fought in the coming days, pierced my chest with bone-deep sadness. And Shimon would not be here to raise his sword alongside mine. I had failed him. Had failed to protect my sister's husband. What would I say when I saw her? How could I tell her that the man she'd loved since she was a girl was no more?

Why did I not find him sooner? Perhaps if I had tried harder to stay next to him when we attacked . . . Perhaps if I had not wasted time with that woman . . .

The midwife's demand barged its way into my mind as I trudged back to camp. Marriage to a Canaanite woman? How could I possibly consider such a thing? Especially when I had just buried Shimon?

She might not even survive the wound she'd received. Her skin had been pallid, her body listless in my arms. Why had she been on that battlefield? I'd kept an eye out for any other women among the dead, but the one laid out in my tent seemed to be the only female among the Canaanite army. Had she truly been shooting that bow she'd clung to with unconscious ferocity? Surely not.

Yet regardless of how dangerous she was, she was still a woman. And a woman alone in this hazardous wilderness was vulnerable. If she lived and I did not claim her, someone else would—someone who might want to hurt or destroy her.

I knew nothing of her, but the thought of leaving her to such a fate curdled my insides, much as the recollection of how close I had been to snuffing out her life earlier unsettled me. I'd thought nothing of cutting down the savage men who met us on the battlefield with tattooed, scarred bodies and the color of hate in their eyes. They were there with only one purpose—to destroy us and thwart the will of Yahweh. They'd been warned time and time again to leave the Land but remained nothing but belligerent. Yahweh had given them over four hundred years since the judgment of Sodom and her repugnant sister-cities. Four hundred long years to repent, and almost forty to flee from the people whose God had broken the back of Egypt. Yet when the woman had opened her eyes for those brief moments, no belligerence had met my gaze, only stark, howling grief. The same agony that now cleaved a chasm in my chest.

Hands on my hips and gaze clamped on the stretch of ground in front of me, I stood before my tent, now forever empty of my closest friend, the man whose marriage to my sister had solidified our brotherhood. These last few steps seemed infinitely more difficult than the thousands I'd taken this morning with an unconscious woman slung over my shoulder. The midwife would no doubt demand an answer as soon as I stepped through the door.

Although my only thought when I rose from my pallet this morning had been vengeance on a faceless enemy, my fate seemed to be determined—by Yahweh, the midwife, or perhaps both. I would be forced to go against the last wishes of my mother and those of my sister, but I had little alternative. I hadn't shielded Shimon from death, but I could at least shield this woman from being assaulted or killed by men with far less mercy than I—and I had met more than a few of those among our numbers.

After the thirty days allotted were fulfilled, I would give her the freedom to stay or to go—the law allowed a captive woman that much. For now, I would protect her. Whether she welcomed the shelter I offered or not.

4

ALANAH

16 NISSAN
1407 BC

My eyes stung; even the weak yellow light filtering
through the seams in the tent wall blinded me. I tried
to shift my position, but a spear of pain plunged
through my shoulder, bringing with it a wave of nausea.

Was the arrow still lodged there?

A bandage encased my shoulder, and my arm was bound
to my chest. The fragrance of strong herbs and honey told me
that a healing poultice had been applied. I sniffed again. No
smell of infection, but how long had I been here?

The large tent was sparsely outfitted—a low stool stood
guard near the entrance, a few pots and baskets, and another
rumpled pallet. Blood-splattered armor lay where it had obviously been shed after the battle, my quiver and bow next to it.
He'd kept my bow?

The tent door flipped open, and a man stooped low to enter.

My pulse stuttered, then pounded. This man had me on a sleeping mat, tied and wounded. What would he do to me? The aftermath of the battle flooded back, the screams, the smell of death. This was the same cursed Hebrew soldier who had found me on the battlefield.

Anger ripped through me. "Where am I?"

My loud demand startled him. He froze, then took one step backward. "In my tent." His tone was defensive but not as arrogant as I'd expected.

"Why did you bring me here?" My voice was steady, thank the gods. I would not let this Hebrew see even a hint of fear.

Head brushing the low ceiling, he filled the space like a wide tamarisk tree, blocking my escape. I was tall for a woman, but I guessed he would stand at least a head above me. How could I possibly overpower such a huge man? I eyed the dagger at his belt; perhaps if I surprised him with a quick attack I could kill him and take out a few more Hebrews before I was caught.

"You were injured." He gestured to the wound that should have killed me, if it had done its job.

"Why bother? I am your enemy."

He folded his arms across his wide chest and tilted his head as if trying to assess my character. "I could not let you bleed to death."

You should have. "So you saved me for what reason? To use me?"

He winced. "I have no such intentions."

Of course not. I snorted. Closing my eyes, I released a breath, slow and steady, through my nose. "Whatever your intentions are, make it quick and be done with it."

"I will not harm you." His voice was closer now, the rumble of it almost soothing. A ruse to lull me into false security, no doubt. I had survived this far without being violated, and I refused to let down my guard for a moment.

I dug my nails into my palm and squeezed my eyes tighter. He was a Hebrew, my enemy, and just as barbarous as any other man. My own father and brothers were fierce on the battlefield, and off. Thankfully, they had wrestled and sparred with me as if I were a boy. I could give as good as I got. *And nothing has changed, Hebrew. I'll fight you to the death.* "How long have I been here?"

"Since yesterday." The whisper of cloth rustling told me he had lowered himself to the ground nearby.

Restraining myself from shifting farther away from his looming presence, I opened my eyes to glare at the woolen canopy above me.

"No one, except a healer, knows you are here."

Why did he keep my presence a secret? "Are you going to let me go?"

No answer.

I shifted my glare toward him, to no effect. He sat on the ground, arms folded across bent knees, head down. A curtain of wavy hair hid his face.

"Will you release me?" I pressed as I darted a look behind him at the tent flap. I shifted my shoulder to test its mobility, but pain speared me again. How could I escape with such a wound? I had already fainted once and had no idea what awaited me on the other side of the door.

"I cannot." His throat moved as if he were swallowing a burning coal.

"Why would you go to the trouble of treating my wound if you were going to kill me?"

"I am not going to kill you."

A fresh wave of memories washed over me again. Cries of anguish, then swift silence as the Hebrews completed their grim task of slaying my countrymen. I attempted to rein in the rush of anger flowing through my chest, but my words flew out like daggers.

"Why not? You put the sword to the other soldiers on the field. Showed no mercy."

He met my furious gaze with a questioning one of his own. "You are a woman."

"It makes no difference."

He cocked his head, studying my face. His brown eyes seemed darker in the tent than they had in the sunlight, the intensity of their appraisal tempting me to squirm. "Did your husband force you to fight?"

I scoffed. "I have no husband." *My cousin made sure of that.*

His brows bunched together. "Then why were you on that battlefield?"

Lifting my head, I scowled at him with all the force of my hatred. "To kill Hebrews." That was all the information I would give this huge man who had dragged me away from the welcome arms of Prince Death. I growled and threw my head back against the pillow.

A pillow? Even as I groaned against the needles of pain my quick action had caused, a question niggled at the back of my mind—if he meant to harm me, why would he provide for my comfort?

The man thrust a hand toward me as if to help, then snatched it back just as quickly. "Are you hurting?" his low voice rumbled.

"I am fine," I said through gritted teeth, ignoring the tenderness in his tone.

"Do you need anything?"

"I said I am fine."

Silence vibrated in the tent for a long while, submitting to the mundane sounds of low conversations outside, sandaled feet scuffling by the tent, and horses nickering nearby. Would he sit there staring at me all day?

A female voice called from outside the tent. "Tobiah? Are you in there? I brought food."

Tobiah—for that must be his name—rose and lifted the door flap.

An older woman bustled in, the tiniest woman I had ever seen, a large pot on one hip and a basket balanced on her head. "Oh, my dear, you are awake? How are we feeling? I brought some food and clothing for you. After I change your bandages, we can get you out of that horrid tunic."

The woman did not wait for an answer, but instead pelted Tobiah with questions about my healing progress.

Yes, I had just awakened.

No, I had not eaten.

No, he hadn't told me.

Yes, my fever was gone. *He'd touched me while I slept?*

"Wait!" I threw up my good hand. "Told me what?"

They exchanged a look. The woman frowned and arched a silvery brow, and Tobiah studied his folded arms.

The woman arranged the lines of her face back into a reassuring smile as she turned to me. Deeply freckled from years in the sun, she reminded me of a little speckled sparrow from the way she flitted her hands about when she spoke. I could see the stories written in the lines of her weathered face, still delicate and fine-featured beneath a layer of age spots and wrinkles.

"What is your name, dear?"

I pinched my lips together, reluctant to reveal anything of myself, even to a seemingly harmless woman. She lifted her brows and waited for my answer. I had the sense she would not give in until I did. I released a huff. "Alanah. Now—what do I need to know?"

"All in good time, Alanah." She leaned down to pat my good hand. "I am Shira, the midwife."

I recoiled. "Midwife? But I am not—"

She released a childlike laugh that did not fit a woman with a silver braid trailing down her back.

"Yes, dear, but no healers were available to help you when Tobiah brought you into the encampment. A few of us midwives came along with the army to help the wounded."

"Oh." I was glad she had been the one to tend my wound. I shuddered at the thought of a strange man taking advantage of my unconscious state. However, Shira was my enemy too. Albeit an enemy who sat next to me unwrapping my shoulder, smiling and chattering about her pleasure that the swelling seemed to be abating.

Tobiah, on the other hand, had retreated as far across the tent as his height would allow. He glowered at the ground, his jaw working as if grinding his teeth. He must be regretting his earlier decision to stay his hand and save me. No matter, I would soon give him the chance to rectify his mistake.

After Shira rewrapped the bandages, she ordered him from the tent so she could help me remove the dirty tunic I still wore. She explained that she had cut my shoulder free but had not been able to undress me without help.

"Since Tobiah forbade that I reveal your presence, I could not bring any other women here. I hated to leave you in that blood-stained garment, though." Her brows pinched as she clucked her tongue in frustration.

With gentleness that contradicted my status as a captive, she helped me sit up. When the tent stopped spinning, I saw what she meant. My brother's tunic had been gray. No longer. Crimson stained the wool from hem to neck.

My eyes went wide. Was this all my blood?

Apparently reading my expression, she patted my hand. "No, dear, Tobiah pulled several dead men off you before bringing you here. The fact of the matter is, however, those bodies saved your life. You must have fallen early in the battle?"

I nodded but winced at the shock of memories her question resurrected.

Yes, I was wounded early, but not early enough to escape the horror. Wails, sightless stares, limbs, arrows whizzing, swords clanging, bodies piled on bodies, and blood, so much blood. My pulse raced as much as it had when I stood in that valley of death.

Shira's intense gaze pierced me, as if drawing out the poisoned images flickering through my mind. She put a warm hand on my face and closed her eyes. She breathed a steady rhythm until my heart slowed its pounding and my hands ceased their trembling.

"You poor thing. No woman should ever experience such things. Your shoulder is not the only open wound, is it?"

I clamped my lips tight against the sob building in my throat.

She lifted the corner of her mouth. Was she laughing at me?

No. There was no mockery in her gray eyes. Her lips curved into a smile that matched the warmth of her gaze, and my shoulders relaxed in response. "You will heal." She smoothed my hair as if I were a child, laid her hand aside my face, and rubbed my cheekbone with her thumb, a gesture that soothed me even more. "You both will."

Before I could ask what she meant, she ordered me to lift my right arm and began the task of undressing me without jostling my wound. An impossible task. Excruciating spikes of pain radiated down my side, across my chest, and up my neck.

Better to die naked than endure more. But Shira persisted, and somehow I bit back the screams while she sponged my bloodied and bruised body and washed my hair over a pot of water spiced with myrrh. She dressed me in a soft woolen garment, a sleeveless tunic the color of ripe olives at harvest.

She fashioned a linen sling for my arm and then tied a wide, woven belt around my waist. I trailed my fingers along its complicated pattern of yellow, red, and green obviously fashioned by a skilled hand.

Shira's eyes lit. "Do you like it?"

I dipped my chin. "I cannot wear this."

"Of course you can. My brother's wife, a master weaver, created this. She would be pleased to see it displayed so well." She lifted a chastening brow. "And offended if you refused."

"Now—" She moved a stool to the center of the tent and pointed at the ground in front of it. "Sit and eat while I braid your hair."

I hesitated.

For such a diminutive woman she certainly commanded obedience. My stomach demanded I comply, but I was reluctant to turn my back, even to this tiny woman. She could just as easily slit my throat as Tobiah in my weakened state.

"I won't hurt you." As testament to her sincerity, she held up a small loaf of flatbread and some dried meat. "I know it's not much. But you must have not eaten anything substantial in days. Best to start slowly."

I accepted the food and sat cross-legged in front of her.

I nibbled at the meat. It was good, salty. Gazelle, if my guess was correct. I tore the soft bread, stirring a sweet fragrance that caused my mouth to water. "What is it?"

"Exactly," Shira responded.

I looked over my shoulder, questioning her with a lifted brow.

A twinkle of humor sparked in her eyes. "It's manna, or 'what is it?' in our tongue."

"Is it made from barley? Or emmer wheat?"

"No. It's made from a substance that falls from the sky." She was teasing me, she had to be. Even so, Shira held a knowing look on her weathered face. "I know it sounds impossible. But Yahweh, our God, feeds us every day with manna. Every morning we gather what we need and discard what we do not."

I scoffed. Was this woman a liar? Or simply insane?

With a low laugh, she put her hands on either side of my head and guided it forward again to keep braiding. "Just go ahead and eat. You will see in the morning."

With a shrug, I took a bite. Nothing I had ever tasted, not fresh honey-raisin bread, not the ripest, most succulent fruit, could compare with the spicy-sweet flavor of the manna. I closed my eyes and groaned.

Shira chuckled behind me, her bony knees vibrating against my back. "Delicious, is it not?"

I did not answer. My mouth was full of bread, but I chewed slowly to savor the ethereal treat. If this fell from the sky every morning, I would be up at dawn.

No one had ever braided my hair. The sensation of someone else's tender fingers weaving patterns into my thick curls was new, and a small bit disconcerting. No one else I knew had hair even remotely as garish as mine—a product of my mother's heritage from some far northern country her ancestors had fled from long ago. Merciless children had teased me about the odd color until, at age nine, my fists ended the harassment, along with any chance of friendship with the other village children. They kept their distance. Either afraid of my ready temper or disdainful of my mother's well-known occupation.

Hypocrites, all of them. Looking down their noses at me while at the same time their fathers and brothers partook of the pleasures at the temple in Arad on a regular basis. Their mothers turned a blind eye to their husbands' disgusting exploits yet tossed epithets at me whenever I walked through the village.

I looked down at my empty hands, heartbroken that even the crumbs of the luscious delicacy were long gone.

"There, all done." Shira patted the top of my head as if I were a little girl. I lifted my hand to explore the intricate braid wrapped around the top of my head. Beneath the plaited crown, the rest of my hair cascaded down like a waterfall to the middle of my back, still damp from washing.

The tent flap flew open and Tobiah poked his head in. "Ready?"

I cocked my head and narrowed my gaze. "For what?"

Shira said nothing. Tobiah seemed to have something very large stuck in his throat, and his eyes went wide before flitting away from me to Shira.

"You did not tell her?" he rasped as he entered the tent.

"It's not my place, young man." They had a silent standoff for a few moments before she stood and began to pack her basket with the remnants of my bloodstained tunic and bandages.

I stood on unsteady legs like a newborn lamb, gauging the troubled look in Tobiah's eyes. Was he turning me over to be killed? If he was not interested in ending me himself, perhaps he would let the other Hebrews do the job.

But why would Shira treat my wound, give me a beautiful dress, and braid my hair for an execution? Perhaps I was to be sacrificed to their god in thanksgiving for victory against my people, or to ensure more of that delicious manna fell from the sky.

I challenged Tobiah with a look, but his gaze slipped quickly away from mine, as if he were loath to look at me. Perhaps he was frustrated with having to give up his war spoils to appease his god. I wondered what sort of bloodthirsty deity they worshipped. Was he even worse than Ba'al? The screech of infant sacrifices suddenly wailed through my head and I shivered terribly. Would I, too, be tossed into the gaping mouth of an idol to perish in flames?

"What are you going to do with me?" I attempted to snarl the words, but they deflated. The assurance I had felt on the battlefield, when I flew in without a second thought for my life, seemed less today, as if Shira's soft hands braiding my hair had rearranged something inside my head.

Tobiah cleared his throat, looked down at his sandaled feet, and dropped his shoulders. "Marry you."

5

His words flew around inside my head like a senseless flock of chattering blackbirds. "What did you say?" I squawked.

Tobiah sighed, loud and long. "I must marry you."

My voice pitched high. "Why?"

"It is our way. If a man takes a woman captive, he must marry her."

Nonsense. Anger flushed through me, and I knew my face was as red as my hair. I stepped forward in challenge, wishing again that I could get my hands on his dagger. "Kill me and get it over with."

He lifted his palms with spread fingers. "I have no wish to kill you."

"Then let someone else do it."

He stepped back as if I'd slapped him, confusion thick on his face. "Why?"

I pursed my lips and balled my fists. Why did he care?

Shira stepped forward to put a gentle hand on my arm. I barely suppressed the urge to yank it away. "Tobiah is trying to save your life, not take it," she said. "We are in the middle of a war camp. No one knows you are here, or other men might lay claim to you. And"—she dropped her voice lower—"some of them would use you before killing you. Not all among us respect the laws of Yahweh."

I shivered against my will.

"Marry Tobiah. He will protect you. I have not known him long, but I believe him to be a man of honor. Please"—she slid her hand down my arm to grasp my hand with a strength that belied her size—"trust me."

An orphan ray of sunlight through the door highlighted a band of green that encircled the gray in her pleading eyes. For some unknown reason, I did trust her. This little Hebrew woman treated me with kindness I had never known. Sincerity permeated her every word.

But the taciturn man in front of me—I knew nothing of him. Only that he'd rescued me against my will. Every answer he gave was short—terse even—and now he seemed to be determined to look anywhere but in my direction.

Did I have any choice? Either I marry this enigmatic Hebrew or subject myself to the humiliation of being passed around. I had few options, none of them appealing. At least this one ended with only one man owning me, instead of many. I would have time to plan an escape later.

I sighed and nodded my head.

Shira slapped her hands together. "Wonderful. I will go find the elders."

"Now?" My pulse sped.

"It's important that you do it quickly, before anyone else sees you." She brushed my hair back from my face. "Besides, I have you all prepared. You look lovely."

My breath snagged in my throat. Shira had been preparing me for my wedding?

I stammered, "But—but isn't there a betrothal period?"

She smiled, but it did not touch her eyes. "Not in these cases. As a captive, you will be married at once, to protect you. There is no dowry or bride-price and certainly no home to prepare since we are still on the journey to our new land."

I raised my brows.

"You must perform certain *mitzvot*, certain instructions, but you are also given protections. The Torah, the law given to Mosheh, our leader, ensures you will be given a full cycle of the moon to mourn your loved ones before consummation of the marriage."

I already had a month to mourn. The wounds on my wrist were healing, no longer tender from the copper blade I'd used to etch the four permanent reminders of grief into my skin.

Tobiah cleared his throat, suddenly quite interested in his dusty sandals. Was he blushing? Surely not. Did he not have experience with women? He must be well over twenty. Why had he not married before now?

Shira threw me a reassuring glance and a tremulous smile before flitting out of the tent with a promise to return quickly with the elders to perform a marriage ceremony.

Once again, uneasy silence reigned inside my black woolen prison. Of course I could attempt to run, but I would not make it far; after Shira's warning that I would be violated by other men in the camp, I could not chance it.

Perhaps if I truly would be given a month to mourn my family, I could find a way to escape. Tobiah could not watch me at every moment, could he? I sat down on the stool Shira had vacated, stifling a whimper at the spike of pain in my shoulder. Running would have to wait until I healed more.

Tobiah stood by the entrance, shifting his weight from foot to foot, large arms crossed and eyes anywhere but on me. I studied my soon-to-be husband. A soldier from head to foot and built like a bear, Tobiah would no doubt be intimidating on the battlefield; although, scanning his bare arms and neck, I saw no markings outlining his battle prowess. What sort of warrior did not display his victories on his skin?

His refusal to meet my eye and his limited answers to my questions annoyed me. Why would he even consider marrying his enemy? He had made no advances upon me, at least since I was conscious, but a month was a long time.

Tension hummed and buzzed in the air. The tent seemed to be closing in on us, and if Shira did not return soon, I might scream. I closed my eyes, trying to steady the rhythm of my heart, breathing slowly and thinking of my father.

He had done his best to persuade me to marry. Even ordered me to do so a time or two. But I refused every suitor he brought before me. I had no interest in playing the part of the dutiful wife to some lecher. And I made it so known to my father.

He blustered, he threatened, but ultimately I won. As much as he ignored his one daughter, he seemed almost relieved at my many adamant refusals over the years. Both Ashrath and Petubah, the wives he took after my mother abandoned us, complained unceasingly about having to feed me as well as Davash, my only unmarried brother. My father told them to keep their tongues in their heads and do their work.

When my cousin refused to provide even one copper deben to secure me a husband after he had inherited the responsibility of my welfare, I had been glad, until I realized that my only option for survival was prostitution. It hadn't taken much to decide to run off to battle rather than submit to such degradation.

And here I sat, ready to marry a man I did not know. A man who was my enemy. I should be exacting revenge on this Hebrew, not marrying him. My brothers' curses howled at me from beyond the grave. Perhaps while I escaped, I could slit the Hebrew's throat as he slept, to silence their cries in my head.

Shira's voice beckoned Tobiah and me outside. We exchanged a brief glance, but not so short that I missed the conflicted look he smothered before ducking out. The nagging feeling that he was as much a prisoner as I was whispered through my mind, but I shook it off. He was the jailer, not me.

I squinted and shaded my eyes with my free hand until they adjusted to the brilliance of the outside world. A semicircle of five older men surrounded us. Arms crossed and glares aimed at me. They all looked the same—long beards and deep scowls. Yet although they were older, none looked sickly, but strong and lean. These men were warriors.

"This is the woman?" said the one in the middle.

Tobiah nodded.

The man raised his bearded chin to look down his nose at me. Black eyes bored into mine. My stomach clenched, but I returned the accusing glower.

"Where are you from?" He seemed loath to speak directly to me. His face bunched, as if tasting bitter wine.

"A village west of the Salt Sea. In the highlands near Arad."

"Are you a *zonah*?"

The accusation of prostitution sliced deep, but I managed to force out a no between gritted teeth.

Another of the long-beards arched a patronizing brow. "Why, then, were you on the battlefield?"

"To fight."

"Against men?" Disgust drew down the corners of his mouth. I answered with an indifferent shrug. They all shook their heads in disbelief, eyes bulging and long beards waggling.

The first man stepped closer. I flinched but held my stance. His thin lips twitched behind his beard, as if he wanted to ask more questions, but instead he turned to Tobiah. "And you want to marry this idol worshipper?"

Tobiah sneaked an indecisive glance at me but smoothed

composure across his face before nodding affirmation toward the elder.

"And are you an untouched maiden?" The elder peered at me, as if to determine whether I would lie.

"Yes. I am a maiden." My face flamed, but I looked him directly in the eye to prove my words true.

The long-beards tightened their circle, whispering among themselves for a few minutes. I strained my ears; a few sharp words hinted that the verdict might lean my way. Perhaps they would forbid this ridiculous union and execute me instead.

One could only hope.

An unexpected "You may marry her" came from the leader's lips.

All the blood rushed to my feet. Hope denied.

"Provided"—he raised a finger—"that she conform to our laws and not be touched for a full cycle of the moon. After that time, if you decide you do not want her, you may put her aside."

Another man interjected, "But she cannot be treated as a slave, mind you. She is a wife, with full benefits of such. She must obey the Torah and put away idol worship."

I resisted the urge to wrap my fingers around the copper amulet that still hung around my neck, the one my father had given me many years ago. Why had Shira allowed me to keep it when she helped me dress if these people were so against our gods?

The midwife's resolute voice came from behind me. "She will. Tobiah and I will teach her."

Tobiah turned wide eyes back to her, then me, but held silent.

The elder tucked his chin, brow furrowed. "See that he does."

The middle elder performed a perfunctory ceremony that included something about a mountain and a cover of clouds and that somehow the marriage tent reminded of such things. As the terms of the covenant were reeled off, the monotony of the man's voice gave way to thoughts of escape.

Perhaps if I was careful, my shoulder would heal just enough in the next three weeks. Tobiah's tent was situated near the edge of camp, it should not be too difficult to steal away while he slept. Perhaps I could even return to my artifice and borrow some of his clothes. Until then, I would play along with this counterfeit covenant.

"Do you?"

I blinked. "Excuse me?"

"Do you accept the terms of the marriage?"

"I do." *Whatever they are.*

"Then you are hereby bound together in the eyes of Yahweh just as Adam and Chavah were bound together in the Garden. You shall cleave to one another as man and wife."

One of the men handed Tobiah a scrap of papyrus—a written contract, perhaps? I would never know, the lines of marks were a mystery to me.

Four of the elders, along with other curious witnesses, scattered as soon as the hasty ceremony finished. However, the head long-beard stood immobile, arms crossed and eyes pinned on me.

He jerked his chin at Shira. "Do it now. So I can return to my meal."

I looked back and forth between them. What had I missed?

Pity pinched Shira's brow. "It cannot be avoided, Alanah. However much I hate to do it. Just tell yourself it will grow back."

"What will grow back?"

"Your hair, dear."

I clutched at my locks. "No!"

She tilted her chin to the side. "Did you not hear the terms?"

"You cannot cut my hair!" As much as I disdained the color at times, it was my only connection to the mother who had left me, a reminder of who I was and who I must never end up like.

"We must, sweet girl. It is the law. A captive woman taken to marriage must put off everything of Canaan and have her head shaven."

"*Shaven!*"

She pinched her lips into a tight frown. "It is for your own protection."

"How can losing my hair protect me?"

"To make you less attractive to the men, Alanah. Until the marriage is consummated, you are still at risk. This is an army camp; very few women among the soldiers can make for a volatile situation. It is why Tobiah had to be so careful. He did not move from your side unless I was there. It also ensures that Tobiah is making the choice to marry you for the right reasons, and not just your beauty."

I glanced at Tobiah. His face blazed as red as the tail end of a sunset and his eyes seemed permanently clamped on his feet. I twirled a strand of my hair around my finger, considering her logic. It seemed I had no choice. Either I submitted to this strange command or find myself in the same situation I faced in my own village.

At least when I took my leave of this place, blending in as a man might not be so difficult. Jaw clenched tight, I sat on the stool in the tent and held my breath, determination alone keeping my chin high. Shira's hand gripped my right shoulder tightly for a few long moments before she began her grim task.

After she untied the amulet of Anat from my neck, she loosened the braid she had so meticulously woven only an hour before. Then, without a word, she held the end of it in her hand, before a slice of shears and a quick breath behind me announced that the hank of hair released from my head.

A tendril fell, floated down to my lap. I grasped it in my good hand, twirling the flame-red around and around my thumb and grinding my teeth against the anger that welled inside me, higher and higher with each snip.

A movement in the corner of my eye snatched my attention. The tent flap.

Tobiah had fled.

6

TOBIAH

I stayed away as long as I could, but Shira would need to return to her own tent. And I should return to my bride. My shorn bride.

Leaving had been a cowardly move. But I could not bear to watch the beautiful red waves float to the ground like withered leaves. So, under the guise of giving her privacy, I fled and sat near a campfire where no one knew me or anything of my unwilling bride, and drank pilfered enemy wine until the sun dipped low.

Shira sat on the stool outside the tent, waiting for me to return. As I approached, she stood. "Alanah is asleep."

"Is she—is she all right?"

Shira looked up at me with a curious expression in her strangely young eyes. "She will be. You must give her time. There is hurt written all over her face. And not just from what has happened here today. She needs time to heal before she can adjust to marriage. Especially marriage to her enemy."

The words stung, although they should not. It was exactly who I was: her enemy, a captor imprisoning her in a marriage she did not welcome. "Did she say why she was on that battlefield?"

Shira shook her head. "She is not ready. She will tell her tale when she is."

Would she tell Shira first? An unexpected desire to be the one she trusted first came over me. Thirty days was such a small amount of time for her to learn to trust me. And I was none too sure I could trust her either. The gleam of retribution seemed to burn in her eyes much of the time.

"You heard the elders, Tobiah. Do not touch her until the time is fulfilled, or you will face consequences." The warning was stark. "They asked me to ensure that vow is upheld. I think you are a young man to be trusted. But since I have many other wounded to tend and cannot stay here, I will be checking on her regularly."

I rolled back my shoulders. "You have my solemn word I will not approach her. I only did this to protect her."

"I thought as much." She tied a worn leather satchel around her waist. "I'll be back in the morning to check on her wound and refresh her bandages."

Alone. I would be alone with Alanah now. No bustling little midwife to buffer the empty space between us. I shrugged off the tension that had gathered between my shoulder blades. *You are a soldier, Tobiah. Act like one.*

The sun rested low on the horizon, outlining the sharp peaks of far-off hills. I pushed back the tent flap and peered into the dark. The remnants of light touched Alanah's form on my pallet, her back turned and her head wrapped in a white linen turban. The head Shira had shaved. My stomach clenched at the loss.

A glint of color on the ground near the center tent pole caught my eye, a stray strand of red. I memorized its position and then dropped the flap behind me and retrieved it in the dark. Just as I had imagined, her hair was soft as the feathers of a newborn bird and fine as rich flax thread. I had never seen its likeness in color among any of my people.

Her stifled moan startled me. A ridiculous spasm of guilt forced me to hide my hand behind my back. Had she seen me? Alanah pulled in short, pained gasps.

"How can I help?" I said.

The sound stopped, as if she were holding her breath. She could not fool me, she was awake, and hurting. I worked to smooth my tone, restrain the urgency that welled up inside my chest. "Alanah. Do you need Shira?"

"I am fine." The strain in her voice belied the statement. From the moment I'd found her on that battlefield, she'd exuded strength and determination. Now she sounded like a little girl, weak and lost in the dark. My arms ached to wrap around her, to absorb her pain.

The strength of that desire startled me. She was no great beauty. Her lower lip, larger than the top one, seemed permanently pressed forward in a frown matching the pinch between her wispy brows. But some of the golden tone of her skin had returned, indicating a woman accustomed to toil beneath the sun, and after Shira had dressed her in a garment that brightened the color of her eyes and arranged her hair into a waterfall of red curls, the change had been startling—and more than disconcerting. She was my enemy. My captive. And, from the flashes of fury that sometimes blazed in her eyes, more than willing to exact revenge for the utter destruction of her people.

And it had been complete destruction—*hormah*. Every soldier—every last soul in their camp—had been either killed or taken captive. For Shimon's sake I wanted nothing more than to celebrate that victory, to lift a full cup to the annihilation of his killers with the others around the fire, but the desire was tempered by this confusing draw toward one of their women. Perhaps it would have been safer to leave her there in that valley to die. But even as the thought floated through my mind, something inside me rebelled. She may hate me, she may want me dead, but I no more wished her destruction than I wished my own.

"I won't touch you, Alanah. You have my sworn oath."

A swish of cloth told me she'd turned toward me, perhaps an attempt to search my face for deception.

"Why?"

I startled at the question that found its way through the dark. I wished I could see her eyes. "I made a covenant with you."

"No blood was spilled."

True, the covenant had not been accompanied by the usual offering of an animal sacrifice. And since this was not a normal marriage, no blood would stain the marriage bed tonight. How could I make her believe my words? To make her understand that she could trust me?

I drew my bronze dagger from the leather sheath on my hip. I placed its point against my palm, wincing at the burn of metal slashing the skin, biting my lip against a hiss. The cut throbbed as I shuffled close to her, my toes brushing the linens upon which she lay. Kneeling, I held out my hand. "Here, give me your hand."

Silence rose like a tide around me. I counted my breaths—ten, twenty. If only I could see her face.

At thirty breaths I almost dropped my palm, but suddenly her strong, slender hand met mine. Her willing touch caused a lump to press up my throat, cutting off my air supply. I swallowed hard against it. "Do you feel it?"

Her voice trembled. "Feel what?"

"My blood."

"Oh." She pressed her warm palm closer to mine. "I do."

With great effort I released her hand.

"Now the covenant is complete."

No answer.

"I will not force myself on you. I vow it to you, and to Yah-weh." I stressed the name of my God so she would understand the seriousness with which I took the vow.

No answer.

"Get some rest." I stumbled my way to the thin pallet that had belonged to my best friend, dragged it just outside the entrance to the tent, and prayed that my wife wouldn't murder me in my sleep.

7

ALANAH

17 NISSAN
1407 BC

I jolted awake. Vivid images of terror and blood and screams retreated at the flood of sunlight, but it happened slowly, as if the dreadful visions refused to release their grip on my mind, letting go one vicious claw at a time.

I'd been back in the valley, with shifting sand beneath my sandals and the screech of rams' horns causing the hair on the back of my neck to stand on end. The dream could not have been more real.

My whole body was rigid. My pulse raced, nausea threatened, and my lungs would not expand. Little sips of air were not enough. As I struggled to draw more breath, flashes of light clouded my sight.

No. I would not faint. I refused to be pulled back into the chasm between dreams and wakefulness where the frightening images plagued me most. I forced a deep breath, looking around quickly when a moan escaped my mouth. Thank the gods that Tobiah was missing from his post outside the door and hadn't heard the evidence of my weakness.

I rolled onto my good arm and pushed myself up with my elbow until I was able to sit straight. My shoulder protested less today than yesterday. But still, I must not damage it further and hinder my escape.

How long would it be before I could use my bow again? I reached past my feet to where it lay next to my quiver. I caressed the wood, smoothed by my father's expert, callused hand and patterned after the one made for the goddess Anat by Kothar, the master craftsman to the gods. Why had Tobiah allowed me to keep it? No other weapons remained in the tent. Regardless, without arrows it was worthless.

A flash of red drew my gaze, a dark circle of crimson splotched across my palm. Dried blood.

Tobiah's blood.

Battle memories flooded in again, conjured by the little smear.

Although the long-beards had been adamant that thirty days pass before the final act of marriage was carried out, I had fully expected to find the Hebrew in my bed as soon as Shira took her leave. Every nerve in my body vibrated when he entered the tent. I had been prepared to fight until he silenced my screams with his dagger across my throat.

When he cut his hand instead and vowed to keep his word, I was almost disappointed that I would not be given a reason to provoke him to kill me.

Almost.

I curled and uncurled my hand, fascinated by the red stain blooming like a *kalanit* flower across my skin. A covenant. An unbreakable pledge forged by the Hebrew's own blood. Why would he do such a thing?

He must see the determination in my eyes, the plan to kill

him and escape; a soldier would not miss such a thing. Yet he'd slept right outside the entrance, snoring like a bear. Either he had full confidence in his ability to fight me off or, like a fool, he trusted his enemy.

My pulse pounded, causing the wound in my shoulder to ache again. Here was my chance. Although my arm may not be ready, my legs were able. Hunting with my brothers, climbing rocks in the wadis around my home looking for game, tending to the crops, and hauling jugs of water back from the village cistern kept them strong and sinewy.

I slung my quiver over my good shoulder, gripped my bow, and peeked through the tent flap, braced for a painful run.

My breath released in a huff. There would be no escape this morning. Tobiah crouched by the fire nearby, forming round circles of dough between his palms. His damp wavy hair hung unbound around his face. He must have awoken early to bathe. Frowning in concentration, he pressed the curtain of brown-gold away with the back of his hand, streaking flour across his forehead.

The hint of a laugh tickled the back of my throat. To cover it, I offered a reproach. "You are burning it."

He slanted an annoyed look at me but grabbed a stick to flip the singed flatbread.

"Shall I finish?" I said.

His eyes met mine and held for a brief moment before traveling to the turban wrapped around my naked head. My face flamed and my fist clenched my skirt. It took all my will not to cover my head with my hand and run from his gaze.

Mercifully, he dropped his attention to his task. "No. I made it—for you." His low voice caressed the last two words.

He made this food for me? He had every right to awaken me at dawn and demand his meal. Yet here he was, huddled on the ground like a kitchen slave, baking bread for me. Manna bread. The spiced-honey smell beckoned me from across the fire. My mouth watered and suddenly I could taste it again. Even such a little bit as I'd sampled yesterday spiked a desire for more. My anxious tongue tingled as Tobiah finished patting the circles onto the fire-heated rock, waited, and then flipped them.

Restraining the urge to reach across the fire and grab the delicacy from his hands, I sat cross-legged nearby and placed my quiver and bow next to me.

Tobiah's lifted brow questioned their presence. I sifted a few explanations through my mind before coming up with one that might deflect his suspicion. "My father made them for me. I feel more . . . comfortable when they are close by."

His mouth pinched as he stood to bring me a piece of bread. He squatted next to me, a trickle of water from his still-wet hair trailing down his cheek. For half a breath I almost reached up to brush it away.

"I promised to protect you," he said with the unmistakable glint of warning in his eyes.

My defenses shot up. "I don't want your protection."

He gathered his brows. "What do you want?"

"Nothing *you* can give me." Gazing at the distant hills to the north, I imagined the roll of the highlands. White, black, and brown clumps of sheep and goats wandering free across grazing lands defiantly green in the face of sparse rain.

My father's farm, nestled against the foothills, waited there to be harvested by someone else's hand. My father, brothers, and I had plowed and planted, tended the wheat and orchards—yet others would enjoy the fruit of our labor. The farm I cherished, the terraced hills I loved, now belonged to a cousin who hated me and had snatched the last crumbs of my life.

I blinked the smoke of the cookfire from my eyes but inhaled the scent, both acrid and comforting. "There is nothing left."

Tobiah leaned closer. His eyes, now level with mine, searched with an intensity that stole my breath. "Then stop trying to run."

Why did it seem like he was looking at my very core, raw and exposed? I broke the connection with the guise of eating the flatbread he had prepared. Once again the taste, like no other, hit my tongue and blocked out any other sensation. A little moan of pleasure slipped out.

Tobiah's cheek quirked. "Good?"

Hoping he would attribute my flushed face to the campfire, I shrugged. *Like nothing I have ever tasted.*

"I gathered two *omers* of manna today. Can you finish here?" He gestured to the cooking rock, tucked against the fire, where he had prepared the bread.

I sighed. Yes, I was a wife now. "Shira tells me this falls from the sky?"

"Every morning."

"Even in this camp, away from the rest of your people?"

He dipped his chin in affirmation.

"And you do not know what it is or where it comes from?"

After a quick shake of his head, he turned to enter the tent, leaving me to my task of grinding the tiny white pearls, as small as coriander seeds, into flour with the stone mortar and pestle he'd left by the fire.

I could not reconcile the fierce soldier persona from the battle-field with his quiet, reserved demeanor. As of yet, I had not seen him even converse with anyone other than Shira, apart from the one-word answers he gave the long-beards during our pretense of a wedding.

He did not seem to have friends among the other soldiers. And yet, there had been another pallet in the tent and a few scattered belongings that made me think another solider had occupied it before me. Who was it? And where was he now?

Everything about Tobiah was a mystery. Who exactly was I yoked to? And how long would I have to endure it?

The more I considered the sharp ridges pressed against the northern horizon, the less confidence I had that I could return to my village on my own. The only way I had reached the battle-camp in the first place was sheer desire to avenge my family. And truly, there was nothing left for me at home.

My father's farm was gone, his two wives inherited by my cousin, Dagan. And due to my mother's choice to abandon me to return to the temple, I was an outcast among the villagers—greeted at the cistern by only whispers behind hands and haughty looks.

Dagan had refused to offer any sort of dowry, making it clear I was welcome in his house only as a slave—retribution for the bloodied nose I had given him as a child. He and some other boys had followed me home from the village with lewd suggestions on their lips toward the cast-off daughter of a *zonah*. I silenced them with one well-placed punch.

I nibbled on another piece of manna to take my mind off my cousin's treachery. The sweet bread calmed the roiling in my gut like a balm. It needed no butter, no spices, no date honey to enhance its flavor. And to think, the Hebrews ate this every day!

All of them looked healthy and strong. Even Shira, elderly and small, sparkled with life and energy, not normal for a woman her age—or someone who had endured the harsh desert heat and sun for forty years. Her skin, although faintly wrinkled, glowed as though lit from behind. Her countenance was almost that of a young girl, full of laughter and vitality.

I mixed the white powder with a bit of water from a nearby pitcher and kneaded it into dough. It was soft and fluffy like I imagined a cloud would feel if I could reach the sky. I pressed it between my palms and enjoyed the lavish feel of the cool concoction spread between my fingers, like a curious child squishing mud at the edge of a stream.

Smothering amusement at my own foolishness, I formed a circle with my thumbs and then patted it, back and forth, stretching it as I did, until a smooth, white disk lay across my hand. I brushed ash off the flat hearthstone close to the fire and flipped the bread onto its surface. A familiar action made unfamiliar by my surroundings and the ingredients.

After a tall stack of flatbread lay cooling on a cloth by my feet, a commotion behind me startled a look over my shoulder. Tobiah had packed all his belongings into two baskets and was now dismantling the tent.

The Hebrews were breaking this war camp, preparing to join the rest of their group in the south. I had little choice but to go with them.

8

Sturdy poles toppled as stakes were pulled from the ground. The tents around us folded in on themselves like weary dancers, skirts billowing as they fell. Soldiers milled around our campsite, shouting orders, packing belongings onto wagons, watering their animals. As the camp flattened, the landscape became clearer.

When I had slipped through the wadi into this valley, the sun had already begun laying herself down at my back, and in the haze of dusk I could not see the expanse of the land where we camped. Nor did I have the presence of mind during the rush of war to distinguish my surroundings.

Now I could see that all around us were high ridges, sharp against the blue sky. The red sand beneath my feet contrasted the brown hills that encircled us to the north.

Shira appeared with a large bundle—too large for her tiny frame—on top of her head. As usual, the radiance of her smile brightened an already lapis-blue day.

"How is our wounded soldier?" She gave a playful nudge of her elbow to my good arm.

"Better." Although my arm did not throb as much, my heart

seemed to have taken up the cause as I thought about leaving this valley and moving farther away from my home.

Tobiah offered to take Shira's bundle and load it on a wagon nearby. She pushed his hand away. "You leave me be, young man. We only have a few miles to travel. In Egypt I balanced huge jugs of water on my head while carrying a basket under each arm." She winked. "I'll be just fine. I am stronger now than I was then."

I did not doubt it. She exuded strength—in more ways than one.

"I've come to travel with you. I don't want to lose track of my charge in the chaos of returning to camp." She adjusted the bundle on her head.

"Are you not traveling with others?" I had seen her only near Tobiah's tent, I did not know where she went when she left.

"I came with a group of older midwives to help the wounded. None of the young mothers I have been tending are close to their times, so I decided to lend a hand where needed." She pursed her lips into a wry smile. "And my hands certainly were needed."

"If only they were used to heal me and not to shear me like a ewe." I rubbed the back of my naked neck, already prickling with day-old growth. When Shira did a job, she did it thoroughly. I surely looked like old Jobab, the beggar who hunched near the village cistern without a wisp of hair on his ancient spotted head.

Shira's melodic laugh and distracting chatter soothed the ache that swelled in me as the company began to move. We were marching south, away from the farm where my every good memory dwelt among the olive groves, the date-palm orchards, and the vineyards terraced on the sides of those rocky hills. To my surprise, Tobiah walked on the other side of Shira, his long stride shortened to match the little midwife's.

I leaned forward to toss a question at him. "Why don't you march with the other men?"

He faltered for a step but recovered. "There is no need."

"I'm not going to run," I said, as much for myself as for him. Home pulled at me, but walking alone in the desert, with no food or water, I would not last three days.

"That is not the reason." He raised a shoulder, dropped it, and then glared at the ground. I looked to Shira for an answer.

"Tobiah has been released from army service for a year." Her eyes, with a wisp of humor, flicked to him. "In order to bring happiness to the woman he has married."

Tobiah suddenly seemed to be more interested in the hills to the east than our conversation.

"He cannot fight?"

"Unless we are attacked in camp, then of course he is free to defend us, but no, he cannot go to war." She squinted with obvious compassion for a solider who could no longer do as he was trained.

I should not pity him—it was one less man to fight my people—but for some reason, guilt slipped between my ribs. *Only a year. Then his life will return to normal. Even if mine never will.*

Another woman called to Shira, and with another wink and a promise to return soon, Shira left Tobiah and me to walk alone. The absence of her chatter amplified the silence as it stretched between us—deep silence that hummed with unanswered questions.

"How long is this canyon?" I said, if only to slice through the pulsating emptiness.

His voice rasped from disuse. "We have a few miles left to cover. But we should arrive before sundown."

"How did you do it?" I asked.

He furrowed his brow in question.

"Defeat the army that had only a few weeks ago crushed you, taken so many captive, and then sent you off like a pack of frightened jackrabbits?"

He gazed over the heads of his fellow soldiers toward the southern route we traveled. "Yahweh."

"Your god?"

He nodded.

I snorted. "Your god didn't fight for you, it was your army that defeated us."

He swung his head to spear me with an intense gaze, too intense for a dispassionate soldier with no thought but to destroy his enemies. "It was our hands, but Yahweh fought for us."

My father had named me for Anat and raised me to be in her likeness, the fierce warrior goddess with a bow. The empty quiver on my shoulder was a reminder of the legacy he expected me to fulfill. Yet even though I'd grown up hearing the tales of the gods—their constant struggle for supremacy, their never-ending lust for blood and power—the tales were mist and legend. The way Tobiah, and Shira, spoke of Yahweh—it was almost as though their god were as real as flesh and bone, as if they could sit down and drink a cup of wine with such a deity.

"How could a god fight for you?" The image of a heavenly body, made from the light of stars and swiping at mortals with a ghostly sword, floated into my imagination, and I scoffed under my breath. What a foolish thought.

"You have much to learn of the Creator and his ways."

Something raw—an edge I'd never examined before—began to throb. The dull ache in my chest dredged up whispers of questions I had never thought to ask, questions born from the sweet breath of mornings as I'd hiked through the fertile valley I loved, from the intricate structure of a purple-fringed passion flower, and from the vibrancy of a varicolored sunrise over the eastern horizon.

A break in our conversation highlighted the crunch of gravel beneath our feet. Changed from sand, the trail had begun ascending out of the canyon toward a low range of hills.

"Your army did crush us," said Tobiah, breaking the silence. "Because we were caught off guard. Our fathers wandered in this desert." He gestured to the east and south. "For almost forty years."

I had heard the stories but did not believe them. A multitude, wandering like nomads in the wilderness for a generation? Without a destination in sight? How could they survive? No water, no food?

"When at last we again neared the borders of the land Yahweh had promised thirty-nine years ago, we were unprepared for the attack by your king. It is surprising that more of us did not die." A muscle at the top of his cheek twitched at the memory.

I was entranced by the telling of his story and the perspective of one who lived on the receiving end of my father and brothers' last battle. A cold shiver meandered up my back. Had Tobiah crossed swords with one of them?

"When we knew we had lost, and that so many were taken, the shofar announced retreat. And we did, ashamed and defeated." All of Tobiah's words strung together over the last few days could not have matched this speech. I pressed my lips together, determined not to interrupt him.

"Armed with the blessing of Yahweh and his promise of victory, we snuck down through the wadis in the night, surrounded your army, and—"

"Decimated us."

A reminder. This man was my enemy. No matter that he had spared me, he was party to the destruction of my family. Tobiah continued in silence until we came up over another ridge. The Hebrew camp spread out before us, in baffling width and depth.

Black, brown, and multicolored tents covered every inch of land, all surrounding a central tent, which towered above the others. A giant cloud high above its black covering shimmered with eerie luminescence. So they were true, the rumors I'd heard, that the Hebrews followed a supernatural cloud around in the wilderness. What sort of magic could conjure such a thing? I could not look away from the peculiar sight.

Shira appeared at my elbow with a satisfied smile tugging at her lips. "Astonishing, isn't it? I've lived among this throng for almost forty years, and still, it takes my breath away."

"Is that main tent your sanctuary?"

"It is. We call it the *Mishkan*, the dwelling place. The tribes are arranged around it, according to the direction of Yahweh himself." She pointed at a banner atop a tall pole nearest the center. "You see, there is the flag of the Levites, my own tribe. We are camped all around the perimeter of the linen courtyard, for we were granted special responsibilities. But all the tribes"—she pointed to each wing of tents spreading to the north, south, west, and east—"have their appointed place."

"And what tribe are you?" I arched my brows at Tobiah.

His chest swelled. "I am of the tribe of Yehudah."

Shira smirked. "The family line of Yehudah, the fourth-born son of Yaakov, holds a special blessing, a royal blessing. Tobiah is right to be proud."

He reddened and turned his face toward the *Mishkan*.

"Tobiah," she said, "where is your family camped? I want to be able to find you again."

Tobiah pointed to a cluster of tents on the edge of his tribe's appointed spot.

She nodded. "And your father's name?"

His nostrils flared. "Malakh of the Shelanite clan."

"Very good." She patted my arm. "Keep that shoulder as still as possible. I will find you in a couple of days to make sure you are healing. Tobiah's family can help with your bandages."

"Are you leaving?" A twinge of loss surprised me. Shira had become familiar to me already, her unexpected kindness lessening the sting of captivity.

"I need to find my family, Alanah. My sons and daughters will be worried for me."

"You have children?"

Pride burned bright in her smile. "I do. Three sons and three daughters." She placed a fist on her heart. "And eighteen grandchildren, as well. I need to kiss their precious faces."

"What of your husband?"

Although her expression remained placid, for one long moment her eyes shouted grief before she responded. "My Ayal is gone, for two years now."

"Oh . . . I am . . . I am sorry," I stammered.

"There is nothing to be sorry for. My husband and I had thirty-seven beautiful years together and built a precious family. He had children from his first marriage and we also adopted another son and two daughters into our family over the years." Her eyes flicked to Tobiah and then back to me. "He was not a perfect man, but he was a man who loved me with his whole life, and I miss him every moment of every day."

Rendered speechless by her declaration and not-so-subtle intimation that the stoic man next to me would somehow be such a husband for me, I glanced away, feigning interest in the landscape and working very hard to erase the unbidden images that her story had conjured in my mind, in addition to the unfamiliar longings they provoked.

With another assurance to Tobiah that she would find us soon, Shira quickened her step, still carrying that huge bundle atop her head, and left us.

Some of my strength and hope went with her. My foot slipped on a stone, and Tobiah gripped my upper arm to steady me. I shrugged him off. "It is nothing," I spat out. But I touched the shoulder sling Shira had fashioned; the misstep had sent pain shooting across my collarbone.

"Should I throw you over my shoulder again?"

Was he mocking me? No, a hint of unexpected mischief glinted in his brown eyes. I glared at him, pursing my lips and looking away. I did not care if this man was my husband, or that he had saved me. I would keep reminding myself, until the opportunity to escape came my way, that he was my enemy.

9

TOBIAH

With every step that brought me closer to my sister, my sandals seemed heavier, forged from lead. How would I tell her Shimon was gone? Alanah glanced at me, as if curious about my sluggish pace. I muttered something about remembering where our family tents were—but I knew, and they were closer than I wished them to be. Close enough for my impatient nephews to find us first.

A wiggling, laughing wall of little boys slammed into me, along with a volley of greetings and questions. "You are back!" "Did you win?" "What did you bring us?" "Where is Abba?" The last question stabbed deep, wrenching inside my gut like a rusty blade.

Sidestepping the interrogations, and after another round of hugs from each of the three boys, I sent them off to their mother with an announcement of my arrival. My twin sister hated surprises. She undoubtedly had sent the boys ahead to warn her. If only I did not carry revelations that would devastate her and steal the shalom from her once-peaceful household.

Would she forgive the bearer of such news? And the brother who was unable to protect the father of her children? I tried to focus on my steps and not the despair that thoughts of Shimon brought to mind.

Would leaving Alanah on the field have made a difference? Or would I have still found Shimon as I did later that day— glassy-eyed, staring toward the heavens? If only the purifying *mikveh* I'd washed in this morning could purge the memory of my closest friend's sightless eyes.

Burying one more person I cared for in this detestable wilderness had taken more out of me than I could bear. Would I trade the life of this woman next to me—my wife—for that of my friend, my brother, Shimon?

Yes. I probably would.

I glanced at Alanah as if she could hear my hateful thoughts. But her attention was trained straight ahead like a soldier pressing into battle. Her face betrayed nothing, but she gripped the strap of the quiver across her chest, white-knuckled and back stiff, as if she were headed into an ambush.

I hadn't even thought of her as I'd greeted my nephews and had not warned her of the news I bore for my sister. But telling Alanah before I told Shimon's wife seemed traitorous somehow, so I kept my mouth closed.

I peered at her again. What could be going through that head of hers? The barest hint of fiery red edged the bottom of the white turban she wore. How long would it be before her lush curls would touch her shoulders again? Did she hate me for such a harsh command? Even though it had not been my own?

Girding myself with as much courage as it had taken to march toward Arad, I stepped into our campsite. My sister stood at the center of the clearing, stirring a pot over the fire.

Tzipi's brown eyes, dark and wary, watched Alanah and I enter the circle of tents. My nephews were already gone, sent off on some false errand, I was sure. *She knows.*

I had meant to take my sister aside, break it gently, hold her while she cried. I was not prepared for the lioness that met me, claws at the ready.

"How did it happen?" She swirled the wooden spoon in the stew again, then tapped it on the lip of the pot.

I turned up my palms. "Sister . . ."

"No. Do not give me words. Give me truth." Still clutching the dripping spoon, she crossed her arms and placed a foot at an angle. Except for the wisps of light brown hair escaping the safety of her head covering, she looked so much like our mother that I felt a sudden wave of longing for my *ima*—yet another victim, along with my father, of the perils of this journey and the fickle people who made up this multitude. If my brothers had not been swept into the rebellion instigated by Korah, one of Mosheh's own cousins, then my parents would be alive to comfort their daughter in her own loss.

I drew a long breath, latching my eyes on the manna-thickened liquid that bubbled in Tzipi's pot. "An arrow. It was swift and shortly after our first attack. We were separated in the crush of the initial assault." I turned my gaze back to my twin sister, willing her to understand, to forgive. "When I finally found him, he was gone."

The sight of my closest friend shot through with a Canaanite arrow was branded in my mind . . . his mouth full of blood from the fatal wound where the arrow had penetrated a weak spot in his armor . . . his infectious laughter and wise words silenced forever.

"Are you injured?" Tzipi asked, her face and tone devoid of expression.

"No." Dragging a hand over my beard, I sighed. "Other than

a few bruises and scrapes, I am whole." A lie. The wound of Shimon's loss throbbed in my chest.

"Good." She dismissed more talk of the battle by jerking her chin to my right. "And who is this woman?"

Alanah's face was a confusion of emotions, and I guessed that she was remembering back to the battlefield during my telling of Shimon's demise.

"Alanah, this is Tzipi, my twin sister. Tzipi, this is my wife."

Both women said nothing but regarded each other like two desert cats, large-eyed and wary.

Tzipi blinked at me, her face somehow now even more devoid of emotion. "Where did she come from?" She spoke as if Alanah was not standing next to me.

"She was wounded in the battle. I rescued her, and if I did not marry her, she would not have been safe."

Tzipi's face contorted in disgust, and she aimed her dripping spoon at Alanah. "Are you telling me this woman is a Canaanite?"

"Sister—"

"You married a heathen woman? Some *zonah* you found on the battlefield?"

"I am no *zonah*!" said Alanah, taking a small step forward. Her eyes blazed with indignation.

"Tzipi." I set my jaw as I stepped between the two women before their claws did real damage. "She is not a prostitute. Her family was killed in the first battle."

"You don't know anything about her. She is probably lying!" Tzipi spat the accusation.

I put up a hand. "That's enough. I have made my decision. It is done."

"And Keziah? What of her?" Tzipi narrowed her eyes to slits.

Like the flat of a blade against my skull, the blow struck hard. I darted a look at Alanah, who was still challenging my sister with a glare. "I will tell her. There is nothing to be done now. Alanah is my wife. We will obey the Torah and the terms laid out by the elders."

Tzipi's mouth pursed as she digested the information, before her gaze swept from the sling holding Alanah's wounded arm to her linen turban. Alanah's hand twitched at the edge of my vision, as if she was tempted to cover her head. Instead, she straightened her back and kept her eyes trained on my sister.

Fearless, this woman—and in so many ways the complete opposite of Keziah, the woman to whom I had been all but betrothed since I was a child. The woman whose heart I must now break.

⁓

"Tobiah! You've returned!" Keziah untangled herself from the clench of her youngest cousin's arms and directed the tiny girl toward her mother. Brushing dust from her tunic and smoothing her dark hair with a fluttering hand, she approached, her pale yellow headscarf billowing behind her. Her bright, welcoming smile and the way she looked me over, as if ensuring I was un-harmed, was a fire-tipped spear to my chest. I held my breath as her brief, but enthusiastic, embrace pressed the scorching brand of regret deeper still.

"I was so worried!" She pulled away with a timid glance at her parents, who sat next to the campfire, unabashedly watching the reunion of their daughter with the man they had no idea had come to lay waste to their expectations. Keziah's mother, once my own *ima's* closest friend, dipped her head in greeting, her smile affectionate—another woman I'd be disappointing tonight.

"Come, sit down and eat!" Keziah tugged at my wrist. "We have plenty!"

"I've eaten, thank you."

"Oh now, I've never seen you turn away another bowl of stew . . ." She pulled at me again with a little laugh. "Between you and Shimon, I don't know how Tzipi keeps up with the cooking . . ." Her words trailed off as the realization that I had not responded to her teasing seemed to solidify. "Tobiah? Is something wrong?" Confusion flickered between her brows, and she dropped her hand to her side.

I pressed my lips together and cleared my throat. "Shimon—" I swallowed again. "Shimon is gone."

Even this partial revelation left traces of ash in my throat—how could I speak more? The torment of holding my expression still as a roar of agony built in my throat was unbearable.

"Oh, Tobiah." With a gasp of disbelief, she covered her mouth with her hands, brown eyes wide and full of tears. "Shimon is dead? Poor Tzipi! Those poor, sweet boys!" Keziah looked up at me with compassion on her lovely face. "And you, oh Tobiah, you must be devastated." She moved close, placing a small, soft hand on my forearm. "What can I do to help?"

My second revelation could wait no longer. With her wide brown eyes and long dark hair, Keziah was a beautiful woman, transformed from the small girl Tzipi had taken under her wing years ago. Somewhere along the way, I'd accepted that my mother and hers would have their way and we would marry. And although I'd put it off for the past couple of years—using the excuse of my military training to postpone—she was already sixteen, and Tzipi had insisted I approach her father when I returned from the battle with Arad's forces.

Now. I was supposed to be asking for her hand now. Instead, I was forced to say, "Keziah. There is something else I need to tell you. I do not want you to hear it from anyone else."

She pulled away, wariness clouding her expression. "What is it?"

I sucked in a steadying breath and folded my arms across the hole in my chest. "I rescued a young woman on the battlefield. She was severely wounded. It was a difficult decision, and one I did not take lightly, but I chose to follow the law and marry her, in order to protect her."

Her lips parted and she blinked again and again, as if trying to reconcile the words in her mind. "Married . . . you are married?"

"I am sorry, Keziah. You have been so patient with me . . . and now . . ." I released my breath in a huff. "I am sorry."

And I truly was. Acceptance of our future marriage had, at some point, transformed into gladness. I'd imagined a life with this woman—her sweet voice greeting me when I returned to camp, her capable hands providing meals and clothing for our family—there was no better choice of wife than Keziah. And yet the picture I'd drawn so clearly in my mind had faded with surprising speed, replaced by one that remained hazy, unknown, yet surprisingly intriguing—one with red hair, audacity, and the unmistakable edge of raw hurt in her caustic responses to my feeble attempts at conversation.

"Doesn't the law say you have thirty days before it is final? Perhaps you can . . ." Although her question trailed away, the plea was as clear as if she'd shouted the words. *Put her aside! Marry me!*

And although it felt like slipping my own sword between my ribs, I needed to make my position plain—to release her. So I lowered my voice in soft censure to discourage any thoughts of hope. "I plan to keep my commitment to Alanah, Keziah. She has no one else, or so it seems. And this camp is a dangerous place for her. Unless she refuses to stay, I will be her husband."

"Of course. That is true." She flinched, taking a step backward as she clasped her hands together in a white-knuckled grip, the delight that had greeted me earlier now drowning in tears.

"I understand." The watery accusation of betrayal trickling down her cheeks spoke differently.

"Please, Keziah, forgive me. This was not my plan." I braved a glance at her father and mother, who were now walking toward us, concern on their faces. I resisted the urge to turn like a coward and run.

"There's nothing to forgive. Nothing was settled." She tried to smile, but the strain of it seemed to break something inside her, and she drew a shuddering breath. However, instead of crumpling, she squared her shoulders. "Tell Tzipi I will be by in the morning to help her with the boys. I am sure she is destroyed."

Her admirable strength caused me to question my decision all over again. "Keziah, I know there will be someone else who—"

She lifted a trembling hand to halt my suggestion and shook her head. "Thank you, Tobiah. I must return to my family." She turned to go but then looked at me, determination evident in the iron set of her shoulders. "You are a good man. I wish you happiness."

I didn't feel like a good man, I felt like a worm as I saw her slip into her mother's arms just before I turned away. I'd hurt a young woman—and a family—that I cared for, and I'd gone against my mother's wishes. And for what? For a Canaanite woman who more than likely wished to see me dead?

10

ALANAH

Tobiah had disappeared halfway through the meal, leaving me at the mercy of his family and without an explanation as to where he was going or when he would return. With the exception of his aunt Nita, who sat next to me, no one said anything to me, no matter how many people streamed through the campsite, eager to bring quiet condolences to Tzipi and to gawk at me—the stranger, the enemy.

Tobiah's two cousins, both nearly as large as he was, sat near me all evening, sharp eyes trained on me as if I were likely to whip out a knife and stab one of their children. Clearly, Tobiah had charged them with watching his volatile wife.

Nita leaned close to me, her dark eyes serious but kind as she took my clay bowl, now empty of the savory stew that'd disappeared all too quickly. "Tobiah explained the situation, and I believe it is best for you to stay with me tonight."

My gaze flicked to the dark pathway that had swallowed Tobiah. The campsite felt very empty without his large presence.

How had a stranger suddenly become the only constant in my life? Everyone else was gone. I missed the weight of my copper amulet around my neck. Somehow I felt more naked without it than without my hair.

Nita must have sensed my unease. "Would you rather wait for Tobiah to return?" Dark, silver-laced curls framed Nita's face, softening the sharp cheekbones and thick black brows that slashed above her narrow-set eyes.

Although tempted to ignore her invitation, my body screamed for rest. The long march from the canyon, along with the ache in my shoulder, demanded I comply. She led me to a small tent nearby but, before entering, she glanced over her shoulder and then turned around with frustration in the harsh set of her mouth. "Noach. Simcha. What are you doing?"

Tobiah's two enormous cousins had followed us. One of them crossed his massive arms and jerked a black-bearded chin at me. "Making sure that one stays put."

Nita puffed out a breath. "She'll be here with me."

"Tobiah asked us to watch her."

"Are you going to run off, Alanah?" she asked me, brows high.

I shook my head, although my mind was still determining how quickly I could slide into the darkness between tents before the two giants caught up with me.

"There now. She's not going anywhere tonight. Just look at her." She frowned at me. "She's exhausted."

"She's a Canaanite. You can't . . ." Simcha said.

"Alanah, these boys seem to think you are going to murder me in my sleep. Is that going to happen?" Her narrowed eyes seemed to deliver a challenge that was half mocking, half razor-edged. "Because I keep a copper blade on me at all times. And . . ." She leaned closer. "I have excellent aim."

"All I want is a blanket to lie on." Although I had considered killing Tobiah to escape captivity, the past couple of days had transformed him from a bloody-faced murderer to somewhat of a protector in my head. I had no more desire to hurt Nita than I did Tobiah. Wouldn't my brothers bellow to hear my traitorous thoughts?

"We'll be right here," Noach said to Nita before directing a glare at me. "All night long."

Although a wave of fear vibrated through me, I maintained a blank expression as the two men stationed themselves nearby, their backs toward the remains of the fire, but watching the tent. Watching me.

"Pay them no mind." The corners of Nita's lips twitched as she lifted the door flap. "You need rest."

As I entered, the covering overhead drew my attention. Instead of the usual black-wool ceiling, a large patch of sheer linen stretched over our heads, leaving the sky exposed.

"It brings me comfort," Nita said. "I have never known anything but living in the desert. I should not know what to do if I lived in a house made of mud brick. I used to sneak out at night when my parents were asleep to watch the stars. My Zakariyah indulged me by having this tent designed for me as a gift."

After clucking and muttering about the lack of a comfortable pillow, Nita prepared a makeshift pallet for me and then laid on her own in silence. Perhaps memories of her husband were made fresh by the loss of Tzipi's.

Tzipi's voice from the tent next to Nita's snared my attention. Although her words were low, from the loud exclamations from her children I gathered she had finally explained their father's death. The insistence from all three that he could not possibly be gone, and the sobbing of the fatherless children, sent echoes of grief through my own body.

I remembered the sensation well—the throbbing ache that gripped me when my cousin came into our valley to announce that my family had been slaughtered, along with the numbness as he gleefully informed me that all the inheritance, every inch of my father's land, was his. Although it was inevitable since I was only a woman, it stung nonetheless.

Shifting on my pallet, I covered my ear with my good hand, but their cries wrenched my heart into a complicated knot. These Hebrews were my enemies and those boys would grow into soldiers someday—soldiers who would no doubt continue the incursion into my homeland. Harnessing my visceral reaction, I imagined a wall between myself and them, a sturdy brick wall that deflected every arrow aimed my way.

Long after the sniffles and low whispers of the boys melted into grief-laden sleep, Tzipi's quiet weeping and heavy breaths soaked through the thin tent walls next to me. There was only a few feet of space between her and where I lay. The sound of ripping fabric cut through the night, the tearing of a garment in mourning.

"I will never forgive" came the breathy whisper, hitched by silent sobs.

Was she talking to me? Did she know I listened?

No, I recognized the whispers that followed as supplications to her god—as if a deity would hear her pleas without a sacrifice. But I could not ignore the vitriol of the words meant not only for me, but all my people.

Why should I care what Tzipi thought of me? Her husband, Tobiah, and the rest of these Hebrews had destroyed everything I knew in their quest to take over Canaan. How dare they? What claim did these Hebrews think they had on our lands? Why were they so insistent on destroying what we built? Hot anger burned away the empathy that had threatened to soften my resolve.

Although every part of my body screamed in exhaustion, sleep refused to welcome me. Trying to avoid the bloody battle scene that jeered at me every time I closed my eyes, I searched the linen covering above me for pinpricks of stars through the translucent fabric of Nita's peculiar abode. The gathering of the gods and goddesses above me was familiar, but tonight they seemed even more distant, more silent, than usual.

A breeze fluttered the tent flap, and with a start I realized that Tobiah's cousins were not outlined against the dim glow of the fire.

My heart thrummed in my ears. Could I hazard an escape? My shoulder was nowhere near healed, but this could be my last chance to slip out and run back north.

With my eyes on Nita to ensure she did not stir, I reached for my quiver and bow and crept toward the flap. Slipping my fingers into the gap, I peeked out, making certain my eyes had not deceived me. But no, the two men were gone. Had they assumed I was asleep? Or decided I wasn't a true threat? I had no time to wonder and no time to care that I had nothing with which to protect myself. *Run. Now.* Sucking in a deep breath, I pushed through the tent flap.

Before I took two steps, I tripped over something and tumbled forward, twisting as I hit the ground. I fell on my good side, but my bow and quiver skidded across the dirt.

"What are you doing?" The enormous lump I'd tripped over jostled me from underneath. Tobiah, lying in front of the entrance again. Why had I not considered that before I tried to bolt?

It was no use dodging the truth while splayed halfway on the ground, halfway across my husband. "Leaving."

In silence, he waited as I pulled my legs off him, stood, and gathered my belongings.

He stood as well. "You are not going anywhere." Although his voice was calm and nearly a whisper, his stance was menacing, as if he expected me to attack him.

Although I could barely see his face in the dim light, I stared at him, defiant.

"You will be killed, Alanah."

My pulse raced. "You will kill me if I run?"

"No. But there are thousands of men in this camp who will see only your heritage and slay you. Spies are dealt with swiftly here."

"I am not a spy." Why did I find it necessary to defend myself to this man?

"I know that. But no one else will stop to question you."

"What does it matter to you? You'll be free of me."

"Have I complained?" Tobiah moved closer.

Although the hair on the back of my neck stood on end, I held my ground, lifting a shoulder with an air of indifference. I refused to let his looming presence intimidate me.

"Then what makes you sure I want to be free of you?"

My thoughts spun like a leaf in a whirlpool. What was he saying? Was he content with this strange, uncomfortable arrangement? I could not believe he was.

"What is it that you want from me?" I said.

"I want you to stop trying to run." He closed the gap further, until all that was left between us was a handspan of charged air. He lowered his voice to a soft rumble. "Do you not remember the oath I made?"

No matter that I'd washed that little spot of blood from my hand, I could still feel it there, pulsing in the center of my palm. I closed my fingers around the foreign sensation and resisted the urge to hide my hand behind my back.

"Have I done anything to make you believe that I would break that oath?"

My mouth was too dry to answer, so I shook my head and stared straight at his broad chest.

"Look at me," he said.

For some reason, the thought of meeting his eyes right now under a sky full of stars seemed more dangerous than running out onto a battlefield. My muscles tensed, ready to flee.

"Alanah," he whispered. "Alanah. Look at me."

I had never heard my name spoken with such tenderness—at least since I had been a little girl, before my father lost interest in me.

"According to the law, you have twenty-eight days left to make your decision. If after that you still want to go, I will not stop you. But for now, you need to heal. So, stay."

Straightening my shoulders, then my neck, and then finally, slowly, lifting my chin, I looked up into his eyes. The fierce sincerity in their brown depths burned my doubts away. The Hebrews may have slaughtered my whole family, but Tobiah would not hurt me.

I nodded and turned to slip back inside the tent, feeling those eyes on my back even as I lay on my pallet, my mind working to untangle the knotted confusion that Tobiah's words had created. Twenty-eight days, he'd said, and then I could go. Twenty-eight days until freedom. Yet somehow the revelation had not stirred the relief I'd expected. And why had it seemed so easy to abandon my plans when he'd appeared?

11

18 Nissan
1407 BC
Camp at Zalmonah

Somehow all the questions I whispered to voiceless stars lulled me to sleep, and I awoke the next morning when Nita jostled me. Dawn had barely topped the horizon, but she was already checking my dressings and refreshing them with clean linen by the time my vision cleared of sleep.

Her eyes sparkled. "Have you gathered manna yet?"

"No." I was exhausted like never before, my limbs heavy and eyes gritty, but curiosity for this enigma sparked and my tongue watered in anticipation. I craved manna as I had craved nothing else before. Not the sweetest dates, the ripest olives, or the freshest barley bread steaming from the oven.

"Come, then." She helped me to my feet, led the way out of the tent, and handed me a large empty basket. "Take only this much manna from the ground, only an *omer* each for you and Tobiah. Any more will be full of maggots by morning."

My stomach recoiled at the thought of worms spoiling the precious delicacy. "Why does it only last so long?"

"So we will rely on Yahweh, every day." She glanced toward the enormous cloud stacked high above the *Mishkan.*

It reflected the colors of the sunrise, yet somehow amplified them, making it twice as brilliant as the rest of the clouds that hovered low in the sky. The column reminded me somehow of a tall army commander standing with arms crossed, waiting for his troops to be ready to march.

I peeled my eyes from the awesome sight as Nita tugged at my hand. "Come now, dear, let us gather manna."

Sitting between his two cousins, who glared at me, Tobiah waved a greeting to his aunt from across the fire, but his small smile was meant for me—a *good morning* from my husband, as if I hadn't attempted to flee from him only a few hours ago. My thwarted escape had been followed by fitful sleep that did nothing to solve the mystery of why I felt so safe in the presence of an enemy soldier who held me captive, or answer the buzzing questions that stubbornly refused to be brushed out of my mind—who was Keziah and what was she to Tobiah?

I turned from his unwanted gesture without matching it and followed Nita as she wound her way through the camp and into the field of manna that surrounded it.

The sun glinted and sparkled off the white that gilded the rocks and the low brush for as far as I could see. The manna lay thick on the ground like a heavy snowfall, almost to my ankles. I scooped up a handful and tasted it. It exploded against my tongue like the most exquisite honey-spiced wine.

Stifling a groan, I rolled my eyes skyward. Nita was watching me over her shoulder with a satisfied smirk. "Do you like it?"

I wiped my mouth with the back of my hand. "It is even more delicious fresh."

She shrugged, indifferent. "I've been eating it since I was a babe. It's the same today as it was yesterday and the day before that."

I blinked at the dichotomy. These Hebrews ate the most

mouthwatering food every single day and yet it had become mundane to them. They had forgotten the pleasure of its taste and texture. Bread was supplied from the heavens each day, but they were blind to the amazing miracle of it.

I had worked the land, toiled each weary day to scratch food from its surface alongside my brothers and my father. The constant threat of destructive storms, or drought, or blight hung heavy until harvest each year. The back-breaking work of harvesting the wheat with a hand scythe. The endless threshing of the golden kernels until they were ready for milling. All this was done in an endless cycle year after year. A cycle that depended on the capricious gods and their whims.

And here the Hebrews were handed food each morning with little effort. I pressed a bit of manna between my fingers. It needed no more than a cursory hand-milling to break it down to a flour consistency for baking. All around us, Hebrews gathered manna without alacrity. As if filling baskets with food that appeared from nothing was drudgery.

My basket was quickly filled, enough for only myself and Tobiah. Nita reminded me of the consequence of taking too much. "My Zakariyah was one of those, on the first day the manna appeared, eager to collect as much as possible in his reckless youth. His spoiled pot of manna the next morning was testament to his foolishness." Her laugh was rueful as she scraped her hand across the top of her basket to ensure that it was only just enough. "The only day we are allowed more is before Shabbat. Then we take enough to get us through the next day, and it stays fresh until the next evening."

How was that possible? "Why?"

She pushed out her bottom lip. "So we have time to rest, enjoy our families, and worship Yahweh."

"You do not work at all that day?"

She shook her head.

A god who insisted that his people rest? Why would a divine being care about such a thing? The *baalim* my people worshipped had never done anything but take, in my experience.

A movement in the corner of my vision caught my attention. Tobiah's cousins again. Had they been following us the whole time? I growled under my breath.

Nita pursed her lips as she followed my line of sight. Simcha leaned against a granite boulder nearby, cleaning his fingernails with the tip of a knife, and Noach stood next to him, his eyes on me.

"What are you two doing?" she called out.

Noach shrugged a large shoulder. "Keeping an eye on things."

My blood boiled, and I strode up to him. "I stayed all night with Nita. I'm not going to hurt her. I may be your enemy but I am not a murderer of women."

His brow wrinkled. "I did not say you were."

"Then why are you here?"

"Tobiah asked us to keep an eye on you while he trains this morning."

"I told him last night I am not going to run."

Simcha looked up from his grooming, the silver knife reflecting the golden sunrise. "He didn't say anything about you running. He just told us to make sure no one touched you."

Tobiah was concerned about my safety? My mind reeled back to our late-night conversation and the comment about the men who might cut me down without a thought. I had taken it as more of a way to control my movement than actual concern for my well-being. The notion somehow lodged in my throat. I had expected Tobiah to treat me like a captive, like a slave, or possibly even like a concubine. But not a true wife.

Noach smirked. "Besides, our grandmother truly is an expert with that knife she carries." He winked at Nita. "I'm more worried about you than her."

My incredulous gaze flicked between Noach and Nita. "You are their grandmother?"

She placed a hand over her heart as she laughed. "Of course, dear. Their father, Asher, is my son."

"B-but . . ." I stuttered. "You don't look that old!"

"Well, thank you for that." She patted her silvery curls. "I think that has more to do with the manna than anything. It seems to give all of us an abnormal vitality. But I was twenty-one when we left Egypt, and my Zakariyah twenty-eight."

Another anomaly to add to the list of Hebrew attributes.

As we walked back to the campsite, with Noach and Simcha following close behind, I noticed something else. I had expected to see slaves out here in the wilderness, a vast disorganized assortment of bedraggled, browbeaten, desperate people. But the regimented structure of the sea of tents gathered around an oversized meeting place in the center and the well-formed, healthy, fearsome men that had met us on the battlefield disproved my notions. The Hebrews had been transformed from Pharaoh's property to a nation of warriors in the space of forty years. Warriors who were more than ready to take over Canaan.

TOBIAH

Uriya struck me in the temple. The butt of his practice sword hit me with the force of a falling cedar. I'd be dead if it were real. With a guttural cry, I slammed my shoulder into his torso, swinging a closed fist toward his ear. Blocking the blow with a rock-hard forearm, he pivoted away while leveling another blow at my head. This time I was ready. The clash of our wooden swords reverberated down my arm.

"Good!" Uriya dropped his defense and backed away. "Much better that time."

"No. Again." I lifted my practice weapon high.

The enormous Egyptian waved at me. "Take a break, Tobiah. We've been at this all morning."

Shaking my head, I advanced. "Again."

With a sigh, Uriya attacked. This time I routed his every swing, anticipated his every pretense, and pushed him back so far he nearly collided with another sparring team.

"Enough!" Uriya threw up a hand. "Enough, Tobiah."

Sweat blurred my vision. I breathed hard through my nose until the blood rushing through my limbs slowed. Uriya tossed me a water-skin and then wiped his face and black beard with a cloth. He was a good sparring partner. The grandson of a general in Pharaoh's army who had defied his king and fled Egypt to follow Mosheh all those years ago. Eager to prove his loyalty to Israel, Uriya had been training in this bleak desert for ten more years than me, but he wasn't Shimon. The yells and grunts of the men exercising around us swept memories of the battlefield to the front of my mind.

"Let's go again," I said, stepping forward.

"Tobiah." Uriya lifted his palms in surrender. "I am done for now. Save some for the enemy, my friend."

The exercises every day were just about the only time I didn't think about Shimon. Or Alanah. And I wasn't ready to consider either at the moment. If Alanah chose to stay, I would not be engaging that enemy. My first year of marriage would be spent defending the camp, not rushing into battle. The thought made me grit my teeth in frustration, but I shrugged it off, craving the release these exercises offered.

"If you are too tired to continue . . ." I let the pointed challenge trail off.

"Yes." He tossed the sweat-soaked cloth at me. "I am too

tired. And hungry. How far are you going to push this old man? You'll have to drag me back to my orphaned sons if the sun gets any hotter."

"Drag your carcass? I'd probably just leave you—"

A quick shofar blast split my taunt in two. The clatter of wooden swords and practice shields around us halted immediately. Avidan, the commander of our regiment, stood atop one of the large boulders that dotted the barren landscape. The fifty or so men who had been practicing around us now gathered around him. Avidan must be here to discuss tactics.

We hadn't heard much from Yehoshua since the victory a few days ago. It couldn't be much longer before we pushed into the Land. The pulse of our first victory was still surging high through all of us; now was the time to strike. Hard. While the Canaanites were still reeling.

"Men!" the commander called out. "Sons of Yehudah!"

"Among others!" returned Uriya with a smile. He had been joined by marriage to the tribe of Yehudah.

"And brothers." Avidan tipped his head in acknowledgment. "I have news, brought from the lips of Yehoshua and from Mosheh himself."

A storm of exhilaration washed through me. This was our time. I gripped the hilt of my practice sword, wishing it were real. I'd welcome the cool familiarity of my curved *kopesh* in my palm right now—the sword I'd inherited from my father. Even more, I wished he were here to use it himself, to see the day that we finally pushed into the Land.

"We are not going north," said the elder. "The chief of the Edomites refuses to let us pass through on the road that cuts through his territory."

Someone jutted a fist into the air. "Then we fight the Edomites!"

I nodded my agreement.

"No." Avidan placed his hands on his hips. "They are our

cousins. Mosheh has been ordered by Yahweh not to attack the sons of Esau."

A murmur of displeasure went up from the men. *And what did Esau do, but threaten our ancestor Yaakov? And sell his own birthright for a bowl of stew?* I scoffed. Obviously his sons were cowards as well. I heard my own thoughts voiced by others around me.

But Avidan stood, unmoved by the swell of anger in his men. "We will not go against the commands of Yahweh. Ever again."

The arguments dwindled as the stinging reminder of defeat clamped our mouths shut.

"We all know what happened the last time we did not wait for Yahweh's direction." The commander circled his gaze about the group. "We lost fathers, sons, and brothers in that first disastrous battle against Arad."

Perhaps if we'd waited, Shimon would be standing next to me right now, probably elbowing me with some suggestive quip. *More time to tangle with your sister before I tangle with the enemy, eh, Tobiah?*

The only thing Shimon loved as much as Tzipi was needling me. As if it had been his personal mission to get a rise out of me. A mission he rarely succeeded in.

A young solider nearby called out. "Then we go west! Take the coastal lands first." Fifty other men lifted voices in agreement, many lifting their dummy swords in salute to his idea.

The elder shook his grizzled head. "No. Mosheh says we are not ready for a confrontation with the seafaring tribes that occupy the coastlands. We must take the eastern route."

Angry outbursts from the men around me tangled with my own frustrations.

"We are ready! Let us loose!"

"We've been preparing for nearly forty years."

"Haven't we proven that we are ready?" said a man next to me.

"Our enemies will think we are retreating!" said another.

It was foolish not to push in now, with the pulse of victory thumping in our chests. The Canaanites would still be licking their wounds. We should strike before their claws were sharp again.

Avidan gestured to a man next to him, who lifted a small shofar to his lips and blew a stuttering blast on the ram's horn—long, long, short, long. Like children brought up short by a scolding, the men ceased their fuming. At least we were well-trained.

The elder waited until every eye was on him. "We are not retreating. We are going a different route. We will go south, head toward the copper mines. We will regroup there. Plan our strategy and then head east in order to skirt Edom. Do not worry, my brothers. It may be a few more months before we enter the Land. But it will be at the time appointed by Yahweh. Our God has gone before us, prepared the way. We have the Ark. We have Yehoshua as the commander of our armies and Mosheh as our leader. We will be victorious!"

A cheer went up from the crowd that had been baying a few moments before. No wonder Avidan had been appointed leader over us; it took skill to reverse the raging tides of battle-thirsty men.

As soon as Avidan dismissed us, with a promise of more directions the next morning, an elbow jammed into my ribs. Levon, one of the younger men who had camped near me during the battle, leaned into me. "You're that one who brought home that woman, aren't you? That Canaanite woman?"

Looking at him from the corner of my eye, I replied with a shrug.

"You are! I can't believe you had that tender morsel under our noses the whole time." He nudged me again with a waggle of his brows.

I didn't answer, hoping he would let the matter drop and imagining the immense satisfaction the snap of the bones in his arm would give me.

"Wish I'd brought back one of those. Did you see some of those women?" He whistled through his teeth. "Barely wear anything, don't they? Of course most of that type don't anyhow." A couple of men nearby laughed.

Ignoring the audience, I stretched to my full height. "She is not a *zonah*."

Undeterred by my show of dominance, his face crumpled into confusion. This young buck was either foolish or foolhardy. "What was she doing there, then? What other use does a woman have in a battle camp?"

"My wife is not your concern."

"Your wife? You married that—"

"Don't." I cut him off with a sharp warning. "Don't say it again."

Uriya's hand landed on my shoulder, but I shrugged it off, determined to keep my wits about me. Shimon's constant taunts had prepared me to keep my head in any circumstance. I wouldn't let this young fool get the best of me.

Levon lifted his palms as if conceding. "You can call her whatever you want, my friend. But what's the point of marrying her?"

Sucking in a steadying breath, I measured my answer before speaking. "To protect her. And obey the Torah."

Levon released a huff of disbelief through pursed lips. Every soldier knew the law, even if it went ignored at times. He arched his brows high. "You really going to wait a whole thirty days?"

I indicated my intent with a firm nod.

He smirked and shook his head. "Waste of time, if you ask me. Just get it over with. Of course, if you change your mind and throw her off, I'll gladly take her off your hands!" He guffawed and spouted a lewd comment about just what he'd like to do to a Canaanite woman.

Fury exploded in my chest, rushed to my limbs. Surging toward him, I gritted my teeth. "You even think about touching her, you'll find yourself skewered on the point of my sword."

Someone grabbed my arms, restraining me from wrapping my hands around Levon's throat. Probably Uriya and a couple other men, but I didn't bother to look. I could barely see anything through the sheen of fury that blurred my vision to anything except the insolent buffoon who had insulted Alanah.

Levon's eyes flared as he took in my expression, which must have reflected the fire that seared my belly at his depravity.

Shrugging off the hands that gripped me, I turned and strode away—my mind focusing on three truths. First, if that fool said another word, no one would be able to hold me back. Second, my decision to marry Alanah had been the right one. And last, from this moment until our covenant was made complete, I needed to stay by her side. No one would be touching my wife but me.

12

ALANAH

A tug on my tunic jarred me as I washed my hands in a pot by Nita's tent. I whirled around, one arm raised to defend myself and water spraying from my palm. Instead of the fierce Hebrew man I expected to see, a small black-haired boy stood there, eyes wide at my overreaction. One of Tzipi's sons. The youngest, if I remembered correctly from their exuberant greetings for Tobiah upon his return.

"What do you want?" I said, dropping my defensive stance.

Swiping at the water droplets trickling down his face, the child shrank back at my gruff demand. Guilt lodged a prickly finger beneath my ribs. "You surprised me." I softened the stiff set of my shoulders and lifted the severe line of my brows.

Relief washed the trepidation from his features, and curiosity took its place. "Is that your bow?" He cocked his head and pointed toward the useless weapon near my feet. I was still a bit confused why Tobiah had let me keep it. Little did he know how fast I could fashion a makeshift arrow—although my knife had been confiscated back on the battlefield. Regardless, I never let the bow out of my sight.

I picked it up and ran my fingers along the bowstring. "Yes. This is mine." A vision of my rough-handed father wrapping tendon cord around the bone-and-wood compound flitted through my mind.

"Do you shoot it?" His eyes grew round, incredulous.

"I do."

He scrunched his face. "But you are a girl!"

"And?"

"Girls aren't supposed to shoot arrows."

I peered down at him. "Well, this girl does."

He sucked in his bottom lip. "I will be a soldier one day." He puffed his chest out in imitation of the uncle he adored. "Like Tobiah, and like my abba was."

At the reminder of his father, the back of my neck prickled and a sudden rush of battlefield memory tied my tongue into a knot.

"And when I am big, I will kill those bad people who hurt my abba." His little chin wobbled before jutting out. The prickles became sharp barbs into my gut. We had both lost fathers.

"Get away from that woman, Liyam!" Tzipi swooped past me and yanked the boy by the arm. "She is dangerous."

"But *Ima*, Tobiah said—"

"I am your mother." Her swift retort sliced through his high-pitched protest. "You do as I say. Now go!"

Liyam's eyes cut to me before he backed away with a look of fear that hadn't been present before his mother barged between us. I glanced away.

"Don't you ever come near my children again, do you hear me?" Tzipi's voice shook with fury as she rounded on me. "You don't even talk to them."

I lifted my palms in surrender. "He approached me."

"Just leave." Her nostrils flared.

My gaze swept the campsite, landing on Noach and Simcha, my ever-present guards, lolling near the fire. "If only I could," I muttered. How much longer would Tobiah be away? Perhaps he'd gone to see that Keziah woman, or to practice killing more of my people. I huffed out a small breath through my nose. Why did I care where the man had disappeared to or who he was with?

"How long are you going to keep up this pretense of a marriage?" she spat out, as if the words themselves were poisonous.

I settled back into a measured but casual pose, arms crossed and chin lifted like a shield. "This was his idea, not mine."

"He already has a woman. He is only doing this out of misplaced obligation, like usual." Tzipi watched me as if gauging my reaction to her revelation. I kept my face carefully composed, hard as granite. After years of practice with brothers who pounced on any emotion that appeared weak, there wouldn't be a twitch—even though my insides felt like twice-kneaded dough.

Did Tobiah already have a wife? Was that where he had gone last night, to tell Keziah that he had taken on another? I had no desire to be a first wife, let alone a second.

Before I could ask, Tzipi strode up to me, arms folded across her chest. I kept my feet planted. I would not retreat. Without fear, she glared with eyes the same color as Tobiah's. "I've already lost a husband. I won't lose my brother. I won't let you destroy him."

I drew in a steadying breath, struck by the grief on her face as much as the poison-tipped words, but I kept my own words smooth, unaffected. "As I said before, you know nothing of me. I am here because I have no choice."

"I know enough of your people's disgusting ways. The way they slaughter children like animals. The perverted ways you worship your gods." Loathing twisted her features into a mockery of their beauty. "Your kind deserves what's coming to you."

The accusations stung, not because of any guilt on my part, but because I knew how true they were—had witnessed them firsthand. The keening of a terrified infant being offered to the flames and the smell of charred human flesh was instantly fresh in my mind. I stiffened, barely reining in the desire to gasp at the ten-year-old memory and the instinct to cover my ears—just as I had the day my father had offered one of his wives' babies to the *baalim* in exchange for a healthy crop.

Latent horror must have played across my face. Tzipi watched me with a curious look before she blinked it away and replaced it with a feral sneer. "He should have left you there to die."

I leaned forward, a handspan from her face. "Then we agree on something." I smirked, holding still as death.

A large hand clamped down on my shoulder and I spun toward the interference. My fist met a man's solid chest with surprising force.

Tobiah grabbed my wrist and held it in the air. "I am going to assume that strike was meant for someone else and not your husband." He looked down at me with his brows raised. Was that a glimmer of humor in his eyes?

Yanking hard, I twisted my wrist from his grasp. "You can assume anything you'd like."

"Well then, I will also assume you and my sister are having a civilized conversation." He divided a chastening look between the two of us. "Since we are family."

Tzipi let out a huff of disgust. "That Canaanite is no sister of mine. She is an enemy, a liar, and an idol worshipper."

Tobiah held his silence for an interminable few moments, his eyes locked on his sister's, as if conveying his innermost thoughts with a look. The two of them stared each other down, as unmoving as two sides of the same stone wall.

Tzipi was the feminine version of Tobiah in so many ways. Yet where Tobiah was built like a bear, her lines reminded me more of a desert panther—sleek, strong, and beautiful. I imagined that before grief had taken up residence in her soul, her Shimon had been a much-envied man indeed.

Tobiah seemed inordinately restrained, yet Tzipi's emotions flashed like a blazing signal fire across her face. I could tell the exact moment she conceded to her brother, when the flame of passion began to flicker and wane.

Tobiah's tone was calm yet somehow infinitely commanding. "Alanah is my wife, Tzipi. She has obeyed the *mitzvot* set by Mosheh. She endured being shaved like a ewe." Another long pause plagued the tense triangle of space between us, yet neither I nor Tzipi dared interject. "If you do not give her a chance to see who Yahweh is and how much better our way of life is under the Torah, how will she ever turn away from false gods?"

Tzipi returned his defense of me with a prolonged silence of her own, as if arguing her side without words. Her neck stiffened and she aimed a look of malice at me, one that instantly reminded me of the women in my village. "There is nothing that could ever make you my sister. Leave. Before the thirty days are up." Without a glance at her brother, she spun and walked away, her head high and her back straight.

I may have left the battlefield behind me, but the war had followed me here. Tzipi had let fly the first shot.

13

TOBIAH

26 NISSAN
1407 BC
CAMP AT PUNON

Nearly a week of plodding through rocky, inhospitable land had brought us far to the south, almost back to the sea our parents and grandparents had crossed on a pathway through the depths. The sea where Pharaoh's army met their well-deserved end.

Alanah paused in her work of clearing rocks for Nita's tent-site. She'd insisted on helping me, even with one arm still locked in a sling. On the long walk south, her demeanor had been more relaxed, even though she remained aloof, but as soon as we arrived in this wide valley, her agitation returned, as if being at rest caused her physical pain.

Standing to stretch, she placed a hand on the small of her back and arched forward with a little sigh. To distract myself from examining the tempting display of her curves, I swung my hammer again, focusing instead on driving the stake into the hard-packed soil.

Swiping the back of her hand across her forehead, she looked off at the orange hills in the distance. Unlike most women, Alanah kept her thoughts locked tight, but wonder at the red cliffs seemed to spill over. "It's like they are on fire," she said in a low but awestruck tone. Was she talking to me? Or herself?

With a glance at me, as if she had just realized I'd heard her quiet exclamation, she clamped her jaw shut and dropped her eyes to the task of unrolling the bundles for Nita's home.

The special tent revived memories of Zakariyah, my grand-father's brother. Stern and unbending with anyone else, he'd been clay in Nita's capable hands. He endured endless ribbing from the other men about his stargazing tent. But from the way Nita had doted on him, I knew he had made the right choice.

When Zakariyah had died a year ago, my great-aunt had endured the thirty-day mourning period as any other Hebrew woman would. But when the moon waxed full again and the appointed time was complete, she continued to mourn, eyes red-rimmed most mornings. I wondered if having that special tent made the ache worse.

But when we reached the edge of the Promised Land, some-thing pulled her out of the darkness that held her—Aharon, the brother of Mosheh, died and the entire nation mourned for thirty days. At the foot of the mountain upon which our high priest died, Nita seemed to lay down her burdens. Her sparkle returned, the tease slipping back into her voice. The slice of her sharp wit jabbed at all of us again, and we loved it. *Doda* returned, full force and stronger than ever.

We worked in silence, stretching the tent walls. Placing the poles in position, we tied them into place, then unfurled the linen covering for Nita's roof and attached the goat-hide flaps that would unroll over the linen in case of a storm. Though we spoke little, Nita's dwelling lifted quicker than most others around us. Pride swelled in my chest at our quiet teamwork and Alanah's ability to assist even with one arm still bound against her chest.

Alanah also seemed to appreciate the fruits of our labor; a little smile budded on her lips as she entered through the tent flap. Curiosity nearly compelled me to follow, see if it had bloomed. But seeing Tzipi struggling to unload a large basket from her wagon, I jogged over to help.

"Here, let me carry that for you." I reached out to take the burden.

She jerked the basket away from my grasp. "How much longer do I have to put up with that—that woman in my campsite?"

"That woman is my wife."

She scoffed, her eyes cutting to Nita's tent. "Not in the true sense."

"She stays until the thirty days are complete, and then she can choose to stay or go. I will not force her," I said.

"How can you tolerate being chained to that idolater? And one taken fresh off the battlefield where my"—she blinked— "where so many were killed."

I imagined that every time she saw Alanah, Tzipi must think of Shimon. How could she not? I did too. I softened my tone. "You cannot blame her for Shimon's death, sister."

"I can and I do."

"It is Yahweh who numbers our days."

"It was not Yahweh who slaughtered my husband. It was a Canaanite!"

I put my palm on her shoulder. "That is true. And Yahweh has given us the task of running them out of the Land. But he has also brought her here. And I can't help but think it may be for a purpose."

She shrugged off my hand. "I do not trust her. And you should not either, Tobiah. She is dangerous." She narrowed her eyes and pointed at my chest. "A snake."

"She is no such thing, sister."

Her lips pinched together and her nostrils flared. My twin sister and I spoke a language that needed no words. Grief shouted even louder than anger in her eyes. It resonated in my gut. Shimon's death was a fiery arrow that had shot us both through the core.

She severed the silent connection with a shake of her head. "Keziah is heartbroken."

"I am sorry to have broken her trust."

"That you did. And our mother's too." Tzipi knew just the angle to push the dagger in. Together Keziah's mother and ours had all but written the *ketubah* marriage contract from the time Keziah was born. At times it seemed talking about our future marriage was the only thing that pulled our mother back from the edge of darkness after the horror of Korah's rebellion. If only it had kept her from slipping over that precipice.

"And now the only son left, after our brothers died, marries our enemy." This comment went deep under my ribs, as did the acrid expression on her face as she slung the large basket onto her hip and ducked into her tent. When had my sister's words become so barbed and poisoned? Grief had sharpened her tongue to a fine point.

Shimon had always been able to keep Tzipi's tempers in check, usually with a well-aimed tease or a soft word. But it seemed as though Tzipi had no intention of letting me blunt the sharp edges for her. I'd never felt so helpless, not since I was a boy and could do nothing to protect my loved ones. Pulled between the sister I loved and the woman to whom I had pledged a vow, I was a fraying rope stretched taut.

Alanah sprang up from a cross-legged position as I entered the tent. To my surprise, Nita's belongings were already unpacked.

Baskets along the walls. Bed mats unrolled and prepared. Everything just as Nita liked it, down to the small fire at the center of the tent to guard against frigid desert nights.

"I did not know what to do with myself." Alanah tugged at the linen binding on her arm. "I am useless in this thing."

"I am sure Nita will appreciate you unpacking." I scuffed my foot on the pebbled ground, suddenly aware of how alone we were. Alanah, too, looked away as if she felt the same tension. I cleared my throat. "I should go scout in the hills, see if I can find any game before it gets dark."

Nodding, she absently rubbed her still-healing shoulder and then adjusted her white turban. The ring of red hair was thicker now at the back of her neck, bringing attention to its long, slender line. Just that bit of fiery color brought new life to her face, accentuated the creamy sun-gold of her freckled skin. I found my eyes drawn to the curve of her throat.

She may not be soft and feminine like Keziah, but she was captivating, with or without her hair. Levon's suggestive comments from a few days ago whispered in my head, as did my resolve to keep her in sight. "Would you . . . would you like to come?"

With a little start, she looked up, a flicker of interest glowing in her eyes—the first I had ever seen of such an emotion. My chest grew strangely warm at the sight.

Remembering Shimon's tactics, I attempted a tease. "Unless, of course, you'd rather sit around here with Simcha and Noach to guard you."

Her gaze narrowed a bit, as if determining whether I was baiting her, but then it cut to her bow lying next to her sleeping mat. *She is yearning to go.*

A shadow crossed her face. "I cannot hunt." She pointed to her bandages. "I am useless to you."

"You still have eyes, don't you? You can search out game."

"How do you know I will be of any help?" She tilted her head. "Just because I have a bow doesn't make me an expert. Perhaps I will only scare game away."

How to explain so I didn't give away my fascination? I had never seen a woman with such keen skills of observation. So completely aware of what was going on around her. Always at the ready with a swift reaction.

Although an uncommon pursuit for a woman, she was a hunter, I had no doubt. Judging by the elongated shape of her upper arms and the strength of her shoulders, that bow was not just a decoration. She was an experienced archer. The flutter of her fingers tapping against her thigh confirmed it. She must be desperate to apply her skills to something other than fending off my sister—who seemed incapable of keeping her opinions in her head.

Feigning indifference with a shrug, I turned my back. "You are probably right, go ahead and stay," I said over my shoulder. "Simcha is out here raising his family's tent, I'll let him know to keep an eye on you."

I didn't even need to turn around to know she had followed me out the tent door.

I was glad she couldn't see the smug grin on my face. I snatched up a spear that was propped against my tent nearby and led her toward the orange hills south of camp.

14

ALANAH

I trailed my fingers along the wall of the narrow canyon, following the pale line of greenish veins that threaded through its rough face. "What kind of rock is this?"

"Malachite—copper ore." Tobiah's voice came from behind me, where he followed a little too closely in this confined space. "This area is full of copper. Before Mosheh led our people out of Egypt, the Egyptians ran many mines here." He paused. "They've been neglected now for some time. Although we've heard a few small mines are back in production after all these years, southeast of here."

"I would imagine the Egyptians want to stay far away from you Hebrews."

"And you would be right." The deep, rich sound of his laughter bounced off the narrow walls. "From what the traders tell us, they are still reeling from the loss of most of their workforce, and their firstborn sons."

What would that have been like? I had heard the tales of the horrific events of the great atrocity committed by the Hebrews and their god. I was no soft-footed Egyptian woman, but even I cringed at the idea of hordes of rotting frogs and locusts swarming the land like a flood.

The narrow wadi canyon opened into a wider area, a protected valley between the steep orange hills that cradled a small green-tinged pool, the remnants of a rainstorm, probably from weeks ago. The water was low, and from the looks of it, stagnant. But in this thirsty land, this would be a good place to find game or fowl.

Instinctively, I softened my steps, my eyes searching in a slow, steady circle for any sort of movement around the spare scrub brush and the few yellow-budded acacias that called this impoverished valley home. My hands itched for the weight of my bow but it stayed tied to my quiver, useless in the grip of a wounded archer.

A brown-streaked rush snagged my side-vision, and I jabbed a finger toward the fleeing rabbit to alert Tobiah. When his iron-tipped spear did not fly past my shoulder, I turned. "Why didn't you aim?" I said in a low tone, wary of scaring off any more prey.

"We don't eat rabbit," he whispered with such passionless authority that I did not bother to ask why. He stooped to pick up a blue-green stone, lifted it to study it in the sunlight, then rolled it back and forth between his fingers before tucking it into his belt. What use would he have for such a thing? Perhaps it was a gift for that Keziah woman.

Brushing the distracting idea away, I squatted next to the brackish pond, my eyes roving its edges, and stilled my body. We didn't have to wait long. A short, knobby-kneed ibex braved the open area and walked to the water, so desperate to slake its thirst that it ignored the two hunters watching him from fifteen paces away. The long, curled horns bobbed up and down as it drank, its tufted beard dribbling with water.

Holding my breath and barely moving a muscle, I turned my eyes up to Tobiah. With a slow, measured movement, he lifted his spear above his shoulder, cocked it backward, and then, in a flash of rippled muscle and a huff of release, Tobiah let the spear fly. The ibex didn't even cry out as the spear pierced its neck. It flopped to the dirt and, with only one or two jerks of its tawny body, stilled. Something like pride rose in my throat at the display of my husband's skill.

The sun had already slipped its hem behind the lip of the copper canyon walls, and it would not be long before it slid from sight. Tobiah retrieved the ibex and his spear and hefted the animal over his shoulder with ease. "Let's head back. I need to bleed this animal out and we don't have much daylight left."

He gestured for me to lead the way, and I plunged back into the narrow canyon that had delivered us to this secret pond.

"See, I was correct about you," he said, unguarded respect in his low voice.

Curling my lips into a smile he could not see from behind, I lifted my shoulder in acknowledgment of his correct assumptions about my hunting acumen. My brothers had taught me well; it was one of the only times they had allowed me to follow after them. Once they realized what a good shot I was with my bow, they took great pride in honing my skills. Tobiah's quiet appreciation of those skills caused an unexpected surge of pleasure to well up in my chest.

A tiny cry caught my attention and I stopped. Angling my head, I listened for the sound again. The light was waning quickly in the wadi and the orange rock beginning to blur into hazy brown, but just as I heard the sound again, I saw a slight movement about five paces in front of us on a small embankment.

A viper.

A deadly horned viper, mottled scales nearly camouflaged into the rock. Coiled for attack, its tongue flicked in and out as he homed in on his prey—two little sand cats, curled against the boulder, completely unaware of the imminent danger. Anger crashed through my body, a sudden protective instinct rushing in like a flood. Without a pause I bent down, snatched up a large rock from near my feet, and aimed it at the triangular head of the snake.

The serpent twisted and sprang off to the side, disoriented by the sudden attack, and then slithered away so fast I barely saw the move. I approached the little sand cats, who mewed helplessly. Their tiny half-opened eyes blinked up at me. "I wonder what happened to their mother?"

Tobiah peered down at the spotted cats as he hefted the ibex higher on his broad shoulder. "Either run off by that snake, or killed by it."

By the time his assessment was voiced, my decision was made. With my good arm, I swept up the creatures and curled the squirming bundle into my chest.

"What are you planning to do with those?" His tone was incredulous.

My response was flippant. "Take them back to camp."

He lifted his brows high. Would he scold me? Or refuse permission?

My defenses reared high, and I challenged him with a glare. "I won't leave them to be devoured by that serpent."

"They are so small, Alanah. It's doubtful they will survive." Concern pulled his brows together.

"They certainly won't if I leave them here."

He dropped his chin, sympathy in the curve of his lips. "But at least you won't have to watch it happen."

"Do you take me for some weak, sniveling woman?" I widened my stance.

His lips twitched with a hint of humor and his brown-eyed gaze echoed the tease. "No, Alanah. Never that."

Was he actually worried I would be hurt if the animals died? Stunned by the thought, I stared at him. Even with the heavy burden of a dead ibex slung over his shoulder, Tobiah seemed relaxed. Almost . . . almost as if he enjoyed sparring with me. "They'll survive." I tightened my hold on the kittens, even as one of them sank needle-like claws into my skin. I sucked in a breath and bit my lip. How could something so tiny hurt so much? To hide my reaction, I spun around to continue walking. But as I did, I could have sworn I saw a grin on my new husband's face—a face that was becoming far too intriguing for my comfort.

15

27 Nissan
1407 BC

Shira's nimble fingers examined my wound. Although it was still tender to the touch, on both the front and back of my shoulder, it was clearly healing well. My oldest brother had once been shot with an arrow in the thigh and it took many weeks for it to be at this stage of healing, and even then, he walked with a pronounced limp until the day he was killed by the Hebrews.

Shira hummed as she worked, her silvery braid trailing over her shoulder. A few wispy curls framed her face, giving her an impossibly youthful appearance. She wound a fresh bandage around my shoulder over a thin layer of honey and herb ointment. The strong smell clung to me constantly.

"How much longer must I wear this sling?"

"Seven more days or so. I want to keep it as still as possible to ensure you have full use of your arm. So you can use that bow of yours again." She darted a look at the weapon on the ground beside me. "But your wound has almost healed. A product of our diet, I assume." She tied a knot at the top of my sling and gently maneuvered my arm into position.

"The manna? It heals?"

She twitched a shoulder. "No one knows for sure. But I will say that since we left Egypt anyone with a cut or broken bone seems to heal much faster than usual. And none of us ages like our parents did back in the land of our birth. I am close to sixty now, but I feel almost as spry as I did as a young girl. Perhaps even more so." She winked at the Egyptian woman who had come with Shira to check my bandages. "Don't you think so, Kiya?"

Kiya suppressed a smile. "I don't think you ever have been without energy, my friend. Even when you were banished to the kitchens, thin as a reed, I'd never seen anyone work so hard." She shook her head, her long black hair, threaded with a few glints of silver, gleaming in the sunlight. I resisted the urge to tug at my own, which was not much longer than my sand cats' speckled fur.

Shira waved a hand and gave a little groan. "Don't remind me. My fingertips still tingle when I think of all the pots I scrubbed with sand."

They laughed together, the sound of two friends connected at the heart. My own ached a little at the reminder that I'd never had a friend, other than my brothers, and certainly never a woman.

I shifted on the wooden stool and looked over Shira's shoulder at the *Mishkan* that had been raised at the center of camp. The rectangular linen courtyard contrasted the orange cliffs with stark whiteness. The tall, billowing cloud pillared high above the newly raised sanctuary.

Shira followed my line of sight. "Ah. Yes. Beautiful, isn't it? I never get tired of the sight of the Cloud over the *Mishkan*."

"How do they raise it so quickly?"

Shira paused in her ministrations to my shoulder and sat back on her heels. "The sons of Levi, which is the only tribe that can take part in the construction and breaking down of the structure, each have a designated job. They work together with such precision, as if they are one body."

"And no matter how inconsequential the task," Kiya said. "There is not one man who is regarded as less important. My husband tells me that it is a beautiful thing to experience."

"Your husband is a Levite?" I looked up at her, trying to keep my jaw from gaping.

"He is. And a leader of the musicians who lift worship to Yahweh with their instruments." Pride radiated from her smile. She was truly one of the most beautiful women I'd ever seen. How had a woman with such regal bearing come to be married to a Hebrew slave? "Were you married in Egypt?"

"No, we came to love each other along the journey." Kiya's golden eyes fluttered skyward. "The more Yahweh drew me in, the more our differences became buried in love for each other."

Tobiah flashed through my mind. *I do not love him. He is my enemy.* But I had to admit that he was kind. Kinder than my brothers had ever been to me, with their rough goading and crass jesting. They had treated me like a younger brother in many ways, and tormented me as such. It wasn't until they came to appreciate my hunting skills that they began to treat me with any sort of respect. But even if they valued my bow, the older I got, the more they heckled me, until I gave up following them on hunts and slipped out to stalk game on my own.

Although Tobiah was silent most of the time, he was quick to offer help, spoke in low, patient tones, and never treated me as a captive. Holding on to my obligatory anger at him was becoming more difficult each day. Especially after the excursion that yielded an ibex and two tiny sand cats who were now mewling loudly from their basket inside the tent.

"What is that noise?" Shira looked around.

Hesitant to reveal my spontaneous decision to rescue the sand cats to these women, I said nothing.

"It sounds like some sort of animal," said Kiya, cupping her long fingers to her ear.

"My cats," I said in a low tone.

Shira bent forward to hear me. "Cats? Did you say *cats*?"

I rolled my eyes. "Yes. Cats. I rescued two of them the other day. They were nearly devoured by a snake."

"Oh!" Shira clapped her hands. "Can we see?"

I was struck dumb for a moment by her enthusiasm, but I shrugged and retrieved my squirming, complaining charges from the tent.

After our foray to the hidden pool yesterday, Tobiah had said little but had brought me a large basket in which to corral them, apparently resigned to my insistence that I would keep them alive.

"How sweet!" Shira reached out eagerly.

"Not when they are sinking their teeth into you." I placed one in her hands and then offered the other to Kiya.

The Egyptian woman raised her hands in refusal. "No, thank you."

"You still hate cats, Kiya?" Shira winked at her. "It's been a long time."

"I cannot believe you don't." She folded her arms and rocked back on her heels.

"It was not the fault of the cats," said Shira.

"They hated me too," said Kiya. "Swiping at my ankles every time I walked by. Snarling and hissing." She wrinkled her nose. "Especially that fat orange one with the missing eye."

"Pharaoh!" Shira flapped a hand in the air and giggled like a little girl.

Kiya laughed, a smooth, pleasant sound. Even her laugh was beautiful.

"What are you two talking about?" I snapped, feeling oddly annoyed by their shared memories. With instant regret for my rudeness, I clamped my mouth shut but kept my face blank.

Shira smiled. "We are speaking of our time back in Egypt. Kiya and I were both slaves in the same household. And our mistress was a devotee of Bastet, the cat goddess. Therefore, cats ruled the house."

"Especially the one Shira named Pharaoh." Kiya smirked.

"Why do you think I named him that?" Shira lifted the sand cat and nuzzled his spotted fur with her nose. "And what is this one's name?"

I pressed my lips together. Was this woman determined to break down every defense I had? There was something about Shira that conveyed such calm acceptance that I always found myself revealing too much in her presence.

Resigned, I sighed. "That one is Bodo. And this"—I pointed to the one now suckling and kneading his claws on my forearm—"is Capo. And obviously they are very hungry."

"Do you have milk for them?"

"Tobiah brought me a jug of goat's milk."

"Good. When you need more, let me know. My sons tend the Levite flocks." She stroked Bodo. "He is a good man, is he not?"

I wrinkled my brow in confusion.

"Tobiah. He seems to be treating you well?" Her thin brows arched high, making plain what she was truly asking.

"He has not touched me." I scratched Capo behind his too-large ears.

She smiled. "I thought so. I could tell he was a young man who values the Torah. It's not much longer though, is it?"

My lashes fluttered. "Twelve days."

"And have you made a decision? Will you stay?"

"Where would I go?" A variety of half-laid plans unrolled in my mind: swiping Nita's knife while she slept . . . taking refuge among my father's Edomite kin . . . settling in some deserted village, alone.

"Indeed. Where?" She pinned me with a glare, as if privy to the machinations in my head. "Tobiah will protect you here, Alanah." She jerked her chin at the northern ridge. "Out there you would be completely vulnerable."

A hundred sharp-tongued defenses sprang up. None of them very kind. I swallowed them all, with huge effort. Perhaps she had little faith in my survival skills, but Shira had been good to me. "As you say." I stretched a tight smile across my lips.

"You are wearing my belt!" Kiya exclaimed.

Startled by her interruption, I put a hand to the intricately woven belt wrapped around my waist. "You made this?"

Pride washed over her lovely face. "It suits you well!"

I looked between the two women whose puzzling connection was finally becoming clear. "You are married to Shira's brother?"

A warm smile played across her full lips. "I am."

"Did he take you captive as well?" I had heard the stories of how the Hebrews plundered Egypt as they fled. Perhaps they had taken Egyptian prisoners too.

"No, Eben didn't put me into bondage. He helped release me from it." She studied me for a moment, as if understanding my true motive for asking. "It is true. We were once enemies. My people enslaved his. And slaughtered them relentlessly for hundreds of years. Yet even in spite of his own prejudices, and my foolish choices, Eben loved me and saved me from an evil man, twice. My husband protected me, time and time again, even when I refused to follow Yahweh."

Instantly grasping the hidden meaning of her explanation, I looked down and stroked Capo. He purred and pressed against me, eyes closing. "I can protect myself quite well."

"Of that I have little doubt . . . But, Alanah, look at me," Kiya commanded with a tone borrowed from some queenly ancestor.

Reluctantly, I obeyed, anticipating a reprimand from this older woman whose elegant presence made me acutely aware of the dirt beneath my fingernails and the loss of my hair. But the warmth of her honey-gold eyes surprised me as she reached out and gripped my shoulder lightly. "Eben protects me because he loves me, not because he sees me as weak."

She paused, as if allowing the implication to settle in my mind.

Perhaps it had. "What changed?" I whispered.

"Yahweh." Her voice trembled with passion. "Yahweh called to me. Brought me out from Egypt so I could be united with the Hebrews, and Eben, in sacred covenant. Though I am a child of Egypt, I am now part of Israel."

She smiled, her eyes traveling upward for a brief moment, as if she was remembering something from long ago. "Someone once told me that Yahweh would make himself known to me, if I searched. And he did. Perhaps he will make himself known to *you*."

What a strange notion, that a god would call to someone. As if a deity would somehow speak to a lowly mortal. To a woman. To me.

16

TOBIAH

Alanah gasped. Wide-mouthed. Eyes open. She was sitting up on her pallet, arms stretched out, flailing, grasping at empty air as I swept into the tent.

I scrambled to her side and put a hand on her shoulder. Sleeping just outside every night, I'd heard her whimper in her sleep before. She tossed and turned on a regular basis, but the fear in her strangled cry this morning had jarred me. I found myself leaping up before I'd even made the decision to interfere.

She turned, vacant-eyed but with horror splashed across her face. Could she even see me? She seemed to look right through me to the other side of the tent.

She swiped at her face as if brushing away flies. "Close their eyes! Close their eyes!" she moaned.

"Shh." I took a chance and stroked her cheek. "*Ishti*, it is a dream. You are here. With me. Tobiah." The endearment *ishti*—my wife—had slipped from my lips all too easily. I darted a look to Nita on her bed, but her back was toward us; she must be deep in sleep to not hear Alanah's distress.

Alanah blinked and shook her head, clearing away the confusion of pre-dawn and throwing off the grip of her nightmare. When her eyes cleared and she realized how close I was, she shrank back, wariness in the drop of her brow.

I lifted my hands in the air, surrendering before she struck at me as she seemed tempted to do. "You were dreaming. I only sought to wake you."

I inched back, sensing she needed more space. She glared a moment more and then relaxed, softening the tilt of her shoulders and uncurling her back. She, too, glanced at Nita's side of the tent, but my aunt still did not stir. I sat back on my haunches, arms folded, studying her face. "Are you on the battlefield?"

Her brows lifted in question.

"The dreams." I tugged at my beard. "Do you see yourself there again?"

She looked down at her hands. "All I see is blood, and so many empty eyes, staring."

What could I say? I visited the same horror whenever my own eyes closed. In fact, she had not woken me at all; sleep visited me only for a few restless hours every night. This morning had been spent as many others, restless on my pallet, swatting away images of Shimon, glassy-eyed and rigid in the blazing sand.

Although I had trained to serve in the army, endured years of pushing my body to its limits during exercises, the battles against Arad's forces had been my first. My nightmares were haunted by broken Canaanite bodies, many by my own hand, screaming or cursing Yahweh with their last breaths.

Divided between the surprising desire to pull her into my foolish arms and the drive to distract us both with some other activity, I chose the latter. "Would you . . . would you like to take a walk?"

Only ten more days stood between our covenant and its consummation, and each day seemed to drag its feet slower than the last. Would she leave after the thirty days were complete? Or stay and continue as my wife?

The agony of the question kept me awake almost as much as my turbulent dreams. How could something that seemed so abhorrent a few weeks ago—marrying a Canaanite—now be such an intriguing possibility?

Every day since our first hunting excursion, I'd invited her to come with me whenever I trekked into the hills. Although our conversation was limited to local game or brief explanations about the ways and laws of my people that baffled her, it was the comfortable silences between us that made me thirst for more knowledge of her past.

"Manna will already be on the ground. We can get an early start." I offered her what I hoped was a reassuring smile, instead of an infatuated grin.

She untangled her legs from the bedclothes and smoothed her twisted dress as she stood. In an unconscious move, she lifted a hand to straighten her hair. Her gaze cut to mine when she realized her turban had fallen off during the night. Swiftly, she bent and retrieved it before wrapping it around her head to hide the brilliant red.

I winced, experiencing all over again the pain of watching Shira cut that first strand—the only cut I'd watched her make. Like a coward I'd fled the tent that day to keep from snatching up the shears from Shira's kind hands and throwing them into the dirt.

As we left the tent, after Alanah had ensured her sand cats were still sleeping in their basket, Nita looked over her shoulder, a satisfied smirk on her face. She'd been listening the whole time. A matchmaker from the beginning, my *doda*.

We walked together, silent in the chill of the desert morning. Alanah wrapped her arms around herself, perhaps wishing she had brought a shawl. I restrained myself from offering my own arm and instead focused on the white field in front of me. Morning already claimed the top of the cliff, and the manna sparkled there like new snow.

A flock of blackbirds burst from an acacia tree, cackling their displeasure. Even this early, many creatures were ahead of us, feasting on the miracle grains before the rest of the multitude awoke to rescue their daily bread.

I followed behind Alanah as she shuffled through the thick of it, scooping handfuls into her basket and sneaking bites when she thought my attention was elsewhere. How could it be anywhere but on her?

The strength that radiated from her drew me like wildfire to desert brush. Everything, from the way she carried her slim body to the way she navigated the rocky path with sure-footed grace, called to me—she was like no other woman I had ever known. I wanted to know her more. I wanted to know everything about her.

As she reached a sunlit spot on the trail, she lifted her chin, eyes closed and hands loose at her sides, enjoying the warmth of the sun on her face. I was held captive by the sight.

And when she opened her eyes—eyes the same bluish-green as the malachite stone I'd snatched from the ground during our first hunting trip—I remembered the first time I saw them, when they made me forget my friend, my brother, on the battlefield in the urgency to save her life.

We smashed through every defense the Canaanites had set in place. Their lines confused, their charioteers decimated by our archers, Shimon and I pushed ahead. I heard his fierce battle yell as he was pulled by the tide of battle deeper into the melee. I was pushed back and lost sight of him as enemy after enemy clashed their angry swords against mine.

*We pushed through the lines of Canaanite infantry, swords
high and the mighty bray of the* shofarim *vibrating through
our blood. There was no sense of time or direction amid the
crush of death and men around me. After the first few men I
sent reeling into the afterlife, faces were only a blur.*

*But Shimon. How long did he take to die? How long after
we'd been separated had his life been stolen? Had he been gasping for breath, calling out for help as I carried Alanah away?
Why had I lived? Why had I not saved him?*

A touch on my shoulder jolted me off the battlefield, and
Alanah's face appeared in front of me. "Tobiah?"

The sound of my name on her tongue completed my journey
back to the moment. It was the first time she had spoken my
name with anything resembling tenderness. She knew where I
had been in my mind; she understood.

Was she softening to me? The look on her face told me she
was, for it betrayed a level of concern I had not anticipated. It
would be so simple to close the gap between us, to wrap my
arms around her. I saw the idea play itself out in my mind, but
before I could summon the courage to do so, she stepped away.
Had she seen the temptation written on my face?

I drew a deep breath, thinking to distract myself by asking
about her family, or her ridiculous cats, but suddenly Alanah
had questions of her own.

"Who is Keziah?"

I nearly choked. What had Tzipi told her? I'd hoped that
the brief mention of Keziah had gone unnoticed. I should have
known better. Alanah missed nothing.

"My mother wanted me to marry her," I said. "When I returned from the battle at Arad, we were to begin a yearlong
betrothal period."

"So she is not your first wife?"

Ah. Alanah thought she was to be a second wife, or perhaps a concubine. "No. You are my only wife. You will always be my only wife."

She looked away, her gaze drawn to the stand of acacias nearby where a large monitor lizard perched on one of the branches, perhaps disappointed that we had startled the blackbirds away. "But our marriage has kept you from your betrothed."

"We were not yet betrothed. I was not . . ." I cleared my throat. "I was not ready to be married."

"And yet, when you saw me lying out in the sand, you decided it was time?" Alanah gripped the elbow of her wounded arm, drawing it across her body.

"No . . . Yes . . . I don't . . ." I stumbled through my tangled thoughts. "No, I was not ready to be married, but when Shira told me I must marry you, I knew it was the right thing to do."

"The right thing?"

"It is my duty to obey the Torah."

"So you married me out of duty?" She pursed her mouth as if tasting a bitter root.

"And to protect you."

"And if I leave?"

"I told you before, I will let you go."

Her brows arched high. "You truly would not stop me?"

"If you were determined to leave, I would release you from our agreement."

"And you would then marry Keziah?" she asked.

I drew in a quick breath through my nose. "I suppose I should, to not bring further dishonor to her family."

"And is she beautiful?"

The abrupt question startled me. Was that a note of jealousy in her voice? I pushed out my bottom lip and folded my arms. "Yes. I would say she is beautiful." *But her eyes don't call my name like yours do.*

She brushed away some manna that clung to her skirt, emitting a low noise from the back of her throat. *Interesting.* I settled back on my heels. Silent. Face carefully blank as I waited. I was a hunter. If anything, I knew how to wait.

"And no doubt a wonderful cook," she said, lifting the basket of manna with a smirk.

She'd snatched up the bait without hesitation. I swallowed a smile. "True." *Yet somehow the manna cakes formed by your palms taste sweeter.* "My mother and hers were good friends and always desired the match."

Her eyes narrowed as she contemplated my explanation. My mother had indeed desired that I marry Keziah. But watching Alanah now, this strong, brave woman, squirming with frustration and feathers ruffled as she weighed whether I would choose another woman over her, I decided that there was no one else for me. I had never gone against my parents, in life or in death. But in this one thing, I would defy their wishes, with pleasure.

My mouth twitched as I realized just how to make Alanah take that one last step into the snare of her own making. "She is also skilled at weaving. In fact she made this tunic." I smoothed the brown fabric against my chest.

Her eyes flared as they tracked the path of my palm. She *was* jealous. My blood surged at the possibility. Alanah was more than softening to me. She was quite possibly as attracted to me as I was to her.

But as swift as the drop of a veil, she drew herself to her full height and spun to continue collecting manna. The move was too fast, however, and she teetered, off-balance for a moment. I grabbed her elbow to steady her. She jerked away as if stung by a scorpion.

"Why won't you let me help you?" I said, frustration leaking into my tone.

She turned on me, one fist on her hip. "I don't need you to help me, or protect me."

"I vowed that I would."

"I don't hold you to any vow."

"It matters not, I am bound to my word. I am your husband."

"You are not my master."

"Have I ever treated you as such?"

"You will. I am acquainted enough with marriage to know what happens after a man has his way. My father's women were no more than property. When he died they were given to my worthless cousin like a set of oxen."

"That is not marriage. That is slavery."

She scoffed "What is the difference?"

"The difference is that, here, Torah is obeyed. A wife is afforded many protections. Yahweh bids us to love our wives. Treat them with care. Consider them part of our own flesh."

She watched me speak, confusion in her eyes.

"I have no desire to imprison you. I have told you before and will say it again: I will not hold you here against your will. My only thought has been your protection."

"Well, there are only ten more days. Then you will be free of me." Something like pain flickered across her face as she glanced away.

I stepped close, unconcerned that many others were now in the field, foraging their own daily rations. Her eyes went wide, the blue-green reflecting the sunrise, yet she did not retreat. A handspan apart, we breathed in tandem, gazes locked.

Her lips parted for a moment, as if to say something, but they quivered and she pressed them together. The movement caused my belly to warm with anticipation.

I could not help myself. Keeping my movements slow, as if she were a frightened doe, I lifted a finger and traced the curve of her ear. Her breathing hitched and she closed her eyes. I slid my finger down the long, smooth line of her neck.

"Yes, Alanah," I whispered. "Only ten more days. Eternal days—but not for the reason you think. I will wait for you. Hoping you will choose me of your own accord." Leaning forward, my lips nearly grazed the top of her cheekbone. "But do not think for one moment that the wait will be easy."

17

ALANAH

You will always be my only wife . . . Eternal days . . . the wait will not be easy . . . Tobiah's words wandered around in my head, traveled with growing intensity through my extremities, and wormed their way into my heart. My chest ached. Had he truly meant what he'd said? I searched beyond the sheer ceiling above me, peering at the silent stars that denied me answers.

I shivered, remembering the scorching trail Tobiah's finger had left on my skin. He had touched me with a feather-light tenderness that I could not reconcile with the bloody-faced warrior who had loomed over me on the battlefield.

I'd always kept my distance from men back in the village. Their leering had been more than enough to remind me of who my mother was and what they expected of me. The knife I'd always carried at my belt had not been for decoration, it had become necessary after run-ins with men who'd not heard of my brothers' fierce reputations or my weaponry skills.

But Tobiah did not look at me the way they had. The way he'd touched me did not make me wish I were invisible, or cause me to curl up inside, wishing for death. Instead, I'd had to close my eyes to restrain the swell of hope that surged upward and clench my fists against the force of desire to make the too-small gap between us vanish.

How had my enemy captured me so completely?

Yet even as I considered my bondage, I remembered that he had vowed to not hold me here against my will. Tobiah had never threatened me. He'd never forced me to do anything, never manipulated me. He had only protected me, as he had promised. He'd appointed his cousins to ensure my safety and watched over me by lying across the opening of the tent every night.

Truth flooded through me. I was not a captive. I never had been.

I knew for certain that if I stood up right now, grabbed my bow, and left the tent, Tobiah would stand by his word. He would let me go. The thought filled me with crushing anguish.

"Tobiah was only four when it happened." Nita's low voice reached through the dark, startling me with its haunting tone in the stillness. Usually by this time of night, Nita was already in the depths of sleep.

Was she talking to me? Or voicing some memory aloud for her own benefit? As I waited for her to continue, the sheer canopy above us undulated from a cool breeze tinged with the slightest scent of the nearby sea. I shivered, and Bodo stretched in his sleep, then curled in closer to my chest.

"I wonder . . ." She whispered, for Tobiah was nearby, stretched across the tent entrance on his mat. "I wonder if he even remembers anything."

"What would he remember?" I whispered back. A brief image of a Liyam-sized Tobiah slipped into my imagination, a small boy who would someday be the warrior who snatched my life back from the precipice of death.

"The night his brothers died. My three nephews, along with their entire families, were killed. Their young wives. Their children." Her voice went flat.

My mouth gaped, although the older woman could not see it in the dark. "How?" The hesitant question somehow pressed through the pinch of my throat.

"My brother married Rivka back in Avaris. They had three sons." A sigh broke from her lips, its tail end curved into an audible smile. "Oh, they were beautiful boys, Alanah. Tzipi's boys resemble them in so many ways. As if Yahweh kept pieces of my nephews and scattered them in Liyam, Mahan, and Yonel as a consolation."

The three boys had kept their distance from me after Tzipi's edict, especially Liyam. But there were times when I caught Liyam's eyes on my bow, one tiny hand tugging at the other as if it were a bowstring. More than once I restrained myself from dropping a wink his way, a rebellious nudge of encouragement for the obvious fascination with archery, and with me.

"Tobiah and Tzipi came late for Uri and Rivka. Rivka was past her thirty-seventh year. It was such a surprise! And twins! What a blessing. Especially after all we had endured under Pharaoh and during our flight into the wilderness."

She turned onto her side, her form silhouetted against the glow of the moon on the tent wall. "We had been in this detestable wilderness for so long, Alanah. And the longer we tarried, the shorter our memories became. One of the Levites, a man named Korah who was a cousin to Mosheh and Aharon, began to sow seeds of discord among some of his tribe. It started quietly, some murmuring, some questioning of whether Mosheh really knew what he was doing. Whether he had become senile in his old age."

"Was there an uprising?"

"There was. And my nephews were involved."

"Did they raise arms against Mosheh?"

"They never had a chance."

"What do you mean?"

"Mosheh ordered the unrepentant rebels to be separated out, along with their families. And then, within the hour . . . the earth began to tremble." She paused as if caught up in the latent sensations of such a terrible thing. "The ground split open. Oh—" She sighed. "Alanah, I will never forget the sight of that enormous gaping mouth slicing through camp, racing toward them. And every single person in Korah's camp—man, woman, child, beast—all of them disappeared into that pit."

Cold shock paralyzed me. My tongue went dry in my mouth. "But—" I swallowed, trying to coax my voice out. "But why?"

"Yahweh himself appointed Mosheh over us. And declared Aharon our high priest. Korah did not just question Mosheh. He raised himself up against El Shaddai, the Mighty God. If he allowed rebellion to slither its way through our camps, we would be removed from his divine protection. We would be exposed to the fury of the Egyptians. Exposed to the vengeance of the Amalekites. We would be slaughtered. It is to protect life that Yahweh has allowed life to be taken."

I thought of the fiery cloud that hovered nearby and the feeling it gave me whenever I looked its way, as if it was a mighty warrior, like Tobiah, standing guard over his people.

"And now it is happening all over again." She made a guttural noise of frustration. "These young ones. They do not understand. There are so few of us left who remember how destructive rebellion is. The slaughter after the Golden Calf was worshipped. The thousands who died. The firestorm that burned the outer rim of camp when the foreigners among us incited a riot."

She kept talking, as if to herself. "They take for granted the miraculous water that feeds this multitude. They have eaten the manna every day of their lives and do not see the utter strangeness of it. They have not felt the desperation of thirst or the hopelessness of hunger. All they do is complain."

"Why would they complain?"

"You must understand, Alanah. My generation is almost completely gone. Nearly forty years ago, Mosheh sent twelve spies into Canaan. Ten of them came back with tales of the people . . . your people and their ferocity. The giants in the land. How the enormous walled cities were too mighty for us to conquer."

"As they are." I did not even attempt to smother my smug response.

She cleared her throat. "No, my dear. I know you do not understand, but there is no army, no fortress, no giant that can stand against our God. No one. I have seen his might with my own eyes." Her voice grew stronger with each word. "I have walked through the bottom of the sea. On dry ground. I have watched as he humiliated Egypt and brought the mighty Pharaoh low."

I blinked into the darkness. The conviction in her voice was difficult to argue with. And truthfully, I had seen the way Yahweh fed them every day. Was this God truly as powerful as the Hebrews insisted?

I'd had little to do with the gods since I was a child. No use for deities who stole everything, ignored pleas and offerings—no matter how bloody—and capriciously withheld rain and devastated crops at their whims. No use for deities that would steal a mother from her child.

Although my father's wives groveled at the feet of their household gods, I ignored the lumps of clay and stone carvings that represented the gods in the heavens and instead spent my time outside, stalking deer, working in the orchards, and honing my shooting skills. The gods took. They took everything.

"Even my own sons are complaining," Nita said. "They cannot understand why we don't just push forward into the land, as we should have forty years ago. They are prepared, body and soul, to fight this fight. And truthfully, we all are tired of the desert. I must admit, even I have been dreaming about lush grass and fields of wheat and barley, lakes and rivers and flowers and fruit . . ." Her voice trailed off. "Even if I will never see it, it's good to know that my children and theirs will enjoy it."

"Why wouldn't you? Since you obviously believe my people will be overthrown?"

She paused so long I wondered if she had gone to sleep.

"I won't live to see it, Alanah. When the spies returned with their report from Canaan, we all were terrified. Myself included, I must admit. And instead of trusting Yahweh, we wondered if perhaps it would have been better had we not left Egypt in the first place. My Zakariyah, too, was among the men who took up the cause with Mosheh, saying that perhaps we should consider returning to the mountain where we had lived after our flight from Egypt."

As they should have. My family would still be alive.

"Because of our faithlessness . . . because of our rebellion . . . Yahweh pronounced judgment upon us. None of us who were over twenty years old will set foot in the Promised Land. I will die. Soon."

18

I'm so glad both of you came." Shira embraced me, careful of the shoulder she'd just this morning finally given me permission to move freely. Although the ache remained where the arrow had pierced me, I was surprised at the range of motion I had somehow retained, in spite of the depth of the wound.

Shira patted Tobiah's arm. "The wedding feast has already begun, but you are both welcome to join us. Come, I will introduce you to our family."

I'd been hesitant to accept Shira's invitation to the wedding feast of Kiya's grandson, but she'd insisted it was my payment for her healing services. This directive was, of course, delivered with a smile and I was glad for the diversion from the unsettling things Nita had told me and the ominous declaration that her life was very near the end.

A blur of faces and names hurtled at me from every side as Shira guided us through the large gathering, gesturing to various guests. "My son Avi and his wife, Liora. My son Dov and his wife, Rachel. Kiya's daughter Nailah, whose own son has just been married."

Nailah was a replica of her mother, tall, slim, and exotically beautiful, the two of them so similar they could have been sisters, except for Nailah's grayish-green eyes that I recognized as inherited from Shira's family.

A swarm of tiny children surged toward Shira, tugging at her skirt, begging for attention with little hands and the name of their grandmother on their lips. She knelt down, speaking with each one in turn, her eyes trained on theirs as she listened to each regale her with stories of some uncle named Jumo who had let them take turns on his drums.

My chest constricted so painfully that I had to press my lips together to restrain a gasp. A memory washed over me with such vivid, bright detail that I was suddenly back in my home in the valley, sitting on a bed, tucked into someone's arms, telling her about something one of my older brothers had done, some minor offense that felt enormous in my small mind.

My mother. It had to be. I could feel the warmth of her body. Smell the flowery sweetness of her bright red hair. Hear the lilt of her voice as she comforted me.

"Alanah? Are you well?" Tobiah's arm had somehow slipped around my waist, holding me up against the heaviness that threatened to press me into its shadows.

I should pull away. Put distance between us. But somehow the fit of my body against his expansive chest felt like the most natural thing in the world. As if the space had been carved out for me alone.

Heat flooded up my neck. "N-no . . ." I stammered. "I can stand . . . I am well." I seized on the only excuse my mind could conjure. "My shoulder hurt for a moment. But I am fine."

His eyes narrowed as if he knew I was lying, but he released me.

Shira gestured for us to sit near her but immediately was

caught up in conversation with a few nearby women. They chattered like a flock of waterbirds, trading stories, laughing, waving their hands in rhythm with jubilant, overlapping words.

Someone handed Tobiah a large bowl of stew and a basket full of manna bread. He placed the meal on the ground in front of us, broke a piece of bread in half and handed it to me. We ate in silence, dipping bread into the bowl of stew time and again. Somehow, even in the midst of a loud celebration, with over sixty people gathered into this large campsite, I felt the most relaxed I'd been in as long as I could remember. Tobiah's quiet presence next to me had a soothing effect—as did the wine that someone had thrust into my hand. Someone else had refilled the wine, twice.

"I've never been to a wedding feast." The words bubbled from my lips like a freshwater spring.

"No?" He twisted his mouth to the side, his expression dubious.

"My father simply brought his wives to our home one day, without ceremony."

"You had no other family? Or friends who married?"

"Most of my father's family lived in the territory of Edom." Except for his older brother, whose son, Dagan, had stolen everything from me after my father's death.

"And my mother . . . I'm not sure where she came from . . . from the far north . . . Sidon, I think? Or perhaps even farther away. I have a vague recollection of a story about her family fleeing on a ship and making their way to Canaan. But I do not know who told me such a thing." I shrugged, surprised that I'd allowed the memory to surface. "My father does not—my father did not speak of her." Where had this sudden compulsion to tell Tobiah of my family come from? I dropped my head and therefore, hopefully, the subject.

My hopes were denied.

"Tell me more." Tobiah's voice was closer than I expected. When I turned my head to look at him, he had moved directly next to me, our arms nearly touching. The look of expectancy on his face was shocking. Was he so interested in my family?

I drew my brows together. "What do you want to know?"

"Tell me about your home."

I paused, feeling as if my toes were dangling over the edge of a steep precipice. If I took a step forward, there was no returning. Everything in me was urging me onward, daring me to take the chance, to open the door to this man who had somehow, against my every instinct, knocked down my defenses.

I sighed as I plunged in. "My home is in a beautiful valley. The hills all around are lined with terraces where we plant fruit trees, date palms, and vineyards. My father spent years and years building the terraces that stack nearly to the top of the hills."

"Why?" Tobiah asked.

For a moment I was confused that he would ask about such a common thing, but then I realized that Tobiah had lived his entire life in this wilderness, being fed manna every day. He'd never held a scythe in his hand. He'd never furrowed the ground or spread seeds and hoped that the gods would be satisfied enough with our offerings to bless the tender shoots with rain.

"The terraces help retain water and keep the soil from washing down the hillsides. The irrigation ditches water the wheat and barley crops on the valley floor."

In the arid desert climate, every drop of rain was gold and silver. It had taken my father many years, longer than my life, to build up the stone fences that formed the wide steps curving up the hills to the west and east of our home.

This year more than any other, Baal had blessed our land with heavy winter rains, and the terraces embraced lush crops—a boon for Dagan, who dripped not one bead of sweat into the soil yet had reaped the benefits of my father's hard work, and mine.

A surge of frustration, mixed with longing for my home, welled up inside me. As if to remind myself, in case the memories faded with time and distance, I began to paint a picture for Tobiah with my words—the arid harshness, the bake of the sun as I hauled stones to patch tumbled-down terraces after a winter of rainstorms, the deafening rush of the wadis during a flood, and the rolling green plains interwoven with wildflowers of every color in the early spring, the red *kalanit* blossoms threading themselves among the tall grasses . . .

I stopped talking midsentence, shocked at how much I had said and how easily it had rolled off my tongue, as if years of pent-up words had gushed out. I blinked, fingers pressed against my mouth. What was wrong with me? Had I drunk too much wine? Or had some invisible barrier crumbled?

"Don't stop," said Tobiah, his tone low but urgent, as if he was afraid that I had reached the end of my words. And perhaps I had.

I scanned the crowd around us, all of them oblivious to the earthquake of emotions reeling through me. Why had I opened my mouth? These people were my enemies. Tobiah was my enemy. I repeated the statement over and over and over in my head, but truly I did not believe it anymore.

Most of the Hebrews, with the exception of Tzipi, who seemed to be pretending I did not exist, had been nothing but kind to me. Nita had welcomed me into her tent. Shira had bound my wounds, tended to my healing, and encouraged me. And Tobiah had protected me in a way that my own brothers had not. That my own father had not.

My father had kept me physically safe—no one had ever laid a hand on me, although my brothers' ruthless reputations probably did more to guard me than anything. But the older I got, the further away he seemed, as if every day he added a stone to the wall between us.

I had worked alongside him. He taught me to shoot and hunt and fight. But by the time he walked out the door to go attack the Hebrews, he barely spoke to me, other than to order me to finish chores and tend the animals. He'd left me to be bossed around by his brainless wives.

A thought struck me as I surveyed the revelers. "Where is the bride? I thought this was a wedding."

Tobiah laughed. "You really haven't been to a wedding feast, have you?"

I tossed him an annoyed look.

"This is the second day of feasting. The groom has already taken his bride into their marriage tent." He gestured across the campsite with a flick of his wrist. "They will enjoy a few days together there . . ." He cleared his throat. "Becoming one."

"Are you telling me that everyone is out here feasting while they . . . ?"

He smothered a smirk with his large hand. "Yes, that is what I am saying."

"But . . . but why?"

"Because marriage is beautiful to us, Alanah. We are glad when two lives are joined together. We celebrate the union of two people bound in a sacred covenant. It is blessed by Yahweh. In fact, marriage was designed by the Creator himself."

I'd never heard such foreign ideas about marriage, yet these notions were filled with such beauty. To me, marriage was nothing more than an arrangement that benefitted the man much more than the woman. Girls were sold into marriage before their first flow most times, could be tossed out for any offense, and often turned to prostitution to stay alive. Men had many wives, used the temple whores without compunction, and offered any unwanted infants to the *baalim* to ensure their crops prospered. It was the way of things. I'd never much questioned it, until now.

Suddenly, I realized that my father had protected me in the best way possible—he had not sold me into the slavery of a Canaanite marriage. Gratefulness burst open inside me like an almond blossom in the sun. My father had his faults—he'd never shown me anything resembling love—but in this at least he had shown me a measure of respect.

Five more days. Only five more days until the consummation of the marriage covenant.

"Will there be . . . ?" Stricken with sudden embarrassment, I clamped my mouth against the question I'd been about to ask.

Tobiah lifted his brows, waiting for me to continue.

I looked down at my hands in my lap, braided my fingers together until I composed an even tone. "Will there be a cel-ebration like this . . . for us?"

Tobiah did not answer.

My skin prickled with mortification. It took every bit of restraint in me to not jump up and run away. But determined not to show any more of my vulnerabilities to Tobiah tonight, I lifted my chin to face him, willing courage to infuse my bones with strength.

"No. There will not be a celebration like this one." His voice dropped low. "Our marriage is not a normal one. And especially after my sister's husband . . . it is best if it is done quietly."

My breath released in a rush of relief. I could not have imagined enduring a horde of Tobiah's family and friends all staring at me during some sort of false celebration of his marriage to an enemy.

"But . . . my beautiful bride . . ." He leaned in close, his shoulder pressing against mine and his warm breath brushing across my lips. My cheeks heated in response. "I have already prepared our marriage tent. We will have plenty of time there to celebrate. Together." His mouth quirked as he lifted his cup. "And I will make sure to have plenty of this wine stocked there." He winked. "I like the way it loosens your tongue."

19

W ho is that girl behind us?" I said to Nita as we walked
through camp with empty water jugs on our hips.
"I've seen her a few times with Tzipi. She will not
stop staring at me."

Nita glanced over her shoulder toward the young girl walking
between Simcha and Noach, the one whose startling silvery eyes
seemed to follow me whenever she was around. With a shining
black braid trailing over one shoulder and her skin a honeyed
bronze, she looked more Egyptian than Hebrew.

"Oh . . . that's Moriyah." Her smile faltered as she faced
me. "Shimon's sister."

Shimon's sister? No wonder she watched me; she must hate
me as much as Tzipi did.

"A mirror image of her brother, that one," said Nita with a
sigh. "There was always a joke or ridiculous tale on Shimon's
lips. There was not a story he told that did not have us all holding
our sides with laughter. Moriyah is just as vibrant, perhaps more

so. Although"—she flicked a glance back at the girl—"Shimon's death has tarnished her sweet smile a bit."

Moriyah was quite tall and already a beauty but could not have been older than thirteen. Somehow, though, there was something penetrating about her attention, something in those light eyes that reminded me of one of the seers who wandered through my village, begging for a meal or a coin in exchange for a glimpse into the future. A shiver skittered across my shoulders as I turned my head. "Is she Egyptian?"

Nita stopped at the edge of a large pool. "Her father's parents were among the few Egyptians who chose to leave Egypt with us. Her mother is Hebrew, of the tribe of Yehudah. Both she and Shimon favor their father, however."

Before I could ask more, I caught sight of the origin of the pool lapping at our toes. From a cleft in the cliff above us came a gushing flow. My jaw went slack. How could such a forceful waterfall bound down the face of the orange rocks when it was far past the season for such a thing to exist? There was no mountain snowcap to feed such a torrent. Was this water from some enormous underground spring that the Hebrews had stumbled upon?

"As unlikely as it is, wherever we travel, there is always a rock gushing water, just like this one, and it's always more than enough for all of us. I don't know how Mosheh always knows . . ." She lifted her eyes to the flow that cascaded white down the slopes, gathering in this enormous frothy pool. "As wondrous as this is, you should have seen the first rock. The one Mosheh struck near the mountain where we spent our first year. The water sprayed so high, it was like a storm cloud shooting skyward. And within days, flowers and grasses sprouted along the path of the stream. Between the rock and the stream that flowed from the mountain itself, the lake that formed southeast of camp afforded us ample water. And my, was it ever sweet . . ."

Her voice trailed off as she dipped her feet into memories and wandered farther downstream, her convoluted explanation doing nothing to satiate my confusion.

Crouching, I filled my jug in the unlikely flow and then bent to wash my face, savoring the coolness on my skin. The midday sun refracted off the red rock walls, intensifying the heat. I dipped my palm in the clear pool, then dribbled water down the back of my neck with an inward sigh of relief.

"It is unbearably hot today, isn't it?"

Shimon's sister squatted next to me, mirroring my efforts to cool myself by patting my face with wet hands. I nodded an agreement but did not reply. I hadn't expected this young girl to approach me, and I found myself with nothing to say. Could it be Tzipi's absence today that lent Moriyah such courage? She seemed in no way fearful of me; her silver-eyed gaze revealed only curiosity. Neither did she seem bothered by my silence—she sat down next to me, cross-legged, and dove into a one-way conversation.

"I liked the camp we stayed at when I was six. There were palm trees everywhere, and tall green grasses that swayed in the wind." She sighed. "My brother used to take me with him when he hunted for quail there." She paused, waiting for me to answer. But what could I say with my tongue tied in knots?

"I am Moriyah," she said, apparently losing patience with my lack of response. She lifted her black brows, waiting.

I flattened my lips. "Alanah."

"I know." Her eyes rounded with surprising enthusiasm. "Nita told me all about how Tobiah found you and saved you and married you." A faraway look gathered in her enormous eyes. "I think it's lovely."

"Lovely? You think it lovely that I was nearly killed and then dragged here against my will?"

She put a hand over her mouth, but her eyes danced. "No.

140

Not you almost dying. That was bad." She furrowed her brow. "I meant how Tobiah is in love with you."

I nearly tumbled backward. "What . . . ? What makes you say such a thing?"

"Oh." She flipped her hand. "I overheard Noach and Simcha talking a few days ago. They said that Tobiah threatened to practically murder a man when he talked about . . . you know . . ." She bit her lower lip and leaned in, brows lifted. "Harming you."

My mouth was a desert. Tobiah had done such a thing? In my defense?

"It takes quite a bit to get Tobiah to explode like that. My brother always tried, but always failed." She pressed her lips together, a shadow crossing her features, and then she nodded with confidence. "He's in love with you for certain. The only reason he left you in the care of Noach and Simcha today was because he was commanded to go to a meeting with the elders."

With a small downturn of her full lips, Moriyah looked toward the waterfall, her long fingers clutching a small wooden whistle that hung from a cord around her neck. "I know how much my own heart hurts right now, I miss my brother so much. And Tobiah considered him a brother as well. But if anything can ease his grief, perhaps it is this marriage."

I gestured to the turban around my head. "Have you forgotten that I am Canaanite? An enemy?"

She frowned. "Forty years ago, as plagues swept through Egypt, my grandparents had a choice to make. They could either stay enemies of the One True God or follow him. Perhaps you have the same choice before you as well."

I was vaguely aware of Moriyah walking alongside me as our small group moved back through camp with full jugs and skins of water. She chattered the entire way, pointing out the different camps, explaining how each son of their ancestor Yaakov was situated around the *Mishkan* and how that related to their position within Israel, but I absorbed little. My mind was instead sorting through her earlier words, attempting to organize my thoughts into a manageable reality. Tobiah could not love me. He was my enemy. He was my captor. He was—

Angry voices suddenly overlapped one another. A large group of men had gathered in the wide open space near the *Mishkan*, shouting at each other and at a few priests who were standing in front of the red, blue, and purple fabric gates.

Noach appeared at my side, his hand gripping my elbow. "We must go back and around. I should not have led us this way."

"Why? What is happening?" I felt Moriyah press closer to me as the shouting grew louder.

Frustration flickered across Noach's face. "There are a few who are angry about the eastern route that Mosheh and Yehoshua have determined to use to skirt the lands of the Edomites."

"And why is that?"

The division between his heart and his mind was plain on his face. "We have been in this wilderness nearly forty years. We are ready to take the land we were promised. The crops are ready to harvest now. If we wait any longer . . ."

"But you have manna to eat."

He made a low noise in the back of his throat. "Many among us are sick of manna. We are ready to partake of the milk and honey we were promised. We are ready to enjoy the fruits of the Land—now."

"The fruits of *my* land, you mean—"

Someone slammed into me, cutting off my angry retort and knocking me sideways into Moriyah. The man's eyes were as wild as his dark hair, his face pale as death, and a spray of crimson smeared across his cheek. Blood? Without apology he pushed past us, scrambling toward the ornate embroidered gates of the *Mishkan*.

I watched in fascination as the man slipped through the large crowd, pushed past the white-linen-clad priests who stood at the gates, and disappeared behind the curtain.

Why would someone who was obviously being pursued run toward the *Mishkan*, where a giant, angry cloud stood guard? That would be the last place I would ever run.

20

A ll this is doing is making me hurt worse." I dropped the infuriating rock at my feet with a groan.

"It may seem that way, but you must work that shoulder more, or you will never pull a bowstring again." Tobiah bent, retrieved my nemesis, and placed it in my left hand. "Now, lift it again."

I rolled my eyes at him but complied, holding the stone straight out in front of me as he had ordered. My shoulder screamed but I held steady, stomach taut, determined to keep the agony off my face and master the endless exercise.

"Good." He took the stone from me just as my muscles began shaking from the strain. "Rest a few moments." He handed me a water-skin.

I tipped my head back to quench my thirst and then swiped at my wet mouth and chin. "Why do you bother with this?" I squinted at him. "Why do you care whether I can use a bow again?"

He tossed the stone from palm to palm. The cursed thing looked small in his big hands. "Isn't that what you want?"

I nodded.

"Then I can help. I've seen others with wounds similar to yours who did not work at training their muscles so soon and it took longer to heal. Sometimes they never regained their former strength."

"Aren't you concerned I will use my bow against you?" I glanced at his sister's tent nearby. "Or someone else?"

He tipped his head to one side. "Will you?"

"Not unless someone tries to harm me."

"Then we both have the same goal. Your defense." He handed me the rock again and gestured for me to lift it, higher this time than the last. My shoulder protested the abuse, but I refused to let a sound pass my lips.

When I could not take the burning ache any longer, I dropped my arm.

The reminder of Moriyah's claim, that Tobiah had defended me to another Hebrew, curled around my heart again, squeezing it in new ways. To distract from the errant thought, I asked the question that had been bothering me since Simcha and Noach had hurried us all back to camp with troubled faces, but no explanation. "Did your cousins tell you about the man who barreled into me at the *Mishkan*?"

Tobiah's cheek twitched as he took the stone from me again. "Yes. Did he hurt you?"

I rolled my shoulder back to diffuse the pain. "He startled me more than anything. I nearly toppled over on Moriyah. But why would someone run like that past the gates? I thought it was forbidden for anyone but your priests to enter."

Tobiah moved to stand behind me and began kneading my shoulder, causing my skin to prickle. "He is a murderer."

My mouth dropped open as I remembered the splatter of blood across the man's face.

"Unfortunately, you were in the way of his flight to the altar."

"An altar inside the courtyard?"

"It is our law. A man accused of stealing the life of another may grab on to the horns of the altar. Plead mercy from those who demand retribution."

"And was he given mercy?"

"No. He was forcibly removed from the altar and taken outside the camp to be stoned."

I spun around to face him. "Why?"

"He was a murderer. There were plenty of witnesses to testify that he killed a man over a woman."

"A woman?"

"The victim had made advances on the man's wife. The man murdered him over it. He attempted to make it seem that it was unplanned—only a fight gone bad. But witnesses testified that the man ambushed the other in a wadi."

"So he was stoned to death? Just like that?"

"Our laws are very clear, Alanah. A murderer cannot be allowed to live among us or they would stain the entire camp with guilt."

"No second chance? Perhaps the man deserved to be killed."

He shook his head. "Our God values life too much."

"Yet the life of the murderer is forfeit?"

"Yahweh will not allow his people to treat life with such disdain. This nation is unique. If we allow men to murder each other, we will be no different than the depraved nations around us—" He stopped with a chastened expression. "I mean no offense to you personally. But the spies we sent into Canaan years ago told of vicious tribes, where murder is not only sanctioned, but celebrated. Where babies are offered to vile gods, where women—children really—are sold to be used until their bodies are broken and they are left for dead." His face was stone, as if he could see these horrors in his mind.

I had seen them with my own eyes.

"I can only assume"—he lifted his brows—"that in the past forty years, it has only gotten worse."

Of that there is no doubt. My brothers' reputations had not been for nothing. The scars on their arms, the marks of pride for the men they had killed, were all too clear in my mind. And the war tattoos, dark marks that covered their chests and backs, testified to the many tribal clashes they'd engaged in—marks that had expanded yearly, as did the boastful stories of the brutality they employed in their warfare.

"Can you not see the difference here, Alanah? Among us, murderers are immediately cut off. Our children are cherished. Our women protected. The laws Mosheh has given us are for our protection. To keep us from the taint of the vile nations around us. To ensure that we are a holy, separate nation. A reflection of the holy God we serve."

"Are you all so perfect?"

"No." He dropped his shoulders. "We are not. I am not. But that is why we were gifted with the priests and the *Mishkan,* where our sins can be atoned for with the blood of sacrifice."

"But why would a God who values life so much be so bent on the destruction of Canaan?"

"I cannot explain the mind of Elohim, the Creator. But I will say this: The people of this land have known we were coming for forty years. Most have left, haven't they?"

They had. Between war with Egypt a generation ago, constant fighting between city-states, plagues that had decimated villages, and fear of the Israelites, many of the people of Canaan had vanished. My brothers spoke of empty villages, some with plows still in the fields and crops ready for harvest, the people having simply taken up their belongings to flee north toward Tyre and Sidon, return to eastern ancestral lands, or migrate to Egypt to fill the empty place Israel had left behind.

"There are still thriving cities," I said. Since word had gone out that the Hebrews were encroaching on our territory, the city of Arad had overflowed with people desperate for the protection the king offered behind high walls.

"And they have been warned."

The words of a wandering prophet filtered through my memories. The old man had stood near the well in our small village, his eyes full of fire and his tattered clothing flapping in the wind.

"A nation of slaves will overcome you . . . Your sin, your hatred for life . . . This land will vomit you out . . . Those who refuse to go will be decimated."

At the time I, like most others, had laughed at the man. Cursed him for his traitorous words and brushed them off as the incoherent babble of a senile old man.

Then someone had beaten the prophet to death two days later. I had walked on the other side of the street and trained my eyes on my feet to avoid the sight of his broken body and bloodied head in the dirt. His body lay in the street like refuse until someone had dragged the carcass away to be burned. It was not the first body I'd seen discarded like waste, and certainly not the last. His words—*hatred for life*—had proven themselves with the loss of his own.

"Yahweh warned the people, through his prophet Noach, a hundred years before the Great Flood. Yahweh warned the people of Sodom and Gomorrah, before fire rained down on their heads. Yahweh warned Egypt through nine plagues before inflicting final judgment by killing every Egyptian firstborn. Yahweh has warned the people of Canaan. And like you, they will be given the opportunity to join this nation, destroy their idols, and worship Yahweh, or to flee."

Although I was not a witness to Egypt's fall, I'd heard the horrific tales of Sodom's fiery obliteration and had seen its remnants on the barren shore of the Salt Sea. Had that been a warning to the people of my land? "And if they refuse?" I asked.

Tobiah said nothing, but a haunted look crossed his face. "Yahweh does not force anyone to believe and obey. He offers the freedom of such a choice. But . . ." His words dropped low. "The alternative will be destruction."

"You would destroy the people who remain?"

"Those who refuse to go, and who take up arms against us, just as the king of Arad did, will soon find that their destruction will be absolute. They all have the same choice to make as you do. Stay? Run? Or fight?"

TOBIAH

She's hiding in the tent again. I glanced at the door flap, willing Alanah to appear with that glint of audacity in her eyes that I'd come to crave.

She'd been quiet since we'd returned to the campsite this afternoon. Giving me the excuse that she was tired after the exercises I'd forced her to do with her arm, she'd ducked inside, face drawn, to hide out with her cats. Although my instinct had been to entice her out to sit with me at the evening meal, she needed some time alone with her thoughts.

I stared into my bowl with a sour stomach. *One more day.* Although the thought of her going away left me wretched, I would not force her to stay. But the idea of my wife—for that's what she had become in my mind—turning her back, walking away from me, was almost unimaginable.

It would be foolish, reckless, to leave the protection of this camp. Although I had every confidence in her ability to survive in the wilderness, I did not trust the Canaanites. Perhaps, even if she did not choose to stay married to me, I would convince her to stay here and live with Nita, where I could at least watch over her from afar.

I plunked my full bowl onto the ground, where the stew sloshed over into the sand. Afar? Ridiculous. How would I ever stay away from her?

"Sick of it too, eh, Tobiah?" Simcha wiped stew from his chin with one palm.

"What are you talking about?"

"The manna," he said. "Even in stew I can taste it. Not sure how much more I can stand."

I shrugged. "Doesn't bother me."

"Bothers me. If we don't move north, we will miss the early harvest. I've had enough of manna and gristly desert animals. Did you try some of those dates the traders brought in from Moab last week? They weren't even that fresh, but I've never tasted anything so delicious. Can you imagine what they will be like right off the trees?" He held up a fist. "Some were nearly this big!"

"Hold your tongue, Simcha," said Noach from across the fire. "You'll get your dates soon enough."

Simcha glared at his brother. "No, we have waited long enough! We are more than ready to move in. What is Yehoshua afraid of?"

"Yehoshua is afraid of nothing. He obeys the orders given by his own commander, Mosheh," I said. "Just as we obey him."

"Mosheh was old when our *parents* left Egypt." Simcha scoffed. "He led a group of ragged, browbeaten slaves into the desert. This is war."

"Have you forgotten that Mosheh was a general?"

Simcha waved a hand. "Different time. Different circumstances."

Tzipi emerged from her tent, and behind her was Keziah.

Suddenly I was more than grateful Alanah was hiding, nursing her sore muscles.

"What are you three growling about out here? We were trying to have a conversation." Tzipi's glance flicked to me for a brief moment. What was she doing?

"Oh, Simcha is bellowing about not being able to run in and crack Canaanite heads together this very moment." Noach guffawed.

The two women sat down next to me. Keziah gave me a smile, a shy one, but one that made me hopeful she had forgiven me for letting her down.

"Why must we trek all the way around Edom? It will add months to this journey," said Simcha. "Those savages are on the run now. Terrified after that victory at Arad. If we wait too long, their fear will have melted away."

Liyam squealed from nearby, a victim of Mahan and Yonel's too-rough wrestling. My sister sprang up to stop the fight. As Noach and Simcha kept up their argument over whether or not we should forge ahead, Keziah scooted closer to me.

Every nerve in my body went tense. Had Tzipi purposefully left us alone? I restrained myself from edging away, pretending that Keziah's presence to my right did not bother me. I had known her most of my life, had spent the last few months preparing myself to ask for her hand, as my mother had expected me to do.

"Those boys." Keziah laughed softly, placing a gentle hand on my forearm. "They remind me so much of you and Shimon as boys. Always wrestling and challenging each other. They are growing up so fast. Liyam is five now, is he not?"

Lifting my arm and pretending to scratch my head in thought, I dislodged her hand. "I believe so. My sister will have her hands full with that one. He never shrinks back from a fight."

"He is so like Shimon."

"That he is." Everything about Liyam was a miniature of Shimon, from his black hair to the humor in his light gray eyes, to the way he pestered his brothers until they wrestled him to the ground. The boy had Shimon's persistence for sure. Shimon had always taken it as a personal challenge to provoke me until my blood raced and my hands shook. Shimon was the only person to ever get under my skin, other than the fiery woman in the tent behind me.

Having broken up the squalling threesome, Tzipi turned around with a look of frustration on her face that somehow transformed into a smirk when she saw Keziah sitting next to me on the ground. With a little lift of her brows, she sat down near Noach instead. I nearly rolled my eyes at my meddling twin and her last effort to push Keziah at me before the thirty days were complete.

"I agree with Simcha," Tzipi said. "I am sick of this wilderness. I am ready to have a home with four brick walls that don't move. I am dreading having to pack up this tent yet again."

Simcha nodded. "And just think, if we go in now, all those crops are just sitting there waiting for us. All we have to do is harvest them."

"Are you a farmer now, Simcha?" Noach laughed again. "I'd like to see you behind a plow."

"Can't be so hard. You plant things, they grow, you pick them."

"You have no idea what you are talking about!" Alanah's voice made me whip my head around. She'd emerged from the tent, fire in her eyes and both fists at her hips. She strode into our circle to address Simcha. "You walk outside every morning and have the most delicious food in the world readily available and you moan about wanting to farm? My father spent every single day of his life working his farm, dragging huge rocks up the hills to build the terraces, hours and hours in the hot sun behind a plow, and sleepless nights when the storms would rage through and knock every stalk of wheat to the ground. You Hebrews are spoiled." She jerked her chin northward. "You sit out here acting as though the fiercest tribes aren't waiting for you, armed to the teeth and ready to grind you all to dust. You may think you are warriors, and perhaps you've had a victory or two, but I have seen men the size of trees in my village. Bloodthirsty men—men without conscience. You have no idea what you are up against."

"Perhaps not." Tzipi smiled as if she had not heard a word Alanah had just said. "But bloodthirsty or not, Yahweh's soldiers will drive them into the ground. And we will make our homes in Canaan and raise our families there in the knowledge of the One True God. Isn't that right, Keziah?"

Alanah's head snapped toward me, her narrowed eyes taking in the sight of Keziah, who was leaning around me to stare back at my wife with a surprised expression. Alanah's mouth twitched as if she had more to say, but instead she whirled around and stalked back into Nita's tent, back straight and head high, one of her sand cats trotting at her heels.

"Enough," I said.

Tzipi's narrowed eyes remained pinned on the place where Alanah had delivered her speech with such passion. No one else in the campsite said a word. Even the young boys went still, their eyes wide.

I stood and moved to stand in front of her, forcing her to look at me and lowering my voice so only she could hear. "I said, enough."

The granite set of my sister's jaw did not waver.

"I have given you grace because of Shimon. Because I understand and share your pain and anger. I have not intervened, hoping that the sister I love would come to accept the commitment I have made to Alanah. She is my wife. If you cannot embrace her, you will at least respect me by treating her with the hospitality you would give a stranger. Your incivility dishonors me. It dishonors you."

I strode away without a glance behind me, my blood racing, both with indignation at my sister and at the thought that, after tomorrow, Alanah—that intelligent, fascinating, and vivid woman—would be mine.

21

ALANAH

15 IYAR
1407 BC

I jerked awake, the dregs of a bad dream still swirling in my veins. How long had it been since I had slept the whole night? Bodo nuzzled my leg, curling into my warmth. The darkness of the tent told me I had awoken before the sun on this last day of my unconventional betrothal. The jealousy that had exploded in my chest last night had left splinters behind. Although I had only seen the woman for a few moments before I had intruded on the argument between the cousins, I had watched her smile at Tobiah, her wide-set brown eyes full of innocent invitation, her dainty hand brushing his arm as she laughed at something he said. Everything about her screamed feminine grace. When Tzipi had announced that it was Keziah practically sitting in my husband's lap—

It had been a good thing my quiver was empty or that lovely girl might have a hole in her perfect head this morning.

Turning onto my side, a flutter of nerves gathered in my stomach as I caught a glimpse of Tobiah sleeping across the doorway, his chest rising and falling in steady rhythm. Only one more day until I would be sleeping next to him. Unless I refused, or he changed his mind and chose her.

Tobiah's challenge—*Stay? Run? Or fight?*—still echoed in my head. I had weighed all three, time and again, a circle of never-ending doubts trailing each one. If I submitted to this marriage, I was turning my back on everything I knew. If I escaped, I would be leaving Tobiah to marry Keziah. If I did what I came to do and slaughtered Hebrews, my life would be forfeit—an option that had become less desirable every day.

Everything I knew of the Hebrews a few weeks ago had been turned inside out. Instead of a mob of faceless slaves, I found admirable warriors and loving families. Instead of a horde of rabid battle-mongers, I found an organized multitude that would go months out of their way to avoid fighting their cousins in Edom. Instead of the vicious tribal warfare that defined my people, I found a nation united beneath one God and united in purpose like nothing I'd ever experienced. A nation willing to accept outsiders as one of them, beneath the protective banner of their Torah laws.

Yes, I had lost my hair. But it was already growing back. Yes, I had given up my gods, but I had little use for them anyhow. Yes, I had submitted to a new way of life, but the differences I saw among these people were fascinating, almost alluring. Babies were not slaughtered on the altar at the *Mishkan* or burned at the feet of their God. There were no temple prostitutes selling their wares in the courtyard.

And when I considered the battle that had stolen my family, I was forced to admit that it was the king of Arad who had attacked first, vowing to crush the wanderers before they set foot on his lands—the same ruthless king who had a reputation for leaving a long, bloody trail of rivals all the way to his throne, and expanding his territory in the same savage manner.

If the Torah of the Hebrews ruled the land of Canaan, would such a thing be celebrated? I suspected not. I'd walked onto that battlefield desperate to die, tossing my life away like refuse and willing to do so in order to avenge the men of my family—men who had thought nothing of murdering and raping.

How had everything I'd ever known been so wrong? So repugnant?

Would I want my own daughter someday to be raised among such atrocities? To be in danger of being tossed on the burning heap at the feet of stone gods? A shiver ran the length of me as I blinked away the awful vision.

I'd never even considered the thought of children. Never given myself the luxury of doing so. But on the threshold of marriage to Tobiah, I found the idea strangely enticing. The image of a small girl, with red curls like mine, and a tiny boy riding atop his father's broad shoulders filled my mind. A smile meandered across my lips. A mother? Me?

I reached down to pet Capo, who always slept near my hip. He'd seemed listless last night and hadn't wanted any milk. I skimmed my hand across his soft fur but he did not press into me like he usually did, even in his sleep. I patted his head, my heart beating faster. Still, he did not move. With trembling fingers, I placed my hand on his body, holding my breath to gauge the rise and fall of the little animal's chest. There was none. He was still and cold.

Bile burned my throat. I'd been so distracted last night after seeing Tobiah and Keziah together, dragging myself to my bed and covering my head with my blankets, that I hadn't thought too much about Capo. He had died and I hadn't even noticed. I was no better than the serpent that had sought his life. What was I thinking? I could not be a mother. My own had abandoned me. What had given me the foolish idea that I would be any better?

Before I could change my mind, I slipped off my mat, placed Capo's little body in a manna-gathering basket, and slid my bow and quiver over my shoulder. Since Tobiah was lying across the entrance, I carefully tugged at the back wall to dislodge the stones that held it down and crawled beneath it. I anchored the wall again before leaving, hoping it would discourage Bodo from following me. Nita would care for him, I was sure. Much better than I could ever hope to.

Dawn skimmed the farthest horizon. If I was to slip out of camp before anyone sought me, I must hurry. Clutching my basket close to my chest, I darted through the maze of tents, heading for the white glow on the edge of camp, the reflection of the manna against the first gleam of the morning. Disregarding the clawing cold that whipped at my face, I plunged into the field, pushing through the grains that swallowed my feet like new-fallen snow. I nearly stopped to gather some, with the awareness that once I was away from the Hebrews I would not taste it again, but I did not deserve such a last pleasure.

I should be rejoicing at the ease with which I had escaped my captors, the sheer width of the freedom that I would now enjoy. So why did my feet ache to turn around? Why did my heart feel like a heavy stone in my chest? Why did the cold wind seem almost warm compared to the screaming void that grew inside me with every step away?

I should have died on that battlefield, yet Tobiah had saved me, cared for me, and protected me, even against my will. But the truth was that Tobiah could hurt me more than anyone, more than I had known was possible.

It was best, my escape. I would never see him turn his back on me. I would never endure the loss of his kindness. He would not be forced to choose between his sister and me. He could marry Keziah and be happy. Be free from the anchor of marriage to a Canaanite.

Doubts, fears, desires, and impossible hopes tugged at different parts of me. Could a person be torn to pieces by such divided emotions? My feet slowed. I lifted my chin to greet the rise of the sun, closing my eyes against its radiance. My chest ached, my breath trapped within a prison of my own making. How could I go when everything inside me cried out to return?

I looked down at my little sand cat and the still curl of his body inside my basket. Poor little one. Broken as I was, I had loved him. Perhaps some kernel of feminine kindness had survived the charred fields of my childhood. The sunrise warmed my face as it rose.

I could not leave.

I would not leave.

I did not want to leave Tobiah. My husband.

A smile curved my lips as I turned around. My footprints through the white manna led back to camp. And there, standing at the head of the path, was Tobiah, hands at his sides, shoulders low, devastation on his face. The desire to smooth the hurt from his brow was overpowering.

I took a step toward him, but something slammed against the back of my leg. Two sharp pains melded into one agonizing burn with tremendous force. Disoriented, I looked behind me just as the double-horned head of a snake sprang toward me again, burying its fangs in my heel.

The basket fell from my hand into the soft, white manna, and a black curtain fell across my sight.

⁓

Fire screamed through my veins as my haze lifted; the pain of the arrow that had pierced my shoulder was a whisper compared with the angry venom tearing through my flesh.

Shira hovered over me, her lively features weighted with concern. "She is waking, Tobiah," she said.

My clouded vision could not register his face, but I sensed his large presence nearby, a silent accusation that, had I not been running from him, I would not be dying now.

Shira wiped my brow with a wet cloth, humming under her breath as she always did when tending me. A habit to calm herself as much as her patient, perhaps. If my heart and mind were not racing so violently, her voice might be soothing, but the blood pulsing in my ears blocked out most of the song, leaving me with a disjointed melody that frightened me even more.

My leg throbbed with sudden violence and, unable to control my reaction, I screamed. Shira lifted my tunic above my knees, her cool fingers examining my burning skin. Her furrowed brows told me the venom had spread farther and that my time was short.

I had seen a snakebite victim back in my village. An old woman who stumbled across a viper similar to the one that had found me this morning. The woman's arm had swollen to three times its size, blistered, and then turned an ugly black before her body had given out hours later. Would I last as long as she had? Or would my heart lay down its fight and give me release from this agony?

On the battlefield a few weeks ago, I had been ready to die, or at least I had thought so. As much as I wanted release from the anguish I was enduring, I no longer welcomed death. Something deep within me begged to see tomorrow. I clung to the slog of my heartbeat hammering an erratic, though rising, pulse in my chest.

My vision blurred, a haze of light and colors flickering around the edges. But the large shadow next to me remained constant. Tobiah. The husband I would never truly know would soon be released from the foolish vow he had taken to protect his enemy. Anguish welled up inside my heart and spilled over, salted with grief, with fear, with regret. Shira's small, cool hand touched my face again, stroked my cheek. I bit my lip to stifle another scream as waves of pain shattered me and consciousness ebbed, inviting me to float on a tide of blackness. Maybe my heart would steady and slow down if I allowed the dark to carry me away.

Snatches of whispered conversation floated around me, as if the words came from lips near the ceiling instead of next to my pallet. Shira was here, and Tobiah, but there were other voices that I could not match with faces. Nita perhaps, a man, and another woman. Words slipped through the haze but toppled over one another like rocks piled high, jumbling and making little sense to my dizzy, overheated mind.

"How many . . . ?"

"Too many to count."

". . . snakes everywhere."

". . . because of the rebellion . . . complaining about the food."

"Mosheh . . ."

" . . . Copper? . . . How long will it take?"

"Not much longer, I hope."

Someone squeezed my hand. I opened my eyes, blinking against the too-bright lamp that hovered over me, swinging gently from the cross-pole.

Shira again brushed the back of her hand across my forehead. "Her fever is so high. Tobiah, please go find more water. But be careful, dear. There are still snakes out there, and dusk has fallen, they will be hard to see. Take a torch. And a spear."

My heart raced faster, so fast that I could concentrate on nothing else. My body responded, demanding that I must move, must flee from the discomfort. My hands tapped against the pallet to release the pent-up energy. The compulsion to stand, to run, was so great that Shira had to hold me down as I thrashed against her.

I tasted salt in my mouth and Shira's eyes went wide.

"Oh no." She placed a firm hand on my shoulder to pin me down and reached over to grab a linen cloth, which she swiped against my lips. It came away scarlet. My mouth was bleeding, the metallic taste nauseating. "Yahweh, save this young woman!" she said. "Preserve her life, for your glory."

Foolish prayer. Her God cared nothing for me. There was no purpose in my life and less in my death, only more capricious dealings from gods who consumed everything. Just as I was being consumed by the venom. My vision blurred and everything swayed above me, tilting sideways. I tried to shake my head against the strange sensation.

Someone tall blocked the light. "Come, it is ready."

Tobiah? No, he is with Keziah. Leave me. Leave me here to die. Mercy.

Hands slipped beneath me, and my body rose into the air as if by magic, but my leg flopped down and I cried out and jerked hard against the rough treatment. Through the haze of torment, I caught sight of my grossly distended, bloody limb. The ominous dark blistering, along with the chariot race my heart was winning, told the truth. Not much longer.

"I'm sorry. We must hurry," said the low voice I craved but should not. "Mosheh has made a snake from copper. Lifted it up on his banner staff. You must look at it to be saved."

22

Something brushed my wounded leg and pain spiked through me, dragging me back to unwilling consciousness. A sheen of red obscured my vision. My eyes must be bleeding along with my gums. A woman next to me screamed at Yahweh to heal her son, and a shofar echoed her desperate plea.

Cries of pain and fear howled around me as if I were in the center of a deranged crowd. Although the screams were human, the familiar faces of the gods hovered in iridescent transparency in front of me. Ba'al threw thunderbolts at my leg, his leer growing wider with every lash. Anat nocked a fiery arrow, the point of it aimed at my chest. She released the flaming missile, which struck me dead center as a mocking laugh split her face in two and she blurred into nothing.

The pounding of my heart would crack my ribs, and my insides would spill onto the ground. I struggled against the restraints around me.

"Alanah! Stop fighting me!" The urgent rumble of Tobiah's low voice yanked me back from the edge of madness. "Open your eyes!"

I tried to comply, but my body refused. My eyes were tight,

my jaw locked, every muscle stone. *You cannot hold me, Prince Death. Let me go! I cannot breathe! No! Yahweh!*

The moment my mind screamed the Name, I felt a release on whatever bound me and a million stars seemed to float across my vision, as if the entire universe were on display behind my eyelids. Ba'al and Anat were minuscule in comparison—nothing compared with such vast, inexplicable beauty.

After what seemed like hours, Tobiah's voice reached through the image, calling me back to earth. "Alanah! You must look at the snake!"

With ambivalence, my eyes fluttered open and I instantly missed the awe-inspiring vision I had witnessed. Blinking a few times to clear the bloody haze that still tainted my sight, I lifted my chin, searching out where Tobiah pointed. Upon a small rise stood a tall banner pole. Torches around its base illuminated a gleaming snake twisted around it, jeweled eyes glittering in reflection of the Cloud of Fire nearby.

A wave of sound rolled back through the crowd, growing as it surged toward us. Pulse pounding in my ears, I could not make out any words, only shouts and exclamations. Tobiah gripped me tighter, his breathing accelerated.

An odd compulsion tugged at me and I fixed my eyes on the snake still reflecting the eerie light from the billowing cloud. The movement made the coppery creation almost come to life, as if it writhed around the pole with evil intent. How could looking at the reason for my affliction possibly save me? Wasn't this a forbidden idol? Or was it a reminder of the sin that had caused such judgment, the rebellion about the manna? How could the source of death renew my life? My head throbbed from the attempt to understand.

Perhaps he will make himself known to you. Kiya's words surged into my mind and I clung to them. It didn't matter how Yahweh would save me, only that he was real and willing.

Yahweh, if you are who your people say you are, heal me. Please. Hear me. Save me. I pledge my life, my bow, to you.

My eyes fluttered shut, too heavy to remain open. Somehow the cries and screams of the people around me began to abate. Were they dying too? I let my head drop against Tobiah's chest. A good place to die, in his strong arms. My heart throbbed and pounded even harder until every sound around me was drowned out by the frantic crashing in my ears and temples.

Then it stopped. Stillness crept down my arms, through my body, and down my legs, until everything inside me was quiet. No breath. No heartbeat. Only bone-deep silence.

Sudden coolness spread over me, as if someone breathed across my face. A peculiar sensation began to fill my body, nothing like the agonizing burn of the venom, but something like the feeling of Shira's kind hands as she braided my hair. The sensation, gentle at first but growing in intensity, washed over me, until the feeling became a Voice speaking words of healing over me. Words of comfort. Words of peace.

But who am I? my still heart cried out. *I am an enemy to these people, to your people.*

No longer, said the Voice. *I have brought you here for a purpose. I will go before you and behind. I will surround you, no matter where you go.*

With a jolt, my heart thudded to life in my chest, its frenetic pace replaced by calm, steady beats. A sweet fragrance filled my nostrils, inspiring me to take a deep breath.

"Alanah? Alanah, can you hear me?"

My mind attempted to hold on to the sound of the Voice, but Tobiah's beckoning words had replaced it. His hand caressed my cheek, and I grudgingly opened my eyes. His face hovered above mine. Just like on the first day I met him. The first time I was rescued from death. "Oh, thank Yahweh, you are alive," he said. "You were so still. I thought . . ."

I was on my back in an unfamiliar tent. A lone oil lamp swayed from a cross-pole, casting shadows on the face of my husband, who sat on the ground next to the wide, soft pallet I lay upon. Casting a glance around the small space, I recognized the stool Shira had sat upon to cut my hair. Was this Tobiah's tent? How had I ended up here?

Had I only dreamed the Voice? And was it my hopeful imagination, or had the pain in my leg disappeared? I attempted to move the limb, bracing for another wave of agony, but none came. Stretching my heel, I spread my toes, but still—nothing. I ran my tongue across my gums; the taste of blood had vanished as well.

"Are you able to move?"

I nodded, astounded that there was no pain anywhere in my body, not even in my shoulder. Instead, my limbs felt light, as if they were feathers ready to be lifted on the breeze. Tobiah slid a hand beneath my back and lifted me to a sitting position. Once again the reminder of his first ministrations came to mind. A rush of gratefulness washed over me—for then, and for now.

"Are you thirsty?" He looked ragged, his long hair loose and wild, fatigue in his eyes. "You've been asleep for hours. The sun will be up soon."

Asleep? No, hadn't I just been drinking at the freshest stream and feasting at a king's table? Or had I dreamed such a thing? There was no hunger. No thirst. Only complete satisfaction. Instead of feeling faint, I wanted to spring to my feet, to run, jump, and twirl like when I was a little girl.

Yahweh had healed me.

Clarity dawned, filling my mind with truth. The household gods I had grown up around, their vacant eyes staring mindlessly at me day after day from their perches, had never spoken to me, never healed me. They were not alive, but simply formed by human hands. But the Cloud that hovered above the camp was not made by any man. The God that took the Hebrews out of Egypt was no figment of Mosheh's imagination. He had spoken to me—to me!

An emotion I had never experienced expanded in my chest, growing in intensity until I felt I might split in half from the force of it. Laughter bubbled out of me like a flooded wadi after a spring rain.

Tobiah sat back on his heels, head tilted, brown eyes wide. He ran his large hands through his sun-kissed mane and down the sides of his face and beard. "What is happening?"

"I am healed." My voice was surprisingly strong after the ordeal I had just endured. "Look." I lifted the linen sheet from my body, knowing exactly what I would see. "It's gone."

My leg was normal. No swelling. No bruises. No angry streaks of poison. Only two small marks on my heel and two on the back of my calf. Fully healed scars, left as a reminder. Forever.

I turned toward him, folding my legs beneath me. My gaze took in the perplexed face of the man who had sacrificed so much for an angry, bitter enemy bent on destroying him. The face of the man who held my heart. He scooted away a few inches, seemingly uncomfortable with my change of posture toward him.

"I heard him, Tobiah."

"Who?"

"Yahweh. He spoke to me."

Disbelief flickered across his brow.

"It's true." I looked down at my hands folded in my lap. "And I understand if you don't believe me. But I must say . . . I must thank you for saving me. If I had gone to my death not knowing what I know now . . ." I sighed. "I don't know why either of you saved me . . . I am not worth it. But I am grateful, even if you send me away after what I did. How I tried to leave—"

"Why?" he interrupted. "Why did you leave? I thought we were beginning to . . ." A grimace halted his words.

"Capo died."

"I know, I saw your basket." His frown was compassionate. "I am sorry. I buried him."

I prayed for an infusion of courage as I inhaled deeply. "My mother left me when I was three years old. Just . . ." I shrugged. "Gone. In the middle of the night. She simply vanished without a word. My father told me that she ran north, back to the temple where he'd found her. Told me a *zonah* never changes. That she couldn't wait to get away and perform her duties again." Nausea swelled in my throat. "It wasn't until I was much older that I understood what that actually meant. What she had chosen over me." I shivered off the memories. "Capo's death reminded me. I don't know how to be a wife or . . . someday, a mother. I am only a *zonah's* daughter."

Leaning closer, Tobiah took my hands in his. "No. No, *Ishti.* You are nothing of the sort." He lifted the same palm that he had marked with his own blood a month ago and kissed it with aching tenderness. "You are my wife."

⁓

TOBIAH

I pulled Alanah into my lap and held her close, whispering apologies that weren't mine to give but welled up inside me anyhow. Apologies for abandonment by her mother, apologies for the loss of her family, apologies for the death and destruction she had witnessed on that battlefield. I rocked her back and forth, wishing I could erase any pain ever inflicted on her and reassure her that nothing would ever hurt her again.

"Why?" she mumbled against my chest. "Why do you care? I am your enemy. I am broken. Possibly beyond repair."

"No." I pulled back to look into her shimmering blue-green eyes. I put my hand on her cheek and, miraculously, she leaned into it. "I took our marriage vows seriously, even though I did not know you. Yahweh led me to you on that battlefield. He had a plan. From the moment I held you in my arms you were no longer an enemy. Alanah, you are my wife. And when that snake bit you . . ." The agonizing fear I'd felt when I saw her body jerk forward and then fall into the white field of manna crashed into me again, and with a groan, I gave in to the compulsion to press my lips to hers.

She stiffened for a moment and I waited for her to put distance between us, but instead she gripped the neck of my tunic and yanked me closer, her lips demanding a response that I was all too happy to give. Since the moment those entrancing eyes had opened on the battlefield, I had craved this woman—a yearning that had only deepened with every fascinating layer she unwittingly exposed. Each excruciating day had tested the limits of my restraint more than the last. Now unfettered, the spark that had crackled between us from those first uncomfortable days burst into bright flame.

"I am . . ." she murmured as she brushed her lips up my cheekbone and to my ear. "I am your wife. And you are my husband. I choose to stay—with you." She leaned her head back—fingers locked behind my neck—with mischief in those eyes and a tantalizing arch to her brows. "And so, my *husband*, I do believe the thirty days are finally completed."

23

2 SIVAN
1407 BC
CAMP AT OBOTH

Alanah lay tucked against my side, her warm breath soft against my neck. Even after two weeks, it still seemed a dream that I was allowed to hold her, that she was flesh of my flesh for the rest of my days. Her head-wrap had long since fallen off during the night and her short red hair glinted in the light peeking through the seams of our tent.

Sunrise had come long ago, but thankfully it was a Shabbat morning and no collecting of manna would be necessary today. Even if I had not collected enough for two days yesterday, I would have been altogether unwilling to leave my wife, hunger notwithstanding, especially after a week of grueling travel through the foothills south of Edomite territory to reach the wide plateau we now camped upon.

Peace graced the planes of Alanah's face this morning, a surprising calm that had enveloped her since the night she was healed. I could not help but caress her cheek and wonder at the change. She smiled before her eyes fluttered open. I ran a finger across her cheekbone again and then behind her ear. She arched an eyebrow but then frowned.

"What is it?"

She grimaced. "My hair. I miss my hair."

I trailed my fingers through the short curls. "I do too. But it is growing back. Soon it will be just as lovely as it was before."

"Am I so ugly without it?"

"You"—I pulled her close to me—"are extremely ugly. So breathtakingly ugly that all I want to do is stay in this tent with you for the rest of my life, so no one ever sets eyes on your hideousness again."

"Is that so?" She laughed, the sound like rare gold touched by sunlight. I was desperate to hear it again.

"It is. For any man will be extremely covetous of such an ugly wife and desire to steal you away." Her silly cat tried to press in between us and I brushed the jealous animal away.

"So the command from the elders did not work? I am still desirable?" She pulled a sly smile. "At least to men who like ugly women?"

"Not one bit. In fact, I think we will keep your hair short."

She lifted a brow again.

"Makes it so much easier to do this . . ." I kissed her shoulder, where the scar from the arrow still glowed red against her skin. I moved my lips up her neck and whispered into her ear. "And this."

She pulled in a quick breath but then laughed and pushed me away. "You can't keep me trapped in this tent forever, you know. I'm not your captive anymore."

"You never were."

She poked her finger into my chest. "You laid across the tent flap every night, Tobiah."

"Don't remind me. That was the longest thirty days of my

life, with you sleeping four paces away from me." I made a guttural noise and nuzzled her ear. "Never again."

"Your words may sour when you are stuck with me for the next year and forbidden to go to war."

Her jibe struck a nerve. As much as I wanted to be with Alanah, the thought of my tribal brothers heading to battle without me was like a dull blade to my gut. Staying behind to protect the women, children, and old people did nothing to stir my blood.

My expression must have betrayed my ambivalence, and Alanah peered at me. "Regretting?"

"Never. You?"

She shook her head, but a shadow passed across her features. I lifted her chin with my knuckle. "What is it?"

Her gaze darted away. "I miss my home."

Disappointment curled in my stomach. Of course she would miss the place where she was raised. I could not expect that she would see this flimsy tent as her home. "Tell me about it."

Her lips twitched. "I already told you . . . at the wedding, remember? The wine?"

"You told me a few things, but I want to hear more." I grinned. "Or do we need more libation?"

She sat up and folded her arms across her knees. "What is it that you want to know?"

"Tell me your best memory."

Her brow pinched with such sadness I nearly apologized for asking such a thing. "Harvest," she said with a sigh.

"Isn't that difficult work?" Other than the stories told around the campfire of the labors of my forefathers in the land of Egypt, I had little knowledge of farming.

"It is. There were times when I could barely use my raw hands after harvesting the wheat and barley. My father was a rich man and employed a number of people to help, but my brothers and I were always expected to be part of the cutting and winnowing."

Propping myself up on my side, I imagined her, red curls whipping about in the breeze and her long, sculpted arms heaving the heavy scythe back and forth. No wonder she was all strength of body and mind after such an arduous life. She had been right the day she argued with my sister and cousins—none of us had a true idea of what a life working the land would be like.

"My favorite part was winnowing. After the harvest was collected, we beat the stalks to release the grains, then tossed them into the air with our forks to let the wind do the work of separating the chaff from the kernels. When I was a child, my father would let me lay across the heaps of gold, sweeping my arms and legs wide to make a winged silhouette on the threshing floor." She smiled to herself and then dropped her chin to her folded arms. "When the winnowing was done, we swept the chaff into burn piles. I remember watching the ash swirl upward, carried on the wind, and then just vanish into nothing."

Weighted silence swallowed her words as she gazed at the tent wall, lost in whatever memories haunted her.

I waited until she looked down at me before I spoke. "You miss your family."

She sucked in a pained breath. "I do. But . . . they knew what they were doing. They were fearless warriors—all four of them were covered with the scars of battle, many self-inflicted to celebrate how many enemies they'd slaughtered."

She turned her body toward me and slid her hand from my wrist up to my shoulder. My skin prickled with pleasure at her soft touch. "Why do you not bear such markings? I've seen very few tattoos on any Hebrew."

"It is a command given by Yahweh."

She wrinkled her forehead. "Are victories not to be celebrated?" Her hand slipped from my shoulder and her thumb absently caressed the four jagged lines that scarred the inside of her own forearm. "Or the dead memorialized?"

"Victories are celebrated by giving thanks to Yahweh, sacrifices of gratefulness to the God who leads us. The dead are mourned for a time, but not worshipped in the way that your people do. We do not carve the images of gods or the names of ancestors into our bodies. We do not cling to death."

Confusion mingled with pain on her beautiful face. I reached up to graze my thumb across her lips. "My brothers died too, did Nita tell you?"

"Yes."

"I remember that day." I restrained a shudder. "The way the earth shook and rolled. The long, jagged crack that split the ground wide open. I thought it would swallow all of us."

The torture of Tzipi's screams as we both clung to our mother still reverberated in my mind. "My mother and father never recovered from the loss of my older siblings. I think large parts of both of them vanished into that pit. They never spoke of any of them again."

Alanah stared at the carvings on her wrist with an inscrutable expression. "My brothers were much older than me as well, sons of my father's first wife, who died before he met my mother. Davash was the youngest, but still five years separated us. When I was very small, I followed them everywhere. They tolerated me, mostly because my father seemed to insist upon it. But as I grew older, I began to realize just how brutal they could be. Pekkel, the oldest, beat one of the field hands to death with a wooden shovel for daring to slip a few trampled heads of barley into his satchel."

She blinked rapidly, as if clearing her mind of the horrific image. "But even if they were ruthless, even if they cared little for me, they were all I had. When they all died and my cousin inherited everything, even my home was stripped from me. It seemed better to die avenging them than to sell my body to survive."

She had been forced to choose between death and debasement? By her own relative? Anger coursed like fire through me. Not trusting my mouth to say the right words, I pulled her into my arms and kissed her, hoping to calm my murderous thoughts with the distraction of her lips. I reveled in the passion of her response after only a momentary hesitation. Perhaps a year would *not* be long enough . . .

"And what was that for?" she said, pressing her long fingers against my chest with a grin.

I placed my forehead against hers. "Never again. You will not face such choices again, *Ishti*. We will conquer the Land. We will build a life together. A family. A home. And I will fight for you, until my final breath."

"Family." She breathed the word.

I lifted a brow. "Of course. My sons will be raised as fine warriors."

"Sons? What of daughters?"

"I cannot teach a daughter to heft a sword." I frowned in mock disappointment, quelling a smile as I imagined a miniature of the fierce woman I held in my arms.

Mischief sparkled in her eyes. "I'll have you know that my father put a bow in my hands as soon as I could walk." The point of her glare pierced me through.

I scoffed. "A bow, of course—anyone could use a bow. Not everyone can wield a sword with skill."

She sat back, arms folded and all softness gone from her features. "Is that so?"

I pressed out my bottom lip along with a casual lift of my shoulder.

"Care to wager on that? Husband?"

ALANAH

"There is the target." I pointed my chin to an empty goat-skin bag hanging over the back of a wagon next to a stand of trees, more than a few paces away from the campsite. "Now what will be my reward?"

"Your reward?"

I smiled. Tobiah had not seen my skill with a bow.

He folded his arms and looked down his nose at me. "If you can hit that, and I doubt it, I will cook for a week."

"Accepted." And I raised the bow.

"What about me?" Tobiah asked.

"You?"

"Yes, what if I hit the bag?"

I laughed. "All right, what would you like as a reward?"

The heat in his eyes lit a burn in my cheeks, so I turned away to take my shot. The whoosh of the arrow whizzing through the air put a halt to his mirth. The bag swung back and forth with an obvious hole in the side.

His mouth hung open.

"It is a good thing you already know how to cook. But please, pay close attention, I do not like my manna burned."

He put out his hands. "My turn."

I reluctantly relinquished my bow, although he seemed to understand how dear it was and held it gingerly, as if it were an infant, not a weapon. The small bow looked almost humorous in his large hands. I handed him an arrow, scrounged from someone in a neighboring tent.

"Now. My reward." And he raked voracious eyes over me again. "You will come hunt with me."

I gathered my brows, incredulous. "Your skin-bag was not my only kill, you know."

He laughed. "I thought not. But I need someone to dress my game in the field."

I wrinkled my nose. Not my favorite thing to do, gut animals, although I had learned the skill from an early age. But I dipped my chin and smiled. "You won't hit it."

The skin-bag hung straight as his arrow arced high above the wagon.

"It seems you must dress your own game, husband. *And* cook me dinner when we return from hunting."

"I want to try!" A little voice called out from across the campsite.

"Me too!"

"And me!"

Tzipi's three small sons raced to be the first to try shooting the bow. Tobiah was forced to hold it high over his head. I thought for a moment the three of them would try to climb their uncle like a tree to get to the treasure, for they hung from his big arms like vines from branches.

"No." Tobiah laughed, a deep sound that seemed to raise the temperature of my blood. "This is your *doda* Alanah's bow. It is special."

They begged and pleaded to be taught to shoot the bow until I could do nothing but acquiesce. Such jubilant shouting followed my quick resignation that many other family members and strangers gathered around to watch.

Tzipi was among them. I caught her eye for a brief moment, sure she would say something to stop us after her violent reaction to my interaction with Liyam before, but following a quick stare-down with her brother, she shrugged an apathetic shoulder and turned away. Either she felt her sons needed a distraction from the still-fresh death of their father or she had ceded to Tobiah's authority.

Moriyah, too, was watching, with an expression of such envy that I determined to take her aside soon and show her how to shoot as well.

Mahan and Yonel, twins of six years old, were keen to watch my every move and solemn as they braced for each shot, trying to outrun each other in their search for stray arrows. But Liyam, barely five, could not even pull the bowstring and threw down the arrow when it refused to comply with his attempt.

"Liyam . . ." Tobiah warned.

I put a hand on Tobiah's wrist and gave a small shake of my head.

"Liyam." I crouched beside the disappointed boy. "Liyam, look at me."

Luminous silver-gray eyes, just like Moriyah's, peeked at me from the corners, but he did not turn his face. It was enough; he was listening.

"When my father first taught me to heft a bow, I was smaller than you. Only four. There was nothing I could do to pull that bowstring, no matter how hard I tried. But my father refused to let me give up. Instead, he gave me a flail and taught me to thresh grain. Let me tag along behind him and help with every chore on our farm. And do you know what? It took almost two years—older than you—but I did it." I leaned closer to whisper. "And do you know what else? I could outshoot my brothers any day."

A broad smile lit his dirt-smudged face. "*Doda?*"

My heart fluttered an odd cadence at his designation of me as his aunt. "Yes, Liyam?"

"When I can shoot a bow like you, can I use yours?"

I stood and tousled his hair, momentarily distracted by the feel of his thick, black curls between my fingers.

"When you are ready, I will help you make your *own* bow, better than this old one."

I knew he wanted to hug me, and I was almost desperate for it, but he eyed his brothers, who would surely tease his soft behavior toward me. I patted him on the shoulder and told him to go find something to carry for his *ima*, to strengthen his muscles.

Tobiah stood behind me, his arms snaking around my waist. "They needed that today."

I nodded. The loss of a father was a wound buried deep in me, I could only imagine the ache these young boys felt and would continue to feel as they searched out their own manhood in the coming years. The reminder that I had been a part of the army that had snatched these boys' father from them grated against my soul. Odd how much had changed in my perspective since Yahweh had healed me, as if someone had poured warm oil on my heart, making it pliable, shaping it into something new and unexpected. Still, at times sadness threatened to pull me under. It was only the presence of Tobiah that staved off its consuming flow.

"You will be a good mother," he whispered, interrupting my morbid thoughts.

If only that were true.

Playfully, he nipped at my ear. "And I look forward to build-ing a very, very large family with you, *Ishti.*"

24

3 ELUL
1407 BC
CAMP AT ABIRAM

The high ridge on which this forest stood overlooked the entire Jordan valley to the northwest. The farther Tobiah and I trekked, and the higher the sun rose, the more clearly the emerald jewel of my homeland stretched out as far as the eye could see. The delicious smell of green surrounded us. I inhaled the freshness deep into my lungs, willing it to cleanse my soul.

The solitude of our hike this morning reminded me of long hours hunting by myself, the hours I had spent listening to the land, learning every blade of grass and every distinct birdsong, every whisper of the breeze and every clue to oncoming storms. But having my husband alongside me was so much better. Although I jested that his large feet would startle away all the prey, Tobiah's light step still surprised me, even after over four months of daily hunts together. A man of his size who could steal through the forest was a rarity. Like spirits, we moved through the trees, alert for game.

As we passed through a thicket of blooming pink tamarisk trees, Tobiah lifted a hand, signaling me to still my body, an exercise I had mastered long ago.

With a slow movement, Tobiah pointed. A fox, red fur gleaming golden in the early-morning sunlight, hunched with her back toward us in the long grass, stalking some small animal. With patience, the vixen waited, not a muscle twitching, black-tipped ears flat. We stood close together beneath the shelter of the tamarisk, breathing slowly, nearly in tandem with the sharp-eyed predator crouched in the grass only five paces away.

With a graceful flash of red and white, the fox streaked forward and pounced on her prey. A soft squeak announced her victory over whatever rodent had tempted her this morning. As she jerked her head upward, her eyes sought us out in the shadows, undoubtedly having caught our scent in the breeze. With a flip of her red and white tail she bounded away, probably off to share the meal between her teeth with kits in a nearby den.

"Reminds me of another red-haired hunter I know," said Tobiah.

"Well, that vixen's hair is longer than mine." I ruffled the finger-length curls at the back of my neck as we stepped out of the thicket. We had ended up on a high ridge that overlooked the entire valley. Green stretched in every direction, ending at the blue hills in the west.

He ran a hand over his thick beard as he surveyed the wide vista. "True. Perhaps we can find you some armor and catch up to the other men. No one would know the difference."

"Are you saying I look like a man?" My eyes flared.

He folded his arms across his chest and surveyed me instead, his eyes traveling over me with a leisurely perusal that flashed heat through my limbs. "No, Alanah, you look nothing like a man." He lifted a playful brow. "But you could fight better than a few I know."

I poked him in the shoulder. "And don't you doubt it. The first time I wasn't prepared for the battlefield, but next time I'll know what I am in for. Besides, with your hair so much longer than mine, it might be easier to shave that beard and throw you in with the women."

He ignored my jest, his playfulness dissipating. "You are never going near a battlefield again, Alanah. Ever. I told you that I would fight to my last breath for you, and I meant it."

My skin prickled as a chill swept over me, along with an image of my strong husband lifeless on the ground. "Mosheh said that Yahweh was going to go ahead of you into Canaan. What does that mean? How many more of these battles must you wage?"

"That depends on the people of this land. From what you've said, and from all the abandoned villages we've come across, many have left. But if King Sihon's arrogant challenge is any indication, the ones who are left will have to be rooted out, and that may take some time."

"More than eight months?" Tobiah's frustration at being left behind when the army of Israel marched against the army of King Sihon this morning equaled my relief that it would be many months before he'd be allowed to fight again. I had suggested this trip into the hills to look for game, insisting that I needed a break from Moriyah, who had become my near-constant shadow, but it was more to keep my surly husband occupied while his brothers went off to war.

Sihon, the Amorite king rumored to be one of the last of the enormous men who wandered this beautiful land, was defiant in his resistance against Mosheh's request to pass through his territory. I'd once seen two of those frightening giants, mercenary soldiers among the army of Arad, both two heads taller than any of my brothers and with black eyes that consumed light like a bottomless pit. Even considering such a beast locked in battle with Tobiah sent a shiver down my spine. Once again I was grateful for the protection of the Hebrews' laws. I had no desire to lose another loved one by the sword.

Tobiah gripped the handle of his *kopesh* at his belt, his thumb caressing its hilt. "Alanah, I am a soldier. I have been training for this war since I was Liyam's age and Shimon and I were cracking at each other with wooden swords. When it is time for me to return to service, I will do so."

Widow. The word reverberated in my head like a shofar call.

"I know you have lost much. And if it is the will of Yahweh, you and I will live a long and happy life together in the Land." He gestured toward the horizon. "But I will fight alongside my brothers. I will fight for the inheritance of my people."

"So you will choose fighting over me?" The image of my father and brothers disappearing up the road that led out of our valley brushed across my memory.

"I choose to obey my God, Alanah. I will do whatever he asks me to do. A lesson that my brothers' deaths taught me." Tobiah was silent for a few moments, his eyes on the western hills across the Jordan valley. "I don't remember much about them. Just a vague memory of sitting on Yonatan's shoulders as we listened to Aharon read from the Torah scrolls one Shabbat. But I do remember that last day well, the day the earth swallowed them for their rebellion against Mosheh. And I remember how my mother was never the same, how she curled in on herself and was practically swept away with grief. She only lived another four years, and my father just two more after she died. My brothers knew the law and they chose, willfully, to rebel."

His nostrils flared and his eyes darkened. "They deserved the punishment they got, for dragging their families into their sin. They were guilty of not only rebellion, but of causing the deaths of their wives and small children." He stared at me. "If Yahweh had allowed Korah and his unrepentant followers to live, their rebellion would have spread like a sickness through the camps. They were murderers. Just as if they killed their families with their own hands. As far as I am concerned, they killed my mother and father too. And a murderer deserves to die."

A shudder traveled through me and I looked away. Tobiah's anger against his brothers was so palpable I could nearly taste the bitterness on my tongue. What could I say? My own family had abandoned me as well, every last one of them. "At least you had Nita and her husband to care for you and Tzipi."

He ignored my poor attempt at hiding my jealousy. "Yes. They treated us just like their own children." Tobiah smiled. "You've experienced a bit of Nita's mothering yourself."

"That I have." Although living with Tobiah was so far beyond what I had expected, I did miss Nita and her stargazing tent. She insisted on hugging me all the time and outright demanded that I get pregnant before she died. The way she talked about her imminent demise set my teeth on edge. Yet another person who couldn't wait to leave me.

My gaze wandered toward the horizon. Had the temple my mother fled to been this far north? Or farther? As if simply speaking of her would dredge up the pain she'd caused with her flight, my father had refused to tell me more than that her family had fled the Hittites from some far country and settled in Canaan, where he'd met her at the temple. Perhaps looking at me had caused him pain too, which was why he'd eventually stopped doing even that . . . I caught myself and shook my head to yank my thoughts back in line. There was no use wondering about the past.

Although I refused to look at him, I could practically feel Tobiah's scrutiny of my face.

"What is it?" he said.

Unwilling to delve into thoughts of the woman who had chosen such degradation over me, I rasped a noisy sigh and rolled my eyes. "Nita constantly reminding me that she is going to fall over dead any day."

"Ah. Yes. Well, I have a feeling we have at least a few months ahead of us before we actually enter the Land. And the curse was that men of fighting age and older would die." His voice lowered with emotion as he slipped his strong arm around my waist. "I think my *doda* may yet pitch her tent beneath the stars Avraham gazed upon."

I lifted a shoulder, unable to say more without revealing the hitch in my throat. Against my better judgment, I had come to care for Nita; her sharp wit and feisty personality paired well with mine, and she seemed to genuinely accept me, even if Tzipi continued to regard me with unbridled suspicion in her eyes.

With a sudden yank that nearly toppled me, Tobiah spun me around by the arm. He pulled me behind him, shocked and stuttering. "Stop, Tobiah. Where are you going?" I stumbled on a root, but he did not pause.

"Back under those tamarisk trees."

"Why? Did you see an animal?" I glanced around, searching for a wildcat or a mountain goat, frowning at myself for not paying closer attention.

"No."

"Tobiah, we need to go hunt. Sunrise is far past. We won't find any game." I ducked a low-hanging branch, laden with dark pink blossoms, as he led me under the shelter of a wide tamarisk enclosed on all sides by tall green vegetation. A quiet, private space, worlds away from the rush and bustle of the Hebrew camp. "What are you doing?"

Turning, he slipped one arm around my waist and with the other slid the quiver and bow off my shoulder. "Distracting you."

"Are you now?" I raised my brows as he lowered my weapons to the ground without taking his eyes off me.

With a little smirk he leaned forward as if to kiss me, but then instead put his lips near my ear. "Is it working?" His warm breath tickled and I restrained a shiver as the hair on the back of my neck rose.

Clearing my throat to mask the effects, I replied with as much flippancy as I could muster. "Try harder."

His grin was audible in his answer. "Challenge accepted."

25

S tretching as I emerged from the tent, I breathed deep, grateful for the cool air here in this thickly forested land where leaves whispered along with the fresh breeze. What a contrast this beautiful country was to the gently rolling landscape and scorching heat of my home. The arduous, seemingly endless uphill trek, the cycle of raising and lowering tents at each stop, the eternal waiting for the long, winding snake of human bodies and animals to move forward—all of it was worth watching the dawn creep over these mountains. The snow-capped hills adorned themselves in pink and gold to match the sunrise.

I drew my woolen wrap tighter around me. The weather had changed in the last few days, and this morning was the coolest yet.

Endless trees stretched tall, shading our tents with long arms. A flock of red-cheeked finches rested in the branches, their journey crossing ours on their way south. Their chirrups were harmonized by a multitude of other birds, more varieties than I had ever seen congregated in one place. They flitted about, changing places on their perches, arguing with each other as they danced through the forest, fluttering branch to branch. Their loud calls echoed. Was it a warning against our progress? Or a welcome?

Tobiah was gone, off to hunt again with a few other men who had also been charged with staying behind during the battle against Sihon's forces. The manna was still fresh to me, even after four months, but this region was replete with game, and the taste of fresh ibex or deer roasted over the fire every night had been glorious. Although I looked forward to whatever he would bring back, I would give him plenty of grief for leaving me behind.

I grinned to myself, wondering how he'd reacted to the new tunic I'd laid out for him after he'd fallen asleep. Kiya had been thrilled when I'd asked her to help me make the garment for Tobiah, and greatly amused when I'd told her it was because I loathed watching my husband dress each morning in a garment made by another woman's hand. And since I'd shredded the thing to rags last night, I'd never have to see it again.

I had awakened to the sound of Moriyah outside our tent before dawn, begging Tobiah to take her on the hunt. She'd become an avid student of the bow, picking it up quickly and eager to practice and, more often than not, hitting whatever dove or quail was unlucky enough to cross her path. Just as he had with me last night, Tobiah had fended off Moriyah with arguments that there were too many leftover enemies lurking in the woods, hungry for retribution against the Hebrews, and plenty of traders of all kinds who streamed through camp, some eager to sell hollow-eyed slaves, male and female, from the back of their wagons. His tone had brooked little argument, and even persistent Moriyah had been silenced by his gruff insistence that she must stay put in the campsite and help Tzipi and her mother.

My increasingly sullen husband had too much time on his hands. It had been painful to watch him doing his duty as guard to the women and children left behind while the soldiers fought Sihon's army. I reminded him that Mosheh had given newly married men a year off for enjoyment, not brooding about like a tethered dog, wishing they were off fighting battles.

I guessed that many of his thoughts strayed toward the loss of Shimon and the last time he went off to war. He confided in me one night, as he held me close on our pallet, his lips close to my ear, that whenever he closed his eyes all he could see was Shimon's eyes as they had been when he'd found him, sightless and vacant. He blamed himself for Shimon's death, and no matter that I tried to assuage his guilt with assurances that he could have done nothing to protect his friend in that chaos, he would not listen.

Liyam flashed by with a large group of other small children, his wooden sword uplifted and a battle cry on his lips. The unfettered laughter of the tiny warrior, and the exuberant wave he offered me, provoked a ripple of excitement deep in my belly. I placed my hand on the area that would soon begin to stretch in ways I could only imagine. Could it be that my body held a little boy like Liyam? A son who would someday walk in the footsteps of the man I had come to love?

I'd waited to reveal anything until I knew for sure that my guess was correct, when my morning portion of manna turned my stomach and my monthly flow had once again not returned, but tomorrow I would search out Shira and confirm my pregnancy, before telling Tobiah that he would be a father. I closed my eyes, imagining the light that would dance in his brown eyes at the news. Although anxiety had seized me when I first suspected, I held tightly to Tobiah's assessment that I would be a good mother, and determined to make it truth. I would do everything for this child. I would never leave it. Never toss

it away like refuse. This child would know all the goodness I
had not.

A gust of wind whipped by, dragging my wild curls into my
eyes. A constant frustration as my hair grew longer. Determined
to tame them before heading down to the well to fill a jug, I
ducked back inside the tent. My headscarf was nowhere to be
seen—perhaps Bodo had dragged it off to one of his hiding
places among our belongings. His spotted fur had matured
into dark stripes and he was growing into his ears, but he'd not
grown out of his playful ways. He'd pestered me all night long,
attacking my feet beneath our blankets. Now he was curled up,
sound asleep in his basket, oblivious to my muttering about his
theft of my turban.

Pulling the front of my hair back with a leather tie was the
next best thing, so I found Tobiah's satchel and dug my hand
to the bottom, hoping to find one of his. I had teased him last
night that someday my hair would be longer than his again and
then finally I would be the wife. He'd pulled me into a deep
kiss that proved my challenge ever so wrong.

My hand met a hard lump at the bottom of the satchel, and
I curled my curious fingers around it. It was a small, oblong
package, wrapped tightly in a linen cloth. A whisper of guilt
swished through me for prying among Tobiah's personal things,
but he had never forbidden me to do so and seemed to hide
nothing from me.

I carefully unwrapped the first layer of cloth, and a glint of
red startled me.

It was my hair.

A lock of hair shorn from my head by Shira's gentle hand
on my wedding day, tied together with a small string.

Tobiah had taken a keepsake from the floor of the tent and
saved it among his possessions. My heart throbbed at the realization of what it meant. He had always been impossibly kind

to me, since that first day on the battlefield, but until now I did not truly understand why. Though my stoic husband had never said as much, from the strand of hair in my hand I knew—he loved me.

There was more, however, wrapped in the linen. I laid the lock of hair aside and rooted through the remaining treasures: a bluish-green-tinted stone from the copper-laced valley where we first hunted together—the one he'd recently admitted to keeping as a reminder of the color of my eyes—a worn braided leather bracelet that I did not recognize, and a small, rudely carved wooden likeness of a lion.

Considering what might be the significance of the previous two items, I reached back into the satchel. The fringe of a feather whispered against my finger as I pulled out the last item from the bottom of the bag. When the discovery lay naked in my palm, the tent seemed to sway around me and my knees buckled.

In my hand lay the end of a broken arrow shaft with a turquoise kingfisher fletching, the edges of which were tinged with old blood. I'd held this arrow before, nocked it against my bowstring, and watched as it slammed into the side of a Hebrew warrior. Watched as the black-haired man had toppled to the ground.

Horror paralyzed me as truth crept slowly through my bones. *My arrow. Shimon's blood.*

I had killed Tzipi's husband—Yonel, Mahan, and Liyam's father.

I had killed my husband's best friend.

26

My only arrow to have connected with an anonymous enemy in the chaos of battle was lying in my hand, testifying to my guilt and threatening to destroy everything.

It was Shimon's demise that I had rejoiced over in the few moments before I was wounded. With his sentimental nature, Tobiah must have retrieved my arrow from his body when he buried him on the battlefield. A token to remind him of all he had lost and why he should fight against my people. Against me.

Heart pounding and head swimming, I returned the evidence with trembling hands, then carefully placed the lock of hair, the stone, the bracelet, and the lion back in the linen cloth and pushed the bundle to the bottom of his satchel. If only I had stopped my intrusion into that parcel when I discovered the lock of hair, satisfied with the revelation that Tobiah cared for me, never knowing the reason why he should not.

The bloody face of the man who had slammed into me on his way to grip the horns of the altar flashed into my thoughts, silent accusation on his phantom lips. *Murderer. Murderer. Murderer.*

What could I do? The only place I could go was back to Canaan, and the only way to sustain myself would be to follow my mother's path to the steps of the temple. The temple where my unborn child's life would be sacrificed in the name of greedy gods.

No. Tobiah must never know.

I could not breathe. The tent seemed to be a living thing, its walls pressing in on me from all sides. Needing to escape the suffocation, I stepped outside and was struck blind by the brilliant midmorning sun. Blinking to clear my sight, I glanced around camp, grateful that Moriyah was nowhere nearby. With the strange way she had of discerning things, she'd no doubt divine my guilt regardless of how well I controlled my expressions. There was too much of a seer in that girl.

Tzipi, however, caught my eye from where she sat in a group of other women, carding wool. She stared at me with a look that bordered on suspicion. Desperate for a diversion to her curiosity, I searched out an empty water jug, slung it to my hip, and set off toward the well just downhill of our campsite.

A group of Hebrew women passed by and, mistaking me for one of their own, smiled and waved, calling out that there was only a small line at the well and that I had picked a good time to come. If only they knew who I was and what sort of burden I carried, they would not be so gracious.

Not anxious to cross paths with anyone else until I decided what to do, I branched off on another path. Birds filled the trees all around, chattering out conflicting tunes, adding to the cacophony of thoughts muddling my head.

Would Tobiah send me to the elders? Have me stoned like the man at the *Mishkan*? Or for the sake of my babe, would he have mercy? Shimon had been nothing less than a brother to

Tobiah; would it be my own husband who avenged the man's blood? Would the man I loved kill me with the same sword he had stayed on the battlefield?

A fallen oak on the edge of a small meadow beckoned me. Finding a seat in the curve of the tree, facing west, I breathed deeply, attempting to savor the freshness of the air. No wonder the Hebrews were set on conquering this area—it was beautiful. Although the weather was cooling, flowers danced in this meadow, dotting yellow and pink and white against the tall green grass.

Their graceful stems brought to mind the *kalaniot* that bloomed blood-red near my home and the way my brothers teased me when I was a young girl by yanking the heads off the flowers and plucking their petals, with jests pointed at my red hair and inferior sex. I responded by reminding them of how the warrior goddess Anat had once threatened to bash in the head of El, the divine father, and echoed the threat with my bow. Although they continued to laugh, they left the *kalaniot* alone after that. It seemed my heart had always been full of murder, black from the start, and perhaps more like Anat than I'd ever considered.

A hoopoe landed on the end of the tree, startling me with the flutter of his black-and-white-striped wings. He seemed unconcerned with my presence and perched there, cocking his fan-topped head at me with a curious expression. Perhaps he had caught sight of a centipede or some large beetle, for he ignored me and began poking his long bill into the crevices in the bark, rooting for his afternoon meal.

"Ah. If only—" I spoke to the hoopoe, who focused on me as if sympathizing with my bitterness. He'd found his reward— a tiny green lizard dangled from his beak. He tilted his head again, studying me from another angle.

I sighed, glad that I had someone to share the burden that

sat on my chest like a boulder, even if it was a bird. "If only it hadn't been me who killed his friend. Or at least I had never found that broken arrow in his satchel. Tobiah would never forgive me if he knew."

The bird startled, the feathers atop his head fanning out in surprise. Stretching his black and white wings wide, the hoopoe lifted with sharp speed and disappeared into the thick trees.

"What broken arrow? What did you . . . ? Who did you kill?"

The rapid demands were Tzipi's. My back straightened but I could not turn. I dared not look at her or my face would divulge it all. But she already knew the answer, as if she lifted it from my culpable heart. Her words were daggers straight into my guilt-weary bones. "You killed my husband, didn't you?"

She came around in front of me, her every slow step pounding the accusation deeper into my heart. "Murderer. You . . . You stole my sons' father. You stole my husband. My friend. My love. You took everything." Each vitriolic statement slammed into me like a cascading series of blows.

Lifting my face but avoiding her eyes, I pleaded, "It was not intentional. I shot wherever I could, it was chaos. War. I didn't . . . I didn't know you, or Shimon, or Tobiah." My voice broke on my husband's name.

"I told Tobiah he should have left you there to rot and I was right. You deserved to die. Not him."

Although my gut shrieked to contradict her, I nodded my head. "If I could take it back, I would."

She continued as if she did not hear me. "I cannot believe I was about to attempt peace with you—thank you, even—for distracting the boys from their father's death with your bow. Instead, I find you were the very one to cause their pain."

Her accusation wrapped itself like a corded vine, constricting my heart, squeezing, jabbing thorns deep—drawing blood.

"Tobiah *will* know." Her voice strengthened, undergirded

by hate. "I will make sure of it. You are a murderer. No matter the law, you should never have been allowed to be among us. You will be stoned. There will be no mercy this time. You will pay for what you did—with your life."

Leaving the empty water jug on the log and without another look at Tzipi, I fled—with nothing but the tunic I wore, the sandals on my feet, and the baby inside me.

27

I jogged downhill on the path, the skill of chasing gazelle through heavy brush serving me well. Vines whipped my face, thorns tangling in my short hair and shredding my skin. It didn't matter. Tzipi was right, I deserved no mercy. Pushing the brush aside, I nearly reveled in the sting of the sharp tips against my palms. I deserved no buffer from their assault. Perhaps it would have been better if my father had allowed me to be thrown to Ba'al after my mother ran off. At least Shimon would still be alive. My eyes burned, but I refused to allow myself the relief of tears as I slapped another layer of brick across the emotion. I stumbled out of the thick under-brush onto a road. Disoriented, I looked both ways. Where would I go?

A snap of a branch behind me whipped my pulse into action. I was being followed. Was this the end? Was Tobiah here to kill me already? Turning north, I braced to run.

"Alanah! Stop!"

Moriyah's voice halted me. I whirled around. How long had she been following?

She crashed through the tall weeds I'd just emerged from,

one hand on her side. "You are too fast." She bent over and breathed heavily. "How do you run downhill like that? I tripped over every single tree root!" She straightened and stretched out a sandaled foot. "I smashed all of my toes."

"What are you doing?" Incredulous, I waved my free hand back up the hill. "Go back to camp!"

She shook her head. "No. Not without you."

"I cannot." *Please, Yahweh, don't make me tell her.* I could endure Tzipi's anger, but Moriyah . . . I didn't want to see the light of friendship go out in her young eyes.

"Yes. You can. Tobiah will understand."

I blinked. "Understand?"

"Yes." She aimed sober gray eyes at me. "You did not do it on purpose."

She knows. I could not force anything to come out of my mouth.

"I saw Tzipi follow you. I wasn't sure what she was planning, so I followed her." A trace of contrition edged her explanation. "I heard your conversation."

I dropped my chin and looked at the dirt beneath my feet. "Then you know what I am. And why I cannot go back."

She slid her hand down my arm to grip my fingers. "Yes. You are my friend."

I yanked my hand from her grasp and turned a fierce gaze on her. "I am not your friend. I murdered your brother."

Tears filled her eyes, and her lips quivered. "I know," she whispered. "But I forgive you. You were fighting in a war. You did not set out to kill my brother specifically."

Guilt crashed hard against my ribs, and I dropped in the middle of the road, arms over my head and knees in the dirt. "No. You cannot do such a thing. I will not allow it."

Her hand was on my shoulder, rubbing, squeezing, trying to console *me*. I was a killer. Deserving of the stoning that Tzipi had threatened. Moriyah sat down next to me, cross-legged, still gripping my shoulder as if to keep me from running away.

"You know," she said, "my grandmother told us the story many times of how they left Egypt. She was younger than you, only sixteen at the time. She told Shimon and me of how the Hebrews had made the mistake of selling their loyalty to Pharaoh in exchange for food, good land, and security. During the many years between Yosef and Mosheh, they allowed Egypt to worm its way into their hearts. It only took a couple hundred years for most of us to begin worshipping Egyptian idols and forget who we were."

I'd heard this story before, as Tobiah had taught me the Hebrews' ways. Yahweh had allowed them to go to Egypt, and when they were there they'd turned from the ancient paths.

"My grandmother always said, 'Did Yahweh leave us there?' No. He did not. Even though our hearts were almost as hard as Pharaoh's, he rescued us anyway. And we were given the invitation to follow him and see his miracles firsthand."

She pushed her face closer to mine, until I was forced to look up at her.

"I will tell you this, one more time and then I will never say it again, because you *will* believe me. Yahweh gave us mercy, sending Mosheh from the mountain to rescue us, he forgave us. And I—" she placed her hand on my shoulder again—"I forgive you."

This girl was barely thirteen. How could she understand the depths of blackness inside my heart? I went to the battlefield to kill, to avenge my brothers and my father. I was not there to protect any life, or even my country. I was there to kill and had rejoiced when the arrow cut her brother down. Yes, guilt had assaulted me soon after, but before the guilt had washed over me, I had rejoiced in his death.

I shrugged off her hand. "I do not deserve forgiveness, and you should not give it."

"None of us deserves forgiveness. And it is already given."

A loud whinny startled us both, and we jumped to our feet. A large man, gray-haired but muscular, approached us. I swiftly pushed Moriyah behind me, and she clung to the back of my tunic. Behind the man, a woman drove a team of horses pulling a long trader's wagon. The baskets piled in the wagon bed overflowed with colorful wool blankets and goods of all kinds. The Hebrews had not sat idly in the wilderness for forty years, and traders were forever streaming through the camps, bartering for well-crafted pottery, fine linens, and weapons.

"Well now, what do we have here?" said the man—Midianite, I guessed from the accent. His slow perusal of my body echoed his lazy drawl.

"Leave us alone," I said. "Our friends are just over there." I pointed over to the empty tree line.

He put a dirty hand above his brows and squinted, pushing his bottom lip out. "I see no one." I shrank back and Moriyah clung tighter, her hand trembling against my back.

The Midianite's leering grin widened and he strode toward us—not even making a show of approaching gently. "There is no use in fighting, ladies. You are quite far enough away from that Hebrew horde that your screams won't be heard. Besides—" smirking, he gestured with a glance behind me. "Kothar here snaps necks with just his thumbs."

Curling my arm back around Moriyah, I turned to look over my shoulder. A giant, nearly three heads taller than I, stood behind us, powerful arms folded across an expansive chest, a broad smile on a mouth crowded with overlapping yellow teeth, and his lone eye trained on Moriyah.

Although my stomach was trembling and my mind twirling

in circles, I stood fast and did not flinch. I would not give him, or the Midianite, the satisfaction of my fear. Whipping my head around, I lifted my chin. "What will you do with us?"

Perhaps if I stalled them someone would find us. Even if it was the man who might plunge a sword into my chest for the death of his friend. At least Moriyah would be safe. *Tobiah, please, rescue her!*

The Midianite tilted his head to the side, a leer twisting his face. He scratched his grizzled chin with his knuckles. "Well, let's see now. We are on our way north toward Damascus. I am sure we can find a place for a couple of lovely girls." His gaze traveled over my hair. "Good thing hair grows back or you wouldn't be worth as much looking like that."

Nausea burned the back of my throat and Moriyah's fingernails dug into my back as she sucked in a gasp.

The man jerked a thumb toward the wagon. "Get in without a fight and you won't die. Simple as that. Or shall I have Kothar help you ladies in?" He wrinkled his brow. "Although I should warn you: Sometimes my large friend is not so gentle."

"What do we do?" Moriyah's whisper warbled with terror.

My hands itched for the bow lying across my pallet in the safety of my tent. We had nothing to protect us. No dagger. No sword. I could try to fight Kothar with my bare hands, give Moriyah a chance to run, she was young and agile. But she might not outrun the Midianite, and if I was dead, I could do nothing to protect her. Our best chance—our only choice— was to go.

When it had been just me, so many months ago, my life had meant so little that I had practically thrown it away with two hands. But I had my baby, and Moriyah, to consider now. Two lives to protect, alongside my own.

"We go. Moriyah, if we fight them, they will kill us." I reached behind me, pulled her cold hand into mine, and squeezed. "One way or the other, we will survive."

TOBIAH

Carrying a small doe over my shoulder, I grinned to myself, thinking of how my skills with a bow had been honed by practicing with Alanah. She'd be proud of the trophy I brought her, even if she'd been annoyed to be left behind while I hunted with a few other men from my tribe.

She had a sharp eye and almost perfect aim. I loved her little ritual—the graceful strength with which she pulled the bowstring, then blinked slow and steady while she found her target, then sucked in a small breath before releasing. I could watch it all day.

Today, I'd imagined her with me, slipping through the tangle of cedar and oak that stretched in every direction. The thought made me smile, and I'd had to glance around quickly to make sure none of the other men witnessed my foolishness. Anxious to hold her, and to mercilessly tease her about the tunic she'd torn into rags while I slept, I quickened my steps.

A commotion greeted me at the campsite. A large group of women were congregated, talking over one another. As usual, Alanah was not among them.

Tzipi rushed over as soon as she caught sight of me, her head-scarf fluttering behind her. "Have you seen her? Is she with you?"

"Alanah?" Why would Tzipi be looking for my wife?

"No, Moriyah. Wasn't she with you this morning? Did you take her hunting?"

"No. She asked to go, even followed me for a while, but we

went up into the hills so I sent her back here. Perhaps she is with Alanah? Gone to practice shooting?"

A shadow passed over Tzipi's expression. "No. No, she is not with her."

I put the doe on the makeshift table next to the fire and rinsed my hands in a bowl. I shook the water from my fingertips. "I'll go ask Alanah if she has seen her."

Again, Tzipi's face registered some emotion I could not place. Unease crawled beneath my skin. "What is it?" I pressed.

She looked away. "I am simply concerned for Moriyah. No one has seen her since she followed you east, hours ago."

"Alanah will know. Moriyah follows her everywhere." Leaving my sister, I ducked into our tent, expecting to see the face of the woman I loved lighting with pleasure at my return, but the tent was empty. Her bow missing.

Emerging, I strode up to my sister, working very hard to quell the apprehension that surged through my limbs as I demanded she tell me where Alanah had gone.

Instead of looking me in the eye, she tugged at her headscarf, tucking her flyaway hair beneath its covering. "She is gone."

"Gone? Where?"

She shrugged, indifferent. "I have no idea."

The look on her face told me otherwise. "Where is my wife, Tzipi? What have you done?"

An ugly sneer contorted my sister's beautiful face. "I did nothing. Your *wife* has run away. And very good riddance to her."

A roar started somewhere in the pit of my stomach, and I clenched my fists tight to keep it from escaping my mouth. "Why would she leave? Did you say something to her? I asked you to be kind!"

"I care nothing for that woman! She is gone and I am glad of it!" The words exploded from her lips with hissing vehemence that I'd never witnessed from my twin. "I only care that Moriyah is missing!" Tzipi's expression abruptly transformed from anger to pleading desperation. She stepped forward and slipped her arms around me, voice trembling and body shaking. "I've already lost Shimon, Tobiah, we can't lose her! What if she's been taken? Please. Go find her!"

Looking north, I squinted. The trail curved to the west, toward Canaan, and then disappeared into the green void beyond, the thick forest obscuring my view. Having split from Noach and Simcha, who, along with a few other men from our tribe had joined the search, I'd followed this trail through the brush and ended at this place. Numerous tracks crisscrossed here, a product of the countless travelers who traversed this wide road that stretched from Egypt up past Damascus in the north. Yet there was a spot where small sandal tracks mingled with larger ones, some so big I could not believe they were real. I had heard stories of giant men who lived in these lands, but I could not wrap my mind around the idea that little Moriyah might be held by one of them. The sandal prints ended abruptly in the middle of the road where the wagon tracks crossed them. She'd been taken. And who knew how long ago?

A small lump in the middle of the trail caught my eye. I knew what it was before I reached it. Moriyah's whistle. Her most treasured possession, a trinket whittled by Shimon when she was an infant. I bent to retrieve it, glad that it was in one piece. She must have dropped it off the back of the wagon she'd been loaded into. She would never willingly part with it, without a purpose. Smart girl, she had left me a signal.

North. I must follow the northern tracks.

Tzipi had pointed out the path Alanah had taken toward Moab. And although I had my suspicions about my sister's culpability in her departure, there was nothing I could do. If Alanah had truly left shortly after I had this morning, she was hours away. I had witnessed the swiftness of her strong legs during our hunts.

As I looked southward, the image of her face crowded my decision, calling with an urgency that shook my bones. Why did she not have the decency to tell me? Or explain why she had changed her mind? The thought of her fleeing, after four months of marriage, four months of oneness, made me ill. Her bow was gone or I would not have believed such a thing. How long had she been planning her escape? Had she been biding her time until she was close enough to her homeland that she could find her way?

Turning my back, I headed north toward a young girl who, without me, had little chance at survival—and away from the Canaanite woman who wanted nothing to do with me.

28

ALANAH

7 TISHRI
1407 BC

I bit my lip, squelching the urge to cry out as the back of
my head slammed against the side of the wagon. Was our
captor working to hit every rut and bump in the road?
Three weeks of rumbling along in this wagon bed, bound and
without benefit of even a blanket to lie on, had rendered me
bruised and hopeless. And for every day of those three weeks
a litany of accusations continued to cycle through my mind: I
should have fought back, I shouldn't have run away, I should
have stayed and accepted my fate. It was my fault that Moriyah
was on her way to be sold as a slave, and who knew what else.

"We'll get more for them if we don't touch them," Shamir,
the Midianite, said. "They pay more for the untouched ones."

"How do you know they are maidens?" said Uli, the woman
I assumed was the trader's wife, or something of the like.

"It doesn't matter. I won't chance it again. Those last couple we brought, I barely got an ear of corn for." His gruff laugh ended in a hacking cough. Shamir seemed to have some sort of illness. He always drove the wagon, and whenever he climbed down to set up camp, his wheeze lingered for hours. It was no wonder he employed the giant to guard his wagonload of goods.

I'd wondered why they hadn't abused us, other than the odd kick or shove if we were too slow getting back into the wagon over the last three weeks. And I had also wondered why they had not attempted to sell us in the last four towns we had traveled through. Their trading supplies were exhausted and gold jingled in the purse around the Midianite's neck, but it seemed he had his eye on a larger prize. Selling us to someone who paid top price for untouched girls—of which I certainly was not. My belly had already begun to swell beneath my tunic.

But why would it matter that we are untouched maidens? Horror swiftly filled the space where the question had been. A temple. There must be a temple where young girls were either used or sacrificed, but only if they were virgins. *No! Anything but that. Not Moriyah.*

The girl was curled against me, one arm slung across my chest. Kothar, the giant, snored like a wounded lion next to us, and I had barely been able to discern Shamir and Uli's conversation over the racket.

Keeping my eyes closed, my jaw slack, and my expression unmoving, as if I too were asleep, I weighed my options. I would never let them destroy Moriyah. I had been watching for any chance to escape these last weeks, but Kothar's eyes were on us every moment of every day. Tonight, however, with his mouth open, back turned, and long legs hanging off the bed of the wagon, he slept.

My hands were tied together, but not as tightly as they had been. I had not struggled one bit since we'd been tossed in the back of this wagon. Hadn't muttered a complaint, hadn't even looked at the scenery passing by. And gradually Kothar had begun to relax, to sleep more deeply.

The moon was bright, and Shamir was taking advantage of this clear night to push farther north. The rush of water to the west had been constant for the past few hours. We were finally following the river north, but from what I gathered from the conversation between Shamir and Uli, we soon would be veering away, toward Damascus.

We would only have one chance.

Still peering through the tiny slit of mostly closed eyelids, I nudged Moriyah with my elbow. She hummed, although her eyes stayed closed. *Such a smart girl.* With the smallest of motions, I moved my mouth closer to her ear and then whispered slowly, "It's time to jump."

She hummed in acknowledgment.

"Go!" I hissed.

In a flurry we were on our feet and over the side of the wagon, both of us slamming onto the rocky ground without the use of our hands for balance. Shamir bellowed at Kothar to wake up and then screamed at the horses to stop, coughing with vehemence.

We ran, plunging into the thick vegetation and toward the sound of water. At our backs, Kothar bawled curses. Without hesitation we jumped into the black river, skidding on the slimy riverbed. Shocked by the contrast of the frigid water against the warm air, I shivered violently. "Let the river take us," I said, gripping Moriyah's trembling fingers with my own and wishing I had time to soothe her fears. "Stay under as long as you can. Now!"

We dove into the rushing water that could whisk us farther away than our legs could. Hopefully the thick reeds and grasses along the banks would keep Kothar from moving ahead of us. Over the past weeks I had observed that it was Shamir who did the thinking for the enormous but dim-witted man; perhaps Kothar would assume we went across the river and not under it. Swallowed up by the icy black water, I could do nothing but pray that somehow he would not see us in the dark.

My sodden wool tunic tugged at me, pulling me downward. Moriyah's frozen fingers kept slipping but I gripped tighter and kicked harder, desperately wishing my hands were free to pull myself deeper. I fought the ropes that bound my hands but they might as well have been made of iron, they would not loosen. Any slack I'd had in the wagon was erased by the swelling of the fibers.

When at last my chest felt as though it would explode without another breath, I lifted my head above the surface and looked around. There was no way to tell how far we had gone, but the water in the center of the river was rushing even faster than near the edges, the black outlines of trees and brush washing by with gaining speed. Moriyah gasped. She too had come up for air.

The giant yelled, much closer than I had hoped, and the sound of his large body crashing through the river vegetation made my heart pound even harder than before.

"Dive!" I whispered before gulping another breath of precious air and dragging Moriyah downward into the blackness. It was deeper now and I could not find purchase on the bottom, but I kicked as hard as my frozen legs would move.

When again I could hold my breath no longer, I kicked toward the surface. As soon as my head popped above the water, a huge boulder appeared in front of us. Without time to react, Moriyah and I slammed hard against it, our hands slipping apart and the rush of water yanking us in different directions; she was pulled to one side of the boulder and I to the other. The river swirled me around, knocking me against another rock and pulling me into a whirling vortex of crashing water. My elbow hit a hard surface and I choked as water filled my mouth. Spitting and huffing, I tried to stand, but even here the water was deep. Had Moriyah been dashed against the rocks? Had I killed that brave girl with my impetuous escape?

Yahweh! Save Moriyah! Help me find her!

A cough to my right answered my prayers. Given courage by the loudness of the rushing water, I called her name softly. She answered but then coughed again. Kicking toward her, I assured her I was coming but then slammed against another boulder. Frozen as we were by the icy water, I knew that tomorrow I would be covered in bruises, even if I could feel little pain at the moment. Horror struck me. Would my baby be hurt by all this buffeting and this frigid water?

Shaking away the terror-inducing thought, I kicked again, calling to Moriyah. Peering into the darkness, I was grateful for its cover from Shamir and Kothar but angry that I could not see her. *You said you had a plan! Perishing in this river cannot be it! Save us! Surround my child with your protection!*

Something grabbed at me and I gasped, seeing Kothar in my imagination, but it was Moriyah's frozen hand gripping the sleeve of my tunic. What was left of my composure nearly fled with my breath as I released thanks to the God who had somehow heard me in the middle of this icy river.

"Swim to the edge," I said, my teeth chattering.

Kicking my numb legs with the remainder of my strength, I did my best to push toward the vegetation on the west bank. When finally my feet met the ground, I nearly shouted with glee, but remembering how long Kothar's legs were, I urged Moriyah forward with a whisper. The weeds tangled around my legs, threatening to drag me back into the black water, their menacing whispers calling out our position, but there was nothing we could do but push forward.

The bank was steep and slick, and my wrists had been rubbed raw by the rope that still bound me. We slipped and stumbled our way to the edge and dragged ourselves to the shore using elbows and wrists. Panting, we lay on our backs, the water still swirling at our feet.

"We have to keep moving. Put as much distance as possible between us and that giant."

She whimpered but nodded.

"Ready?"

Another whine. "I'm frightened."

"Look at me," I ordered.

Her eyes were pale with moonlit terror.

"We are going to live. Both of us. You are going to see your family again. Do you hear me?" I said the words with as much conviction as I could with my teeth chattering and my body convulsing with shivers. "We must survive."

She nodded her head.

Rolling over, I propped myself up and somehow dragged my knees under my body to stand.

"Which way?" Moriyah asked.

"They'll expect us to stay close to the river. We go west."

As much as I felt like we needed to run, my feet would not comply. My waterlogged leather sandals grated at my skin, sliding and squeaking loud enough to alert anything out on the hunt in the middle of the night. I feared, too, that if we stopped, we might succumb to the cold. The only way to get warm was to move our bodies.

Straining my ears, I heard nothing more than the hush of night sounds, a few restless birds and insects. Had we truly lost Kothar back on the other side of the river? I could not chance it.

We walked until Moriyah's knees buckled and she toppled forward. The smallest wisp of light on the eastern horizon highlighted a hill in front of us, covered in thick trees.

"Moriyah," I said, pulling her back up. "We need to get around that hill and start a fire." Not giving her a chance to argue, I pressed forward. Our progress was slow, but by the time we reached the small hill, the sky had lightened enough to reveal limestone caves, like gaping wounds, in its side.

"Gather kindling," I said and began to search for tools to start a fire.

By the time Moriyah had a handful of twigs and dry grasses, I'd found a piece of flint and a large stone. We climbed up the side of the hill, sliding on the limestone rubble as we made our way to one of the larger caves with hands still bound.

"What if there is an animal in there?" she said.

"Our chattering teeth will scare it away."

She grinned at my jest, a small measure of the terror replaced with a glimmer of hope in her light eyes.

The cave stank but was empty. Although it was shallow, it afforded us a dry place to start a small fire—another skill learned from my father. Before the sun had fully risen, Moriyah and I were tucked together next to the fire, too exhausted to deal with our restraints. I hoped Kothar had given up the chase, or at least was blind to the wisps of smoke curling out of the cave. An easterly breeze swelled and dragged the smoky trail with it.

Yahweh truly had protected us this night, or at least had honored my request to save Moriyah and my innocent babe. But I was grateful that he cared for them, for he certainly could not care much for a murderer like me.

29

TOBIAH

A surge of energy from the center of my bones answered the call of the thundering war drums. *Shofarim* screamed their response and the men around me pounded a pulsing rhythm with spears on shields. Everyone reeked of sweat, dust, and righteous anger. After the victory over King Sihon's forces, Yehoshua had issued an order to travel north and take the kingdom of Bashan from King Og, a man whose legendary height caused the tiny thread of foreboding that niggled at the base of my spine.

Now that Alanah was gone, I had thrown off the armor of the first year of marriage and donned the battle gear of a man who needed to forget the faithless wife who had fled.

This was where I belonged, alongside my tribal brothers, sword in my belt and spear in hand, my body ready to push forward into whatever lay ahead, with no thought of anyone or anything except my goal—especially her.

After three futile days of searching for Moriyah, Noach, Simcha, and I had conceded defeat. None of the traders we questioned had admitted to seeing any young girls in a wagon and, truly, whoever had taken her could be anywhere by now. First I'd failed Shimon, and now I'd failed his young sister. What good was a warrior who could not protect the people he loved? That poor girl, so innocent, so full of life . . . The thought of what she might be enduring nauseated me, and I could not let my mind linger on such hideous imaginings. As morbid as it was to think, I prayed that instead she was in the arms of her brother, wherever that may be. It was the only thing that kept me from shattering to pieces.

And Alanah, the woman to whom I'd offered my protection and my love, had chosen to return to Canaan over marriage to me. How could she do such a thing after those months together? Especially when she had told me of how the only option left to her there was so repugnant.

Yet even though anger at her incomprehensible decision had cycled through me again and again, my gaze was constantly drawn to the edge of camp, hoping to see her burst through the tree line, returning to me with that rough-edged smile on her beautiful lips.

Don't think! Forget her face. Forget the feel of her in your arms.

Instead, I focused on the tall mountain range to the north; the three giants were laden with caps of snow and sweeping skirts of green that sloped toward us. In the distance, Edrei perched atop a high hill, the enormous city surrounded with walls of astounding height.

We had marched for days, through the richest, lushest countryside I'd ever beheld. Abundant crops stood at attention. A vast array of fruits—most of which I had no names for—shone from the trees like tiny points of sunlight. We'd scavenged in the orchards as we'd passed through, and I'd been surprised at the variety of tastes on a tongue accustomed to a steady diet of manna—from crisp, sweet globes, to tangy citrus fruits, to small red ones whose juice stained our teeth bloody.

The land was rugged, lined with hills and valleys. The sounds of rushing streams and rivers had become a common occurence, a contrast from the days without water as we trekked barren deserts.

I could see myself living here, breathing the clean air, taking in the sight of the majestic mountains, and hunting the plentiful deer and mountain goats that populated this land. The thought of hunting without Alanah soured the vision and I blinked it away, just as the quick double-blast of a shofar drew my attention from the mountains to the men standing on a ridge above us.

I'd seen Yehoshua before, the tall, dark-haired commander who answered to Mosheh alone. He'd been present for some of our training sessions, his silent perusal of our skills causing a rush of nerves in my belly. The man inspired me like no other. This faithful leader, along with Caleb, the revered warrior, had stood firm against the cowardice of the other ten spies forty years ago. He was the man my brothers should have been, had their ears not been bent by the likes of Korah and his band of rebels. But instead they had chosen their own destruction, like Alanah.

"Brothers!" Yehoshua's voice rang out across the valley and every man hushed to absorb the words that would usher us into battle. "Look to the city there, called Edrei. Do you see the towering walls? Do you see the impregnable bronze gates? Can you envision the vicious man-beasts there whose heads top yours by two cubits, or more? Can you count the swarms of their armies who fight in the name of a god whose depravity you cannot fathom?"

He paused, scanning the crowd slowly, as if searching out cowardice among us. I schooled my features even as the bleak visions he'd conjured marched through my head. Would this be my last day? My last moments on this side of the river that separated this life from the next? Would one of those horrid beasts spear me through?

"Sihon was nothing compared to Og," called out Yehoshua. "A puppy. Og himself is twice your height. The spies we sent brought back toe-curling stories of daily human sacrifice in this place. Blood runs through the streets of that city like rivers during their profane festivals. But we do not serve a filthy, man-eating god of iron and stone." He held up his sword, pointing toward the enormous peaks that edged the northern horizon. "We do not serve false gods who live on top of mountains. We serve the God who *made* the mountains. We serve the God who rescued us from Egypt with the very unraveling of the Creation he began. We serve the God who built the foundations of the earth with a mere word."

As he described Yahweh, my apprehensions began to recede, replaced by the reminders of the glories my parents had seen in Egypt. The mighty Nile replete with blood, the swarms of locusts, the sky-blackening clouds of flies, the conquest of the sun itself, the sea congealed into walls with a blast of Yahweh's nostrils.

Yehoshua continued, his voice as strong as a man of twenty. "We have nothing to fear. Yahweh has already won this war for us. We will trample the gates of Edrei today. Our feet will tread upon the necks of our enemies. Our swords will remove the blight of their evil from this beautiful land."

Once again Yehoshua gestured with his sword, but this time toward the group of priests, two thousand cubits away, who carried the golden chest built to house the tablets of the covenant laws. The distance swallowed up any details of the holy object. I knew only from rumor that it was decorated with two winged creatures and carried by two fixed poles on either side. What courage those priests must have to approach such a deadly vessel! Tales of men charred to the bone by a flash of light from its core had haunted me since early childhood.

"And there," he called out, "on the shoulders of the sons of Levi, is the reminder that Yahweh stands with you this day. That he will deliver these enemies into your hand. So brothers, I ask you now . . . Will you lend your sword to this victory?"

With one accord, we lifted our swords and spears, and a rumbling shout of solidarity burst from every mouth. The drums began to pound again, their summons to war melding with the many *shofarim*, and my blood pulsed in time to the driving cadence. But just as the signal was given to march forward, a clear image of Alanah's blue-green eyes looking up at me on the battlefield crossed my vision. The memory of the resignation in her expression once again hollowed out my resolve to forget her. I missed her. I missed the taste of her mouth, her rare laughs, the wicked tease in her voice when she challenged me to a footrace or a shooting match. I even missed the temper that flared whenever I managed to best her in one or the other.

Tzipi may stomp and demand that I marry Keziah, like she had two days ago—a vain attempt to keep me from this battle and ending up like Shimon. But I didn't want Keziah.

I wanted my wife. I wanted the vivid woman who made my pulse spike and my chest ache with longing. I wanted the woman who took on a serpent to protect two helpless sand kittens and who had seemed to give me permission to scale the walls of her heart. I wanted the woman who did not want me.

Every step toward Edrei compounded the ones Alanah had taken away from me, and the closer I came to the dark-hearted men who guarded the city, the hotter the flames of anger kindled in my veins. Grief, betrayal, pain, and rage corded themselves together in my limbs. The writhing mass of emotions, coupled with my disgust of the abominations presided over by the king of Bashan, stoked a fury that burned away every trace of fear, leaving only the sight of the priests and the golden ark that housed the *shekinah* presence of El Shaddai, the God Most High.

There was not a doubt in my mind—even if Yehoshua decided to send me into battle alone. Og's men would meet their end today. Yahweh had already won.

30

ALANAH

8 TISHRI
1407 BC

The shard of flint split from the rock in a perfect, sharp-edged break. Reining in a cheer, I scuttled back into the cave. The cords that bound my hands had dried into an impossible knot; no matter which way I tried to loosen them, my hands were still imprisoned and my wrists raw from the chafing.

"Moriyah, wake up. Help me cut this."

The girl peered at me through the cracks of her eyelids. "I'm so sore. I cannot move."

"You'll have to, my friend. We must put more distance between us and that giant. Who knows how far we have to go to find the Hebrews?"

"We are going back?"

"Of course. Where else would we go? You need to be with your family."

"And you need to be with Tobiah."

I didn't answer but offered her the makeshift knife. "Here, hack at this rope."

"Does Tobiah know?" Moriyah didn't move. "About the baby?"

I sucked in my cheeks. I'd hoped she hadn't noticed, but I should have known better. Moriyah missed nothing. "No. And he won't."

"What are you talking about?"

"Nothing. Come now, cut this cord so we can go."

If I didn't know better, I would have thought Moriyah was related by blood to Tzipi. The girl's targeted glare cut me to the marrow. "You *are* coming back with me, aren't you?"

"I'm taking you back, and then I will go."

"So you will abandon me?"

Sympathetic pain shot clean through my chest. "I'm not abandoning you. You have a family who loves you. I can take care of myself. Tobiah is not interested in being married to a murderer. He's probably already betrothed to Keziah." I swallowed the acrid taste of the words. "Or married, if Tzipi has had her way."

"No. Tobiah wouldn't do that. He loves you."

"You know nothing about love. You know nothing about me or Tobiah. You are a little girl who is confusing marriage with the games men and women play."

Ignoring my caustic response, Moriyah set her jaw. "I may not yet be a woman, but I am not ignorant and I am certainly not blind, like you."

My mouth went slack. I'd never heard such impertinence out of the sweet girl's mouth.

"I may be blind, but if we don't get out of this cave and farther south, we'll both be dead. Now, cut the cord." I jiggled the flint knife at her.

With a scowl between her dark brows, she complied. It took

longer than I had hoped to cut me free, but I nearly cried out at the relief. In turn, I cut Moriyah loose. What I wouldn't do for a soothing salve to calm the enflamed skin around both our wrists.

"How will we make it back? Won't someone see two girls traipsing through the countryside?" She waved a hand between us. "What if we get taken again?"

"I have a plan, but you won't like it."

Moriyah lifted a brow. "What is it?"

"Two girls will surely draw attention, but two ratty boys will not."

Understanding registered on her face, and her eyes darted to my hair. "You mean . . . ?"

"It will grow back." I scrubbed at curls that now reached my ear lobes. "Mine has."

She pinched her eyes shut but nodded.

With admirable restraint, Moriyah sat very still as I hacked at her hair with the sharp edge of the flint knife. Although I had honed its edges once my hands were free, I could tell by her twitching shoulders and the fingers tapping against her knees that it was painful. Dark clumps of hair fell onto the cave floor.

"There. You look awful," I said.

Tears sprang to her eyes.

"No! I meant the haircut is a mess, just like a boy would do with his own knife." I scooted closer. "Your mother will fix it. You are beautiful, Moriyah, with or without hair."

Silvery eyes blinked at me. "I am?"

"Of course." I gave her a tight smile. "In fact, we should do a little more work, or no one will believe you are a boy, short hair or not."

Using the flint knife again, we trimmed our tunics just below the knee, then I used the excess to wrap my breasts close to my body and another strip around my belly. Thankfully my tunic was loose enough that Moriyah declared my abdomen looked as flat as my chest. The binding was painful—almost unbearable—but at the same time felt like secret armor protecting the life inside my body.

We scrubbed dirt onto our faces and under our fingernails, and then I showed Moriyah how to walk like a man: wide stance, long strides, moving her shoulders and arms instead of her hips.

"Good," I said. "Now keep your chin level but eyes more on the ground. Men don't look people in the eye unless they want your attention or are asserting their dominance. We must blend in, avoid notice."

A sheen of fear shined in Moriyah's pale eyes. "What if . . . ?"

I grabbed her shoulders, giving her a little shake. "No. We will not think of the what-if. Do you not remember what we endured last night? In that river? You and I should either be dead or in that wagon headed to Damascus. I called out to Yahweh in the water and I immediately found you. So even if my only purpose in this life is to get you back to your family, then that is what I will do."

The morning was cold but bright. A huge three-peaked mountain range loomed white-headed in the distance to the north—Har Hermon, the throne of Baal himself. I'd always heard tales of the Storm-god who lived atop that mountain. As a child I'd envisioned it as some mystical place, where the peaks extended to the heavens and storms raged day and night as the gods battled against one another. Seeing it now with my own eyes, I realized it was only a mountain. A beautiful mountain that, as Tobiah had told me, was created by Yahweh. A god who was limited to a mountain—a god who demanded the flesh of children to be satisfied—was a god who was too small. But a God who deigned to hear me in the middle of a furious river, without benefit of idol or offering, was a God truly worthy of worship.

Turning my back to the myths of my past, I set a quick pace. I kept the river to the east of us, as far away as possible while still keeping it in sight. Although I had no idea how we would find them, the river was my only guide toward the Hebrews. Once we moved farther south, I hoped to search out someone who might point the way, but I could only trust that the God who had ushered us through the rapids in one piece would guide me now, somehow.

The land sloped downward, but the rugged hills alongside the river made for slow going, and the vegetation was so thick in places we were forced to climb higher to avoid getting mired in the underbrush. Moriyah never complained, although her stomach was as empty as mine. She walked next to me in silence, working hard to keep her stride long and straight. By the time I stopped to rest beneath a sycamore, Moriyah held herself more like a boy than I would have thought possible.

She beamed at my encouragement. "Shimon would be proud of me. He always teased me about acting like a little girl."

The reminder of the brother I had killed knocked painfully against my ribs. "But you are a girl."

"No," she laughed. "Shimon was always messing about. In fact, I think he considered it a personal challenge to make Tobiah explode. I remember one time—Shimon put indigo dye in Tobiah's washing pot one night. Tobiah's hair had a distinct bluish tinge for days."

I cleared the amusement from my throat. "Did it work? Did he get angry?"

She shook her head and grinned. "Tobiah acted as though nothing had happened at all. He just sat down next to us and ate his manna portion, blue hair shining in the sun, even though Shimon laughed so hard tears ran down his face."

"And he let Shimon get away with humiliating him?"

She waved a hand. "Oh no. We'd been camped near a swampy area at the time, a place where the water was so murky we could not use it. Tobiah gathered as many frogs as he could find and let them loose in Shimon and Tzipi's tent." She shook her head. "I thought Tzipi would murder them both. She was pregnant with Mahan and Yonel at the time, or she might have."

The image of a blue-haired Tobiah being ear-dragged by his twin sister surged into my head but was quickly replaced by such acute longing for my husband's embrace that my heart contracted painfully. A flutter in my abdomen answered the emotion and I gripped my belly. "Oh!"

"What is it?" Moriyah grabbed my arm.

"It moved." I blinked at her through a haze of relieved tears. "My baby moved inside me. It's alive."

Moriyah's smile lit up the shaded canopy beneath the tree. "She will be *natanyah*, a gift from Yahweh."

"A girl?"

Her lips twitched. "Yes. I am certain of it."

"Well, let's hope we don't have to chop her hair off someday as well. Come, Mikal." Calling Moriyah by her chosen male name, I patted my swaddled belly. "Natanyah is ravenous."

As we finally exited the narrow river valley, the landscape opened up before us to reveal a sparkling blue lake. The wide basin was a blur of every shade of green.

"Look!" Moriyah pointed at a stand of trees. "Fruit!"

My stomach snarled, overcoming the trepidation of running heedlessly toward the food. Moriyah reached the trees first, snatching a red globe off a low branch. Holding it up to the light, she studied it from every angle.

"What is it?"

I laughed. "A pomegranate."

"It's beautiful! I've only seen the dried seeds that traders brought through camp once in a while." She smelled the rind and then tried to bite into it, scowling when the tough skin refused to relinquish its treasure.

I took the pomegranate from her, used a rock to crack it in half, and handed her one side, but I waited to eat, anxious to watch her discover her first-ever mouthful of fresh fruit.

Her eyes grew as large as the fruit in her palm as she scooped the red seeds into her mouth. "Delicious!" Bright red juice dribbled down her chin as she pointed south. "Look! There, what are those?"

Just past the pomegranate grove stood long rows of vines laden with purple clusters that sagged nearly to the ground. Saliva surged in my mouth and my feet walked toward the dark jewels without conscious thought.

With a flick of my flint knife, I severed the arm-long cluster from the vine and held it in the air. The sun shone through the orbs, turning the skin a translucent red. They were almost too perfect to eat. Almost.

Popping one into my mouth, I groaned at the tart sweetness and then lodged in another two. I had grown up nibbling fruit ripe from the vine my whole life, but somehow these were far and above the most delectable I had ever tasted.

"How have I gone my whole life without eating these?" Moriyah's words were slurred around the mouthful, and her cheeks bulged. "What are they?

"Grapes. They are the fruit used to make wine."

"Oh! My grandfather owned a vineyard, back in Egypt!" She tilted her chin, curiosity twisting her face into a frown. "How do these become wine?"

I resisted a laugh. Truly, what would these Hebrews do with farms and vineyards they had no idea how to tend? "Well, after they are harvested—"

"You boys!" a booming voice called from a few rows away. "Get away from my grapes!"

Grasping Moriyah's juice-slick hand in mine, I ran, tugging her behind me but clutching the remainder of my grape cluster to my chest. Peering over my shoulder, I saw a large older man behind us, waving his arms, calling out for other men who were tending the fields farther up the terraced slope. In the distance, a small fortress stood guard at the top of the hill. How could I have been so careless? Hunger and fatigue had overtaken my normally acute senses.

"Run!" Certain she could keep up, I released Moriyah's hand and headed for the shoreline, the clearest path I could see away from the furious Canaanite farmer.

Behind me, Moriyah was making a strange noise, but afraid to slacken my pace I simply yelled out. "What is wrong?"

She released a loud laugh she must have been attempting to restrain. "They thought we were boys! It worked!"

A rumble of thunder sounded off to the east and a sudden wind whipped across the water toward us. The clouds were gliding northwest, darkening with astounding speed. Relief sped through me just as quickly. The angry man would no doubt leave us be; two pilfering boys were not worth the effort of running into an oncoming storm.

"We must find shelter."

Near the end of the lake, craggy cliffs jutted against the blackening horizon, pitted with dark holes and wide caves. "There!" I pointed. "Go!"

Another boom of thunder shook the ground as a deluge broke free. Skidding on rain-slick rocks, we climbed, panting but pressing forward until we hunched inside a small cave. I swiped at the water dripping from my hair into my eyes. An awe-inspiring vista spread out around us. The white peaks of Har Hermon were hidden behind the dark clouds, but rebellious rays of sun still shone through, glittering across the wide lake in large swathes.

Terraced farms dotted the whole basin, and a village clung to the curve of the lake, hovering at the shore as if waiting on its edge like a patient fisherman, toes in the water.

Moriyah gasped. "Alanah, you are hurt!"

I looked down at my tunic. A dark red stain was splayed across my chest. Blinking, I spun the memory of our flight from the farmer backward in my head. My ankle throbbed from twisting, but I did not remember hurting myself otherwise.

Sudden realization dawned. "The grapes, Moriyah. I must have smashed the cluster of grapes in my hand. I dropped them along the way."

She sighed loudly, her shoulders drooping in relief. "I don't know what I would do if I was all alone in this land. If those men had caught us . . . discovered we are girls . . ."

"I will not leave you alone, I promise. No matter what happens, I will not let anyone hurt you. We must be more careful from now on. It was foolish of me not to pay closer attention." My mind finished Moriyah's thought. If we had been discovered as women, there was little doubt we would be violated.

"But Alanah—" Moriyah's face was twisted into an expression of pain.

I slid my hand into hers, reassuring her with a squeeze. The poor girl must be beside herself with fear after our second flight away from men who meant us harm, in as many days. "Yes, Moriyah?"

"Did you have to drop the grapes? They were so delicious."

31

I'd almost forgotten the taste of manna. Canaan was replete
with crops: silver-leaved groves bursting with olives and terraced hills stacked high with rows upon rows of vineyards.
Moriyah and I had become swift as larks snatching fruit from the
fields. We'd learned from our first encounter with that farmer
that one of us must be a lookout while the other harvested
our meal.

Moriyah had become so adept at holding her body like a boy
that I had every confidence she would pass as one if we were
accosted. She told me that she meditated on her brother's facial
expressions and the confidence of his stride each night. The
more she spoke of Shimon, the less razor-edged the reminders
of my part in his death were. I almost felt as though I knew
him personally, with all her stories of him and Tobiah and their
friendly competitions.

At the last village we'd come across this morning, I'd gathered the courage to approach an old couple on the outskirts.

Under the guise of begging for work in exchange for food for myself and my "brother Mikal," I asked, in the lowest tone my voice would allow, if they had heard about the enemies crouched on the edge of the land. As we helped the old man haul water back from the village cistern, I'd been regaled with tales of the Hebrews' destruction of King Sihon and his forces and then another huge battle for the northern lands of Bashan, where, incredibly, the Hebrews had won against King Og, a giant rumored to have a taste for human flesh.

Please, Yahweh, let Tobiah have married Keziah, so he will have another year without war. The thought had cycled in my mind ever since, etching deep grooves of pain that were filled only by a small amount of hope. I would forever think of Tobiah as my husband, but I would rather he be in Keziah's arms than in the arms of Prince Death.

The old man and his wife were petrified of the Hebrews and asked, again and again, if I thought they should flee north. Grateful for their unexpected hospitality, I assured them that they should indeed leave the area. Their four sons had left them to their own devices years ago, caring nothing for their elderly parents when fortunes could be made elsewhere—another stark example of the superior laws of the Hebrews, who were commanded to honor their elders and care for them until their journey in this world ended.

After refusing the couple's kind offer of a place to stay the night, we took our leave with the knowledge that the Hebrews were encamped across the river near Shittim, on the plains of Moab opposite Jericho, and within easy walking distance.

Avoiding the trade road that led south toward Jericho, we edged our way along the western hills, scuttling into the brush or behind boulders whenever we heard anything that resembled a person or a wagon nearby.

When the plains of Jericho opened up in front of us, we

finally stepped into the open, drawn out by the massive date-palm orchards that crisscrossed the valley. It would be easy to hide among the thick groves as we made our way toward the river.

Jericho stood atop a hill, flouting its high position and enormous walls in the center of the plain. A thick outer wall and tall gates stood guard around the mass of flat-topped buildings. An inner wall protected the middle of the city, and from our position I could see nothing more than the tops of two tall buildings; one, from its size, I assumed was a palace, and the other, from the tall wooden *Asherah* pole, a temple. A cold shiver worked its way through my body, for I was well aware of what transpired in temples such as that one. Even at the smaller temple in Arad, the temple priestesses loudly advertised their skills dressed only in sheer linen.

I had always been disgusted by such things, appalled that women would so fully degrade themselves, but even more now that I had lived among the Hebrews where acts like those were punishable by death. And yet my own mother had left me to return to that sort of life.

After we had slipped into the afternoon shade of the orchard, Moriyah and I sat with our backs against the broad trunk of a palm, munching on dates we'd cut from a bough heavy with fruit. My feet ached after walking for days, much more than when I had walked with the Hebrews. Now my sandals chafed my toes and heels, rubbing the skin raw, reminding me of my foolish push toward the battle with vengeance in my heart— never suspecting a Hebrew warrior would be at the end of my heedless path. No matter how much I wished that my arrow had not found Shimon's side, I could not force myself to regret landing in that valley with a Hebrew one in my shoulder.

"Do you think we might see the Cloud from here?" Moriyah craned her neck to peer through the fronds toward the eastern ridge that lined the horizon with hazy blue, the place where the kind couple had told us the Hebrews were encamped. "Perhaps when we come closer to the river?"

"Getting back to the other side of that river will be a challenge." I shivered at the thought of our first crossing. "I hope the current is not as strong as it was through those rapids."

"Yahweh helped us cross the first time. He will do it again." Moriyah's confidence bolstered my own. "How are you so brave? You have lived among the Hebrews your whole life. You had your brother and Tobiah to protect you, and Yahweh watching over you at all times."

She looked down at her grimy fingernails with the first hint of embarrassment I'd ever seen on her face. "I pretend that I am you."

Taken aback, I laughed. "That is ridiculous."

"No," she said. "It's true. The first time I saw you, you walked right up to Tzipi with the fiercest expression I'd ever seen on a woman's face. I was terrified of you and thought you might cut Tzipi down right then and there. But I kept watching and saw that, beneath that warrior-shell, your heart is kind. The way you spoke with Liyam that day, before Tzipi swooped in like a screeching hyena, convinced me."

I smirked at the memory. Tzipi truly had acted as though I was planning to roast her little boy over the cookfire and gnaw on his bones.

Something yanked my hair and jerked my head painfully to the side. As my mind caught up with the realization that I had been grabbed by someone who had crept up behind us, I caught sight of Moriyah's silver eyes, wide and terror-stricken. She sprang up and skittered backward, far out of reach of our only weapon, my flint knife still on the ground next to the large cluster of dates I'd sliced from the tree. The hand that gripped my hair shook me, sending ripping pain through my scalp. A voice ordered me to my feet with a curse against "filthy thieves."

Although I tried to comply, he kicked me in the hip and I collapsed on the ground. With another kick to my ribs that made me fear for my baby, the man yanked me again by the hair and dragged me to a half-standing position. I could not see his face, only his large, dirt-encrusted toes on the ground beneath me.

"This is not your property," he said as he jammed the point of a dagger into my cheek. "I'll string you boys up by your necks."

Moriyah stood helpless beside me, her eyes darting between me and the man who held me captive. He seemed large, but not a giant like Kothar.

"Mor—Mikal! Run, go!" I managed to grind out between my teeth.

She took two steps backward but shook her head. I restrained a snarl. Infuriating girl. Why would she not protect herself?

"Smart boy," said my captor. "You run off and I'll gut this one like a lizard."

"We only had a few dates," I said, digging into my chest for a low vocal tone. "Let us go. We won't come back."

"No. My master says to bring him every thief. And that's what you are, and that's what I'll do." Not the owner of the palms then, but a guard. "You there," he said to Moriyah, whose wild expression matched the turbulence in my gut. "You try and run and you'll pay for your meal by finding out if this boy's ugly red hair matches his blood." He laughed at his own morbid humor. "And you—" He came around in front of me, without letting go of my hair. The man's grimy hair hung to his chin, and his eyes seemed to bulge from their sockets. He smiled, revealing teeth more brown than white. His breath and body reeked. "If you fight me at all, your little friend will suffer even worse. Understand?"

Nausea sprang to my throat. I fully understood his meaning. This valley may be full of beauty, with fields that boasted fruits of every color, but I had heard tales of Jericho from my brothers, dark tales that pitted my stomach as they flooded my mind.

Foolish. I had been so foolish to come near this evil place.

32

J ericho's walls loomed above us. The guard had tied our hands together with a rope he wore about his waist and now led us into the city tethered like animals. No one gave us more than a cursory glance; judging by some of the other human cargo being carted into the city, two dirty boys at the end of a short rope was a common sight.

I kept my elbows tight against my body; the wrapping around my breasts was loosening and I feared my secret would spring free at any moment, but even as I did, I kept watch for some way to escape the lumbering guard ahead of us. There were so many people jammed together here; perhaps if Moriyah and I pulled on the rope as one, it would slip from his hands. My hopeful idea melted into reality as I saw that our smelly friend had the rope looped twice around his own wrist.

As soon as we passed through the wide outer gates, the stink of the place assaulted my senses. Donkeys and horses and sheep and cattle were being driven straight through the city, droppings everywhere. Urine-soaked mud clung to my sandals and squashed between my toes. Against the sweeping vista of the gorgeous land outside the walls, Jericho was a festering refuse pile.

Stumbling along behind the guard over uneven cobbles and ascending steps that led higher into the city, Moriyah and I dodged a pack of dogs that nipped at our legs before speeding off into the chaos to chase a fugitive chicken that had escaped its cage.

Homes huddled together without a breath between them, and human waste and discarded animal carcasses tinged the air with decay. I longed for the neat rows of Hebrew tents and the orderly care taken to ensure that refuse was buried outside of camp.

A second set of gates with impossibly thick bronze doors led to the inner ring of the city, guarded by a contingent of soldiers who scanned the streaming masses with wary eyes. The reminder that the Hebrews planned to soon take over this land, and therefore this city, made me wonder how long they would be forced to lay siege. With nearly unscalable double layers of walls and gates that would shut tight against their entry, there would be little chance of direct invasion. They would have to encircle the city and wait, cutting off the food and water supply. If, that was, the army of Jericho did not march against them first.

And yet, the old couple had assured us that the Hebrews had won against that giant king in the north. Was Tobiah a casualty in that battle? Was my baby's father with Shimon in the underworld? Again, I took up the plea that had become a constant rhythm in my head. *Please, Yahweh, let Tobiah have married Keziah.*

The guard led us into the heart of the market. Tradesmen called out their wares, jostling each other to be the first to reach our ears. Frankincense, cinnamon, and handspun linen were offered in insistent tones, all of the finest ingredients and much better than the man down the road, as if two captives had anything to offer for such things. One wagon boasted a white mountain of salt, gathered from the Salt Sea to the south of Jericho.

As we passed one stall, a small boy with a bony spine rippling through his thin tunic slipped past us to reach out and snatch a cluster of grapes in a grimy fist. The merchant saw the tiny thief and smacked his hand with the flat of his sword. The boy howled and ran off, clutching his hand to his chest instead of a meal.

The contrast between this bustling city with wood carvings or bronze idols gracing every other market stall, and the Hebrew camp where such things were forbidden, was stark. Many of the women we passed kept their eyes on the ground, as if well aware that any eye contact was an invitation. Others, however, brazenly displayed their wares, lounging in doorways or windows, vacant-eyed and loudly advertising their services alongside the fruit sellers and goat traders.

More than anything, I wished to have my hands free, if only to cover Moriyah's innocent eyes and ears. "Why didn't you run when I told you to?" I said, hoping the guard would not hear me over the clamor of voices.

"And leave you alone? No. We are going home. Together." The stubborn girl set her jaw.

Home. Did I have such a thing anymore? Dagan had stolen my beautiful valley, and I was no longer welcome among the Hebrews. Would there ever be a place I could truly call home again? I doubted it. Home was a broad-shouldered warrior with cinnamon-brown eyes that exuded warmth and humor, who had loved me although I had been his enemy. I yearned for his arms around me and his lips on mine. But as much as I wished to be home again with Tobiah, even if by some miracle I returned to the Hebrew camp, the desire and the acceptance I had seen in his eyes would be gone forever, replaced by accusation for my unforgivable sin.

The guard stopped and jerked the rope, hauling us toward a stall that stood at the end of the market. The tables were laden with huge clusters of dates, their sweet smell somehow cutting through the grimy air of the market.

"Found these two boys eating your fruit, Master Urdu." The guard yanked the rope again, aggravating the burn on my wrists. "Brought them right to you, I did."

A short, balding man with a rotund belly came out from under the shade of the canopy. "Ah, Pavel. You did well." Squinting, he bunched his face into a frown. "I don't tolerate thieves in my orchards."

Pavel beamed. "I told them I'd gut them like lizards, Master, just like you said."

"There will be an extra pot of beer for you tonight." Urdu took the rope from Pavel and then patted the larger man on the shoulder, as if speaking to a child. "Head on back to the orchard now." Pavel clomped away with a ridiculous grin on his face.

"Now." Urdu scratched his fleshy chin. "What should I do with you two worthless clods of dung?"

Swallowing the fiery retort that sprang to my lips, I kept my expression blank.

"Haven't you seen what we do to thieves around here?" Urdu poked a fat finger into my collarbone and then pointed over his shoulder.

My eyes followed the gesture. A pole stood at the center of a small open area. Four bodies hung from it, arms stretched high above them and feet dangling two handspans above the ground. Two men still squirmed at the end of their tethers. Carrion birds circled around the pole, dashing in to poke at what was left of their mutilated faces. The other two bodies were bloated and limp and looked as though they'd been hanging there for days.

"Not a pretty way to die, is it?" Urdu smiled, as if delighted at the prospect of adding to the body count.

Fear bubbled to the surface, busting out of my mouth. "We only ate a few dates. We will work off the debt, if you wish. My friend and I are hard workers."

He leaned forward with a curious look on his face. A look that reminded me that I had not lowered the tone of my voice when I spoke. His eyes searched my face, then traveled down to my chest. His brows flicked upward, then he grabbed my tunic and yanked me forward. The swift movement caught me off guard, and since Moriyah was pulled with me, I lifted an elbow to steady her. The binding on my breasts released, sliding to my waist, just as the man peered down my neckline.

Lustful glee replaced suspicion on his face. "Just as I thought. A woman."

Icy panic spread through my body. I should have just let him hang me on the pole. I glanced around, desperate for a way to escape. A small crowd had gathered around us and my gaze snagged on a flash of color. A woman with a dark purple turban stood nearby, a market basket in the crook of her elbow. She stared at me boldly, her face portraying some sort of confusion before her jaw sagged slightly. Before I could consider the bewildered expression on her face, Urdu turned to Moriyah.

"And what about you?" he said with a flick of his tongue across his lips. "Somehow I get the feeling you aren't a boy either."

"Don't touch him," I said, letting my rage surface.

The man ignored me and reached for Moriyah. Swinging our bound hands toward him, I kicked him in the shin, but not before he grabbed the neck of Moriyah's tunic and ripped it down to her navel, exposing her gender to everyone in the market. Mortification burned red in her face as she cried out.

"What is going on here?" came a voice from nearby. An older woman, with hair dyed an unnatural shade of black, strode toward us. A younger woman followed, her head shaved on both sides, revealing curling tattoos above both of her ears. Both women wore sheer garments, layered with tiny pleats and clutched at the waist with thick beaded belts. Their eyes were slathered with kohl that stretched all the way to their ears, and large amulets of Ashtoreth hung from carnelian-beaded chains about their necks. Temple priestesses. Two blank-faced, burly guards stood behind them, gleaming *kopesh* swords in their belts.

"Mistress Mishabel." Without letting go of Moriyah's destroyed tunic, Pavel's master bowed his head toward one of the women. "These thieves were discovered in my orchard, and I have just found out that they are women posing as boys."

The priestess turned toward me, peering at my face and then skimming a critical gaze down to my feet and back up to my hair. With a slight narrowing of her blackened eyes, she addressed me. "Where do you come from?"

I saw no reason to lie. "The southern highlands. Near the Salt Sea."

"And you?" She turned to Moriyah.

"She is my sister," I said, knowing Moriyah's accent would give her away.

Mishabel ignored my obvious lie. "And you, my dear, where are you from?" Her tone was grating in its condescension.

Apparently realizing the woman would not relent, Moriyah replied in a soft tone. "I am Hebrew."

Mishabel's eyes flared wide and she glanced about, as if discerning whether anyone else had overheard Moriyah's answer. She turned back to Urdu. "I'll take them off your hands. What do you want for them?" Her tone was flippant as she gestured toward me with the back of her hand, revealing a fading tattoo, a sun-disk embraced by a crescent moon, the united symbols of Ba'al and Ashtoreth.

A swirling pit of disgust swelled in my gut. *No. Anything but that.* Ceding to instinct, I stepped backward, but Urdu yanked on my tether again, forcing me to stand still as I waited for them to dicker over us like two loaves of bread. After sucking his teeth in contemplation, Urdu laid out an exorbitant price for us—one I was sure the old priestess would refuse.

"Done," she said without a twitch. "I'll have one of my men bring you the silver right away."

I nearly gasped at the casual tone of her voice. She couldn't be that eager to buy two ratty, smelly women with their hair cut like boys. We looked anything but seductive. What possible reason would she have to toss so much silver at Urdu?

Mishabel led us around the back side of the temple complex, through a wooden gate, and to a large house. Gesturing to the guards, who situated themselves on either side of the doorway, she smiled with false sweetness on her red-painted lips. "Don't bother running. They have no problem killing runaways. You won't make it out this door. Although you certainly wouldn't be the first to try."

She led us inside, leaving us bound together with Pavel's rope, and pointed at a flat pallet in the corner of a room with only a tiny slit at the top of the wall for a window.

"You have tonight, ladies, to sleep. Tomorrow we will clean you up and you will begin work." The woman sneered as she ran her eyes over me. "You remind me of someone I once knew, and if you are anywhere near as talented as she, you will do well here."

I'll die first.

"This one, though." She put her finger under Moriyah's chin, forcing the girl to look straight into her eyes. "You, they will pay more for. Untouched, are you?" When Moriyah blushed, the priestess patted her cheek. "I thought so. Yes, I must find just the right worshipper to change that."

Moriyah's face blanched, and the priestess chuckled loudly as she left the room; her short companion followed without a word, only a backward glance with kohl-rimmed eyes at Moriyah before she closed the door.

Moriyah's knees collapsed as soon as the lock clicked, pulling me down with her. She retched on the floor beside her, sobbing.

Yahweh? Is this your plan? The destruction of this innocent girl? Why did you not just let us drown?

I cleared the fury from my throat so as not to frighten Moriyah. "Come now, lay down on the pallet. There is nothing we can do now but sleep."

"But tomorrow—" Her voice warbled and cracked.

"Don't think about it." I pressed closer to her and put my forehead against hers. "I will think of something. You *will* see your family again. I promise."

She nodded and with a bit of maneuvering we laid down on the pallet that wasn't much more comfortable than the dirt floor. Twisting her fingers into mine, she closed her eyes, her body jerking every so often—from physical pain or from soul-agony, I could not tell. Eventually her breathing lengthened and she slept.

I, however, continued my silent rebuke of Yahweh for not protecting Moriyah—and for lying to me about some mystical purpose. Silence met my ears. A flutter in my abdomen jerked my attention back to the fact that I was carrying a child. Tobiah's child. What would these depraved people do to my baby? Would they give me herbs to rid my body of its presence? Or would they allow it to be born and then burn it on the altar? My blood raced and my breath came in short spurts. No. I would kill that woman if she came near my baby.

My litany of inaudible grievances against Yahweh grew longer, and louder. I screamed at him in my mind until I could think of nothing else to say. Once my noiseless fury was spent, I tried to force sleep on myself as the last dregs of sunlight disappeared from the window-slit and darkness consumed us, but I could not keep my mind from cycling through different ways to escape this room and get past those armed guards.

What seemed to be many sleepless hours later, the door swung open and a shadow loomed in the doorway, silhouetted by a dim light.

"Alanah?" a woman's voice whispered.

I did not respond. I had not told my name to either of the priestesses—who would know what to call me in this house?

"Alanah. Come here, hurry. Bring the girl." The urgency in the woman's low voice caused me to sit up on the pallet. Moriyah moaned in her sleep but did not wake.

"Who are you?" I asked.

"We must hurry. The guards are occupied for now but we cannot waste time."

A rescue? The dim light moved forward into the doorway, casting light on the face of the person holding the small lamp. Black kohl-smudged eyes met mine; it was the shorter priestess, the one who had said nothing as she had trailed behind Mishabel.

A trick! I leaned over Moriyah, shielding her.

Another woman took the lamp from the priestess and approached me, but her face was in shadow. "Please, Alanah, we are here to help. Dayatana led me here to help you."

"Who are you?" I yanked a veil over my fears to challenge her with a glare. "Why would you help us?"

242

She held the lamp close to her face. It was the woman who had so boldly met my eye in the street earlier today. She reached up to push back the purple headscarf that covered her hair. The lamplight glinted off bright red curls now uncovered, and eyes the same color as Tobiah's malachite stone stared into mine.

"I am your mother."

33

After cutting our bonds and giving Moriyah another tunic to slip over her gaping one, Dayatana led us through the dark household. I could not grasp fully the realization that my long-lost mother was behind me as we crept down the hallway. How had she known it was me in the market? She had not seen me since I was three years old, the day she left me.

And this was where she had flown to? Jericho? My father had said she'd run back to serve Ashtoreth, but he had never told me where. Yet when I saw her on the street she was not dressed like Dayatana, but simply like any other Canaanite woman in a colorful, one-shouldered woolen tunic. Only her brazen stare and purple turban had stood out in the crowd.

Dayatana opened the front door and poked her head out to peer into the black night. "You must run, quietly. I had a few of the girls distract the guards, but it won't be long before they come back around this side. I unlocked the back gate."

My mother cupped Dayatana's cheek. "Thank you, my sister-friend. Your debt to me is paid."

"If you get caught I will not protect you—I cannot." Dayatana glared at me. "Mishabel is unforgiving, and I must pre-

tend that someone stole you away without my knowledge."
She looked around the corner. "Go! I hear the guards!"

Without hesitating, I grabbed Moriyah's hand and we ran,
following my mother through the dark.

"Here it is. Come, girls," my mother whispered, then took
my other hand and dragged us through the gate. We stumbled
into the street and sped through town. I wanted to ask where
we were going, to ask how she knew me and where she had
been for most of my life, but all I could do was think about
the feel of my mother's hand gripping mine and how familiar
it seemed, over nineteen years later.

Even this late at night, people packed the streets, doing business by torchlight—yet no business that should be carried out in
the day. Again I wished I could cover Moriyah's eyes and ears,
protect her from the perversions of this cesspit, laid out for all
to see in the alleyways and empty marketplaces.

More respect for my father's choice to isolate me budded
in my mind, as did gratefulness that I'd been sheltered on the
farm. Yes, the temple and its wares had been at the center of
Arad, where we'd traveled a few times each year to trade our
wheat, barley, and wine, but I shuddered at the openness, the
audacity, of such behavior here in Jericho.

Drunken fights plagued almost every corner, but my mother
sidestepped them without flinching. She must be used to such
horrors after living here for so long. A drunk bumbled into
our path, and with a strong, steady voice my mother ordered
him away. To my surprise he startled at her tone and tripped
off into the night.

The darkness in the town was suffocating. Torches everywhere cast yellow light on black deeds, but I felt as though a
heavy shroud stretched wall to wall over Jericho, blocking out
every good light. Even the stars hid their eyes.

We passed through the bronze gates into the outer circle of

the city. Holding my breath, I cringed at the filth I knew my feet were stepping in as we descended toward the outer rim of the city. My mother stopped at the foot of a stone staircase nestled between two tall buildings. "Quickly, let us get out of the street. I don't think anyone saw us, but Mishabel will not give up easily. She does not relinquish silver lightly."

As we climbed the stairs, I realized this house was built against the outer wall of the city, not too far from the main gates. On the other side of the thick barrier lay freedom, and beyond that, the Hebrews—and Tobiah.

My mother knocked softly on a wooden door at the top of the stone steps. "Let us in. It's your mother. Quickly." The door swung open and we bustled inside. I blinked against the brightness of three tall floor lamps flickering in the large room.

Another woman stood in front of me, my own shock reflected on her face. Her hair was red and curly, and her eyes, although dark brown and lined with kohl, were shaped just like mine. She was almost my mirror image, as well as my mother's.

"This is your sister, Alanah. This is Rahab."

"My . . . sister?" I gaped at my mother.

"Yes, I was pregnant with her when I fled the valley. She is your full-blooded sister, and this is her home." The revelation was delivered with curt frankness that nearly knocked me to my knees. *A sister?*

Incredulous, Rahab stared at me. "I cannot believe you are here. When she said she saw you in the marketplace . . . I did not believe . . ." She stepped close and placed a hand on my grimy face. "We look so much alike. No wonder she knew it was you right away." Sheer bewilderment kept me from jerking away from her touch. As if noticing my discomfort, she dropped her hand.

"And who is this?" She turned to Moriyah, who I had almost forgotten was standing next to me. The girl was looking back and forth between the three of us, amazement painted on her dirty face.

"This is Moriyah. She is the sister of my husband's brother-in-law. Which makes her—I don't know exactly?" I laughed, a nervous and pinched sound.

"You are married?" My mother's face brightened.

"I was . . . to a Hebrew named Tobiah." I could practically hear Moriyah frowning beside me.

"A Hebrew? How could you be married to one of them and be here?" Rahab asked, jerking a thumb over her shoulder toward the eastern window.

"We were kidnapped by Midianite traders and driven far to the north. We escaped through the river and walked here."

"Are they coming now?" Fear sparked in Rahab's voice as she ignored my improbable explanation.

"The Midianites?"

"No, the Hebrews. They are coming, are they not?"

I looked back and forth between the two fire-haired women. "We were told they are camped across the river on the plains of Moab."

"They've been there for a month now. No one knows what they are planning. We also heard there was a battle between the Hebrews and the forces of Bashan in the north." My mother shook her head. "The wine merchant said the destruction was unheard of."

My blood sank into my feet. Had the old man been wrong? "The Hebrews were defeated?"

"No. They bested Bashan, even though Og, the king, is known to be ruthless in battle and astoundingly tall. The warriors of Bashan don't even bother offering sacrifices to the gods anymore before battle, they know they will win."

"But they didn't win?" I sighed with relief. "The Hebrews defeated them?"

She shrugged her shoulders. "I can't explain it."

"I can." A smile tugged at my mouth. "For now, though, can we wash? I cannot stand the smell of myself." I gestured to my feet, covered in filth from the streets.

"Of course!" Rahab called out to someone named Ohel and a tall, broad man with skin the darkest brown I'd ever seen strode into the room.

"Take these ladies to a room and make sure they have plenty of water to wash with, and clean clothing." Rahab smiled at me, her kohl-lined eyes conveying humor at our unsightly garments. "We will talk in the morning."

Ohel nodded and led us to a room that boasted a luxurious bed swathed in fine linens. After a few moments, he returned with an enormous pot of water, thick cloth for drying our bodies, and two clean linen tunics. As soon as the door closed behind him, Moriyah and I stripped. Removing the tight band around my swollen belly was bliss; my entire body sighed at the freedom from the painful binding. Moriyah and I scrubbed our skin pink, turning the pot of water a murky brown. I hoped Rahab did not mind that the wood floor of her home was covered with slimy muck from our bath. After slipping the clean tunics over our heads and moaning at the softness of the linen against our bruised bodies, Moriyah and I lay down on the lush bed and stared at the ceiling. I groaned at the impossible softness and the contrast to sleeping on cave floors, dirt under trees, and Mishabel's flat pallet.

"I am never, never leaving this bed," said Moriyah, patting the soft linens on either side of her body. "Ever."

"That makes two of us." We laughed together freely, as if we had not been prisoners in a temple brothel only two hours before and dreading the horrors of tomorrow.

"Alanah?" Moriyah turned onto her side, her silvery eyes shining in the flicker of the oil lamp next to the bed. "There are times when I know things. I just have a sense of the answers to questions deep in my bones, sometimes before the questions are even asked."

This I had guessed from the first time I'd sensed her uncanny eyes on me.

"But today—" she continued, her voice sounding more like a little girl's than I'd ever heard. "I just don't understand. How are we here? How is it that your mother and your sister found us? Rescued us?"

I blew out a regretful breath and placed my hand on the swell of my belly. "Yahweh," I answered as I gave silent, chastened thanks to the One who I'd spent hours berating earlier tonight. "It can only be Yahweh."

34

My eyes popped open as Rahab's servant, Ohel, pulled the scarlet curtain away from the window and sunlight spilled across the floor. The huge man did not look at me but said, "A meal is waiting for you," in a low tone and then left the room before I had a chance to react to the strangeness of his presence.

I toed Moriyah's leg. "Wake up, sleepy." She moaned and threw an arm over her face.

"Leave me be. I told you I am not leaving this bed."

I laughed. "All right, but I smell food."

She rasped a little growl but sat up. "Only food could make me get up. I have never slept on anything so comfortable in my life."

My mind went back to the pallet in Tobiah's tent. True, it had not been the softest bed, but I had never been more comfortable, more surrendered, than while lying in his arms. I brushed away the bittersweet memory. No use dwelling on fleeting shadows.

Two dresses had been left on a chair in the corner. I was

hesitant to take off the linen tunic, but perhaps the thin garment was meant only for sleeping. Rahab's husband must be quite wealthy to afford such decadence. As I slipped the soft green dress over my head, I wondered whether he would be angry about taking in two ragged women fleeing the temple.

"It may be too long, but this is the most beautiful thing I have ever worn." Moriyah smoothed the striped blue and white fabric of her dress against her narrow hips with excitement in her eyes. "Do you think your sister means for me to keep it? It would not be difficult to trim it shorter, would it?"

"I don't know. I have only made one garment in my life." Shrugging off the memory of the tunic I had made for Tobiah, I tied a cord around her waist, pilfered from the scarlet curtain that hung at the window, and billowed the fabric out around the makeshift belt until she was able to walk without tripping.

"Oh, my mother is a wonderful seamstress. She would love to—" Moriyah stopped, her eyes flooding.

I put my arms around her and she pressed her forehead into my shoulder. "Don't give up hope. You will see your mother again."

She sniffed and nodded but kept her head down.

I slipped a finger under her chin and forced her to look at me. "We are here. In the home of my sister. Is that not a miracle? Yahweh has brought us this far, has he not?"

I have a plan, the Voice had said the night I'd been healed from the snakebite. Was this all part of his plan somehow?

A knock sounded before the door opened and my mother stepped inside, her presence causing my stomach to contract with nerves. "I'm glad you girls are finally awake."

My mother smiled at Moriyah, seeming to avoid my gaze. "We have not been properly introduced, Moriyah. My name is Tashara."

"I am so grateful to you, Tashara, for saving us from that

awful place." Moriyah twisted the tassel of her red-cord belt. "If you hadn't come . . ."

My mother placed her hand on Moriyah's shoulder. "I was not about to leave you both there. As soon as I recognized Alanah and realized what Mishabel planned, I knew what I had to do. Thankfully, Dayatana owed me a great debt." She patted Moriyah's face, revealing a dark tattoo on the back of her hand, one identical to the old priestess who had purchased us in the market—the mark of her identity as property of Ba'al and Ashtoreth. "You are a beautiful girl. How did you ever pass for a boy? Even with your hair chopped like that?"

Grinning, Moriyah displayed her masculine stride for my mother. "Alanah taught me," she said. "But I perfected it."

My mother laughed and the sound tugged at my memory with a mixture of longing and irritation. "Well, you won't have to use your skills here. Rahab and Ohel have a wonderful meal prepared for you. May I have a few minutes alone with Alanah?"

It took every bit of my strength to not leave as well, but I stayed rooted to the ground as my mother closed the door behind Moriyah. She stood with her back to me for a few moments before turning.

"We must talk, daughter."

I flinched at the word. "I have little to say."

"You are angry with me," she said, arms folded across her chest.

I matched her guarded stance. "You abandoned me."

She winced and then dug her fingers into her bright curls on either side of her face, her expression tormented. "It was agony. Leaving you there. If I had turned a dagger on my heart and plunged it in a thousand times, it would not match the pain. I did not want to go. I fought it for weeks. But I was near to showing with Rahab, and your father was desperate."

I wrinkled my brow. "He knew?"

"No." She sighed. "I hid it well. But the rains had been gone for a long, long time. After those prophets came through town, the land dried up and hot winds blew every trace of green away. Most of his crops were languishing, and there was no sign of a reprieve. He was desperate enough to wish that he had something to give to Baal, an offering."

Rahab. She ran to save my sister from death? "But why—"

"Did I not take you? Because he adored you, carried you about like a doll from the moment you were born. I knew he would never give you up. If I hadn't been absolutely certain, I would not have left. I have never seen a father love a daughter so much—ever."

She came closer, her steps tentative, and then slowly reached out to put a hand on my cheek. The feel of my mother's hand, gentle on my face, brought a rush of unbidden memories. "I could not have made it to Jericho with you. You were too small and too many dangers lay along the path. My only option was to run."

I searched her face. Now that I stood in front of her, that face was completely familiar to me. A few flickering memories had clarified in my mind as she spoke: her lullabies, walking with her among the olive trees, my father slinging me over his shoulder with a hearty laugh, even tracing that hideous tattoo on her hand with my small fingertips and asking her what it meant.

"Why did you come here?" I said. "To Jericho? Back to the temple? Wasn't Rahab in just as much danger here?"

She lifted her chin, an echo of my own stubbornness in her expression. "It wasn't my intention to go back to the temple. This was where my parents had settled after fleeing the Hittites when I was just a little girl."

I lifted a brow. "But if your parents were here, then why . . . ?"

"My father sold me to the temple when I was thirteen."

Moriyah's age. My heart bled at the thought. "How? How could he do such a thing?"

She shrugged. "My family was starving. A plague had swept through the entire country, decimating thousands. I had five younger brothers and sisters who needed food. There were no marriage prospects for me, so I was sold."

My mind screamed out against the injustice, the revulsion. Girls, no more than a commodity, were sold every day, sometimes to protect the family, other times to further a father's fortune. It was the way of this land that I sprang from. A land where human life was held in such little esteem that infants were fed to a fire to placate greedy gods.

Yahweh's laws insisted that women be protected, daughters not be sold as slaves, and men stay faithful to their own wives. I longed to be there, among the Hebrews, where my baby would be protected from such evils. But in this city, the level of degradation seemed to know no bounds.

I would do anything, anything in my power, to protect this life inside me. I would never allow anything to befall this child, even if it meant losing my own life. My mother's justifications for leaving did not satisfy. "You should have taken me."

She shook her head. "I could not."

"Why? You could have paid a traveling caravan to escort you, found one with a few women perhaps, so you would have been safe—*we* would have been safe."

"I knew they would not allow it."

"Who would not?"

"The head priestess."

"I thought you came back here to be with your family."

Her voice quivered. "It was my hope that they would welcome me . . ."

"But they refused?"

"They did. They still could not afford to take me on, especially with Rahab on the way. I knew this was a real possibility when I left. One child was enough. Two would have been out of the question."

"So you went back."

Guilt hung heavy on her face, pulling at the corners of her eyes. Something I had noticed almost immediately when she'd shown up in that dark room—a depth of sadness that haunted even her laughter.

"I did. I wished I could have found a way. It was all I knew, other than your father. I met him here, you know, in Jericho, soon after his first wife died. Did you know that?"

"No. He never spoke of you except to say that you had run back to prostitution."

She paused, taking a trembling breath. "I deserved that. I am sorry that I hurt him, but I did what I felt was right at the time. Perhaps I handled it poorly, did not give him credit. He cared for you well, didn't he?"

She put up a hand again, to caress my cheek, but I stepped back.

"My father took care of me. He protected me, sometimes even from my brothers, but he could not take the place of the mother who left me. You have no idea the pain you caused. The isolation, the mocking that I endured at the hands of the people in the village. I was 'the daughter even the whore didn't want.'"

Tears filled her eyes, but I ignored them. The words begged for release, I'd held them in too long. "Perhaps you thought you were doing what was best for me, but what you did, abandoning me, was worse than if I had been offered to Baal."

My mother wept, the kohl around her eyes dripping a black stream onto her pale yellow dress. I was almost glad for it; for as many tears as I had shed as a child, she deserved to weep. My breath was coming fast, and I threw my words like knives at her, each tip a little sharper.

"You left me. Alone. In a village that despised me. With a father who saw me only as a reminder of your abandonment. You stole my childhood, left me nothing, and walked away. I will never leave my baby." I placed my hand over my belly and my mother's eyes followed. I watched understanding dawn on her face. "I will never leave this child in the care of someone else, for anything. My heart beats for the child."

She backed away, slowly, as if unsure of her balance, then turned and walked to the doorway. With a hand on the latch, she paused. "My heart has always beat for you, and for Rahab, as much as yours does for the child you carry. Perhaps I made the wrong choice." She looked back over her shoulder, determination in the set of her jaw. "I know you have suffered, and Rahab has suffered. But you are alive, and Rahab is alive, and for that I cannot regret my decision."

35

TOBIAH

27 SHEVAT
1407 BC
CAMP AT ABEL-SHITTIM

The fire cracked and popped, sparks shattering from one of the logs as it disintegrated and tumbled into the ashes of its predecessors. Smoke burned my eyes as I stared into the glowing embers, wishing I could blink away the memories they stirred of the fire in Alanah's eyes during the last of our hunts together six months ago—the day we came across the little fox in the woods and shut out the rest of the world beneath the tamarisk tree.

Tzipi startled me with a toe into my back. "You planning to guard that fire all day?"

I ignored her and leaned back on my palms, stretching my legs out as if settling in. There wasn't much else I *could* do. The thrill of victory over the forces of Bashan had long melted into boredom. We'd been camped here on this large plain at

257

the foot of a mountain range for months, watching the leaves fade and wither, shivering beneath our blankets as the snow glazed the tops of the nearest peaks with white, and then into a new season where an astounding number of birds traveled north above our heads. The river to the west had begun to rise as the snows melted, hurrying through the valley on its pointless rush to the Salt Sea.

"Tobiah," she insisted.

My sister's persistence had become grating. For the thousandth time I wished Shimon were here to diffuse her relentless nagging.

"What do you want, Tzipi? Are you here just to harass me over Keziah again?"

"No." She returned my scowl. "I want you to come with me to the traders that arrived yesterday, to see if I can barter some spices for these wool blankets." She lifted a bundle in her hands to give testament to the statement.

"Oh." I relaxed my fisted hands on my thighs. Perhaps for once I might avoid the cycle of arguments she constantly instigated. She didn't need a guard to go to the traders' wagons, her tongue was sharper than any sword lately, honed by grief over Shimon and Moriyah.

"But now that you bring up the subject—" She tucked the blankets beneath her arm with a pat.

"Tzipi . . ." Her name came out like a growl.

She lifted a palm like a shield. "Brother, I understand you are still upset over that Canaanite woman—"

Another protest kindled in my throat.

She pursed her lips. "I mean . . . over Alanah. But how much longer will this go on? She is not coming back and Keziah has been more than patient. She has loved you since we were children, Tobiah. She will be a good wife to you. You know this."

I did know this. Keziah was everything a man could want in a woman. Sweet-natured, intelligent, attractive, Torah-abiding—and she had waited, far longer than I had expected.

Tzipi knelt down beside me. "I know I have been no better than a crow cackling in your ear over this, Tobiah. But I want what is best for you. You need a wife. You need a partner, like I had in Shimon. These battles will come to an end. You will not be a warrior forever." She pointed toward the river in the west. "Over there is a new life. A home. Land where we can raise our children in the knowledge of Yahweh, just as our parents wanted. Let the past go and cross into your future. It is time to do the right thing."

The right thing. I had always done the right thing. After my brothers wasted their lives on rebellion, my parents were heartbroken. Even as a four-year-old boy, I'd been keenly aware of the change, especially in my mother. She had wasted away to nothing, many days refusing to eat and spending her days lying on her pallet, vacant-eyed, staring into the void.

There were days she had rallied, smiling and chatting with us around the fire, but her laughter was hollow, as if all her joy had disintegrated. Less than three years later, she'd walked off a cliff.

My father had lasted only a few more years. If his spirit was crippled by his children's and grandchildren's deaths, my mother's had destroyed it. It didn't matter that I had always obeyed him, protected my sister like a lion, and never spoken a word of disrespect to either of them. It wasn't enough to keep him from embracing death with both arms.

My sister reached over to ruffle my hair. "Come now. What's the use of having a huge bear of a brother if he won't protect me from those menacing traders?"

"I've heard most of those new traders are women, Moabite women, and a few Midianites as well."

"Truly?"

I nodded. The Moabites must be cowards to send in their

women to do their trading. Although after the way we had crushed Og's fearsome army, I could barely blame them.

She shrugged a shoulder. "I would still feel safer if you came with me. You never know what could happen."

"You are probably right." I allowed a teasing smile to crawl across my lips. "Women are far more dangerous anyhow."

I had always stayed away from the traders that frequented the edges of our camps and was surprised at the amount of wooden idols brazenly displayed on the tables. Surely no Hebrew would buy such a thing, especially in full view of the Cloud hovering over the mountains to the east, as if keeping an eye on the dealings. The strong smell of exotic spices stung my eyes as Tzipi fingered a headscarf with intricate purple embroidery.

"Do you like it? What do you have to trade?" said a Midianite woman behind the table. Her eyes were heavily rimmed in green and black kohl, and gold rings lined her ear from top to bottom. I attempted to keep my eyes only on her face, but the dress she wore was practically sheer on top and tied at the shoulders with only the thinnest of straps.

Tzipi glared at her but kept stroking the headscarf. "I have a wool blanket, but this scarf is not worth such fine craftsmanship."

"What do you mean?" asked the woman. "This scarf was made by the Phoenicians, the masters of purple dye. They harvest a snail that emits this color and have perfected the process to ensure complete saturation. There is no other color that comes close to its beauty, do you not agree?" She raised a brow, challenging Tzipi to barter back. Once the spices my sister had been searching for were included, the deal was completed with ease. Tzipi turned away with satisfaction on her lips and the expensive headscarf tucked in her basket.

Before I could follow Tzipi into the crush of people gathered around the traders' wagons, the woman slipped out from behind her wagon and grabbed my arm. "Will you be coming tonight? There is to be a festival, over there." She pointed to the south, where the acacias grew in dense groves along the foothills. She looked me up and down, grazing my arms, chest, and face with unapologetic appreciation.

The hair on the back of my neck stood on end. "No, I will not be coming. I have a family to tend to."

"A wife?" She tilted her chin to the side and peered at me.

The word pierced me. "No."

"Surely a strong man like you has a wife?" She put a hand on my bicep, and I felt it flex without conscious thought. Her eyes glittered, black and dangerous.

A smile curled on her lips and she raised both brows. "Come," she said, honey in her tone, "we are all related, are we not, sons and daughters of our father Avraham?"

Yes, the Midianites were related to us, descended from Ketubah, Avraham's concubine. Illegitimate relations, and far from the worship of Yahweh.

Her teeth tugged at her lower lip as she stroked the beads that hung low around her neck, drawing my eyes where they should not go. "Perhaps we can find a way to meet later?"

The ache for Alanah had not ebbed since she had walked out of my life months ago, an ache that even the bloody battle of Bashan did not assuage. I missed everything about her, the curve of her full lower lip, those bewitching eyes full of mischief and allure, the smell of her skin . . . Perhaps Tzipi was right that I needed another woman to wash my mind of her—

No. This Midianite woman offered only a temporary solution to a lifelong problem, a solution that would cause me only more pain. This was certainly not the right way to erase my cravings for Alanah, and surprisingly I had no desire to do so, nor to entertain thoughts of replacing my wife with another. Perhaps I'd consider such a thing after we had reclaimed Avraham's inheritance, but for now my place was alongside my brothers, sword in hand.

I jerked away from the Midianite woman's clutch. "Take your wares somewhere else, they cost more than I am willing to pay."

I walked straight west, pushing through the long grass until I could walk no more and the swollen river blocked my escape. The plains across the river were so green, so lush, it was almost painful to look and not be able to cross right away. The Promised Land my father had died before seeing was right there, in front of me now.

The river rushed through the landscape, threading between us and Jericho. I squinted at the city I knew lay far off in the distance at the foot of the western hills, a city rumored to be ringed by two fortress walls, guarded day and night by a huge standing army.

After seeing Og's forces trod into the dirt by our own, with few casualties on our side, I had no doubt Jericho would be taken and, with the rush of frustration in my veins running as high as the water below me, I could not wait to plunge into the fray.

36

ALANAH

27 SHEVAT
1407 BC

Arms folded, I leaned on the worn stone sill. A breeze caressed my face, bringing with it the fragrance of the almond groves bursting with soft pink blossoms as I stared off to the east. Rahab's inn was built against the high outer wall of Jericho, her windows exposing the view toward the orange hills of Moab off in the distance and, below them, although too far away to see, the Hebrews' encampment. Jericho's army lay between us, blocking any lingering idea I had of returning Moriyah to her family and giving truth to the rumors: The Hebrews were coming. *Tobiah is coming.*

Moriyah squeezed in next to me and patted my belly. "How much longer until she comes?"

I laughed at her dogged insistence that this squirming, kicking person inside me was female. "Not too much longer, I hope. This baby is a warrior, I assure you. My insides are one large

263

bruise." I arched my spine and rubbed my lower back, where a throbbing ache had taken up residence since yesterday.

"Well, *she* will be just like her *ima*, then." Moriyah nudged me with her elbow. "Look at the Cloud over there. It's so clear today. I think I see the sun sparkling off the river."

The column of unearthly swirling colors hovered over the tallest peak directly east of us and, although it seemed small from where I stood, I knew its actual size well. Every morning for four months I had watched it, hoping it would move closer, signaling that the Hebrews were on the move. Every day it stayed anchored to the top of the ridge. *Why are they waiting?*

"When will they come?" Moriyah echoed my thoughts.

"If I knew"—I gestured behind me, in the direction of the palace—"the king of Jericho would be first in line to hear the answer, I am sure."

My mother had informed me that the city practically vibrated with tension. Wild rumors abounded in the streets—tales of the vicious Hebrews and how they bested Pharaoh by smothering every firstborn in Egypt by hand, how they used powerful spells to walk through the sea on dry land, and how they destroyed King Og with fire from the magic box they carried at the center of their multitude. Mosheh was heralded as an ageless sorcerer with control over the glowing storm cloud, and Yehoshua, a giant descended from Ba'al himself.

After seeing the swirling Cloud with my own eyes and comprehending Yahweh's power, the idea that Ba'al was the god of storms was almost laughable. There was only one God who had commanded the sea to split in two and one God who had crippled Egypt with hail and fire. And that God was no deaf and mute idol of wood and stone. He spoke to me. He heard me in the river. He was alive.

I corrected each convoluted rumor with the truth as far as I understood it and told Rahab and my mother of my own encounter with the God who had spoken directly to my heart. The distinct scars from the snakebites on my leg testified to the truth of my healing, but I suspected both of them had trouble reconciling everything they had known with my impossible experiences with the Hebrews.

"They *are* coming, Moriyah," I said, placing my hand over hers on the windowsill. "I can feel it in my bones. You will embrace your family soon." I only hoped they would not hold it against her that she had been living in a brothel.

At first, I had attributed Rahab's fine clothing and beautiful furnishings to a wealthy husband, but it did not take long to realize that she was unmarried, and where exactly the gold and silver came from. The back of her hand was tattooed with the same mark as my mother's—the crescent moon embracing the sun-wheel, the symbol of Ba'al and his consort, Ashtoreth. Rahab had been a temple prostitute at one time as well.

This inn was situated near the gates of the city and guests were lodged in the rooms below us, where Rahab and a few other women tended to their comfort. Although Rahab was discreet with her business, and Ohel guarded us and Rahab's two little girls when she was gone, Moriyah was anything but ignorant.

But we truly had no other place to go. The day after my mother rescued us, she had returned to her husband's citrus orchard outside the gates and discovered that Mishabel had offered the guards a special prize for finding one red-haired woman and one raven-haired girl. We were trapped inside Jericho's walls. Trapped inside Rahab's home, no matter what disgusting things went on below us.

For her part, Rahab was unrepentant when I confronted her, to the point of flippancy, but I could see the toll this life had taken on her. Although she was three years younger than I, she seemed aged beyond me, beaten down by the life she led and the burden of the business she'd built with her own degradation. The same shadows haunted her brown eyes that haunted my mother's—regret, shame, loss. All things I was well acquainted with.

My ambivalence toward my mother's presence was a constant thorn beneath my skin. Though my heart flipped with mystifying delight whenever she visited, I could not bring myself to say more than a few words to her and, more often than not, escaped to the other room when she came.

Moriyah intruded into my thoughts with the last words I expected. "Tobiah is coming too. Perhaps he will be here for his daughter's birth."

There was nothing I wanted more than for her hopeful words to be true. Every night I lay in my comfortable bed, wishing to be in Tobiah's arms instead, wandering through every moment of our brief months together—hunting, laughing, reveling in our oneness.

I exhaled. "Moriyah. He has surely been married to Keziah for months. He probably already has another child on the way." I winced at my own conclusion. "He will want nothing to do with me, or this one." I covered my belly with a hand, as if I could protect the child from the truth, but my insides twisted into knots until I nearly groaned.

"That is a lie. And you know it is." She pushed away from the window with a scowl. "I'm going to entertain Amaya and Lissa. At least they listen to me." Rahab's two small girls adored Moriyah and were never far from her side.

I turned to apologize for my brusqueness, but the twisting inside me suddenly became a deep pressure that shot up my back with the force of a bolt of lightning. I bent forward, gasping for breath.

Moriyah's eyes locked on mine. "I'll go get Ohel," she said. "You need Rahab."

I grunted as a wave of pain reverberated through my body, along with a fresh realization. "And Tashara," I ground out through my teeth as I sank onto the bed. "I need my mother."

An arrow through the shoulder was nothing. I would take ten arrows if it meant this fiery pain would cease—twenty! I hissed out a loud breath through my teeth and then bore down as Rahab commanded. It was too dangerous to summon a midwife; my mother and sister had to do. If anything good came of their profession, it was experience birthing children.

"The top of the head is visible, Alanah," said Rahab. "You are doing well."

Shira's melodic voice sprang to my mind, and I longed for her calm presence and the wisdom built from nearly forty years of guiding children to mothers' arms. What if something went wrong? Would Rahab know what to do? What if the child did not breathe? Another contraction seized my body in its maniacal grip and I bit my lip against screaming out, tasting blood from the effort.

Rahab let out a little gasp of breath, a sound of surprise and confusion. My mother tilted her head to examine what had shocked my sister, and her eyes widened as her jaw dropped.

"What is it?" My heart beat a frantic warning signal. "What's wrong with the baby?"

"The baby is fine," said my mother with a tight smile. "Keep pushing."

I glanced back and forth between the two women. Their eyes guarded secrets. "You are lying! She's dead, isn't she?" My voice went shrill, but I could not control the rise of panic boiling higher and higher. "I knew it! I killed her too!"

"Alanah." My mother leaned down, putting both hands on either side of my face. "*Kalanit*. Hush."

The endearment reached into my earliest childhood memories, brushing its soft fingers along my mind like the petals of a *kalanit*, one of the graceful flowers that washed the highlands in red-headed beauty every spring—the flowers my mother had always compared me to as she whispered love into my ear at bedtime. Although I had not heard her nickname for me since I was three years old, the sound of it washed over me like a cool stream. I blinked acceptance of her quiet command.

"Good," she said. "Now push. I want to meet my grandchild."

After a few more excruciating pushes, the baby slid free of my body. Release thrummed through me, followed by immediate terror. Why were Rahab and my mother so quiet? Where was the baby's cry?

"Alanah. Look." Rahab gestured for me to move closer to the end of the bed. "You must see this."

The sight that met my eyes was beyond comprehension. My baby squirmed on the soft blanket where Rahab had placed her. But the tiny body was fully enclosed in a transparent sac. She yawned and flexed her foot, as if unaware that she had emerged from the womb.

"It's a sign," whispered my mother. "A sign from the gods."

"No." I smiled through tears that I could do nothing to prevent and suddenly had no desire to stop. "It is a sign from the One True God. He heard my prayers and preserved this child. He was with her. He enclosed her in his protection."

Rahab pressed a long fingernail against the membrane that surrounded the infant and it burst, releasing a gush of waters. After freeing the baby from the film that clung to her, she lifted her up to me, just as the tiny girl voiced her displeasure at being deprived of her warm enclosure. I curled her against my skin, feeling as if my heart were beating outside my body. A rush of enveloping love spread through me as I examined her tiny features with one finger; her snubbed little nose, the full bottom lip that pressed out from beneath a thin one—just like mine—eyes the same shape as the man I loved, and the damp traces of wispy red curls smashed against her scalp.

"My daughter," I whispered. "Natanyah. My gift from Yahweh."

37

25 ADAR
1406 BC

Natanyah squawked beside me, grasping the air with tiny fists, entertained by the shaft of sunlight that flooded across the bed. A surge of emotion swelled in my throat, until my eyes were swimming. I was smitten. Her every sniffle and coo put me on alert. I heard them even in my sleep. She was everything good and beautiful and graceful wrapped into one sweet bundle of flailing arms and legs. She turned her face toward me, perhaps distracted by the sway of shadows and light cast by the crimson curtain fluttering next to the open window. No—it was me she watched, her large eyes, still a muddle of midnight blue after three weeks, glittering. We stared at each other, both of us captivated. If only Tobiah could see her just once—

Rahab entered the room, interrupting my fruitless yearning. "It's about time you two layabouts awakened. Moriyah has prepared a delicious meal with no one to eat it." Moriyah had been thrilled to learn cooking from Ohel, whose knowledge of herbs, spices, and many exotic ingredients fascinated the girl.

Since that first taste of pomegranate during our escape, she'd been nearly obsessed with discovering every new flavor this land had to offer.

"Where are Amaya and Lissa?"

"The girls went with *Ima* and Ohel to the market this morning. The early crops are coming in, so they went to fetch some barley."

I frowned, unable to hide my disdain about the origin of the silver that paid for that barley.

"Don't make that face. I have no other way to provide for my girls." Rahab knelt down to caress Natanyah's downy head, already sprouting fine red curls.

"Perhaps you will meet someone—"

"No." She put up a palm. "I won't live the life our mother does. Scrabbling in the dirt with some lonely farmer, relying on the gods' miserly rainfalls to make enough money to survive." She placed her chin on her bare shoulder, casting her gaze around the room. "My girls have a nice home here—their every need is taken care of, they have beautiful clothing and food brought from every corner of the world. It's a small price to pay for their comfort and safety."

"No, it is a horrible price to pay. I have seen another way." I pulled on her hand, forced her to face me. "Tobiah gave up everything to ensure that I was protected by the laws of Yahweh. He loved me, even though I was his enemy—" My voice choked, but I cleared the emotion away. "And I have heard the voice of the Creator, willing to heal me, even though I set out to kill his people. And look—" I brushed my palm over my daughter's soft head. "Look how he took care of us."

Rahab's brown eyes filled with tears. "Perhaps there is such grace among the Hebrews, but here . . ." The shadows weighted her gaze again. "Here, there is nothing for me but this life."

"And Amaya and Lissa? What will be their fate? Watching

271

the stream of men flow in and out downstairs as they grow older? What if one of those men harms them?"

She shook her head, the wild curls bouncing. "No. That is why I employ Ohel. He ensures the girls are occupied and safe when I . . . entertain."

My stomach flipped. "They are tiny now, but do you think they will remain ignorant? Do you not think they will question all this?" I swept my hand around in a circle, gesturing to the richly appointed curtains, the intricate wall-hangings from Egypt, the patterned rugs, and finally, the gold jewelry gracing Rahab's neck and the extravagantly woven dress she wore.

Rahab folded her arms across her chest, displaying our familial obstinate jaw-set. "I have done what I had to do. Just as you have done."

I sighed. "Perhaps. But I have learned that there is always a choice, and Yahweh has a plan. Even if I am not among the Hebrews, there is a reason for all of this. I know it. Otherwise, I would not have been kidnapped and ended up here practically at your threshold, and our mother would not have recognized me."

Rahab's glare began to melt, until a forlorn expression crossed her face—a face that seemed so much older than it should, older than mine in many respects. "Well then, your God, this Yahweh, had better show up soon, because I am tired. If I could give it up and just run this house as an inn, I would do it. But my reputation goes before me, visitors want more than just a bed to sleep in and a meal. I have tried to stop, I have, but I am afraid. And who would ever want to marry me?"

"I know, sister." I could not imagine the humiliation Rahab had endured, but I understood desperation, worthlessness. I covered her hand with my own. "I know."

I had known nothing of this sister; my mother had fled the farm before my father even knew she was pregnant. But in the past few months we had kindled a friendship—a stilted one at first, neither of us knowing how to reconcile the gap between us, but something that had been broken seemed to be mending on its own. Something I had not even known was missing from my life.

"Why? Why did you choose this path, Rahab?"

A pained look contorted her face. "I was snatched, one day in an alley when my stepfather brought me into town to sell olives from our groves. I had sneaked off to chase a stray cat. One of the temple guards saw me and took me. I was not even twelve. I was hidden inside the compound, the same one you were imprisoned in." She pulled at the necklace around her throat as if it suffocated her suddenly. "Over the next few months, they convinced me it was what I wanted. When my mother . . . our mother . . . found me and begged me to come home, I sneered at her and turned my back on her."

"How did you get away from the temple, if you were so convinced that it was the life you wanted?"

"I got pregnant."

"With Amaya?"

She shook her head. "The first one . . . they took it. Before I even held him in my arms." She turned her face away. "He was offered to Ba'al the same day."

The horrific memories of the sacrifices filled my senses again, plunging me back into the sights and smells of evil. Rahab had lost a child to such barbarity? I gripped her hand, wishing I had more than platitudes to offer.

She sniffed, smiling and blinking away the evidence of grief. "Then, when I became pregnant with Amaya, I asked to be set free."

"And the head priestess? Why did she let you go without a fight?"

"A few weeks before, I'd overheard two of the priests planning to assassinate the king. He owed me a favor for saving his life. Mishabel was forced to go along with his demand for my freedom. If she had protested, it would have brought attention to the fact that she was most probably part of the plot. Instead, she had to let me go, publicly thank me for my service to the king, and congratulate me after he gifted me a chest full of gold and jewels. I bought this old inn with my reward, since the proximity to the gate makes for a steady stream of customers."

I winced at the casual indifference with which she described her trade. "Since I have a head for business, I've done well for myself, as you can see. But Mishabel would do anything to get back at me for the deaths of her two favorite priests—another reason I employ Ohel."

The door opened and my mother strode inside, holding Lissa in one arm and gripping Amaya's hand with the other. Two dark-haired men followed her, their wide eyes taking in the well-appointed room. Almost as one, Rahab and I moved to stand in the doorway between the rooms, between the men and my infant daughter. Behind the strangers, Ohel stepped inside and shut the door, the stony expression on his face unreadable. Moriyah stood off to the side, a basket of fresh bread in her hands, shrinking against the wall as if she could melt into the mud brick to hide. If only she could.

"Who are these men, Mother?" The authority in Rahab's voice was unmistakable—this sister of mine had no fear.

Instead of answering Rahab, my mother turned to me. "Alanah, you must listen to what these men have to say."

What tale had these men spun that had persuaded my mother to bring them here? What if they were spies for Mishabel? "Mother, why did you bring them here? What if they tell—"

"Go ahead, Shaul," she interrupted, gesturing toward the taller of the two men. "This is the daughter I told you of."

The men glanced at each other, wide-eyed, before the one called Shaul stepped forward, his brown eyes boring through me with an intensity that nearly made me step backward. "Shalom. We have come here from the land across the river."

Were they Moabites on the run from Yehoshua's army? Their tunics were similar to Ohel's, but something about the way Shaul spoke, slow and careful, as if searching for the correct words, along with the way the younger man shifted from foot to foot, gave me pause. I searched their clean-shaven faces for signs of deceit. A long scratch along Shaul's jaw caught my attention, as if he'd nicked himself with a blade like a man unused to shaving his beard.

With a quick glance at the open window, Shaul allowed his voice to drop low, slipping into a dialect with which I was very familiar, one I had heard every day for the four best months of my life. "We are Hebrews. And we are coming to take this city."

38

The men ate the meal Moriyah had prepared as I fidgeted in my seat, desperate for news of the Hebrews. The idea that Hebrew men sat at my sister's table, men who could possibly know Tobiah, swirled around inside my head until a question bubbled out of me. "How long until they come?"

They startled at my use of their own dialect.

Shaul raised a thick black brow. "So, it's true, what your mother said—you were among us?"

"I was. I was married to Tobiah, of the clan of Shelani, tribe of Yehudah."

Shaul scratched his chin, scowling as if the sensation of being clean-shaven annoyed him. "I don't know him. Do you, Peniah?"

The younger man shook his head. He seemed almost loath to speak to any of us, and his dark eyes roamed the room with evident disgust, touching on the rich fabrics, the Egyptian-style furnishings, and the exquisite imported bowl that contained the well-spiced lamb he was devouring like a ravenous lion. Although Rahab's profession disgusted me equally, I felt a spike of defensiveness for his dismissal of my sister.

Shaul asked for the story of how I came to be with the

276

Hebrews and how Moriyah and I had ended up in Jericho, since my mother had given him only the barest of details. As I recounted the tale, Shaul's jaw slackened and even Peniah stopped eating long enough to ask how we could have possibly escaped notice as we ran through the countryside. Shaul laughed when I described our days dressed as boys and our escape from the furious vintner. Some of the tension that had entered with the Hebrews dissipated with the telling, so, with a proud little smile, Moriyah went to put a fussy Natanyah to sleep in the other room.

"Tell us," said Rahab after Moriyah closed the door, "what do you mean that the Hebrews are coming to take this city? When?"

"We have not been told when, only that it will happen. We have been sent, by Yehoshua himself"—Shaul lifted his chin, obviously full of pride that he had been chosen from all the men of Israel—"to spy out this city and report back as soon as possible. Our mission is secret. Only Yehoshua knows we have come."

Rahab refilled Peniah's wine cup. "Do you actually think you can take this city?"

He looked her up and down with a little smirk, one that trumpeted his opinion of her. "Edrei, the stronghold of King Og, was no match for our army, and Heshbon, the mighty fortress of Sichon and its surrounding cities, are now inhabited by Hebrew families. Yahweh goes before us. This city will fall as well, one way or the other. Even the treachery of the Moabites could not deter us."

"The Moabites? I thought Mosheh wanted to avoid conflict with them. Aren't they related to Avraham as well?"

"Indeed they are," said Shaul. "But the Moabites and Midianites conspired together to send in their women to ensnare our men and entice them into worshipping their foul gods. Sent their own wives in as traders to trick us into participating in their perverted practices. Unfortunately, many fell victim to the ploy." His eyes narrowed as he thunked his cup onto the table, red wine splashing over the lip. "Nearly twenty-four thousand of our own were struck down as a result of their rebellion. A final culling of the multitude before we set foot into the land."

I barely restrained a gasp. Twenty-four thousand? Was Tobiah among those losses? Surely not. Tobiah had nothing but respect for women, and the laws of Mosheh. I could not imagine him being lured in such a way. Besides, he must be married to Keziah by now. He would be safe. He must be safe.

Struck with a sudden need to see my daughter and to escape the red-tinged shadows of the battlefield that swirled in my head, I left the room, furious at the tears that burned behind my eyes.

I found Natanyah snuggled against Moriyah on the bed, asleep with her little arms over her head and sweet mouth pursed. How did the sea of love I felt for such a tiny being expand its borders every time I saw her? After kissing her forehead, I sat next to the bed, leaning against the wall and folding my arms across my bent knees. I didn't have the heart to say anything to Moriyah about the devastating losses the Hebrews had sustained.

Rahab had trimmed the girl's hair into a more attractive style, and she had grown in the few months since we'd been captive in this house, womanly curves beginning to fill out her figure. Her family would barely recognize her.

"Can you believe it?" Moriyah whispered, her silver-gray eyes shimmering with excitement. "Hebrew men, here, in this house? Yahweh must be providing a way for us to return home."

Did I have a home anymore? Tobiah had been my home for those months among the Hebrews, and the house I had been born in had been given to Dagan. I was Canaanite, no longer married to a Hebrew who would protect me. If the Israelite army came through to destroy this town, would I be counted among the dead? Would Natanyah? Moriyah?

No. At the least, I must find a way to return Moriyah to Tzipi and Tobiah. Would the spies take her with them? A flutter of regret at sending her away unfurled itself in my chest. I had come to love this Hebrew girl. Her guileless ways, her strange near-prophetic perceptions, her willingness to forgive me when there was no reason to do so . . . She seemed almost like a daughter to me now, even if I was only a few years older than she.

I stood quickly and strode back into the room where the men still sat around the table with Rahab and my mother, interrupting their conversation. "You must take Moriyah with you. She needs to be back among her people."

"We cannot. I don't even know how we will make it out of here alive." Shaul crossed his arms. "We were spotted in the marketplace, I am sure of it. There were two men watching us very closely as we spoke with your mother. It's one of the reasons we stopped here to ask for lodging, hoping to make it seem that we were soliciting a woman, not spying for the enemy."

Peniah wiped his lips with the back of a hand. "There is no way we could escape with a girl between us, even dressed like a boy. We will have to find a way around Jercho's army." He gestured to the east. "We traveled along the shore of the Salt Sea in the middle of the night to approach from the south. Getting out of this city and back across the river will be difficult enough."

"I have a better idea," Rahab interjected. "Save all of us."

Shaul laughed. "If we cannot take one girl, we certainly cannot take all of you."

"No, I do not mean now." My sister's brown eyes sparkled. "When you return, you must spare this household."

"And how do you propose we do that?"

"There must be some sort of signal we can make, to ensure that your people know to spare us."

My mother put a hand on Rahab's arm. "How do we even know that they will succeed? Jericho has been attacked before, and never has she been taken."

"Were you not listening, Mother?" said Rahab. "They defeated Og, Sihon, the Midianites, and numerous other armies that came against them. Not to mention that Egypt was brought to its knees. You've heard yourself how terrified everyone is in this city. Their God is powerful. And I believe—"

"Believe what?" My mother's voice was small.

"I believe that this God, this Yahweh, spoke to my sister"— Rahab rested her large brown eyes on me—"and told her that he had a plan. Otherwise, I do not believe she would be here now, with Moriyah and Natanyah, especially now that these men are here. There is a reason."

"It certainly is a coincidence," my mother said.

"It is no coincidence," I said. "These men were sent here by Yehoshua. Yehoshua is second in command to Mosheh, who talks with Yahweh himself."

"Mosheh is dead." Peniah put his cup down and dropped his eyes.

"What?" I gripped the edge of the table. "How can that be?"

Shaul sighed. "It is true. Mosheh went to the summit of Har Nebo and did not return. Yehoshua inherited the authority of Mosheh and is in command of us all."

The front door crashed open and Ohel, who had been standing guard, strode in. "There is a commotion down the street. They are looking for these men. Going house to house."

I felt the blood drain from my face. "They will kill us all if they are found here."

"Quick," Rahab said. "To the roof. I can hide you there." She led them to the ladder that leaned against the wall. "There is a hatch here, follow me."

The three of them climbed the ladder and then she returned

within a few minutes to tell us that they were well hidden among the drying flax bushels on the rooftop.

The ladder was concealed under a few blankets and pillows on a bed made up to look like no one had touched the linens, and all trace of the large meal spread on the table was taken away. I tucked my bright hair beneath a green linen headscarf and Rahab painted my eyes and lips with an expert hand before moving on to Moriyah's. I prayed that Mishabel had long forgotten the two of us, but we could not chance recognition. We must look as if we worked downstairs, no matter how much it made my stomach turn to see Moriyah disguised in such a way.

The four of us women waited in silence, until someone pounded at the door with such force that the hinges wobbled.

Ohel stood to approach the commotion, but Rahab shooed him away. With a measured calmness that I envied, she brushed the hair away from her face, checked her kohl in the copper mirror, and walked across the room with her head held high, even as the pounding and shouting continued. How was this woman three years younger than I? She had the backbone of a queen and the resolve of a warrior.

As soon as she opened the door, soldiers pushed her out of the way and poured through the doorway.

One, a commander, yelled at Rahab. "Where are the spies?"

"Spies?" she said. "What are you talking about?"

"We received a report from one of your neighbors that two men were seen coming here a few hours ago."

"My dear, lots of men come here." She touched his arm with a tone smoothed by practice. "In fact, a few have already been here today. But they left"—she winked—"plenty satisfied."

The commander narrowed his eyes. "And were they all Canaanite?"

She feigned deep thought. "Hmm. I really couldn't tell you. We didn't talk much."

A few of the soldiers snickered, and the commander barked at them to be quiet. "We are looking for two Hebrews."

Rahab's eyes widened with innocent horror as she clutched her hands together. "Hebrews? You mean those crazy slaves who follow a cloud? The ones who defeated King Og?"

"Two of them were spied in the marketplace today, speaking with a whore."

She looked at me. "Sister? Those two men who came by earlier. The ones with such foreign accents? You don't suppose they were Hebrews? They were so quiet."

What was she doing? I shrugged my shoulders at her.

"They did seem to be in quite a hurry. They ate a meal and then left, without even staying to enjoy the inn's amenities." A seductive flutter of lashes delivered the meaning of her statement.

"Where did they go?" The commander stepped closer, his eyes blazing. "How long ago was this?"

"Oh, about three hours ago, just before the gates closed for the evening." Rahab pointed at the window. "My daughter watched them run toward the river." She smiled with maternal pride. "Always watching, my little Amaya. She counts the travelers coming in and out of the gates all day long. Why, just yesterday she told me a story about a camel sliding off the ramp—"

"We will be searching this house now," he interrupted, gesturing to his men to follow his orders.

"You are welcome to." She waved a hand, giving them permission to have free rein. "All you will find is a few women and a couple of children. And of course my bodyguard. Any guests we entertained before are long gone now."

All the commotion had woken Natanyah, and she howled with hunger. I took the opportunity to take her into the bedroom and sat on the bed containing the ladder to nurse her, my legs folded beneath me in an approximation of comfort. A young soldier came in, searching behind the scarlet curtain, but with a quick perusal of my activity on the bed, he left, without asking me to move. Liquid relief eddied through my veins.

I heard the commander question Rahab again. She gave them false descriptions as the soldiers spent a few more minutes searching the house, but when no men turned up, they left, without ever noticing the hatch built into the ceiling. A miracle if ever there was one.

Rahab waited until the sun had gone down to retrieve Shaul and Peniah from the roof. "You must go now," she said as she backed down the ladder. "That commander was far too suspicious. I cannot put my girls in any more danger."

"How will they escape? The gates have been locked for hours," I said. "They are being looked for in the streets. It's too dangerous, even in the dark."

Rahab looked out at the last reflections of the sunset against the low eastern clouds. Then her eyes brightened. "The window."

Rahab ordered Ohel to retrieve the ropes the flax bundles on the roof had been tied with, and we knotted them together with the red cords from the curtains. Although it would reach only halfway down the wall, the rope was the only chance for Shaul and Peniah to escape into the moonless night. As tempted as I was to once again beg them to take Moriyah, she would likely break her leg leaping from such a height and put all three of them in more danger.

Rahab gave the men instructions not to return the way they had come, but instead to run north and hide in the hills three days before returning to the Hebrews, for they would no doubt be hunted by the king's men.

Peniah descended first as Rahab, Shaul, and I held the end of the rope. After a few moments of burning palms and measured breaths, the rope went slack as Peniah released his grip.

We waited, wide-eyed, listening for any commotion at the foot of the wall. I prayed that Peniah had made it safely across the deep ditch that encircled the city and was waiting for Shaul in the almond grove as they had planned.

Rahab snagged Shaul's arm before he climbed onto the sill. "You must promise to save us."

Shaul nodded. "I will tell Yehoshua himself of your kindness and insist that he protect you."

"How will they know who we are? If you Hebrews breach the walls, we will be killed in the chaos."

He scrubbed at his jaw and looked around. His face brightened as he gripped the curtain that fluttered in the evening breeze. He pointed at the red cord braided with the papyrus rope that would aid his escape. "Hang this outside your window. It will be easily seen from far off against the stone. Everyone will be told to spare the inhabitants of the house that displays this blood-red cord."

Rahab studied his face for a moment. "How do I know that you will do such a thing? What if you forget?"

Shaul's lips pursed and a crease formed between his brows, his expression solemn. "I give you my oath in the name of Yahweh, you and anyone inside this home will be spared." He raised his palm, skin shredded by the rough rope his friend had just escaped by. "May my own blood attest to this oath."

Rahab's eyes flitted to Moriyah with a squirming Natanyah in her arms and then touched on her two little daughters huddled on the bed together. She reached out to grip Shaul's bloodied hand. "I believe that you will do what you say you will do. Your God brought my sister here to tell me of this Yahweh and of his mighty power and his love for his people, and somehow . . ." She turned her eyes to me, new emotion shining through the shadows. "Somehow, I believe."

39

TOBIAH

1 NISSAN
1406 BC

The nation of Israel spread out along the riverbank for as far as the eye could see, ordered by tribe and clan, waiting for the signal that would end our forty years of wandering. Two thousand cubits to the north, the priests who carried the ark stood at attention, white robes fluttering and eyes trained on their destination.

We had been told to prepare ourselves to ford the river this morning when the *shofarim* sounded the call. The swift water had days ago overcome its banks, runoff from the white-capped mountains we'd seen in the north. For days men had hacked away the tall rushes that lined the banks, leaving us with a relatively clear view of the opposite shore—Canaan, at last.

Earlier this morning I'd seen Shira on the bank of the swollen river, her small arm around the waist of her Egyptian friend. Too far away to hear what the two women were discussing,

I considered the long journey they had taken to come to this spot, to the very edge of the Land. What stories they must have to tell.

The last words from Mosheh, before he ascended a mountain one final time, still circled through my mind. He had spent the last days of his life recounting the trials in Egypt, the subjugation of Pharaoh, the wilderness wandering, and the laws that would protect our nation and our lives. It was hard to imagine my parents suffering under such oppression but almost as difficult to believe the generation before us had been so cowardly at the gates of their inheritance. I believed Mosheh's last words with everything in me. Our enemies would indeed cringe before us, and we would trample down their high places. And looking around at the other Children of the Wilderness, faces expectant, heavily armed and practically twitching to move forward, I knew I was not the only one.

If only Shimon were here to experience this moment, this culmination of the grand journey. Tzipi stood nearby, her brown hair whipping her face in the cool breeze coming off the river, her arms around her three boys, boys who would become men in the Land without the benefit of their father's guidance. I would do all I could to fill the immense hole, but there would be gaps, to be sure.

I had already worked out with Tzipi how we would get the boys across. I'd come back for each one in turn, and then her and the wagon. Hopefully all of our belongings would not be swept downstream. I trusted Yehoshua's leading, but I anticipated that crossing here would be chaos and wondered why we had not moved forward in the winter, when the flow had been more amenable. But I was determined not to question and prayed no one else would either. Hopefully we had learned well from the example of the ten spies whose cowardice had cost us all so much. I refused to spend another forty years wandering,

I was ready to dig roots deep into the soil of the beautiful land across the river.

The *shofarim* lifted a synchronized melody into the air, the sound causing the hair to lift on the back of my neck. A few sheep lent their calls to the sound of the rams' horns, and cattle and donkeys brayed as if they, too, were ready to move, heedless of the rushing river they must cross to reach the sweet grasses of the Promised Land.

A low rumble began somewhere nearby, the vibration of it traveling through the ground. Before I could place the origin of the sound, the earth shook with a curious rolling sensation that caused me to lower my body and widen my stance to keep from falling. Children and animals screamed all around us, and I whipped my head around to ensure Tzipi and the boys were safe. My sister's arms were a protective circle around my nephews as they huddled together in the dirt. Throughout the chaos, the *shofarim* blew.

After one more violent jerk, the ground stilled, as did the ram's horns. For a few moments we all stood silent, waiting for another shaking, but none came. Everything had returned to normal, as if the earth hadn't just growled and quivered like a beast awakening from slumber.

Buzzing conversation surrounded us as everyone righted belongings and comforted children. "Look!" someone cried out. "Look at the water!"

All heads turned northward, toward the place where the priests were standing with their feet in the water up to their shins. But upriver, a wave seemed to be approaching the men.

"What is that, Tobiah?" My sister's voice was suddenly next to me, small and fearful. She slipped her hand into mine, a silent reminder of my vow to her as a small boy—to protect her always. "What is happening?"

I shook my head, as astounded as she was. I felt my own

body stiffen in preparation for the wave that threatened to bowl over the priests and wash away the golden ark that contained the laws written by Yahweh himself.

But by the time the wave reached the priests, it had lost its initial power, and although the men bobbled back and forth in the current, they stood firm.

Suddenly, the river disappeared before our eyes, the flow ceasing completely. A shout of jubilation swelled among the multitude, even as I blinked to ensure that the sight of the rocky riverbed was not a mirage. All of our preparations to ford the river were unnecessary, for Yahweh had already provided the way. And why not? He'd split the sea for the generation before us.

It was our time to walk forward, to break the hold the wilderness had on us. It was time to claim Avraham's promise.

Again, the *shofarim* sounded, this time a call to march.

40

S weat-drenched hair clung to my bare neck and shoulders, making me wish I'd tied it back before sparring with Uriya in the heat of the afternoon. But anything was better than dwelling on the revelation those two spies, Shaul and Peniah, had dropped on my head.

Moriyah is alive.

Alanah is alive.

And not only alive, but together, living in a brothel with Alanah's mother and sister. A million questions had careened around and around in my head since the men had left our campsite. Shaul assured me that Yehoshua himself had declared Alanah's family would be spared when the city fell, out of gratefulness for their aid of the spies and the information they had provided on Jericho's defenses and siege preparations.

After taking a long draught of fresh water from a skin-bag, I gestured to Uriya to attack again, already bracing myself for the collision of his thick-muscled body against mine. Between the frustration of waiting to move on Jericho until *after* the feast memorializing our escape from Egypt and the news that my wife was behind the city's impregnable walls, I needed a release. Wrestling with Uriya, who never held back, was my best option—other than scaling Jericho's ramparts alone to retrieve Alanah and Moriyah.

But instead of rushing forward, Uriya placed his hands on his hips, raised his brows, and nodded at someone behind me. I twisted to look over my shoulder. Tzipi stood a few paces away, a linen-wrapped bundle in her hands and a bleak expression on her face.

When Shaul had come into our camp today with the unbelievable story that Moriyah and Alanah had escaped Midianite traders and found their way to Jericho, I'd expected Tzipi to weep from relief that Shimon's sister was alive. Instead, she'd become strangely quiet and without a word had slipped into her tent before the men left. Assuming she needed some time to absorb the shocking news, I'd come here to work out my own confusion by trying to wrestle Uriya to the ground.

My sister approached me, clutching the bundle to her chest, her half-wild expression making me wonder if *she* needed to pummel something, or someone. She released a groaning sigh that backed up my assessment. "Tobiah. May I speak with you?"

I flicked a glance back at Uriya, meaning to let him know we were finished, but a surprising expression crossed his face as he regarded my agitated sister—desire, wrapped in thick concern. The realization that my Egyptian friend was interested in my sister shook me for a moment, and I narrowed my eyes at him. With a shrug and a half-smile that confirmed my suspicions, Uriya walked away, slipping his tunic over his head as he did so.

"Tobiah, I have something to tell you." Tzipi's solemn tone halted any thought I had of teasing her about Uriya's designs on her, and his status as a widower. The sheen of tears in her eyes erased the thought completely. She cleared her throat and then held out the parcel to me. "I should have given you this that day." I took the bundle from her and unwrapped the linen. Alanah's bow lay in my hands. The bow I had thought she'd taken with her when she fled from me, fled from our marriage.

"I don't understand." The weight of Alanah's most treasured possession in my hands split open the wound that had only just begun to scar over, making my chest ache with longing for her. "Tzipi, why do you have this?"

"She killed him." Her expression became stone. "She found some arrow in your bag and realized that it was her own, that Shimon died on that battlefield with *her* arrow in his side."

The words spun around and around inside my head without coming to roost on steady branches. I asked her to repeat them.

"Your wife killed my husband, Tobiah. It's why she ran. When she admitted it to me, I told her that you would afford her no mercy—that she would be stoned."

Fresh grief crashed into me, and I stumbled backward. It was *Alanah's* arrow I had retrieved from Shimon's body that awful day? How could this be true?

Torn between wanting to console Tzipi, who looked nearly as undone as I felt, and screaming at the sky for the injustice, I chose the latter. *Why, Yahweh?* Out of all the Hebrews for Alanah's arrow to connect with, it had to be the man I regarded as a brother? Why had everyone I had sworn to protect ended up broken or destroyed? I had done everything in my power to live up to my promises, but it was never enough.

You are not a god.

The words appeared in my mind with uncanny clarity, as if drawn in the air before me. I had no control over anything—not my parents, not Tzipi, not Shimon, and surely not Alanah. Had I been trying to be my own god? Determining my own steps instead of ceding to Yahweh's plan?

I lifted my eyes to the outline of Jericho's walls to the south-west of our encampment, wishing I could see the crimson cord that hung from one of the windows, the mark of an oath made between Alanah's sister and Shaul. Somehow Yahweh had brought Moriyah and Alanah to the very city we planned to attack. Although I had no idea what they had endured, they were alive. Where my strength and ability to protect them had ended, Yahweh himself had taken up the cause. And perhaps he had a greater reason for guiding them to that place, even if I did not understand it now.

I caressed the smooth wood of Alanah's bow, the evidence that she had not left me because she did not love me, but out of guilt and fear, for she would never willingly leave behind such a thing. "Why, Tzipi? Why would you hide this from me?"

"Because I knew what I'd told her was a lie." She dropped her gaze to her hands. "I knew that you *would* be merciful. I knew you would not hold it against her, that you would forgive. And I just—I want my husband. And she took him. She took him, Tobiah!" Tears spilled down her face, and her shoulders jerked as she walked forward into my arms, finally allowing me to comfort her as she mourned the man she had loved.

ALANAH

28 NISSAN
1406 BC

Crowded around the open window, Rahab, Moriyah, and I watched the Hebrews march around the city in eerie silence. How could such a huge army walk without making a sound, other than that of their insistent feet trampling a wide circle around Jericho? The golden ark shimmered in the sunlight, and the white robes of the priests who carried it gleamed.

Tobiah was here! I could feel his nearness in my bones. Although they were too far away to distinguish faces, I could not help but watch for the man I loved—his long sun-streaked hair, large build, and confident stride—among the thousands that followed the ark at a distance.

The gates had been shut tight since the night the spies had slipped out Rahab's window over a month ago. Another contingent of men had appeared at her door the next morning, insisting on searching the house again, and even Moriyah had played her part, flirting with one of the young soldiers with shocking brazenness. She'd laughed when I'd chided her later, reminding me of how skilled she was at being a boy. "This time I imagined I was Rahab," she said. "Much easier than pretending to be Shimon."

In the days since the spies escaped, people had been streaming in from the surrounding valley to take refuge from the coming onslaught. Although many were able to prove their Canaanite heritage and were allowed through the gates, unarmed, we'd seen quite a few calling out at the foot of the wall, screaming to be allowed entry, cursing the king of Jericho, who would leave his subjects to be slaughtered by the Hebrews. Once the Hebrews had crossed the river, Jericho's army had been called inside the walls and the enormous bronze gates locked and fortified. Anyone outside would be left to their own devices.

Among those who had been fortunate enough to be admitted were my mother's family, her husband Terran, twin sons Tannar and Danell, and three young daughters—five more siblings I had not been aware of—along with a few other family members that I could not keep straight. The boys, who were twelve, regarded me with wariness, but the three girls studied me with keen interest, and although none of the children had red hair, there was certainly resemblance between all of us.

Both levels of Rahab's inn were full of people desperate to be saved when the Hebrews attacked. I marveled at the thought that if Rahab did not own this home, the spies might not have survived and Moriyah would have no chance to be rescued. Perhaps Yahweh had used the tragic circumstances in Rahab's life for something good, for his own purposes. And somehow my own life had been a part of that.

The change in Rahab since the spies left had been drastic. Not one man outside the family had crossed the threshold downstairs, and neither had she been summoned away. Instead, we spent long hours lying on the bed together talking, learning to be sisters. She questioned me about every aspect of my time among the Hebrews, fascinated with Yahweh and the way of life that differed so greatly from Jericho.

And now they were here, a long, slow snake of men winding around the city. Would this be the day Moriyah was delivered back into the arms of her family? Would the man I loved set eyes on his beautiful daughter? I had the sudden compulsion to climb out the window, the same way the spies had, and search out Tobiah. I placed a hand on the rope that hung over the sill, dangling blood-red down the mud-brick wall, pleading silently with Yahweh that Shaul and Peniah would hold fast to their oath to save us.

With a shocking urgency, the *shofarim* screamed from the contingent of priests. The army followed suit, adding a multitude of insistent calls to the jarring noise. But instead of turning toward the city and rushing toward us, as I expected them to do, the priests at the head of the column turned northward and marched away, the rest of the long rope of soldiers following their lead.

Were they retreating? No! They couldn't leave! Tobiah was walking away instead of coming closer! Jeers rang out from other windows close by, and from the soldiers stationed nearby at the gates. "Cowards! Go back to the desert! Take your little horns with you!"

My heart pounded out a call as I gripped the windowsill. *Come back! Come back! Don't leave!*

An arm slipped around my waist. "They will return, Alanah," said Moriyah with that odd far-off look that accompanied her most decisive statements. "Have faith. They are coming for us."

41

For six days, the Hebrews repeated their baffling circuit around the city each morning. Rahab finally chanced an excursion into the center of town late one afternoon and returned with one sack of barley and a small pot of dates.

"Three days ago," she said as she came in the door, "when I ventured into the market, there was laughter, mocking of the Hebrews for blowing their horns and marching in circles. But not today. The streets are barren, except for grim-faced soldiers just standing around, anxiously awaiting orders."

"What do they think will happen?" My mother relieved Rahab of her load since I was still nursing Natanyah.

Rahab blew out a breath. "I don't know. One man said he thinks they may try and starve us out. We have deep cisterns fed by the underground springs, so we should have plenty of water." She gestured to the barley. "And as you can see, people are hoarding what they have. There is not much to come by, and what is left is going for two and three times its worth."

"Will the king send the army back out there? Defend the

city?" Raising the shoulder of my dress, I lifted a satisfied Natanyah to my shoulder and gently patted her back. Strange how natural the movements seemed, as if I had always been a mother to this warm treasure cradled against me. Her wispy red hair tickled my neck as she curled into my embrace.

"Heshbaal is a proud man. When I was working at the temple, I witnessed how ruthless he is with his political enemies. I saw many a man taken out to be thrown from the top of the palace walls or slaughtered at the feet of the *baalim* in the temple. So many—" She sat on a stool, as if weary from the burden of memories she carried. "But I also saw Heshbaal waver. There is an underlying cowardice to the man, and never did I see him more fearful than when stories of the Hebrews came up the trade road."

"He should fear," I said. "Look what Yahweh did to Pharaoh."

"I know. He was obsessed with the stories; the water turning to blood, the frogs, all the firstborns dying. Whenever someone claimed to have been there or related to someone who had, he insisted on hearing their tale firsthand."

The stories had been told to me around the campfire, by those who had direct knowledge of the fall of Egypt. Shira—oh, how I missed Shira—she had been there, had seen the water bloom red and the frogs overtake the country. She had told me of how Yahweh had allowed them to experience the first three plagues and then placed a protective hand over them. Would that protective hand extend to us, in this house? Or would we be destroyed along with the rest of the city?

One of our small sisters tugged at Rahab's sleeve. "Can we go outside now? I am tired of being indoors."

Rahab frowned. "I am sorry, Pilar, but right now it's just not safe." She turned away from the little girl, but the frown remained.

"What is it?" I asked.

"I think, perhaps, and I could be wrong, but I think someone is watching the house."

Instinct caused me to grip my daughter tighter against me. "Who?"

"I'm not sure. I saw the same two men the last time Mother and I went down to the market. They seemed to be following us, but I attributed it to recognition of my profession. However"— she pulled at her arm, as nervous as I had ever seen her—"today they were there again, watching me. And as I came up the stairs, I looked over my shoulder and they were just across the alley."

A chill crawled up my back. "Do you know why they would be stalking you?"

"I know what I fear, but I am hoping it is not the case."

"That Mishabel knows that it was our mother who rescued Moriyah and me? And that we are here with you?"

"That is exactly what I fear. One of the soldiers must have reported seeing the two of you after their search for the spies. Or perhaps Dayatana revealed what she knew." Rahab's eyes darted behind me, where her two girls tossed painted stones into a cracked pot in a corner with our young sisters.

"If she really wanted us so badly, I am sure she would have already sent her men to the door. With the Hebrews camped outside Jericho, I don't think they will bother with us." I laid a comforting hand on her shoulder. "I cannot imagine it will be much longer until they attack. They can't loop around the city forever."

"I hope you are right. And Ohel will let us know if anyone tries to approach. He is guarding the house." Her body relaxed and then she smiled at me. "I always knew about you, you know. *Ima* has told me stories of you as long as I can remember. It is so strange that you are no longer a dream or a tale, that you are here in the flesh, comforting my fears as an older sister should."

Tears blinded me for a moment, until I blinked them away. "I never knew anything of you. I wish I had. I wish that *Ima* had not—"

A loud crash sounded against Rahab's door before it burst open with an explosion of splintering wood. Four large men with swords drawn barreled through the entrance.

The children screamed, all pushing behind Moriyah, who had joined their tossing game across the room and was now standing with her arms out, like a young mother hen protecting her chicks. Terran rushed in from the bedroom, the boys behind him, but skidded to a stop when he saw the soldiers. Instead of confronting the men, he took two steps backward.

Rahab, however, boldly walked forward. Pride for my sister's courage surged through me, but almost immediately a cold wave of fear washed it away.

"What do you want?" There was no tremble in her voice.

"The Hebrew," said the leader, pointing his sword at Moriyah.

Moriyah? Why only her?

"No, you will not touch her," said Rahab.

The leader pointed his sword at her chest. Blood tinged the edge of the blade and my stomach dropped as I realized that Ohel had been guarding the door. "I will touch whoever"—he raked her with greedy eyes—"and whatever I want to touch."

Rahab lifted her chin, fury in her glare. She, too, must have realized her faithful bodyguard was dead. The bloody sword tip moved to her throat.

With Natanyah in my arms and the soldiers between Moriyah and me, I could do nothing but watch in horror as the girl rushed forward. "No! Leave her alone, I will go with you. Don't hurt anyone else, please."

One of the other men grabbed her, and as quickly as they had entered, and before any of us could react or plead for her life, they were gone. Moriyah was gone.

"I have to get her back. I have to go," I said, already pushing Natanyah into my mother's arms. My mother and Rahab protested, insisting there was nothing I could do.

"She is my responsibility. I cannot abandon her. They will kill her, I know it. They will destroy her, and then they will kill her. Especially if the Hebrews attack."

"But you could be killed, Alanah." My mother's voice wavered. "You cannot win against Mishabel's guards."

"That is true. But at least this time I am going into battle for the right reasons." I pressed a swift kiss to my daughter's temple and breathed in her sweet fragrance. "Take care of her. She is . . ." My voice cracked, along with my heart, as I looked into my mother's eyes. "She is everything."

Slowly she nodded. She, out of anyone, understood the ripping pain that was shredding me to pieces. She would keep my beautiful girl safe. Just as she had kept Rahab safe by breaking her own heart and leaving me behind.

Moriyah had no one. I could not let her suffer without at least attempting to rescue her from the situation I had caused.

Rahab urged me to wait a moment while she rooted in a large crate in the corner, then handed me a small but well-crafted bow and a quiver with two arrows. "A guest left these behind months ago." She pressed a kiss to my cheek. "I wish I could do more."

I gripped the bow and slung the quiver over my shoulder. With one final look at Natanyah squirming in my mother's arms, I stepped over the remains of the shattered door, past the crumpled form of Ohel at the foot of the stairs, and ran into the night, heading toward the only place I was sure Moriyah would be taken. The temple.

42

I stole among the darkening streets, sliding shadow to shadow until I reached the center of town and found the same gate we had exited that first night in Jericho. I scrambled over the gate and dropped into the lush garden that we had fled through as my mother rescued us.

The living quarters where we'd been held were directly across the courtyard, but the windows were all dark. Instead of crossing out into the open, I held to the wall, feeling my way along the brick through the garden and around the side of the tall *migdol* tower that guarded the entrance to the main sanctuary.

I peered around the corner and breathed a prayer of thanks. Moriyah's arms were pulled behind her, tied around a tall pole. But she was alive and, so far, unharmed. The wooden column was carved with intricate depictions of Jericho's many gods, their hideous faces leering over Moriyah's shoulders. A young, bare-chested priest stood in front of her, holding a rod over the flames of a large brazier and chanting something over and over that I could not decipher.

A woman's voice from close by commanded him to "Get it over with." Was it Mishabel? Taking advantage of the shadows

301

between torches, I moved closer, trying to get a glimpse of the old priestess and judge how many guards I was up against.

The priest lifted the rod—a brand, still glowing red from the searing fire he'd been using to heat the metal. Even as I whipped an arrow from my quiver and nocked it, a scream that froze my blood emanated from Moriyah's lips.

I shouted at the priest and he spun around, searching out the one who called to him from the shadows. Sucking in a quick breath, I released the arrow and the priest toppled backward, my arrow protruding from his head.

I nocked another arrow and moved toward Moriyah. The poor girl was in a near-faint, slumped forward against her bonds, whimpering from the searing burn she'd received. My chest roared with rage. How could they destroy her sweet face?

"You can't do much with one arrow." I spun toward the voice. Mishabel stood on the temple porch, a feline smile on her red lips. She laughed and flicked her long nails at us. "Guards, take her."

"Stop!" I ordered, and to my surprise the men halted. "Have you looked at your friend the priest there?" I said to Mishabel, jerking my chin at the body.

With a furrowed brow, she did, and the satisfied smile melted from her face.

"That's right. Directly through the eye. And I did it from over there, at least fifteen paces away. It doesn't matter if you try to flee. I can hit a deer at a run."

She sneered. "The guards will kill you both immediately if you harm me."

"I don't care. I would rather both of us die than what you are planning to do to Moriyah. It won't happen."

She cocked her head. "So we are at an impasse?"

"Let her go."

"I cannot, I have already promised the king an eyewitness. This little Hebrew will share what she knows and then will be sacrificed to protect us from invasion. A young virgin, and an enemy at that—Heshbaal will be pleased. And I waited until the time was just right to take her from your sister's house. I'll have my revenge against you, your mother, and Rahab while repaying a debt to the king." She clucked her tongue against her teeth. "It's perfect."

My stomach hollowed. Dayatana must have revealed what she knew. All those months of trying to hide and Mishabel had known the entire time where we had been.

Moriyah whimpered. They had branded her like an animal. One side of her face was flaming red and blistering, a permanent scar that would forever mark her as a temple slave covering her cheek and the corner of one eyelid. It was a miracle that two silver-gray eyes streamed with tears instead of just one. I would not let them hurt her again. I may have stolen her brother's life, but I would not let anyone steal hers.

"Take me," I said.

Mishabel threw her head back and laughed. "You? What use are you? You are certainly no virgin."

"I am a witness too. I lived with the Hebrews for months." She quirked a brow.

"I was married to one of their soldiers. And my sister is Rahab. She told me much of your king and how much he enjoyed her . . . company."

Her eyes flared wide but then she shook her head, one fist on her hip. "No. I want the girl."

"It's either me and you release her, or we all die. Your choice." I pulled back harder on the bow, aiming at the center of her chest, at her blackened heart.

She studied me, gauging my sincerity, then waved a hand at one of the guards. "Cut the girl loose."

"No, Alanah. I can't leave you," Moriyah said as the guard freed her, tears glutting her voice. "I won't."

I kept my eyes on the priestess. "You must." I used the only weapon I knew she could not stand against. "You must care for Natanyah, so she knows the ways of Yahweh. She needs you. Please. Go back to your family. Tell Tobiah—"

A few moments of silence followed, but then I felt a kiss on my cheek and her whisper in my ear. "I will tell Tobiah that you love him." And then she was gone, off into the night.

With my eyes still locked on Mishabel, I waited, giving Moriyah as much time as I could before I surrendered. My muscles began to quiver, and I cursed myself for being out of practice. *Please, Yahweh, guide Moriyah's path to Rahab's house. Protect her. Protect them all.*

With as much strength and courage as it had taken to step out onto that battlefield, I lowered my bow and bowed my head. *Forgive me for ever fighting against your people, for being selfish and ignorant. I offer you my life, in exchange for Shimon's.*

The guards charged me, relieved me of my weapon, and wrenched my arms behind my back. Mishabel strolled up to me and put her cosmetics-laden face directly in front of mine. Every line and wrinkle showed beneath the caking mess slathered across her skin. The kohl around her eyes only drew attention to the age spots and slack skin, and the red stain on her mouth did nothing to hide the two large sores on her upper lip. She was even older than I had guessed, and likely the priestess who had enslaved my mother all those years ago.

"I will make you wish you never did such a foolish thing," she said.

I just smiled at her as incomprehensible peace flooded through me. Moriyah was safe, Yahweh was watching over her. Natanyah would be safe with my mother and Rahab, and the Hebrews would rescue them all. My debt was paid—these people could do what they wanted to with me.

I was marched back to the house I'd been held in before. With an almost gleeful flourish of her hands, Mishabel ordered a few servants to prepare me for a meeting with the king in the morning. "You know what he likes," she said. "Make sure she is marked as well. She belongs to our Lord Baal and his Divine Queen now. Just her hand, mind you. This face . . . I have plans for this face." She scraped a long hennaed finger down my cheek, her dark eyes glittering. "Rahab's sister. Tashara's daughter. Oh, this will be lovely. I've waited a long time to collect on those debts." Satisfaction oozed from her sore-laden smile before she strode out the door, ordering two of her largest guards to ensure I behaved myself. Both men stood inside the door, leering as the servant girls forced me to undress, washed me with icy water, shaved every bit of hair from my body, and then dressed me again in a filmy gown that left nothing to the imagination. By the time they finished, I was past shame and had taken to boldly glaring at the guards with my jaw firmly set and my shoulders back. These people may own my body, but I wouldn't let them break my spirit.

The girls braided my hair, which was now down to my shoulders, and applied thick cosmetics to my face, a foreign feeling. Other than the time I wore kohl to disguise myself from the soldiers, I had never even lined my eyes. I preferred the mud-beard I had slathered over my chin as I prepared for battle so many months ago.

Then, without warning, the guards approached and held me down in my chair. My ears and nose were pierced and gold hoops inserted. I refused to cry out at the pain each time the needle stabbed me, instead focusing all my energy into glaring a hole into the back wall.

But I could not help but whimper as they tattooed the back

of my hand, almost wishing they'd given me a brand like poor Moriyah. Yet, even as the bone needle sliced over and over into my skin before ash and indigo were smeared into the bloody wounds, I concentrated on holding my body as still as stone. I refused to give my captors satisfaction by surveying the damage they had done to my hand. Besides, I knew what I would see, the same crescent moon and wheeled sun-disk that marked my mother and sister as temple prostitutes. Forever identified as the thing I hated the most.

When the servant girls had finished their hideous tasks, I was led to another room. The guard unlatched the lock on the door and swung it wide. Eight young girls slept on two pallets, jammed together like mice in a hole. A couple of them raised their heads and shielded their eyes from the guard's oil lamp. They were shockingly young, two of them nearly the same age as little Pilar, and most younger than Moriyah, all of them strangely silent. Were these children sold by their own parents like my mother had been? Or snatched from the street like Rahab? My stomach clenched with disgust and fury. This—this was what Rahab had endured. No wonder Yahweh was coming to destroy this city. The depravity of Jericho knew no bounds.

If only I had my bow and the two men on either side of me were not so heavily armed, I would begin the battle right here. Instead, I was pushed inside, ordered to stay presentable or face the lash, and locked in the darkness with a roomful of girls who I was helpless to protect from the evil that lurked outside.

43

After sleepless hours with my swollen breasts aching every time I imagined Natanyah's sweet voice and my hand stinging from the ugly tattoo that sprawled across my skin, the door jolted open and two new guards ordered me to follow them. Although all of the girls awakened at the intrusion, eerie silence filled the room full of children that should be laughing and playing in the sunshine. Filled with bone-aching pity, I let my eyes travel around the room, meeting the curious kohl-lined gaze of each precious child before obeying the guard's command. *Yahweh, rescue these girls.*

With outrage and terror roiling in my gut, I was led through the courtyard, wearing my flimsy gown, back to the temple. Mishabel met me on the same porch she'd threatened me from last night. Her slow perusal of my transformation made me ill. "Good," she said. "Very good. You'd better hope the king is well-pleased, he will be angry you are not that Hebrew girl."

With a flick of her wrist, she led me up the stairs that stretched between the *migdol* towers and into the temple where the stench of incense and blood was so strong I grew light-headed. I held my hand over my nose and kept my eyes on the floor. I did not even want to consider what was going on in the dark cells that lined the temple walls and wished I could cover my ears against the sounds that emanated from them.

A constant humming chant grew louder as we moved closer to the back of the temple, where the light from the main entrance was overtaken by shadows and flickering torches.

Mishabel led me into a wide room, where a towering statue of Ba'al sat enthroned next to Ashtoreth, his sun-crowned consort, with one upraised fist clutching a silver lightning bolt. I'd seen many iterations of Ba'al, large and small, and never felt any fear. But this menacing idol glowering down at me with glittering eyes made from some dark jewel caused a shiver to run from the top of my head down to my heels. Evil filled this room like smoke, and every breath I took seemed thinner than the last, as if these awful gods were stealing my air.

"This is no Hebrew girl, Mishabel."

Mishabel bowed low as a man entered the sanctuary. "No, my lord. I am very sorry to say that the Hebrew girl died escaping last night." Her lie was flawless, delivered with just a hint of false compassion.

The king was not nearly as old as I had expected, close to my oldest brother's age perhaps. His bald head was tattooed, his beard shaved on both sides and braided a handspan below his chin, and his heavily muscled arms were marked with many scars. I had no doubt why this man ruled Jericho, for even wearing a sleeveless blue robe with golden fringe, he was terrifying. The Babylonian-style garment had been woven with such tight precision that it shimmered in the flickering light. It was the robe of a high priest.

He approached me, frowning. "Then who is this?"

"She lived with the Hebrews and has offered to give you valuable information about their army."

"You? Aren't you Canaanite?" He raised his brows at me. His eyes were light brown, but his pupils were large and black and madness hovered in their depths.

Although tempted not to answer, I decided courage was my best course of action. I held my head high. "I was taken captive many months ago and traveled with them from the southern desert."

"And you saw the cloud?" His tone was oddly enthusiastic. He stepped close to me, tilted his chin, and peered into my eyes. He smelled of exotic oils and his breath was sweet with mint, a stark contrast to the foulness of the air in this temple and, I guessed, the putrid blackness that colored his soul.

"Yes, I did." *The Voice within it spoke to my heart.* I concentrated on not flinching as his peculiar eyes traveled over my face, as if he were studying me, trying to discern whether I was lying.

I must have passed the test. He swung around and clapped his hands together once, like an overeager child. "And you know something of their warfare tactics?"

"I fought against them before I was taken captive. And I am—I was also married to one of their soldiers."

He cocked his head to one side. "You remind me of someone . . ."

I sighed. "I am the sister of Rahab, who used to serve in this temple."

"Ah! Yes! That is who you remind me of!" He smiled and spread his hands wide. "How could one ever forget Rahab? And you are her sister? Hmm. Yes, very good." His eyes roamed over me with excruciating leisure. I barely contained the instinct to cover my body with my arms.

"Mishabel," he said without taking his eyes off me. "You may go."

She dipped her head and began to back away. "Thank you, my king."

He snapped his fingers at her, halting her groveling exit. "You and I, we are even now. There is no more debt between us."

She acknowledged him with a patronizing dip of her head, threw me a satisfied glance, and swept out of the room.

The king stood with his back to me, staring up at the statue of Ba'al, hands clasped behind his back. "So you lived among the Hebrews?"

"Yes, for four months."

"And you married one?"

"I did."

He turned and then circled around me. "And you loved him?"

"He was my enemy." *My rescuer. My love. The father of my child.*

He folded his hands together and placed his chin on the point of two fingers. "Tell me what they plan to do."

"I cannot. I was taken by Midianites seven months ago. I have no idea what their strategy is."

He made another circle around me, closer this time, determination in the set of his mouth. "This is the seventh day they have come to parade around and blow their horns. Why do they wait?"

I shrugged. "Yahweh seems to do things in his own time."

A shofar blew at that moment, a low sound that seemed to come from all around. Another joined, and then another. How could the sound of a few shofars resonate so clearly all over the city and reach us here inside the sanctuary of the temple?

"They have surrounded the city again. They've been marching around and around and around this morning." His voice lifted over the noise.

They had not left after one circuit today? They were still marching?

"I will not let those slaves take my city." His wild eyes locked on me as he came closer, and I backed up a few steps. "I will ensure that Lord Ba'al protects us." I retreated again, but my bare heels struck the platform that held the enormous statues. I could go no farther. To the right of me was a crimson-stained stone altar.

"That virgin Hebrew girl would have been a better sacrifice, but blood is blood." He slipped a long dagger from his belt and lifted it to my throat. "How kind of you to put yourself in just the right place." He chortled, a maniacal sound, and lifted his brows twice. "It's almost—almost as if you are eager to die for the sake of Canaan."

The *shofarim* were louder now, so loud that I almost had to shout to be heard over the tumult. "No. I won't die for Canaan. It may be my homeland, but it's no longer my home. Israel is my home."

Fury cut across his features, and he pressed the tip of the dagger into the base of my throat. I sucked in a breath and closed my eyes, conjuring up the images of my daughter and my husband to dwell upon as I died. The *shofarim* were so loud now I wondered if the Hebrews were right outside the temple.

A deafening crack shattered my concentration. My eyes fluttered open just as a large fissure split the northern wall and daylight spilled inside. The king gasped, and I spun to see what had the man so startled.

Ba'al's head separated from his body and tumbled to the floor, followed by the thunderbolt and his outstretched hands. The sun-crowned head of Ashtoreth followed suit, crumbling from her neck as if lopped off by a giant invisible sword. Her hands, too, disintegrated into a pile of rubble at her feet.

The king fled the room, his face drained of all color. With only a moment to consider, I followed him, hoping that in the confusion, no one would see me sprint through the temple. If the Hebrews were coming, I needed to be in Rahab's house, the only house that would be spared in this city. Pushing aside priests and priestesses staring at the destruction behind me, hands to their ears to block out the swelling sound of the rams' horns, I headed for the gaping entrance.

Vicious snapping and cracking sounded behind me, but just as I reached the porch I heard my name being called out. Casting a glance over my shoulder, I caught sight of Mishabel at the center of the temple, black hair disheveled as she pointed at me, ordering her guards to catch me. But the roof suddenly caved in, swallowing her in splintered cedar wood and dust.

What was happening here? Surely a few thousand *shofarim* could not make such a terrifying noise, a noise that would destroy a temple.

The sound continued to swell, vibrating the ground beneath my feet as I tore through the temple courtyard. Although many guards and soldiers filled the area, none tried to stop me. For all they knew I was just a *zonah* trying to save myself. A worthless girl who meant nothing to them.

The girls!

Without conscious thought I spun around and headed for the house. I barreled inside, pushing aside panic-stricken servants to throw aside the bar on the door that held the children captive. Eight pairs of kohl-lined, terrified eyes met mine.

"Come, girls. It's time to go!" I shouted over the noise, beckoning them toward me. "If you stay here, you will die!"

I herded the girls toward the market, still surprised that they'd all trusted me and followed me out of the house without question. By the time we reached the outer stalls, the *shofarim* had grown impossibly louder and the entire city began to shake, just as the temple complex had done.

The girls screamed, and I hollered at them to hold hands, but to keep moving. The stones beneath our feet seemed to be rolling like a wave, so I grabbed the closest girl's hand and ran, hoping the rest of the children would follow.

Everyone around us was screaming and shouting, dodging to hide beneath wagons and merchant tables, but I pressed forward, determined to reach the outer rim of the city and Rahab's home.

Glancing over my shoulder as we passed through the gate, I realized the two smallest girls were falling behind. Letting go of the hand I'd been holding, I doubled back and swung one of the girls onto my hip. Clutching the other's hand, I bellowed at the others to run faster, toward the outer wall.

Around us houses were crumbling, mud bricks shattering into dust. A horse galloped past, his eyes swirling in fear, barely missing one of the girls as he thundered by. Screams emanated from every window as walls tumbled down. Everyone was running a different direction, in a desperate and futile bid for shelter.

The shaking halted for a brief moment, but instinct told me the worst was yet to come. I blinked my eyes against the dust that billowed from the wreckage around me. Between the bright sun and the swirling clouds of debris, I could see nothing. Could not see Rahab's home. *Please, Yahweh. You told me you had a plan. Is this that plan? That we all die here in Jericho?*

In answer to my plea, my vision cleared and I saw the house. Even though all the other homes nearby were destroyed, it still stood. My heart pounded. They were safe. They had to be safe. My arms ached for my baby.

The door to the bottom level of Rahab's inn had swung open from the shaking. I pointed to the doorway and the girls ran toward it. I clutched the small girl whose arms encircled my neck like a vise and muttered assurances that I knew she could not hear over the unearthly *shofarim* and the violent trembling of her body. The seventh girl entered the house at the same moment another huge jolt of the ground wrenched me from my feet and I tumbled forward. Cradling the girl close to me, I crawled toward the door, which had slammed shut.

Just as I reached the doorway, the *shofarim* sounded again, a blast of sound that seemed even louder than the last. The world shook as I huddled against the door, shielding the tiny girl with my body, my bloodied hands braced against the wood as the sky itself seemed to quake.

Something hit my head and the world went dark.

44

TOBIAH

I pulled in a deep breath to blow the shofar one last time. Jericho had fallen. Not by my hand, or the hand of any other Hebrew. But by the mighty hand of Yahweh.

We had simply watched as Jericho was destroyed by the sound of our rams' horns. When the last trumpeting blast died away and the walls finished tumbling, we stood in reverent silence as dust and smoke rose into the air. There was no sound. The birds had long since fled from our braying noise, and everyone in the city was smashed beneath a pile of rubble.

Orders were given to go in, to ensure no survivors.

No survivors.

No one could live through that devastation. No one. The area in which the two spies told us Moriyah and Alanah were hidden had crumbled along with the rest of the city.

I dreaded every step toward the remnants of Jericho. We climbed through the broken ramparts, slowly, avoiding the precarious landslides of rubble that had pitched down the slopes all around.

There was no movement that I could see, although a few

deep-voiced screams from far off told me that Canaanite soldiers had been discovered alive, and dispatched.

Yehoshua had given strict orders that not one item be taken from the city, not one person taken captive. And seeing the destruction that Yahweh had caused here, surely no one would be tempted to disobey.

My feet moved toward the portion of the city the spies had indicated. To my relief and surprise, one large house stood. It was leaning, but stubbornly clung to the only portion of the outer wall that remained upright.

The door hung by only one hinge but I moved toward it, drawn by the last shred of hope that clung to my heart. A pile of rubble lay across the threshold, the remnants of a corner of the roof that had disintegrated. But it was not only bricks on the ground. Someone lay trapped beneath the pile, halfway inside the doorway. A pair of bare feet were visible along with the hem of a dress. I moved closer. It was a woman. A woman with flaming red hair.

I pulled mud bricks and shards of wood off her, calling her name, desperately watching for movement. I brushed debris from her face, surprised by the amount of kohl she seemed to be wearing. But it was her, it was Alanah. She was clutching a small girl to her chest, a girl whose open eyes were staring into a world beyond this one. Carefully I lifted the small body and placed it to the side.

I leaned over Alanah, begging Yahweh for some sign of life, and nearly shouting from relief when I felt the slightest wisp of air on my cheek. She was alive!

Gently, I turned her over. What was she wearing? A sheer linen gown fitted tightly around her body, leaving most of her exposed. Long gold earrings hung from her ears, a gaudy beaded hoop pierced her nose, and beneath the dirt, her lips were painted red and her cheeks smudged with color.

What had she done to herself? Had she been prostituting herself to survive? Disgust and anger coursed through my veins.

I had promised that she would never have to make such a choice again. Another promise I had failed to fulfill.

Yet, even as I railed at Yahweh for not guarding her against such debasement, I remembered the words he had given me. *You are not a god.* Perhaps there was more here to understand than what my eyes could see. Perhaps, even in this, Yahweh had a plan. I'd seen the river stop its flow and the walls of Jericho crumble before my eyes. I had no right to question his will, or the power and methods with which he accomplished it.

I crouched down and picked up the battered body of my wife.

Alanah stirred in my arms, her eyes fluttering open. She stared at me. "Tobiah?"

My pulse pounded in my ears at the sound of her voice, as well as the sight of those clear pools of blue-green that had called to me on a battlefield and upended my world. "Yes, Alanah. I am here."

"No . . . I'm not . . ." She grimaced, straining at her words. "You are . . . you are gone. Natanyah . . . the girl." The ramblings made little sense, but at least she had spoken before her eyes closed and she lost consciousness again.

I brushed my lips across the purpling bruise on her forehead and pulled her close. "I have you, *Ishti.* I am not letting go."

ALANAH

6 IYAR
1406 BC

A warm hand caressed my face. "Are you awake now, sweet girl?" The voice was familiar, but I could not place it, it did not belong to the palace in Jericho—or had I already left that evil place? Yes. I was running and the world was falling apart. And all the girls . . . My baby! *Natanyah!*

My eyes snapped open and Shira's gray-green ones smiled back at me. "There now. You are back in the land of the living." She smoothed my curls away from my face. "Your hair has grown so quickly! I did hate cutting it."

I tried to sit up but weakness overwhelmed me, forcing me back to the pallet. "Where am I?"

"Home," she said. "Back where you belong."

"How did I get here?"

"Tobiah brought you."

He was here? He had seen me?

It had seemed only a dream, Tobiah holding me, calling me *ishti*. But the last thing I could remember clearly was the palace and the king leering at my sheer clothing before the heads of the gods tumbled to the ground. My clothes! Instinctively I grabbed at my chest, but the horrendous filmy gown Mishabel had forced me into had been replaced by a soft woolen shift. Relief touched every corner of my soul. I hoped the thing had been burned.

Compassion pulled at the corners of Shira's mouth. "Moriyah told us everything, Alanah. And—"

"Where is—?" I pushed up on my elbows. Rahab sat cross-legged across the tent, with my mother holding Natanyah next to her. A relieved sigh expelled from my lungs. "Can I hold her, please?"

"Of course." Shira's face lit with excitement. "She is so beautiful! Just like her *ima*."

After laying Natanyah in my arms, my mother knelt next to me. "We have been so worried. I cannot believe you were right outside the door and we did not see you." Tears filled her eyes.

I brushed my lips across my daughter's soft cheek and breathed deeply of her sweet scent. "Those girls, from the palace—are they safe?"

Sadness crumpled her brow. "Most of them are, *kalanit*. But the little one . . . she did not survive."

The knowledge pierced my chest. Poor child. Such heartache for such a short life.

"She is safe in the arms of Yahweh," said Shira. "And you saved seven other lives, Alanah. Seven girls who would not be alive without your courage. And each life is precious."

"As I have learned," I said, drawing Natanyah closer to nurse her. The familiar tug at my breast soothed the loss of the little one who had clung to me so tightly, as did Shira's reassurance that Yahweh cared for even a tiny, nameless girl.

I trailed my fingers through Natanyah's red curls and she sighed as she suckled, her tiny fingers curling and uncurling as her eyes drifted shut in contentment.

"We will leave you to rest now, dear, and enjoy some time with your precious girl," said Shira. "Kiya and Moriyah have been asking after you constantly. Although you have quite the bump on your head, when you are feeling up to it, there are a few people anxious to see you."

Tobiah? A spring of hope welled inside me but was quickly quenched by the hint of sadness that crossed Shira's features.

"What is it?" I tensed my body, preparing for the news of Tobiah's marriage.

"We will talk later," she said. "We have much to tell you. For now, you enjoy your precious baby and Bodo there." She pointed toward the basket-cage in the corner, where my sand cat slept curled into a ball. Nita had kept him?

With an encouraging smile, the midwife led my mother and Rahab outside, a strange mixture of family, old and new.

It was as I had guessed, and dreaded, and hoped. Tobiah had taken Keziah as a wife, which in turn had kept him from dying in battle. All the pleas to Yahweh had not been in vain; the man I loved still lived. And that was enough. It must be enough.

"Has he seen you?" I said to Natanyah, who was studying me with wide-eyed curiosity. "Even if he is not my husband anymore, he will always be your abba." I pressed a kiss to her smooth forehead. "A man who could love his enemy will have no trouble loving you."

With a gurgle, Natanyah smiled for the first time and bent her elbow back with a flap of her arm to smack her tiny palm against my chest. I laughed. "Oh, don't you worry, I will teach you how to pull a bow, no matter what your abba says."

When I lifted my hand to caress her cheek, the ugly tattoo caught my eye and shame filled me once again. How would I ever face him?

I stepped into the bright sunshine with Natanyah against my shoulder. My head still throbbed, but my vision was clear. The Hebrews were encamped at the bottom of a hill, their vast well-ordered numbers a welcome sight. To the south lay Jericho, a crumbled waste amid the fertile beauty of the valley. The tent I had been in seemed to be on the very edge of camp, facing away from the rest of the multitude. Above us, to the west, stood the *Mishkan*, gleaming brilliant white against the blue sky and green land. Yet the Cloud that usually hovered above the *Mishkan* was absent. I scanned the valley but the only clouds were feathered high above us, moving slowly across the heavens.

Panic seized me. Where was Yahweh? Had he left his people? But my pulse slowed as I considered the destruction at Jericho. Nothing but a divine hand could have caused the obliteration of such a heavily fortified city. And once again, he had heard me when I'd called. He'd saved those girls—or most of them.

His Cloud may not be visible anymore above the *Mishkan*, but surely his presence hovered above this assembly and over his people. A whisper of something holy—something beautiful—thrummed in my veins, as if here at the foot of this hill Yahweh was closer than ever. And since this was the land promised to Avraham hundreds of years ago, I suspected that, along with the inheritance the Hebrews were now living in, a divine presence surrounded them in this place, watched over them like a loving father.

"Alanah! You are awake!"

I looked behind me to find Moriyah approaching. Her horrific wound was covered by a thin headscarf she'd arranged across her face. My stomach churned. *If only I had been a few minutes earlier, faster with my bow . . .*

"Oh, Moriyah . . ."

She lifted a hand to push back the veil, revealing the crescent moon and sun-disk that had been etched into her skin. Salve shimmered on the flaming wound, exaggerating the swelling. She grimaced as she rearranged the veil. "It is awful, but it was not as bad as it could have been. That horrid priest had only just begun branding me. Without your intervention, I could have been blinded, Alanah. Shira says it will scar, of course, but I am alive." She shrugged.

Alive and marked as temple property for the rest of her life. "Forgive me—"

She put up a hand. "There is nothing to forgive. You saved me in the river. You protected me all throughout our journey. And you offered up your own life for mine. No—I will not let you apologize." She grazed a knuckle down my baby's cheek with a soft coo, as if eager to distract from the subject. Natanyah yawned and settled against my shoulder.

Shaking my head, I let the matter drop, for now. "Where are the girls? The ones from the temple?"

"Oh, Alanah." She clapped her hands together. "What a miracle. I cannot believe you made it through that earthquake with those children! They are being well cared for by your mother and sister. And Yehoshua himself thanked Rahab for protecting those two spies and invited the whole family to live here, on the edge of camp." She gestured to the tent I'd just emerged from. "If they choose to stay, and become one of us, they will be welcomed."

Just as I had been welcomed, even when I was an enemy.

"Where is Nita?" I said, eager to see the woman who had been so kind to me in spite of my rough edges.

Moriyah's face fell. "Nita is gone, Alanah. Tobiah said they found her in her tent one morning a few weeks ago, gazing up at the sky with a look of absolute peace on her face. She caught a glimpse of Canaan, but she never set foot inside it."

Although she'd assured me it would happen, grief struck me hard. Nita had been a true friend to me and her loss tarnished a bit of the shine from my joy at being among the Hebrews again. "She is with her Zakariyah, then." My voice wobbled, and I paused, working to choke back the tears that seared my throat. "I wish I had thanked her for her kindness to me."

Before I could say more, Moriyah's gaze drifted over my shoulder, just as a voice I had not been prepared to hear spoke behind me.

"Moriyah, may I speak to Alanah for a moment? Alone?"

My back stiffened, and everything in me stilled. Did I have the strength for this confrontation? Here and now? After handing Natanyah to Moriyah, I closed my eyes for a moment and breathed slowly through my nose, hoping to dredge up a bit of the courage I'd summoned when facing down an army, an evil priestess, and a bloodthirsty warrior-king.

Empty-handed, I turned to face my greatest regret.

45

Tzipi stood before me with an inscrutable expression on her face. I braced myself, anticipating the words that would fly from her lips, echoes of her last conversation with me. *Murderer . . . pay for what you did . . . no mercy . . .*

"Thank you," she said.

I flinched in surprise, then clenched my jaw to prevent it from sagging open.

"Thank you for saving Moriyah. She would not have survived without you."

I stumbled over my response. "I could not—I would not have allowed anything to happen to her."

"She told me everything. The traders, the river, Jericho. How you took her place in the temple . . ." She choked on her words.

"I would have done anything to protect her."

Tears glittered in her eyes. "But to offer yourself in place of a Hebrew?"

I shrugged. "Her life is worth more than mine."

Tzipi pursed her lips and shook her head. "Moriyah is precious, but the sacrifice of your own life was a weighty thing. Do not discount it."

"How can you say these things?" I felt a surge of something hot and defensive in my chest. "You know what I did."

The corners of her mouth twitched down. "My Shimon was my heart. He was everything good and kind and strong and I loved him with my whole being. But he died in war, Alanah. It may have been your arrow that pierced his side, but it would have been someone else's otherwise. Yahweh chose that time for him to die." She paused, pulling in a heavy breath, looking toward the wasted city in the south. "I don't know why, perhaps it was because Tobiah needed to find you so that you would be in Jericho at the right time to meet your sister and share what you knew with her."

Facing me again, she took a step toward me, her voice growing stronger. "Think, Alanah, of how many lives were saved because of your presence in that city. The spies, your sister and her family, those girls from the temple."

The memory of the Voice whispered in my ear. Yahweh had used me, even when I was an enemy of his people. He had surrounded me in protection, even when I had no regard for my own life. He had swept up the ugly chaff of my life, burned it away, and somehow what was left was worth more than I could ever imagine. The depths of such mercy astounded me.

Tzipi's brown-eyed gaze fluttered to the ground. "I must ask your forgiveness."

"My forgiveness? I killed your husband!"

"Yes, your forgiveness. Mine has already been given."

"But why? I stole your sons' father!"

"No. What you did, you did out of ignorance and hurt. If Yahweh gave you mercy, then I have no right to withhold my own." The sincerity in her clear eyes astounded me, and I wondered for the first time if she and I could build a friendship from the ashes of such destruction.

"Tobiah loves you, you know," Tzipi said.

I jerked back as if she'd slapped me.

"I must also ask your forgiveness for pestering him to marry Keziah after you left."

"It is for the best," I said, my heart plunging to the pit of my stomach. "I am glad that he was spared from more battle for the past few months. I'd rather he be married to Keziah than dead." Tzipi's face contorted with confusion for a moment, before mystifying humor dawned in her eyes. A sly smile played across her lips.

"Tobiah is not married to Keziah, Alanah."

"What do you mean?"

"Keziah was betrothed to another man, right after we crossed into Canaan. No matter how much I pushed him, Tobiah refused to ask for her hand."

I heard her words but they did not make sense; they seemed garbled somehow, twisted. "But—but, why?"

"Because even when he thought you had left him because you did not return his love, he could not let you go."

Tzipi's form blurred in front of me, and the dam of my heart burst. I bowed my head and let the tears flow. The woman who had hated me with such passion rubbed circles on my back, speaking words of comfort and reassurance into my ear.

"But Shimon . . ." My voice warbled. "I killed his closest friend. How will I tell him?"

"He knows, Alanah. I told him after Shaul and Peniah told us they had seen you and Moriyah. He was devastated, but it did not change what he feels for you. If anything, it helped explain why you ran away and gave him hope that if he found you in Jericho, you would return to him."

Hope? Was there such a thing left between Tobiah and me? I wiped my face with the back of my hand, my gaze cutting to the black mark tattooed there. How could I ask him to bind himself to such shame? What could bridge the river of pain and loss between us? My head snapped up as the answer came to my mind, along with another question. "Does he know about Natanyah?"

"We all decided to leave that revelation to you. He has mostly avoided camp since he brought you back from the city. I think he believes the baby is your sister's."

At least I had a small measure of leverage. "Where is he?"

"I believe he went up over that ridge." She pointed to the southwest. "Someone spotted a pack of gazelles grazing there early this morning. He went to hunt."

"Good. I'll need a few things before I go look for your brother." I lifted a brow. "One should always be well-armed for battle. Don't you think?"

Tzipi's lips curved into a genuine, conspiratorial smile. "How can I help?"

46

TOBIAH

The herd of gazelles had left me trailing behind long ago. I'd given up easier than I should have. But for some reason I did not care, I only desired to get as far away from camp as I could. Lush green flooded the valley, all the way to where the river glittered under the midday sun. A field of flowers, their red heads bobbing in the quiet breeze, spread out in front of my resting place beneath a stand of flowering trees.

I was tired. More tired than I had been after crossing swords with some of the fiercest soldiers on the earth. Today my body felt the weight of my heritage dragging behind me and pushing against me from ahead. What would this beautiful land hold for me? And how long would it take before I could lay down my sword and simply rest in its abundance?

I leaned my head back against the trunk of a tamarisk and peered up through the feathery leaves, inhaling the sweet fragrance of its resin. Honeybees bumbled around between the pink blossoms.

The last time I had enjoyed the shade of such a tree, Alanah had been my wife. After delivering her unconscious body to the tent appointed by Yehoshua to her family, I'd spent the last two days in the wild and the night under the stars, away from the draw of the woman who caused such a violent reaction in my soul.

I missed her with every fiber of my being, but I would not force her to stay with me. She had found her family, a family that, by all appearances, seemed to love her. Her mother and sister had hovered around her like ruffled hens as we'd returned to camp, regarding me with protective suspicion in their kohl-rimmed eyes.

Moriyah, with her poor, damaged face, had sought me out to tell me what had happened after they were taken on the road. Her assurances that Alanah had done everything possible to protect everyone around her with little regard for her own safety and dignity, made my respect for her deepen even further.

But from the beginning, I'd told her I would not hold her to a vow she'd made under duress if she chose not to stay, and I would hold to my word, even if it slayed me all over again. I would release Alanah to Yahweh's safekeeping alone.

A blue and green sun-bird fluttered into the sky from a branch above me, startled by some sound nearby, its wings flashing like metal in the sun.

"Tobiah? Are you there?"

Alanah? I hesitated, gathering my composure before coming out from under the tree. The contrast of bright light after the shadows under its canopy caused Alanah's form to swim before my eyes for a moment. Was she truly here? Fording through a sea of red flowers to find me? Her fingers grazed the petals of one of the taller blossoms as she approached. Disturbed by her intrusion into their perches, a few orange-winged butterflies danced into the air behind her.

A mixture of nerves and eagerness that had no business thrumming in a warrior's chest struck up a steady beat. Her hair had grown to her shoulders, and the sight of it shining red-gold in the sun added desire to the hum of anticipation in my limbs. The soft blue woolen tunic she wore reminded me of Tzipi, but as Alanah came within a few paces, I realized that the gaudy earrings and beaded nose-ring were still in place, though her eyes were no longer smudged with kohl. Surging indignation replaced the pleasant sensations from before. She was not returning to me. Moriyah had assured me that it was the priestess who had dressed her in such indecent garb, but after living all those months with her mother and sister, she must have assimilated back into life in Canaan. It still held her in its grip. A leather satchel was slung over her shoulder. Had she come to say goodbye before her family fled together?

"Why are you hiding?" she said, as if seven months had not passed behind us. As if she were simply wondering where I had been during a hunt.

I shrugged a shoulder, playing the game. "Getting out of the heat."

Her gaze dropped to my dark green tunic, and one corner of her mouth turned up. "You are wearing the tunic I made."

I smoothed a hand over my chest, remembering the pride and amusement I'd experienced when I'd discovered what she had done. "Of course I am, I found my brown one in pieces the morning you disappeared." I lifted a brow in challenge.

A spark of mischief flared in her eyes. "Oh? I wonder how that could have happened? Perhaps wild animals? Surely not Bodo?" She frowned in mock concern, the tease in her tone giving me the smallest measure of hope.

"Oh, to be sure, a wildcat claiming her territory got her claws on it. But it wasn't Bodo." I pinned her with a look, my blood racing with the thrill of sparring with her again.

However, instead of volleying back, she turned to look out over the valley and the sparkling river to the east. She cupped a hand above her gaze. I watched her from behind, glad for the freedom to run my greedy eyes over her without notice. The breeze tangled her thin woolen dress around her legs and floated red curls in wild spirals. How I had missed this woman! How would I possibly let her walk away from me again?

The sun-bird she'd startled before returned. Hovering over us for a moment before landing again amid the pink-tipped boughs, he watched us, head cocked and one eye focused on us. He seemed to be deciding who might break the silence. I resolved that it would not be me.

"I cannot say that I regret going to that battlefield," she said, but she did not face me. "I was hurt, confused, and alone."

I held silent, not ready to betray my own confusion.

"And if I did not make such a foolish decision, I would not have been wounded and you would not have found me."

A flash of memory stung me: her blood, those captivating eyes, a bright curl around my finger.

"But I wish I'd had the courage to tell you about Shimon. If I could go back to that moment, that awful moment before I released that arrow, I would. There is nothing I can do except beg your forgiveness." She dropped her chin. The sun-bird in the tree chirruped, turning his head this way and that, as if gauging my reaction to Alanah's words.

I felt the gentle push of Yahweh on the wall of my heart, the same push I had heeded when Alanah had exploded into my life. I obeyed the nudge. "I do not hold it against you."

Alanah whirled, curls flying—oh, how I wanted to bury my face in their softness. "You truly forgive me?" The relief on her face was plain, she had not expected this reaction.

"You know as well as I do the risk Shimon accepted when he stepped onto that battlefield. You did not aim your arrow at my friend. Only at the people you felt had stolen your family. What you did, you did out of ignorance, Alanah. I just wish you had come to me, trusted me, when you discovered the arrow . . . instead of running away."

That broken arrow. Why had I kept such a thing? A morbid keepsake, a reminder of the evil that had felled my brother-of-the-heart. I'd held onto it as some sort of tangible reminder of our mission to clear the Land of the Canaanites and their bloodthirsty gods, but instead it had cost me Alanah.

To my surprise, she moved forward. I planted my feet, folding my arms across my body, determined not to reach for her without invitation. Keeping her eyes on mine, she removed the gold ring in her nose.

"Put out your hand," she said. Although I paused for a moment, I complied. She dropped the thing onto my palm. "When you found me on that battlefield, I was dead, Tobiah. As dead as if my bones had been plucked clean and left to dry in the sun."

She removed one large gold earring and placed it in my hand. "But then Yahweh brought you to me. He granted me mercy, through your kindness. Through you, he lifted me out of my grave."

The other gold earring landed in my palm.

"As you, and your God, began to chip away at my walls, something inside me began to be restored. And when that snake bit me, my heart stopped—it stopped, Tobiah. But Yahweh breathed life into me, revived me. He preserved my life, along with Moriyah's and Natanyah's, in that river. He surrounded us in protection. He never abandoned us. And since we emerged from that water, he has been continually making me into something new."

She reached into her leather satchel and pulled out a pair of shears. "I cannot undo what is past. When I first married you, all I wanted to do was find a way to escape. But when I was taken by those traders, all I could do was think of ways to get back to you. To return to the husband I love."

She took a step closer, her eyes swimming in tears I'd never before witnessed. I longed to drag her to me and drown in them, but her speech was not finished.

"The first time," she said, "I complied out of desperation. But now, I want to shed everything of Canaan. I want to be your wife, with nothing of the past between us."

She knelt down in front of me and held the shears in upturned palms, a look of raw, honest vulnerability on her face. "I offer you all of me, freely."

Sliding one hand into her fire-colored hair, made all the more brilliant by the blaze of the sun, I accepted the shears.

"And you are sure this is what you want?"

She dipped her chin, blue-green eyes shimmering. "The outside of me does not matter, only that my heart is bound to yours for the rest of my life."

I tossed the shears and the jewelry into the dirt, dropped to my knees, and pulled her into my arms. "You are my wife. The covenant was made the very first night, sealed with my blood. We are one."

She trembled in my arms, tears flowing for the first time since I had known her. I brushed my lips across her cheek, tasting the saltiness of her surrendered burdens and broken-down walls.

Then I kissed my wife.

Seven months of separation melted between us like wax under a flame. Alanah, my warrior, my love, came alive under my touch. Although the feel of her lips beneath mine was familiar, something new sparked in the air, a result of the lack of barriers between us, and I could not wait to explore the depths of the heart she had finally, truly opened to me.

Behind us, the sun-bird chittered a loud chastisement as he winged into the sky. I dropped one last kiss on Alanah's lips before relaxing my hold on her. "I guess our little friend there does not understand what it is like to be away from his wife for many months."

With a small laugh she lifted her hand to caress my face. "Perhaps not. But I am sure his mate will be glad that he did not fly off with another."

"Keziah is a lovely woman, but you . . ." I pulled her hand from my cheek and kissed her palm. "You set fire to everything I thought I wanted in a wife."

Eyes locked with hers, I once again placed my lips in the center of her hand and then turned it over to survey the tattoo there. She grimaced and tried to pull away, but I refused to let go.

"It is the only thing I cannot rid myself of." Disgust edged her voice. "I'll forever bear this mark of shame."

"I am glad," I said.

She looked at me as though my beard were on fire.

"Now that I know what you did for Moriyah, I will look at this and remember what a warrior I have for a wife and what pride I have to be married to a woman who would have such courage." I kissed the black mark with a smile. "And I will ask you to repeat the story, so I can hear it all over again."

She rolled her eyes. "Tobiah—"

"There is still one thing I do not understand," I said as my mind wandered back through the story of her journey back to me. "Who is Natanyah?"

A mischievous grin spread across her face and she sprang to her feet. "Come," she said with a jerk of her head that made her red curls shimmer sun-gold. "I'll introduce you."

Alanah's family had been given permission to live on the outskirts of the camp, among the few foreigners who still traveled with us but had not chosen to bind themselves to Israel.

Their numbers had dwindled significantly over the years, either
through intermarriage with the tribes, the choice to submit to
the Covenant and its laws, or the decision to part ways with us
and return to wherever their ancestors had originated before
they had been enslaved in Egypt. Alanah's family would have
to make the same choice in the coming days.

The campsite bustled with activity and, much to my surprise, Tzipi was among the women preparing a meal near the
cookfire, along with Shira and her Egyptian friend, Kiya, who
both acknowledged us with smiles before turning back to their
animated conversation. During the walk back to camp, Alanah
had told me the two women had been helping Rahab care for the
temple girls and of course Shira had tended to both Alanah and
Moriyah's wounds. I'd be forever grateful that I'd crossed paths
with the wise and strong-willed midwife the day of the battle.

Tzipi turned to watch us approach, and I questioned her
presence with a lift of my brows. She turned her back to me,
making a show of stirring a pot of stew over the fire, but not
before I caught a playful smirk toward my wife. The expression may have been small, but the gesture was not—the two
women I loved most in this world had made peace. I prayed it
would last, or I'd not have a moment of rest until they placed
me in my grave.

Perhaps now that Tzipi had found some measure of healing
over Shimon's death, she would be open to the possibility of
accepting Uriya, who I'd decided would indeed make an excellent choice of husband for my sister. My beautiful sister was
young and full of life, and although Uriya was older and no
match for Shimon's wit and audacity, he was a good man, a
man who'd deeply loved his wife who'd died in childbirth and
was a strong yet compassionate father to his nearly grown sons.
After months of her bothering me about marrying Keziah, the
least I could do was repay her in kind . . .

A small group of children, including my nephew Liyam, paraded through the campsite, earning chastisement from Tzipi to not run so close to the fire.

Liyam caught sight of Alanah and me and with a wide grin headed for me, wrapping his small arms around my knees. "Tobiah! Where have you been?"

I slung the boy over my shoulder, amused by his squeals of delight. "I have been hunting wild creatures like you."

"Catch anything?" he called from behind my back, his dirty toes wiggling near my chin.

"Only the most elusive prey of all." I tipped a sly grin at Alanah. "A red-haired vixen." I flipped Liyam back over to set him on the ground. The boy ran off to rejoin Alanah's young sisters in their game of chase, farther away from the fire—and my sister's wooden spoon.

"I do believe I tracked you this morning, husband." Alanah poked my chest with a finger. "Although it wasn't too difficult— a blind man could follow your trail."

"Oh now, I believe that is a challenge." I leaned close, my lips grazing her ear. "Perhaps we should do more hunting later. I did find a large tamarisk tree to take shelter beneath . . ."

I reveled in the deep flush of her cheeks, but before I could deliver another teasing quip, Alanah's mother and sister emerged from their tent, their wary eyes on us and their red hair announcing their familial tie to my wife. As usual, Rahab clutched her baby close to her chest, as if I was likely to snatch the infant from her arms. Alanah had described the suffering both women had endured, so their defensive posture and guardedness was understandable. Alanah had learned to trust me after a time— perhaps these women would find healing among us as well.

"*Ima*. Rahab. This is my husband, Tobiah." The pride in Alanah's voice made a lump swell in my throat. "He came to meet Natanyah."

I glanced behind the women into their empty tent. Where was this person Alanah spoke of? Moriyah had not mentioned meeting another woman during their escape, but Alanah had said something about the three of them safely crossing the river. Rahab stepped forward and handed her baby to Alanah. The infant burbled and smiled up at my wife. Understanding smashed through the thick wall in my mind, just as Alanah turned to me with unmistakable joy on her lovely face.

"This is Natanyah. Your daughter." Before I could protest, Alanah lifted the tiny girl and placed her in my arms. I was afraid to breathe. Afraid to hold her too tightly. Afraid I might drop her.

"Daughter?" My thick tongue stumbled over the word. "You were . . . You were with child when you left?" Alanah nodded, truth shining in her eyes. My courageous wife had endured even more than I had guessed.

The warmth of the baby's small body against my chest scrambled my thoughts until I could do nothing but stare at her, searching her features for traces of myself. And although the wisps of red-flame curls were Alanah's, I was there in the shape of her eyes, the same as my twin sister's, and the cleft chin that was hidden beneath my beard. This child was mine. Mine and Alanah's.

I am a father.

Alanah moved closer, until only the baby—only Natanyah— was between us. Everything in my world shifted again, expanding to make room for the change.

EPILOGUE

ALANAH

1 NISSAN
1399 BC

The houses had long since crumbled; a mixture of fire, rain, and time had toppled nearly every mud brick to the ground. I was glad they were gone and every harsh memory with them. The evil had been burned out of this valley and swept away on the wings of the wind, leaving only the promise of a new life among the hills I loved.

The fields were overgrown, plagued with tall weeds that stood like bushy giants among the once-graceful stalks of wheat and barley that had swayed in tandem under spring breezes.

Even the long lines of rock fences, so carefully stacked and tended by my father, showed their age, many of them lying sprawled on the ground or missing stones like gapped teeth. The olive trees had survived the neglect but were in desperate need of pruning. I restrained a groan, but Tobiah must have seen the frustration on my face.

"We knew this would be a lot of work, Alanah." He slipped his arm around my waist. "And we have many hands to help us."

"I'm not concerned about the labor involved," I said. "I only wish I were able to help more right now."

He splayed his warm hand across my ever-expanding belly. "Only a few more weeks." He kissed the side of my neck. "And then I'll put you to work. Can't have you getting lazy on me. I need someone to dress my game."

I elbowed him in the gut. "Don't you mean dress *my* game? These are my hunting grounds, you know. I know every wadi, every trail, every secret cave."

"Ah. You'll have to make sure to acquaint me with such places—" He took a nip at my ear and then whispered, "Alone. Without the children."

"Abba!" Natanyah howled. "Mikal hit me!"

My ever-patient husband turned to quell the sibling argument between our two oldest children. Naming our first son after Moriyah's false identity had been Tobiah's idea; he'd insisted that Shimon would have found the idea hilarious. I still smiled every time I thought of that girl striding through the countryside, all masculine legs and shoulders and clapping with glee whenever she managed to trick someone into believing she was a boy.

Watching her wave goodbye as we left her behind with her family at Shiloh had been one of the hardest things I'd ever had to do. In spite of the painful ostracism she suffered, and the ever-present veil that covered her scar, her sweetness endured. Although she found solace in her talent for cooking and insisted that she was content with her lot and did not need a husband, I prayed that Yahweh would provide a man who would be blind to the brand and see only the gem hidden beneath.

What grace Yahweh had, that this portion of the new land had fallen to the tribe of Yehudah. Tobiah had petitioned Yehoshua himself for permission to settle back in the valley of my childhood. Due to my husband's loyal, fearless service in the army of Israel, along with the influence of Rahab's husband, Salmon, one of the leaders of the tribe of Yehudah, the request had been graciously obliged.

My mother, with our youngest son Lev in her arms, appeared beside me as I surveyed the winding terraces that embraced the hills. Terraces that I could already imagine would thrive again soon, with the help of Tzipi's strong boys, her husband Uriya, and Uriya's two grown sons.

"I never thought I would see this valley again," my mother said as she leaned her cheek against her grandson's reddish-brown hair. "I had forgotten how beautiful it is."

"I am glad you are here, *Ima*." I linked my arm through hers. "I know this must be difficult for you."

She released a weighty sigh. "My time here was short, Alanah, but every inch of this place is filled with memories of you." She smiled. "My tiny *kalanit*, her red head bouncing through the green fields, barely visible above the wheat stalks."

I cast a glance back at Natanyah, who was exploring the ruins of the houses with Tobiah, her little hand clasped in his enormous one. Her red hair glimmered in the sun as she chattered to him with wide gestures and vivacious tones. The two of them had been smitten with each other since the moment he'd held her in his arms, and I prayed fervently that the battles with the remaining Canaanite tribes were over for now. My little gift needed her abba to walk by her side as she grew into whatever purpose Yahweh had planned for her.

Just as Yahweh had devised a purpose for me, before I had even known he was beside me—I'd never been alone.

A Note
from
THE AUTHOR

The forty years of wandering are, in many ways, a giant blank space with only a few tantalizing clues as to where exactly the Hebrews went and how the people of God changed during that period. We know that after Sinai they made a number of encampments and endured the horrific fallout from Korah's rebellion (Numbers 16), but we do not know the exact timing or location of any of these events. My choice to place Korah's rebellion in the last third of the forty-year wandering was completely artistic and it could very well have happened much earlier. Without a doubt, the memory of watching the earth swallow men, women, and children would have greatly impacted the Hebrews, as it did Tobiah.

Throughout the wanderings, God fed his people every day with manna. What exactly was this food? We have only a vague description: that it was small like coriander seeds and tasted sweet. To be a substance that would sustain a person, it must have been the perfect balance of fats, carbohydrates, proteins, vitamins, and minerals. I considered how such a food like this would affect the human body and imagined that it would provide abundant energy for the long journey, aid with building and maintaining muscle, and give the people who partook of it a health they had not experienced in Egypt, where they lived on slave rations. And considering that the Word of God, and therefore Jesus himself, is compared to manna, the spiritual implications of daily consumption are of critical importance to those who follow Jesus. To Alanah, who has only begun to taste of the "bread of life," its flavor is exciting and the newness of its mystery fascinating. If readers get anything from my books, I hope that it is a desire to taste the Word again and regain that sense of wonder about the mystery of a God who desires his children to be fed from its nourishment daily. May it never be mundane to us, or a drudgery, to collect the freely given treasures tucked between its pages.

Although it may have been difficult to read about the atrocities of Canaan, as much as it was to write some of them, I felt it was necessary to depict the brutal nature of the tribes that made up Canaan. As Tobiah says in Chapter Three, the people of Canaan (specifically the Amorites) were given over four hundred years to turn from their evil (Genesis 15:12–16). Think of how long that is— about the same gap exists between the Pilgrims setting foot on Plymouth Rock in 1620 and today. God gave them four hundred years of grace before kicking them out of the Promised Land. And although the Bible says nothing about prophets warning the Canaanites, from the pattern established since the days of Noah, I believe that God may have repeatedly warned them to repent or face coming judgment. The destruction of Sodom and Gomorrah would have been a visible and lasting reminder to the people who lived in this area of just what could happen. Yahweh is a God who values life, and from the beginning, when Cain slew Abel, he insisted that those who spilled the blood of innocents be brought to justice. Throughout history, civilizations that destroyed human life in sacrifice to their gods disappeared, in one way or the other. The various tribes of Canaan were absolutely numbered among them. The implications for our own culture is sobering.

Rahab is a fascinating historical figure. This book began to spin around in my mind after a conversation with my mother, who was discussing this Canaanite prostitute in a Bible study group. What would make a woman, whose people were the enemies of God, choose to put her own life in danger to hide two Hebrew spies? Without a doubt she would have been rewarded if she'd turned them in to the king of Jericho. Of course the Bible says that the people of the city were terrified of what they'd heard of the Hebrews, but I wondered how God was at work behind the scenes, and how the foundation was laid, years before, that led up to the decision that would put Rahab within the royal lineage of Messiah Jesus.

It is fascinating to me to consider how our lives affect one another and even the lives of people we do not even know—and also how sometimes our poor choices may end up being used to glorify God in ways we never thought possible. So I wondered, who could have possibly influenced Rahab? Who could have brought her news of the Hebrews and the miraculous ways of Yahweh and convinced her that life among the Israelites was preferable to Jericho? My answer of course was Alanah, an unknown sister inspired by the command in Deuteronomy 21:10–14 that Canaanite women could be chosen as wives for the Hebrews but were to be treated with a dignity unheard of during this era of brutal warfare, where most captive women were enslaved, raped, and/or killed.

We have no other clues about Rahab's life, other than she chose to live with the Hebrews, follow Yahweh, and ended up marrying Salmon (Matthew 1:5) to become the great-grand-mother of none other than King David. But undoubtedly the life she'd lived prior to Jericho's walls tumbling down was a sad and painful one. Sex slavery in all its forms is an assault on human life. Unfortunately, the horrors of human traffick-ing are not relegated to the ancient past. By some estimations, nearly thirty million people are currently enslaved worldwide, the majority of which are women and girls. If your heart, like mine, is broken by such an atrocity but you are unsure how to be a part of the solution, I would encourage you to start by watching the documentary *Half the Sky: Turning Oppression into Opportunity for Women Worldwide*, which was inspired by the book *Half the Sky* by Nicholas D. Kristof and Sheryl Wu-Dunn. You can also go to my website, www.connilyncossette.com, where there is information on how you can be involved with setting the captives free, one precious life at a time.

It is so bittersweet to be wrapping up the OUT FROM EGYPT series, and I am so grateful for all the people who have worked to make it possible, including Raela Schoenherr, Charlene Patterson, and Jen Veilleux, the most excellent of editors; Jennifer Parker, who designed the beautiful covers; Noelle Chew and Amy Green in Marketing, and all the rest of the fabulous Bethany House team who have supported and encouraged me in so many ways. Meeting you all in person this year highlighted just how blessed I am to be a part of Bethany House.

Special thanks to Tammy Gray and Nicole Deese for being such excellent writing partners, for keeping me on my toes and challenging me to be a better writer, and for being such precious sisters in Christ. I am overjoyed that you both are a part of my life. Thanks also to Tim Deese, who read my battle scenes and made sure they weren't too girly and gave me excellent ad-vice that enhanced those scenes greatly. Lori Bates Wright and Dana Red, thank you, my beautiful friends, for your constant encouragement and your excellent critiques. I am so grateful that the Lord brought such wonderful writers and friends into my life. Thank you as well to my beta readers—Juli Williams, Ashley Espinoza, Kristen Roberts, and Karla Marroquin—for your willingness to trudge through my early drafts. Thank you to my mother, Jodi Lagrou, for sparking the idea of this story in the first place. Thank you to my fabulous agent, Tamela Hancock Murray, for your constant support and encouragement. And last but certainly not least, thank you to my precious family—Chad, Collin, and Corrianna, you are my heart and I love you all to the moon and back.

QUESTIONS
for
CONVERSATION

1. *Wings of the Wind* was inspired by Deuteronomy 21:10–14, which gives the Hebrew men directives on treating a captive woman with dignity. Alanah begins her journey with the Hebrews as a captive but comes to see how God's laws are for the protection of women and children, which is a stark contrast to her own culture. How does Alanah's story change your perception of the ways God's laws protected and provided for women in a brutal tribal culture that viewed them as property and commodities?

2. Along with having to shave her head, Alanah must give up the goddess amulet she wore, submit to the Hebrews' laws, and adopt their lifestyle and culture. What things have you had to put aside to pursue new life in Jesus? As you examine your own heart, what things are you strug-

gling to leave behind? How have you seen your life and desires change since you came to faith?

3. Although Alanah begins the story as a hardhearted enemy of the Hebrew people, the kindness and guidance of a number of other characters cause her to question her opinions and gain new understanding of Yahweh. Who did God use to influence your own journey toward faith? What was it about that person that was different? Who else in your life has been an influential reflection of Jesus?

4. One of the biggest differences Alanah sees between the gods of Canaan and Yahweh is that false gods are "consumers" of their worshippers while Yahweh is abundant in his love and provision for his people. As you consider the false gods of this modern age, such as media, celebrity, money, technology, and drugs, can you see the ways in which they consume those who follow after them? What idols do you see in your own life that consume your time, energy, and joy?

5. The destruction of Canaan is a complex and controversial topic both within the community of faith and outside of it. What new insights did you gain into Canaanite culture that might explain why God would give the Hebrews such commands? Do you see any parallels to Canaan and the culture in which we live? How do you think God feels about that? In what ways does our culture devalue life?

6. Although Tobiah is certainly a fallible human being, he is depicted as a warrior, a pursuer, a protector, a defender, and a vehicle of grace and mercy to the ones he loves—all characteristics of our Messiah Jesus. How have you experienced these attributes in your own walk of faith?

7. It is easy to look back on Israel and judge their continual lack of faith and obedience without considering our own. What struggles do you see coming up again and again in your life? How is God using these struggles to show you his faithfulness and mercy?

8. In Joshua 2, Rahab the prostitute gives aid to the Hebrew spies in spite of the danger. She ends up being rewarded for her faith and, despite her past and her heritage, was ultimately named in the lineage of Jesus himself (Matthew 1:5). When have you had to make a stand for your faith? In what ways does the story of Rahab inspire your resolve to stand firm against persecution? How did you feel about Connilyn's imagined reasons for Rahab to help the Hebrew spies?

9. Rahab is described as a prostitute in the Bible, someone whose life was undoubtedly defined by sin and pain, yet was given the opportunity to shed her past, find new life, and be called an ancestor of the Messiah. How does the way God used Rahab for his purposes and glory, even in her brokenness, encourage you?

10. When have you, like Alanah's mother, had to make a decision with no clear-cut, easy answer? Did you experience fallout from that decision? How did God use the situation for his glory?

11. *Wings of the Wind* draws a picture of God's sovereignty in Alanah's life and how he was at work in her life long before she knew him, to accomplish his long-term purposes. How have you experienced God's sovereignty in your life? How does knowing that God sees the end from

the beginning affect your daily life and choices? In what ways has he proved his loyal presence in your life?

12. The description Alanah uses of the harvesting process is symbolic of how God changed her heart and how the truth of her identity and purpose is revealed through difficulty. What "chaff" in your life has God burned away, and what treasures have you reaped from the process of being "winnowed" by trials? Are you facing any trials in your life currently? In what ways might God be using these experiences to bring you closer to him?

13. How do you think Moriyah's experiences in Jericho will affect her life in the future? What might be the ramifications of the trauma she endured, in light of her culture and the time period in which she lived?

Connilyn Cossette is the CBA bestselling author of the OUT FROM EGYPT series from Bethany House Publishers. Her debut novel, *Counted With the Stars*, was a finalist for the Christy Award, the INSPY Award, and the Christian Retailing's Best Award. There is not much she enjoys more than digging into the rich, ancient world of the Bible, discovering new gems of grace that point to Jesus, and weaving them into an immersive fiction experience. She lives in North Carolina with her husband of over twenty years and a son and a daughter who fill her days with joy, inspiration, and laughter. Connect with her at www.connilyncossette.com.